Also by Gerda Charles

THE CROSSING POINT   (1961)

This is a Borzoi Book, published in New York by
ALFRED A. KNOPF

A

Slanting Light

A

Slanting Light

GERDA CHARLES

1 9 6 3

ALFRED A. KNOPF
NEW YORK

L. C. catalog card number: 63-18439

THIS IS A BORZOI BOOK
PUBLISHED BY ALFRED A. KNOPF, INC.

FIRST AMERICAN EDITION

A

Slanting Light

23rd April

I FOUND your letter awaiting me. My landlady who is too lazy and too old to carry it up five flights of stairs left it balanced on the knob of the banisters. I picked it up and opened it as I climbed—not because I was in a hurry to get at the money (you know very well that I accepted it only to give you less pain) but because up till now I have liked hearing from you—not as a husband but as an old friend. Why, incidentally, have you always sent the money in notes? Was it because to make out a cheque, a money order, you might have felt yourself obliged to use *his* name? It was bad enough to write it on the envelope I suppose: Mrs. Oscar as I was known here, instead of Mrs. Holland.

Well, you won't have to do so any longer. *Yes* I am quite determined to take this job. *No* you cannot dissuade me. No, I will not come back to you. But the moment I leave here—

next Tuesday—I shall cease (as in fact I wished to three weeks ago the day Danny left me, escaped from me, sailed away from me to South Africa, to freedom from me) to use his name—it was only a gesture, he never lived here—and revert to my own . . . which is also yours. This small thing at least should please you.

You see! I still want to please you in some things. As you yourself write, here in this letter lying by my hand, the habits of sixteen years cannot be broken by the disruptions of sixteen months. I still prefer not to think of you—as you cannot bear to think of me—alone. You suffer, you truly suffer at the thought of me alone. I think you kept sending me money all this time in order to keep me company. Danny was neither generous nor particularly amenable even when he was here. But at least your money took me to a cinema those evenings he was at the theatre; or those evenings when he wasn't in work but still didn't come. Yes, your money helped me to feel less alone. That too should please you.

Write, you say again in this letter as in all the others. Write everything, write every detail, spare you nothing. "If I only know I don't mind so much. It is the not knowing which kills!" Are you sure you want to know? Everything? Will it hurt you more—or less—if, now that he is gone, I allow myself the luxury of saying everything? Are you sure it will hurt you less if I hurt you more? I don't know, I simply don't know. After all these years I don't know whether you are masochist or saint. To know all might truly give you a black-grained, morbid pleasure.

You say the only thing you cannot bear is not knowing. Do you realize that this is imposing an impossible condition of wisdom on me? How can I tell if, by some error of judgement, in my frankness I cut, one day, too deep? How much can you take before suddenly it is too much? Can I trust your self-knowledge? I do not *really* want to hurt, Francis. At least . . . I don't think so. I am not like Danny who never

4

minded or rather did not understand the components of hurting. For an actor he had really very little imagination. That is probably why he is a rather unsuccessful one or comparatively so. The South African tour isn't anything like a Number One Company. I find I am glad about that. I'm glad he hasn't deserted me for something rampagingly successful. Six months of fit-ups and one night stands and not very high salary; that pleases me.

"Detail," you say. Every detail, no matter what, of thought or experience.

Yes, I know, you have always liked detail, done your best to train me into it. I have often wondered whether this is because you are an artist or because you are a schoolmaster. I know—you have told me often enough—that to paint well, to draw well, one must have an exemplary patience over detail. My vagueness over some things, my occasional woolliness invariably irritated you just as it irritated my father during his life. A printer has to have this absolute accuracy over tiny detail too. He liked you for appreciating that even more than he liked you for being a cut above us. Art master in a grammar school . . . that was a leg-up for a small-time, Liverpool printer's daughter. From lower-middle to middle; that was something to him.

How bewildered and annoyed he would have been about this living-in job which I am determined on taking up next week. Here are some further "details." It is a sort of housekeeper-cum-general-bottlewasher situation with an American dramatist and his family over here for a year. I haven't seen them yet though he is here already. The others arrive on Tuesday and I am to move in the same day. He is having a play put on by the Vauxhall Theatre Company in a few months' time. They have taken a furnished house in St. John's Wood—of all the districts in London! You know how I feel about St. John's Wood and the year I lived there; the year I was young. When the woman at the agency mentioned the address I felt immediately: God is compensating. Though why He does not punish instead I do not know. Though I have no doubt He will in the end. One does not cause pain as I have done without payment being exacted. But perhaps just being with Danny was punishment enough. Do I hurt you when I write like that? I still don't know. I think I hope so. You bloody saints!

I put down my pen a moment ago to look at myself in the mirror. There came such a torrent of bitterness behind my face that I felt I must see what it looked like.

I am very far from beauty—though you would never allow this. No one has ever looked at me twice in the street. My best points are such odd ones: my arms and my forehead and the modelling of my body across the chest and collar bones. I am not exceptionally tall—as you are—but I have the arms of a tall woman, slender and very beautiful. You have tried to draw them a thousand times just as you have tried to draw the contour of my throat and chest. My breasts are too small. Nothing much to get hold of as I used to tell you sometimes hoping that it would discourage you, not knowing (though I know now) that the mere cupping of the palm about such small delicacy can be an experience more inflaming than any other to such men as you—or Danny. (Is *this* too far? Does *this* detail hurt?)

My nose is too wide at the nostril and my legs too muscular and I am too pale and my brown hair is rapidly becoming too grey. But you and Danny have both loved my face, both I think for the same reason. You gave my face an adjective once. You called it "gentle-browed." This is a very nice adjective which I don't like at all.

My face has always presented me with great difficulties. I have never understood why—except in the crudest ways—there is an almost universal conspiracy of silence about the effect of one's physical self on one's destiny. I should have said that it is of the very first and most primary importance.

6

Our fates are literally in our faces. Who was it said that had Cleopatra's nose been a quarter of an inch longer the history of the world would have been quite changed? Politicians and historians don't understand this; they don't take enough account of Napoleon's smallness, of Hitler's ugliness.

Imagine for instance a woman who has all the tastes and talents necessary to become one of the great courtesans of history—and who has been given the mild, stupid, long-nosed face of a sheep. Think how she must spend her life— if she is born poor—selling stockings behind a counter or typing letters about insurance, because her body denies her soul its opportunities. How beauty—or the illusion of beauty —counts. Even Freud, whom one might have expected to value other qualities, was highly affronted at even the smallest hint that his wife was not madly attractive to other men.

But apart from beauty . . . how important to one's life are the limits and deceptions of one's face; as important as the limits of one's class. There! I am touching on our old argu-ment. The middle-middle have never understood, or ob-stinately refuse to understand, the difficulties of the lower-middle. Poor old lower-middle; the worst class of all to be born into. But I won't start that all over again!

"Gentle-browed!" This broad, dreaming forehead which makes me look so yielding, so malleable, so gently restful . . . it lies, doesn't it, Francis? The fact is I am not gentle at all— though even my voice has managed to match itself to my looks. I am *gently* tough, *gently* determined, gently and violently imaginative, romantic, selfish. Yes, selfish. Though you have never used the word others have, your sister, my brother. . . . If I were not selfish would I have left you? Would I have refused you so often, even before Danny? Would I even write as I am writing now, using you instead of refraining from using you as, bent on pain, you insist I do, telling you the truth as I am going to tell you *now, again,*

7

for the thousandth time: I cannot stand you. I cannot bear you near me. (Still no hate?)

"Gentle-browed!" Behind the pale, dewy sheen of this tender skin, behind the delicate bone, above these soft, brown, feathered eyebrows, I am a monster. Why don't you cast me off once and for all instead of asking me, for ever asking me to come back? If I were black-haired you wouldn't ask me. If I were fat and sleepy with currant eyes and a tiny mouth you wouldn't ask me. *Then don't ask me at all.* You don't love me; you love my collar bones.

The playwright's name is Zold, Bernard Zold. I imagine he is Jewish which inclines me in his favour. Danny is half Jewish. Oscar was his father's first name. He took it as his stage surname rather than Radzikowalski or something Polish and impossible like that which it really is.

I have a weakness for Jews just as I have for coloureds. Do you remember a Cingalese, an education officer visiting Liverpool schools to examine teaching methods over here? You brought him home from Medford Grammar with you one afternoon and left me to give him tea while you scrubbed the crayon dust off your fingers. I had barely set eyes on him when an uprush of pure, sensual feeling so took possession of me that I could hardly pour from the teapot without spilling.

I like them dark . . . the darker the better. Why did I marry you—who are bleached-fair, light-eyed, long, chunky, stiff-moving? I will tell you something. Before I got to know you properly the other typist and I in father's office always used to laugh at the way you walked when you came in to get your class stuff printed. We used to say you had a wooden leg—no one could walk like that without one—but we couldn't decide on whether it was your left leg or your right. *There* is a detail for you you never suspected.

Yes. I like them dark; dark and strange. But not yellow, never yellow, yellow frightens me. You wouldn't know, you

8

only came to Liverpool during the war, but there was always a mixture of colours there even in the days of my childhood; Chinamen, negroes, Indians . . . I remember once, when I was about ten (I just realized that I could have said "thirty years ago" . . . "I remember thirty years ago . . ." I am thirty-nine, Francis; I am in my fortieth year, Francis!) I was sent to collect some washing from a Chinese laundry. In those days we lived quite near the centre of the city, over the shop. My bedroom was directly over the machine-room. When there was a rush order the presses would throb half the night. It was a very nice, steady, drumming, enfolding noise. The shop was on a corner and my bedroom faced a main road. In the evening, trams (I adore trams, I cannot forgive the councils who have destroyed them) would pass with such a lively rattle and ping and lurch, their lights, no more than six feet away from my window, brilliant. I would lie in the dark and watch the heads of the passengers on the upper deck. I hated Sundays when the machines stopped and the trams were few. Ah, those sad, brown, Liverpool Sundays before the war. I think it was then that began that long hatred I have always known for week-ends. To this day I come alive on Monday morning, my blood beginning to flow with the hum and brightness of midweek.

You never knew Parkstone Road. Blitzed and bombed we'd moved and separated works and home before you came to the city.

But about the Chinese laundry, when I was nearly ten. An English-woman was behind the counter, thin-faced but decent-looking; respectable. I can see her now. A salesman was trying to sell her some cheap children's clothes he was hawking about in a shabby, cardboard suitcase. "Lun," she called into the room behind the shop. A hideously ugly, pock-marked Chinaman came out. "These might do for our Ireen," she said, holding up some white cotton socks. In those days they cost about threepence a pair. Her tone was quite ordinary. She wore a wedding ring. She was married to him. They discussed the socks. The idea of this terrible face as a husband terrified me. How could such a thing come about, that was the thought which haunted my child's but yet not childish mind. How could this come about? I have, unfairly, never liked the Chinese since.

I am meandering. But I find it pleasant to talk to you—as long as you are not there. I find I don't dislike the thought that you are my husband—as long as you are not Chinese and as long as you are not here but in Liverpool in the pebble-dashed, three-bedroomed house in the flat, neat little street. Perhaps you don't miss me too much after all. You have the school and your handsome collection of art-books in the extra-high shelf, standing so tall and rather offended-looking as if they know they are only bought by connoisseurs and third-rate artists. The real ones don't bother with all that classy, four-guinea, reproduction stuff. They're too busy creating their own brilliance of life. Ah! that was nasty. I should not write that. But it is how I feel in my heart, Francis. And that is what you want to know, isn't it?

Don't send me any more money. I shall have no expenses and a salary. St. John's Wood—and "theatre" again! Isn't that strange? The whole of my year in London at the drama school, the year I thought I was going to be an actress, I lived in a room off Abbey Road. And then . . . the war, father's illness, Tom called up—and it was over, the candle blown out and never lit again. I married you instead of striking another match.

Though this house where I have been living is not so very far away I have not dared to go even *near* Abbey Road these past sixteen months. And now, so easily and smoothly (just a turn on my heel in the street less than a week ago, just a sudden decision blown in on me from nowhere, to enter the agency) . . . St. John's Wood waiting for me!

It is too much! I must placate the gods, make a small

sacrifice. Shall I burn Danny's letters? Or yours? This raises
an interesting point, doesn't it? Would you prefer me to burn
yours and so know that even that much of you isn't with me
any more . . . or would you prefer me to burn Danny's, with
the knowledge that they represent to me the more potent
sacrifice? This is almost a metaphysical problem, isn't it?
Which would you rather be, given the choice . . . important
in the abstract or very small in the actual?

Yes, yes, I will write again when I am settled in the house
or when I feel like it; or even just to please you. But there is
a condition. *You must not write to me again.* Do you hear,
Francis? From now on I do not wish to hear from you. The
slightest jerk at the end of that thin, attenuated line by
which we are still joined . . . the faintest possibility of re-
minder . . . this seems to me *intolerable.* I feel myself becoming irrational, hysterical, almost frenzied at the thought.
I am beyond argument in this matter. Do as I say.

Ruth

❂❀❂❀❂❀❂❀❂❀❂❀❂❀❂❀❂❀❂❀❂❀❂

29th April

MR. ZOLD has gone to the station to meet the rest of his
family. This consists of: his wife; his daughter, aged eight;
his mother. I arrived this morning. The house is in one of
those adorable, blossomy small streets I remember, yes, very
vividly, from that year when I was young. The houses are
small and square and stand like the charming, elegant,
sturdy little ladies with their sensible, glossy heads well
screwed on, the frou-frou favourites of dukes and monarchs,
for whom they are supposed to have been built.

The rent, which Mr. Zold let slip, is enormous and he
seemed a bit worried about it. His agent over here took the

house for him. I suppose he thought an American playwright must be rich. But I don't think Mr. Zold is at all; or only moderately so.

I don't know quite what I expected a highbrow (he must be highbrow if he's being put on at the Vauxhall) American dramatist to look like; but it wasn't quite what I saw. He is of medium height, fat—no, not exactly fat but giving an impression of softness, fatness: not well-dressed; a light, loose, pale grey suit, very baggy. He has a habit of bending and straightening his knees like a diffident lecturer before a class. He wears a deprecating look on his face which is pear-shaped, his cheeks very full. His forehead—I look so much at my own (since you taught me to) that I am peculiarly observant of other people's—his forehead though broad is narrower than his face and has a curiously naked, bulging look, like a very young baby's. I think if he were fair he would look porcine but though his face is pale, his hair is black, coarse, but thinning in streaks across his scalp and his eyes are not small and pig-like at all but large, heavy-lidded and very dark.

I have not taken to him. (Are you glad? No, damn you, you will be sorry.) I suppose I hoped for too much. A high-brow dramatist, St. John's Wood. . . . But he is very polite. He showed me round the house with placating, absent-minded little half-sentences. He did not, for that matter, appear to take to me either. We fought a polite, nerveless battle over carrying my suitcases upstairs. I wasn't at all sure that, as a sort of servant, I shouldn't insist on carrying them myself, but in the end I let him take them.

The house is quite small. My room, the spare room and the second bathroom are on the top floor, there are three bedrooms and a bathroom on the first floor and two rooms at ground level. There is a big (comparatively; nothing is big in this bijou house) living-room running through from front to back and giving on to a minute, paved courtyard complete with trees in tubs at the back; a small, square dining-room communicating with the living-room by double doors, and a good big kitchen. In one respect at least, my employer is typically American. He became most animated over the hot water system (and incidentally least animated when I mentioned his family).

When we had inspected the rest of the house Mr. Zold led me back into the drawing-(living-?) room which has white walls, cream furniture, oatmeal silk settees . . . the decorating has not been too well done anywhere, gay-modern in intent but poor workmanship. A jobbed-up little house really, certainly not worth the rent except for its architecture and its neighbourhood.

I was thinking this when there was Mr. Zold suddenly standing in front of me with an exaggerated, screwed-up look on his pale, full face, a somehow too young expression which did not suit it at all.

"I don't know how these strike you, Mrs. Holland, but I feel I need my sunglasses."

He was holding up two cushions by their corners, one terra-cotta, one purple. I had noticed that there were a great many of them in the room.

"Aren't they just terrible?" he said. His voice has that peculiar, soft-high, feminine, Yankee tone I remember hearing so often during the war. "Sick-brick and sad-purple. For God's sake what'll we do with 'em?"

I thought they looked rather striking, not at all displeasing in that beigy, creamy room and for one moment nearly said so. Then I remembered what I was doing there—I can see that I shall have some difficulty in remembering my footing in this household—and said instead with a housekeeper briskness: "I'll take them away, shall I?"

"If you please," he said, hunching his shoulders, and dropping the cushions fastidiously from a height he walked away in a sort of burlesque tip-toe moving his hips with a

heavy swinging from side to side. "I feel they're going to
bite me!" he said, looking back over his shoulder.

There was an instant when, rapidly collecting an armful
of terra-cotta, I could have paused with arms full of cushions
and laughed—but I didn't. I didn't even smile. You know
(and I sometimes think have almost feared) my too quick,
gently responsive manner. Have you ever suspected that it
was touched up, slightly cultivated? You are so *stiff*. Did I
warm and smile so often only to stab you, I wonder? No, no.
I do myself an injustice there. I respond only to give other
people's wit an importance. It is my way of pretending that
the world is more attractive than it is. But with Zold . . . his
small joke irritated me. He is—I see this already—not the
man to make jokes. They do not fit him, are out of place
with that full, melancholy face and naked forehead. He
ought, I felt irritably, to know this. Perhaps he did because
his shoulders slackened immediately. Then he said, moving
towards the door with his small feet: "Well just put them
behind the gas meter or some place. I guess it's time for me
to go meet the train."

"Is there anything you want me specially to do?" I said.

"No. No. My agent sent his secretary along this morning
to do some shopping. She got a lot of groceries and stuff."

"What about the beds?"

"The beds?" He looked surprised.

"Yes," I said still in my efficiency role. (You will remember these attacks, Francis. Dirt in the corners for six weeks
and a tremendous drive and dust and turnings the sev-
enth. All, all to avoid routine, boredom, suburbanism.) "If
you'll tell me where the linen cupboard is I'll start making
up the beds."

He looked slightly at a loss then said: "Why, yes. That's a
good idea. I guess the sheets and all that are in the closet or
somewhere. Maybe you'd hunt around and find them, Mrs.
Holland. I forgot to ask."

"All right. I'll have them all ready by the time your family arrive." He was still standing, his hand on the door knob, looking down thoughtfully at the floor so I added conversationally: "Are they good travellers?"

He looked up and said absently: "Oh sure, sure. That is. . . . I don't know about my mother, she's so seldom been away from home. But the others will be O.K. Especially my wife, nothing *she* likes better than travelling. Suits her down to the ground. She'd be perfectly happy travelling the world for ever. Kid'll like it too I guess, now she's over this tonsillectomy. That's why I had to come on ahead without them."

"What's her name?"

He blinked his eyes and said, "The kid? Virginia. I call her Ginny. *She*," he emphasized the word meaning me to understand his wife, "wanted it. I'd have chosen something simpler myself. Like Ruth, say. Now that's a nice, simple name, Ruth."

I lifted my eyebrows and gave a small, cheerful laugh. "It happens to be mine!" I said.

"Well isn't that nice!" he said. He tilted his head sideways. "But perhaps your wife wanted a name similar to her own?"

"Nothing like," he said. "She's Jessica." The lids came half down over his eyes and he seemed to lose interest in the conversation. "Well," he said looking at his watch, "I guess I'd better be getting along. Just"—he lifted his arm and made a vague, hunched gesture towards the kitchen—"just help yourself to anything you want. Tea or whatever. . . ."

"Thank you," I said.

As soon as he had gone I made my way upstairs and unpacked, looked for and found the linen cupboard and made up the beds (*what* linen, scanty, poor quality, patched; he has certainly been done over the rent) then toured the house all over again seeing it through three different pairs of eyes; yours, Danny's, mine.

15

Danny now . . . he'd have liked it. It's got just that tarty, chipped paint, shady-smart, *mews* quality he thinks the last word.

You would go around rather gingerly determined to be accurate over its date and saying, correctly, that the "character" of the house has been ruined. The bedroom walls would please you: expiring lilacs, starved yellows, emaciated, waxy greens. There is a black bedspread in the yellow room and a poison green to go with the lilac. For once I do not dislike the arty colours. They add a kind of glint to this house which—perhaps because there is no one in it—seems somehow *pale*. Personally I think after a few weeks in that cold-porridge drawing-room Mr. Zold will be screaming for his terra-cotta cushions back.

The house through my eyes? Pale as I have said. Fragile somehow. Francis, I have a feeling this house somehow does not fit Mr. Zold and will not fit his family. There is going to be some vast discrepancy somewhere between this house and the lives lived in it during the next twelve months.

I am waiting for them now, sitting before the electric fire in the living-room which I feel I can use till they are actually here, have actually taken possession. After that my place will be in the kitchen, I suppose. Perhaps I should have stipulated "as family" as they say in the advertisements. But perhaps it's better not. I don't know.

Something happened to me an hour ago. Exploring the house, alone, free, strange, after Mr. Zold had gone, had given me an intense, nerve-stretched delight. When I came at last into this room and sat down on the big settee before the fire a deep, clanging pleasure seemed to boom with great strokes in my heart. And then, quite suddenly, it left me and I have been sitting here for a long hour filled with anguish.

The April afternoon is almost over. The room is not quite dark. I can see a metallic-grey rift of light in the dark sky beyond the rough hedge which holds the front garden from the street. I stretch one palm to the fire. And, as I had known they would, the questions, the dislocations have begun. Who am I *really*? Where is my place? What am I doing here before this stranger's fire in this strange room which, only two hours ago, I had never seen. It is not even someone else's home into which I am trying to fit my otherness. Until they come this is no man's land. There is a square, heavy, glass ash tray on a small table near me. That is where I always arrive with my questions; at a solid, transparent, barrier, heavy and glassy-cold against me.

Well? Again the question, like a small fist beating on the thick, slabbed glass; "What are you doing here before this stranger's fire?" And the answer—as I have always known it—"No more strange than any other fire, any other room."

You are ready at this point to cry out to me to come back to where I am not strange. You will not believe that this happened no differently, no less often, in the living-room of the little house in Liverpool. Those "artistic" grey walls and the great, scarlet panel over the fireplace, all painted—not very skilfully—by ourselves . . . they too are as strange to me as these skimmed milk surroundings.

How long since we first moved to Eversley Road? Nine years? Nine years for you, seven and a half for me of living with the grey walls and the square, vermilion "patch of colour." The neighbours (whom you never noticed—but I was brought up in a milieu where the neighbours counted) were curious, very slightly resentful, kind. I think they became after a time quite pleased to have us. We became topics to talk to visitors and families about at Christmas and holidays. Can you not imagine Mrs. Palmer (*what* a name! exactly like her own anonymous house) saying from her deck-chair to Mrs. Thing, knitting in the sun: "Oh yes, we've got nice neighbours. Can't complain. I suppose one or two're a bit funny like. Like next door to us we've got a couple that's sort of arty. They're quite nice, mind. I can't say a word against. But they've got these sort of . . . well not exactly contemp'ry . . . well he *teaches* art. At the Grammar. Bit of an artist himself so you can understand it really. Well, they've got these . . ."

You do not know how I hate Eversley Road. You are the "artist," you are the higher class of the two of us. But you have never hated Eversley Road or that . . . that *mouse* suburb as much as I.

You want me to come back because "my presence makes life for you." But what makes life for me? Where, in that meagre, satisfied little street can I soar to a sense of travel, illumination, a free, bright wing lifting, lifting. . . . In Eversley Road what can make life for me? *You* think because no one has ever loved you (that's true isn't it, Francis?) that just to be loved by anyone must be bliss beyond all measuring. Like everyone else you overvalue what you have never had. Being loved is not enough. *Being loved is nothing.* But of course you won't believe this. You think I ran away with Danny because we loved each other. Rubbish. I ran away with Danny because he is a life-giver. The unscrupulous always are. I have often tried to analyse this out, to find out why, but the answer eludes me. I have heard it said that we are really sorry for the cads—of both sexes—and that's why we find them so attractive. This is not so. The truth, as near as I can get to it, is that cads are both quick-witted and self-sufficient; they find themselves marvellous company. They seem to enjoy *themselves.* They are always having a party, inside. How delightful to be a cad and never bored!

They will be here soon. Perhaps, if I'm feeling good-natured I will write more when I go to bed. It would be cruel to send this letter and leave you wondering what the rest of the Zolds are like. And I am not cruel. I am not cruel. Am I, Francis?

Yes, I am cruel. I feel myself, have always felt myself so, even as I drive in the daggers, knowing on the plunge that I should hold back, be just, not wound. But you are there, you offer yourself. You are my Jew; the scapegoat I have always (knowingly, helplessly, with shame) used to ease the monstrous pressures deep within my red heart. I warn you, Francis, I warn you now. Tear up my letters unread. For—not wanting to—I will drive in the daggers again. I do so now to relieve the intolerable humiliation, the pain— not of love but of insult—of my abandonment. I savage you now in revenge against Danny. But at other times there will be other reasons.

I did not love him, I tell you. I disliked him if anything. Great blocks of granite, adolescent stupidity—not to say ignorance—lay beneath those dark, sardonic good looks and restless, cad's charm. Yet I am as outraged and fevered as if I had loved. It is the vacuum I cannot bear; the vacuum.

Has it occurred to you that in fact you are lucky? At least you love. You have a constant star in me; a known want. This must be steadying. But I have had no such luck, no love . . . only a tawdry, outraged possessiveness. You see! You are better off than me after all!

Later

Well, I have had a little luck. That is . . . I think there will be at least one person to like in this *ménage*—something I was for some reason beginning to doubt.

Have you ever noticed (it is odd how I can write to you things I can never *say* to you: that somehow slightly absurd and self-conscious fingertips-together judiciousness of yours so often dried me up in actual talk) how impossible it is to judge what a person is like without knowing the people they associate with, live with, are related to? How clear and *true* the clichés come out after all: "we are judged by the company we keep." The places where I have most often tested this are the holiday hotels, guessing, before the wife or husband comes down to breakfast or the one sits waiting in the foyer for the other, what kind of human entity is going to establish its relationship with the one before me. One speculates . . . but only when the two halves come together can the categorization be complete. I am speaking of surfaces, of course.

And yet, having written all that, I see that it is all false; or at least only half true. Who could categorize you by your conjunction with me? Or vice versa?

From what I have already written of Mr. Zold could you make a guess at his family, his wife? I will admit she came as a surprise—but a nice one. She is a tall woman, as tall as he, and rather heavy-figured. I imagine she must be round about forty which is, I think, roughly his age too. She moves with a slow, deliberate, yet somehow—this adjective may surprise you—*demure* step; a kind of hesitant girlishness which, though it does not go with that deep bust and rather broad hips, is appealing.

Her colour is brown. She has a straight-nosed, high-cheek-boned, brown-skinned, Red-Indian looking face; a squaw woman, but sweet. She wears her black, sleek hair in a big coil into the nape of her long, brown neck. Her mouth is big, slightly loose and crinkly. Her eyes, which slant, are small. She smiles often in a short-sighted, wide-lipped way. And from the moment she came in, folding the eye-veil back over her small velvet hat, she talked; about the crossing, about the packing, about the weather in New York, about the train . . . on and on—but in one of the most charming, soft, purling voices I have ever heard. Yes, I must say I have taken to her immensely; something I hardly ever do with women. And I am reasonably certain that this feeling will last. She is so . . . there is simply no other word for it, *nice*. She has no "personality" in the rough, strong sense of that

word. I doubt if she is clever. She is not pushing, not amusing. During the whole evening we spent together unpacking
and so on, she did not make one funny, witty or penetrating
remark. And yet, there is something so brown, wholesome,
pleasing about her one cannot help feeling charmed. I was
not surprised when, at one point during the mad scramble of
the evening—I will tell you about it in a moment—she told
me that she had been a physiotherapist before she was
married. She has a soothing effect. Her favourite words are
all superlatives. "It's great to get to know you, Mrs. Holland,"
were her first words to me when I came out of the kitchen
(rather nervously, I confess) into the confusion of luggage
and people in the hall. "Welcome to London, England," I
said holding out my hand. She laughed a little, seemed shy
too, then our hands managed to meet. Could I make her
some tea? "Wonderful! I'd just love a cup of tea." Could I
help her unpack? "That's just too kind of you. But have you
the time?" (As though I were a visitor just dropped in to say
Hallo!) "Oh well that's marvellous, Ginny," she called. "Come
over and say Hallo."

The child who had been standing, rather silent and
lumpish, by the door, giving sideways glances at me, came
forward. She is like her mother, heavily built with a solid,
square body. She is tall for eight and to my surprise, not-
withstanding two black-haired parents, has Scandinavian-
blonde, straight hair, hanging heavy and glossy to her
shoulders. She had a cheap box camera slung over one
shoulder and a plastic child's handbag over the other.

"How d'you do, Ginny," I said holding out my hand.

She hesitated before putting out hers, shook mine but said
nothing, only lifted one shoulder. Her features are firm,
pale, straight and thick. Her neck is short and thick and
creamy, hardly like a child's. She wore a gold heart on a
chain hanging round it—plus several bangles on her wrist
and a small gold ring.

Turning away from me immediately she moved to a large, wooden crate and stooping to it cried: "This is mine. I *know* this is mine. It has all my things in it. Please, Daddy, can I have it open now?"

(It was most uncanny! To recognize "the American child" right out of a movie, there in the flesh!)

Mr. Zold who all this time had been talking rapidly to his mother now looked over at me. "In a minute, Ginny," he said absently. "Mrs. Holland—"

I went over to him.

"Mrs. Holland, I want you to meet my mother. Mother, Mrs. Holland is going to look after every one of us while we're here. She's a very" (he gave a quizzical, slow shake of his head from side to side), "very competent person. She's been making up beds all afternoon."

I had held out my hand to Mrs. Zold senior and she was shaking it and looking at me with a rather curious set of her jaw as though she were biting her side teeth together very hard on a piece of cotton, but on the word "beds" she gave a kind of jerk forward.

"I hope," she said with an air of screwing herself to it as though it needed great courage to tackle me, "I hope they've been well aired?"

"Aired?" I said, wondering somewhat impatiently what she expected me to do about it if they weren't. Some trace of this thought must have shown on my face for her manner became even more fussed.

"It's very, very important," she said looking down with a nervy, dipping movement of the head at her handbag. I saw that it was a very large duplicate of Ginny's shoulder bag, a big, transparent, plastic square with crude red roses stamped by some process on the sides. It was crammed to bulging point.

She looked up at me and said rather desperately: "Wouldn't you say so?" She bit the imaginary piece of cotton again.

Feeling exactly the same irritation with her as I had felt earlier with her son—and I must admit for as little reason—I looked at her rather absently, my tongue slightly in my cheek (I mean literally) and didn't answer right away. My "gentle" look protected me, as always, from seeming rude and Bernard who was calling across to Ginny didn't notice; but the old lady, to my surprise, did. Her nose, which is high-bridged and with an extra knob on the end, all at once looked shiny and pitiable. I suddenly noticed that her hair was grey, frizzy and untidy, that she was very thin, her shoulders bowed over in a pronounced hoop, that she wore a cheap, rayon-y sort of dress most unsuitable for travelling in.

"Yes, of course," I said as warmly as I could to make amends (though I think the damage has been done). "Actually I've discovered that all the linen is kept in the big cupboard in the bathroom which holds the hot water tank—and that's been very hot all day. Someone must have switched it on early this morning." I turned to Mr. Zold as if to say: It must have been you, but he gave me a "Now you've done it," look.

"You mean the electricity's been burning all this time for just nothing?" she said agitatedly. "Bernie, you go right up now and turn it off. Nobody's going to have a bath tonight anyway. We're all too tired. Anyway we all had baths this morning on the boat. I saw to that. I had to stand over Ginny. 'Now just you go along and get into that tub,' I said. I saw to that all right," she repeated. "So there's *no need* to waste all that—"

"Now stop worrying about the bills before you've even sat down," he said with a laughing-frowning, patient look. "It's a thermostat anyway. Did you say tea, Mrs. Holland?"

He half helped her off with her coat to encourage her, then darted after me to the kitchen to mutter in my ear (though it took some dignity from him, this fleetingly pleased me): "Fool enough to let drop about the rent soon

23

as we met and she just hasn't stopped about it all the way here," then he went back and began taking the family over the house.

I took tea in at last to find a heated argument going on in the big living-room . . . drawing-room . . . I don't know what they'll call it.

"I want the yellow room. I want the yellow room. It's my very favourite colour. Daddy, I want the *yellow,*" Ginny kept intoning against young Mrs. Zold's mild counterpoint of "You can't want to sleep under that black spread, Ginny. You just won't like it at all."

"I don't care. I want the yellow."

She went on chanting, sitting on the *pouffe* with her straight, solid, bare legs stuck out in front of her. I took a cup of tea over to old Mrs. Zold who was sitting straight up, quivering and watchful, on a hard chair with her back to the window. She gave me an equivocal glance as she accepted the cup. I offered her the sugar bowl. With a gesture of impatience, as if she had told me this fact a thousand times before and I still couldn't remember it, she said: "No. No sugar. I gave up sugar a long, long time ago."

"Mrs. Holland! *You* try and talk some sense into my daughter!" said Mr. Zold in a light voice. He again, as with the cushions, tried (without quite succeeding) to make a gay thing of it. "What do *you* say? Don't you think Ginny's a bit young to be playing Mata Hari the Beautiful Spy with that exotic, black bedspread and those black drapes with the lightning streaks on 'em? Calculated to give her nightmares, I'd say."

"They could give me nightmares too, if that's the room you've in mind for me," said Mrs. Zold senior, staking her claim for consideration but disowning responsibility by looking fixedly at her cup.

"As a matter of fact," I said in a reasonable voice, "I was a bit puzzled myself, you know, about the rooms. The biggest one, the one at the front, has only *one* single bed in it. The room at the back—which is actually much smaller —is the one with two beds. And the smallest of the three has a *double* bed in it. It's really a very odd arrangement indeed. I can't think why they had them like that. Perhaps the owner was a widow or something."

"Well anyway, that settles it," said Jessica Zold. "All we have to do is change the single in the big room for the double in the little room. Then Ginny has the little—"

The other three all spoke at once.

"That still leaves me with those nightmare drapes," said old Mrs. Zold.

"But I don't *like* that little room with those old, green walls," said Ginny with heavy obstinacy.

Mr. Zold, wearing a curiously artificial look of thoughtfullness, said hurriedly: "No, I don't think that'll do."

Jessica looked at him mildly. It struck me that she is used to being overruled.

"A better idea," he said, "is to move one of the single beds from the yellow room into the big front room; give Ginny her heart's desire and the rest of us some peace by putting her in the yellow room, and"—he turned to his mother with a placating expression—"give mother the green room. Only it's smaller, Mama. Would you mind that?"

Getting up he crossed over to her, sat down on the arm of a chair next to hers and took her hand. She sat looking away from him but her mouth quivered; perhaps with pleasedness . . . I don't know.

"I want you to be comfortable, Mama," he went on.

She said nothing.

Ginny said: "I want some milk," and went out to the kitchen before I could forestall her. Jessica, calm and silent, drank her tea.

"Look. If you don't think you'll be comfortable in that little room, say so. Just *say* so, Mama."

Mrs. Zold turned her head slightly and I caught a curious look in her eye: undecided, obstinate and . . . what? Mocking, I think, but I am not sure. Then with a kind of Jewish, sideways shrug as if wanting to give in but without losing face, she said: "Well, if you think it's airy enough. I should care . . . big, little . . . I've slept in small rooms," putting her chin up then down. "All I'm concerned is a good bed and fresh air."

"It's a smallish room but it's got a huge window," I said.

"Well, all right then! The green room! What difference?"

Mr. Zold who was still holding her hand, unexpectedly, and I must say, quite unself-consciously, lifted it to his lips and kissed it.

"Good, Mama," he said gratefully.

She gave no sign of noticing but suddenly (I *think* by way of apology) became voluble.

"I've got to have air when I sleep," she said. "If I've told my family once I've told them a hundred times—" ("A thousand," said Ginny lifting her nose out of the glass of milk she had returned with)—"will you stop her being rude to her grandmother, Bernie, fancy furniture, fancy linen, that I can do without. So long as it's clean, so long as—"

"Yes," said Bernard. "Yes. Now look, Mama, I'd better go see about moving those beds around. Would you help me, Mrs. Holland? I'm sure sorry we have to do this all over again when you spent so long in making them up. But that's kids for you."

"That's all right."

But it wasn't! No sooner had we got the beds moved, rearranged and made up again than old Mrs. Zold decided that the double bed in the small room gave her no room to move. Also it took away the air! It would have to be changed for the single in Ginny's room!

"What you must think of us," said Mr. Zold, who'd hardly

stopped apologizing, as we finally got all the beds into place at last, "I just daren't think."

"Oh, go on!" I said, lifting on a sudden bubble of cheerfulness. "Think nothing of it. I enjoyed it."

In fact I had. The more running about, lifting, folding and unfolding, rolling and staggering under mattresses, the more a happy energy welled inside me. I liked, yes I liked the comic strangeness, the whirl, the four strange, yet-to-be-explored people, the laughing collisions, the intimate confusion with bedsprings and sheets and Ginny's toys, the scrappy supper with everybody in the kitchen. How I love untidiness and scramble. As much as you hate it.

(But above all, perhaps, the escape from a spring evening? For a few hours, the defeat of time?)

Before we all went to bed Jessica thanked me with the sweetest charm, Bernard with almost embarrassing gratitude, Ginny not at all, and old Mrs. Zold rather grudgingly but determined to show she knew her manners.

Do you feel you know them at all? I don't. I don't think they're a particularly attractive family, apart from Jessica, but there must be *something* to Mr. Zold. I keep forgetting that he is a playwright and attached to the Vauxhall. When I remember, it jolts me. They are so ordinary, somehow. How childish that sounds! As though writers, actors, painters—and their families—are beings divorced from ordinary life. Yes, yes, yes, I *know* they're not. You have patiently been telling me for years that they're not. (You adore the thought that they're not, don't you?) But I will admit that I could wish that the Zolds were more . . . oh, I don't know.

Well, anyway . . . here we all are, strangers together under a strange roof. Did I tell you that *my* room is pink? I hope Ginny doesn't come poking around and decide on a new favourite colour! I don't like that child.

Ruth

P.S. I wonder why Mr. Zold didn't want the double bed for himself and his wife—and she did? Just the reverse (isn't it?) of you and me.

R.

◊┤◊┤◊┤◊┤◊┤◊┤◊┤◊┤◊┤◊┤◊┤◊┤◊┤◊┤◊

18th May

AFTER nineteen days I can only say that God has certainly tempered the wind to these short-coated lambs by sending them *me*. What *you* would think of these Zolds gives me some amusement to contemplate.

To begin with . . . they do not cook! That is one reason why they are lucky to have someone like me who—you must admit—has a talent for cooking. (How many times have I wanted to splash out . . . gnocchi, blinis, escalope de veau . . . but I cannot bear the thoughtful way you eat. You *chew*, yes, somehow more than other people chew. You . . . concentrate on the act somehow.)

Their respective attitudes towards home cooking are: Mr. Zold hates eating in restaurants but has been partly conditioned to it. Jessica dislikes (I cannot say hates, I doubt if she "hates" anything) kitchens and women's work generally and is rather incompetent but in a quiet, unspectacular way so that you don't notice (much). She adores eating out and will make any excuse to do so. The child Virginia equally adores restaurants or in her case self-service "eateries" as they call them, and consumes hardly anything but pop and peanuts at home. And old Mrs. Zold who, she tells me, has never had the time to do much cooking (why?) desires—or so she says—only a boiled egg from time to time on a tray.

Whatever I make for them is praised to the skies by Mr.

and Mrs., rather resentfully eaten to the last shred by the old lady, and messed about by Virginia. It hadn't occurred to me that there might have been some difficulty over their being Jews, but apparently they're the kind who've long since thrown overboard most of the Jewish customs—except they still don't touch anything connected with the pig. So ham and bacon are out for the duration. This delights me! I have a sense of travel, of being in a foreign country. Nothing could please me more.

Otherwise. . . . Well, they are not very difficult to *work* for but there *is* some difficulty—I hardly know how to define it—about the *living* with. I think this is partly because my standing *vis-à-vis* the family differs with each of them so that speaking to more than one at a time I am seesawing rather wildly between different levels. Let me define (in detail!) what I mean.

Though I am, so to speak, "hired help" as they would put it, Mr. Zold is entirely and unself-consciously democratic with me. In fact he hardly notices me about the house but that is probably because our orbits don't collide very much anyway. He is a late riser—and, it seems, feels perpetually obliged to excuse this, to me, sympathetic habit, when we do happen to meet—and by the time he comes down to breakfast (fruit juice, cold milk, cereal, and coffee left ready in the percolator) I'm upstairs doing the bedrooms. By the time I'm down again he is either out or working. The spare bedroom on my floor he has taken over as a study. This occasioned some argument with his mother who kept saying: "I don't know, Bernie, why you just can't work at that little bureau in the dining-room instead of that poky little room up there. Why, it's no more than an attic!" And she gives me a rather accusing look as though I've stepped out of my place in having the bigger and better room on that floor.

She is the only one who interrupts him up there (I gather

he is drafting a new play) taking unwanted cups of coffee
to him at intervals and opening the window which he
promptly shuts again as soon as she's gone. He is patient
but not too angelic with her. "For Heaven's sake, Mama, will
you go downstairs and gimme a bit of peace," I heard him
shouting after her this morning. She came down and into
the living-room which I was dusting, gave me a side glance
to see if I had been listening, fidgeted about the room
wearing a childish, scolded look, and finally sat down with
her sewing, making a summer dress for Ginny. I watched
her hands on the soft, pinky cotton, stroking the gathers
into place with a needle. Those long, very long fingers which
might have been elegant in youth but are now very ugly,
the bones ending in big milky finger-nails, made curiously
spasmodic patterns of movement over the material. Then I
realized she was trembling. Quarter of an hour later *he*
came down, put his arm around her shoulders, smoothed
her forehead, asked if she was feeling all right—she nodded
but said nothing—and went back upstairs again. It's ridiculous the way he cossets her.

Most of the time I feel a slightly vexed amusement at her
attitude to me which is both placating and superior. I do
believe she is frightened to be too friendly in case I "pre-
sume"! What do you think of *that* for American equality!
There is, really, something very odd about her attitude—
taken in conjunction with her clothes, her undistinguished
mien, her insistence on some "manners" and ignorance of
others. For instance . . . all Americans are curious eaters
with their right-hand-fork technique, but she has the oddest
habits; heaping everything onto one plate and then taking
it over to the chair by the window and eating it there with
the plate on her lap.

Jessica treats me in her friendly way (she has a manner
like whipped ice cream; cool, bland, very soft) as if I were
an old school friend spending a few days with them. But

even her attitude is modified a bit when her mother-in-law is in the room. The other day J. came into the kitchen where I was having my usual early lunch before giving them theirs. I hadn't quite finished and went on eating, a book propped in front of me. She hovered a moment but said nothing, then went over to a cupboard and rummaged inside. Only when the old woman followed in after did she turn hurriedly and say: "I wonder if we could have lunch now, Mrs. Holland? We want to get out early this afternoon."

I jumped up immediately, my mouth full, and set about serving them, old Mrs. Zold looking determined and uneasy and triumphant as she ate carefully avoiding my eye.

The child takes no notice of me at all; nor for that matter much of anyone else. She is a radio and television addict and does little else—despite her crateful of toys—but listen and watch . . . when she is not at the rather expensive private school—but they couldn't get her into any other— to which it is my not particularly enjoyable duty to take her each morning. They say, though I have not yet seen any samples, that she has considerable artistic talent and they are arranging for her to have extra art lessons here at home. Useful, as always (though the more helpful I am, the more the old woman resents me!) I have told them which agency to apply to. Well . . . I suppose there *may* be talent in that child. She has had a picture in a New York exhibition of child art. I shall see her "portfolio" as they call it when it arrives here next week.

Before I finish—I have had such an odd thought! It has just struck me . . . this kid Virginia, might be your daughter! That solid-fleshed, thick-white-skinned body of hers with the heavy, clomping legs; her straight, linty hair, the jerked, awkward stiffness of the child's manner sometimes; the "talent for art." How very . . . disconcerting. I thought I had run away from you; and here you are!

There is something I don't like about this; some nasty,

complacent moral is being drawn somewhere and thrust at me. I don't like it at all. No wonder I disliked her on sight!

R.

❂❦❂❦❂❦❂❦❂❦❂❦❂❦❂❦❂❦❂❦❂

25th May

ONE OF MY less than charming, lower middle-class attributes is vulgar curiosity. I snoop. Just like the neighbours I despised in Eversley Road. How are you managing about them, by the way? What a lot of nosy questions you must have had to parry these last seventeen months. Poor you! I could almost feel sorry for that ordeal I have forced upon you if for no other. What, I wonder, did you tell them? That I'd had a "breakdown"? That my old grandmother was ill and needed me? Or perhaps they think you murdered me and buried me in the garden one dark night! Perhaps I'd better come and show myself to Mrs. Palmer for five minutes one day just to stop the very curious glances which I'm sure are being directed at you behind your back!

As I was saying—I snoop. The rewards for this are that, for one thing, I now know just how old everybody is because I had a quick look at their passports the other day. Old Mrs. Zold is older than I thought: 72. Her dear son Bernie is 41. And Jessica, believe it or not, is five years older than her husband. She is 46. That's interesting somehow.

I am beginning to wonder very much about nearly everything to do with this family. They don't seem to add up anywhere. "Bernie" had his first play produced by a local repertory—or stock as they call it—company only three years ago and his second, only last year. That's the one they're doing over here. How it will go in London is of course anybody's guess. It has had, I gather, a rather odd history for an American production, being neither a raging success nor the reverse. It was put on at a "fringe" theatre in New York (something like the Vauxhall here), was cheered by every intellectual in town, and—this is the odd thing— neither flopped nor otherwise, just staggered along keeping its head barely above water for something like four months before finally folding. This is *most* unusual in the New York theatrical world where you're either top or out before the first night audience has got home and taken its shoes off.

(You hate this theatrical gossip, don't you? Whenever I used to talk "theatre" you would wince and tighten inside like a sea anemone sensing danger. The theatre was always your enemy like the sea to a man who has married a mermaid. And of course you were right. Your instinct knew truly. I have returned to my element in the accidental, inevitable way of pure destiny. You could not keep me from it. Surely you see now how stupid it was to try?)

All my information, I need hardly say, comes from Jessica who is able to talk to me because the weather has suddenly become very warm. One effect of this is that the old lady now goes out to sit in the front garden immediately after lunch in order to *get more air!* She has a positive fixation on fresh air, that one! She won't, however, go to the little courtyard at the back for it. She likes the street. (I wonder if she's ever lived in a slum?)

Anyway, as soon as she settles herself with her sewing, Jessica comes in to the kitchen with her slow, heavy step and head-held-sideways girlish manner and talks to me over the washing up. A kind of perfume of pleasantness comes in with her. I find her company very smooth, very easy; like honey.

One thing I have begun to see is that the members of this family have been leading a curiously confined life ever since they arrived in this house. Apart from Bernard's occasional contact with his agent (they haven't even started casting

yet), apart from one or two routine tourist trips on Sundays
to the Tower and Westminster, apart from bus conductors
and shop assistants—and me—they have hardly spoken to
an English person yet; indeed they have hardly been beyond
the confines of this neighbourhood. This is particularly hard
on Jessica who was telling me this morning how she missed
her friends. Did I tell you by the way that they do not come
from New York City itself as I had rather stupidly assumed
at first. They live in Allegra, a fair-sized town in upper New
York State, which is Bernard's home town but not hers.

"I was a Philadelphia girl," she told me today, picking up
plates and wiping them with slow gestures. Anything she
does domestically looks as though she's never done it before
and is only just learning how, now. "It was quite a wrench
to leave there when I got married, I can tell you. Philly's
such a fine, beautiful city. I just wish you could see it. You
know, Mrs. Holland, I enjoyed my life very much when I
was single," she went on. "My, that was a wrench, leaving
all my brothers and sisters and *their* families and children
and all. My family's very well known in the town," she said
with a kind of naïve pride. "Everyone in Philly knows the
Levys."

"What about your husband's family?"

"Just the one brother. He's ten years older than Bernard.
We don't see much of him—and thank the Lord we don't.
He's just not like Bernard at all."

I'd like to have asked her just how he differed from his
brother but she turned the subject in a gentle way—I am
undecided whether it was also deliberate or not—and went
on: "I guess you've noticed, Mrs. Holland, that I'm not crazy
about domestic life?" I laughed on an indulgent "Oh well
. . ." note and she smiled too. "But I just never had to do a
thing before I was married. I had this job of mine that I
simply loved every minute of, visiting just about every hospital in the city and I *loved* it."

"I'm vague about physiotherapy," I said. "What was your particular work?"

"I worked with the visiting consultant," she said enthusiastically. "It was fine. I'd see the patients and have a chat and coffee with nearly everybody—and a good gossip with the nurses!" she added with that beguiling, gently skittish look of hers, resting her long hands on the washing up bowl. "Christmas and New Year's I was invited to all the ward parties—every last *one* of them. All the internes danced with me!" she added with such naïve, girlish delight that I felt delighted too!

Suddenly I felt happy again. The spring sunlight filling the square kitchen, Jessica's voice which is exceptionally musical, my hands in the warm, soapy water, pictures of Jessica's early life which she managed to make by some magic of voice or personality sound so cheerfully sweet, so radiantly simple and busy and calm, floating across my mind. . . .

"It's a wonder you didn't marry a doctor!" I said teasingly.

"That very nearly happened—more than once!" she said. "Why, I was practically engaged to one when Bernie happened along. He was sent to this clinic in Philly when he had trouble with his knee—we had this very famous Doctor Smythe that people come from all over the world to consult—met me there and honest, before I knew what was happening we'd got married. He'd just made up his mind that I was the one—*you* know!—and there we were! He gave me no time at all to think about what I was doing or whether I was making a right choice . . . or *any*thing. Of course it's worked out. And of course every girl should be married and I wouldn't want you to think I've ever regretted it. . . . But I must say I was ve-ry happy as a girl. It wouldn't be true if I said otherwise. Of course I've made lots of friends," she said, with a sudden, upward flourish of her left hand, "in Allegra. Bernie isn't too pleased sometimes when he comes in, finding the girls around. He takes one look and goes off and locks himself in his study. Well he'd be there anyway so I've got to find my own company, haven't I? We're just opposites in that way I guess. The Zolds are anti-social and I'm not."

"Does old Mrs. Zold live with you?" I asked. "In America, I mean."

"Yes and no. Not exactly. That is, she did at first—or rather we lived with her. But when Ginny was coming I said to Bernie: 'Look, there just isn't going to be room for all of us here any more. You've got to find another apartment for when I come back.' "

"Come back?"

"Ginny was born in Philadelphia. I wasn't going to have my baby without having my own family around. Anyway I was that homesick when I first got married I was more in Philly than I was in Allegra those first years. Bernie came over week-ends of course. *So.* We started looking or rather Bernie did. I was at home. Well I guess you know the housing shortage was very acute over there for a long while. I was back in Allegra, Ginny was going on three months (and was *that* a picnic with Mother Zold and the diapers all over the place!) and we still hadn't found anything at all. Then we heard of this one room apartment on the first floor (what you call the ground floor over here) of the same apartment house. No use to us of course. But then Bernard had this idea of our taking over Mama's apartment and her taking the single downstairs. How he finally talked her into it I'll *never* know," she said, wiping her hands on the roller towel. "It's not that she objected. I mean there wasn't anything that you could put your finger on. That's not Mama Zold's way *at all*. But it was just: 'How'll I carry on the business, how'll the customers manage with only one room? ...' "

"Does she run a business then?" I said in surprise.

"You can hardly call it that now. But she's a very, very

good dressmaker. Why, she had some of the best people in town come to her at one time. You can see the quality work she does if you look at Ginny's dresses. She still makes everything for her. Oh she's very good at her profession."

(I have indeed noticed Ginny's frocks, far too fussed and frilled with enormously unnecessary lace edgings on the collars and big, stand-out skirts, all wrong on that solid little chunk of cheese.)

"Why, you couldn't get workmanship like that on anything from a store," she said. "Of course Bernie's always on at her to stop doing it. But you know what old people are like. You couldn't stop her with a machine-gun if she wants to do something."

"It must have been quite a job persuading her to come to England with you," I said casually.

"Again yes and no. Plenty of protesting till he's worn himself out, but where her son goes she goes. That's the law in this family and well she knows it. He'd no more have left her living alone in that one room without him seeing her at least once a day than he'd have left Ginny. In fact I do believe he'd sooner have left Ginny behind than his mother. He's just about *the* most devoted son you ever saw."

"Yes, I've noticed that," I said.

"My girl friends say they've never seen anything like it. They say they don't know how he took time off to marry me! But he certainly put his foot down over Europe. 'Are you going to spoil my whole career at this point, Mama?' he said. Did he *plead* with her. 'You know darned well I wouldn't have an easy moment if you weren't with me. Anyway, don't you *want* to see Europe? What've you had in your life that you want to pass up an opportunity like this that anybody else'd give their eyeteeth for?' he said. Well it's true she's had a hard life. Left to bring up two children without a cent but what she could earn. *He* was never any good by all accounts." She drew in her breath. "She certainly had a life from that husband of hers. Best day's work he ever did was the day he died. Bernie was only twelve and that brother of his had already beat it to Pittsburgh. Fat lot he cared what happened to them for all he was making plenty of dough even then. Bernard has to get his picture in the paper before *he* shows up again. He had his picture in Art Kenno's Column after the New York premiere," she said with her crinkling, rather charming, boastful look. "Maybe you don't know but that column's syndicated right across the U.S. It's one of the biggest honours a writer can have."

"It's just an *ord*-inairy little gossip column with *ord*-inairy news items like anywhere else," said Mr. Zold just behind us. We had been so absorbed in talk that we were still standing before the sink though the dishes had all been put away minutes ago and it was clean and empty. He had stretched out his arms behind our backs and now gave us each a light, awkward thump on the shoulder. Then, bringing his hands down abruptly he said: "Don't let yourself be kidded by any tales of *my* glory, Mrs. Holland. Listen to *her* and you'd think I was Eugene O'Neill and George Bernard Shaw rolled in one. And"—he shook his head solemnly— "apart from Mr. Shaw's middle name there is *no resemblance whatever* between me and either of those two."

"That's not what some of the critics said about *The Curtain*," she said in mild, musical protest. "Show Mrs. Holland the clippings, Bernard, why don't you?"

His face, with its loose, fattish flesh, tightened immediately and he gave her a look of exhausted anger; then with an impatient turn of his shoulder, walked to the door. When he had gone she said, quite serenely: "Couldn't you just scream! He can't bear me even to *mention* his success. Can you imagine any other man *not* wanting people to know about it? But not my husband. He won't even give his own family the pleasure of talking about it. After all . . . we're

all part of it, aren't we? You'd thing he'd be *glad*. But no. It
was just the same at home. Anybody said anything he'd just
turn it aside, perhaps say *one* word as though it gave him a
pain to have it dragged out of him and change the subject.
And he can say what he likes, he did get some wonderful
notices. Why else would the movies have bought it?"

"Oh! has he sold the film rights?"

"Oh, sure. Though I don't think they're going to use it
after all. You know movie people! But how else could we
have afforded to come to Europe for a year? Not on what
he was making in his job—*or* what he made in the theatre,
what with taxes and all. I still say it was a risk—but *you*
try and stop him! And *The Curtain* being put on here in
London he just had the perfect excuse."

"What *is* Mr. Zold's job? Or was?"

"He was sort of, well I guess sort of librarian you'd call
it, in a Scientific Institute just outside the town. Oh," she
said with a little, backward flip of her hand, "it's a very
responsible job. They wouldn't have given it to Bernie in
the first place (he's no scientist you know, he's had no train-
ing *at all* in that field) if they hadn't thought him highly
capable of it. They had applicants who'd been to graduate
school and trained and I don't know what all . . . but it
was Bernie who got the job. They just think the world of
him at the Institute. The pay wasn't all that good, mind;
and what with everything going higher and higher it hasn't
been all that easy for us with four mouths to feed and two
sets of rent—at least it wasn't till that lousy brother of his
began doing what he should've done years ago.

"Well, anyway, here we are," she said gaily, "in London,
England. Though for all the difference it's made so far we
might just as well have stayed home. Oh now don't think
I don't like your country and this house and St. John's Wood
and all. It's so *pretty*. But I do miss having the girls around.

She talked on till old Mrs. Zold, becoming suspicious,

came in from the garden and, although she said nothing, broke up the conversation in thirty seconds.

"The girls" is one of Jessica's pet subjects. I seldom hear her speak for three minutes without some reference to them. At first I thought it was her way of talking about her women friends in general; as in fact Bernard uses the word. "Where are the girls?" he asks me sometimes when he comes in, meaning his wife, his mother and his daughter collectively. But no. Jessica, I have discovered, uses the word in its strictly literal sense. Back in Allegra she has a whole gaggle of young, unmarried girl friends who seem to revolve around her, a flotilla of small craft guiding this big, sweet, helplessly inefficient woman through the ordinary hazards of everyday life. It probably all started with baby-sitting but has by now ramified in all directions. I find I am doing it too. One reason is the somehow irresistible docility with which she receives direction. This is something I have not met before; someone who can be bossed without losing their dignity. Amenable and twinkling she notices nothing and is never cast down. Is not this remarkable?

Her husband, I am reasonably sure, is quite different. Like his mother he notices everything, not with a quick, snapping observation but with a slow-blooded sensing of whatever's going on. Yet he too has surprised me. Take this evening. The others were in bed and I was just about to go up myself when he came into the kitchen. He wished, it seemed, to apologize for his behaviour that afternoon, for not being amiable and charming over his press cuttings, for his abruptness, for walking out. He could not rest without apologizing.

In such circumstances what would one expect from someone so generally awkward in manner? Stumbling? Hesitancy? A graceless plunge? (Such as you have so often taken.) Not a bit of it. He came in with a quick, simple step, one hand in his pocket, and said with a great, sincere ease:

"Mrs. Holland, I hope you will forgive me for this after-noon. I have an idea I was rude."

"Oh please—" I said standing up.

"Sit down," he said in a mock-bullying voice, pleased at being able at once to set a lubricating, comic tone into the situation.

Surprised, I sank down again so hard that I thumped on the wooden, kitchen chair. The sound caught his attention. Looking round the room with a frown he exclaimed impatiently and walked out very rapidly saying "Wait a minute." He returned with the comfortable, padded, fireside chair from the hall, dumped it down in the corner at the side of the fireplace, said briskly: "You should have done this yourself," and went on immediately before I could say anything at all: "About the clippings—I don't care to show them around. Jessica ought to know that by now. It wasn't because it was you. I wouldn't have you think that."

"I understand absolutely," I said, as indeed I did. He thought—it was obvious—that I had thought of myself as being treated like a servant. And I saw that this notion had horrified him out of self-consciousness. Concern made him brisk and active. (I have had the idea as I write these words that he may possibly be one of those few men whom power would not corrupt.)

"I hope you don't; not absolutely!" he said. "That would be a hell of a dangerous thing to do, to understand anyone absolutely."

There was a curiously expectant expression on his face as he finished this sentence, his mouth slightly open, his jaw thrust forward, his tongue pressing against his lower teeth. His heavy, black eyes were alight.

I said, laughing slightly: "Don't you want to be under-stood, Mr. Zold?" and he made a gesture with his right hand, throwing it up light-heartedly and taking a quick clutch at the air as if catching a fly. All at once he seemed entirely delighted about something; perhaps no more than the fact that he had discovered an intelligence in his kitchen. He took a boyish step towards the fireside chair, almost sat down in it, glanced at the door—and returned to lean against the table on the opposite side to where I was sitting. "Most dangerous," he repeated.

"I haven't ever quite thought that out but I think if I had I would disagree with you," I said.

"The European—not to say British!—optimism! *Reason; understanding; logic* even. You still think these things work."

"Well, don't they?"

"In minute quantities—yes. In impersonal, say governmental transactions—perhaps. Between individuals . . . I would say, no."

"Oh, but surely. . . ."

He began to walk with his loose, prowling, lecturer's step up and down his side of the kitchen table, touching it lightly with his finger-tips at each turn.

"Unless," he began, "you are born into some Jamesian never-never land"—he stopped abruptly, cocked his head at me in sudden doubt, then, as he saw that I was with him, continued—"inhabited by creatures of exquisite fineness of feeling—and who is, for heaven's sake?—an excess of sensibility, an acute understanding won't do you any good at all. Believe me. You think people like being understood? Nothing on God's earth is going to make you more unpopular more quickly. In ordinary society if you understand people too well, and show it, what happens is that you make yourself ambiguous, easily used and—above all —suspect."

Talking—or rather lecturing—he had looked away from me but on the word suspect he caught my eyes. Immediately his slightly excited but even flow of talk seized, so to speak, in midstream. He stopped, drummed self-consciously on the table, seemed about to go. And in a curious way, what he instantly felt about himself—that he was being pompous, theoretical, pedagogic—communicated itself to me and I too suddenly felt that he was being all these things.

There was a pause. Neither of us could think of anything to say. I began to long for him to go. He took another shy, hooded look at me, realized (I swear) immediately that I wanted to get rid of him, forced down an inclination of his own to run (I realized why later) and started again on another tack, looking around him saying: "You really must make yourself as comfortable as you can in here, Mrs. Holland. Why, for heaven's sake you haven't even got a radio."

"I have in my room," I said. "I don't stay down here an awful lot in the evenings usually."

"What *do* you do?" he said becoming animated again. "In your spare time I mean?"

"Read a good deal." (You will be interested in these answers too, won't you Francis? Though you may not believe their simple truth.) "Walk sometimes. I adore the neighbourhood—"

"Yes. It surely is a beautiful part of London. Though I can't say I've seen much of it yet."

"Oh but you must," I said. "You don't know how lucky you are, living here. I do believe it's the most charming district in the world!"

"And the highest rent!" he said dryly. "Well, I guess I might as well enjoy it. Where d'you recommend I walk?"

"If you want to see one of the loveliest sights on earth," I said—and paused.

"Yes?"

"If you walk up to the main road, turn sharp left, twice, you'll find yourself in an L-shaped cul-de-sac. Walk right to the end, turn right and you'll see a row of little houses—"

"And?"

43

"And a cherry tree," I muttered.

"A row of little houses and a cherry tree," he repeated.

The sentence sounded so abominably sentimental that I felt suddenly furious with myself and said brusquely and rather hastily: "It's no good your seeing it now anyway. You're too late. The blossom's over."

He gave a rather barking, artificial laugh which I disliked and said: "Too late again! The blossom's over! Oh, well."

From what odd sources come the reasons of behaviour! It would have been more honest of me at that moment to have left Mr. Zold with a slightly *un*-pleasant view of my nature, my personality. Do you want to know why I didn't? Because I could not resist a small, nasty triumph. Because Zold's nose was shiny! Yes, he looked, with his shiny, bulging forehead and nose, rather ugly, rather vulnerable. And I could not, I *could not,* with a kind of vengeful vanity, resist the smoothing of my "gentle-browed" look to point the contrast. I suddenly fancied being beauty to the beast.

"Yes, it's a pity," I said in my "soft" voice, my far-princess manner. "It was really something to see . . . all that dazzling, luscious bloom shining against the sky. It looked so thick, clustered . . . crunchy almost, like some marvellous meringue . . ."

I looked up and caught his gaze full on me. With absolute surprise I saw that he knew exactly what I was doing—and probably why. The fact that he was obviously not going to do anything with the knowledge—just note it behind those heavy, black eyes and leave it at that—somehow annoyed me still more. How this man provokes irritation! And the less justification the more exasperated one gets. (You always irritated me by *not* knowing. He angers me unreasonably because he *knows*.)

Changing the subject (and, with an undercurrent of temper, abandoning the princess) I said: "I seem to be express-

44

ing myself rather theatrically. Moving into your field. As
a matter of fact I once had ambitions . . ."

"Yes," he said, his eyes lightening a little with a kind of
intimation of amusement (could it have been *at* me?), "I
rather thought you might."

"Did you?"

"Writing for it or acting?" he said with some interest, his
manner becoming brisk again. He enjoys, I think, conversations of finding out rather than opinion.

"Acting. I had a year at Drama School once."

"But no go?"

"No."

"Now why was that?"

"Oh . . . things. The war. Being a provincial; I come from
Liverpool. Marriage . . ." (I added after a pause).

He pressed his lips together and glanced at my ring but
refrained from asking about my circumstances. For a
moment I felt that you deserved some loyalty, that I shouldn't
tell anyone I had left you. Then I heard myself say: "I've
left my husband."

"And is this the only kind of job you could undertake?"
he said with immediate practicality. His total ignoring of
the emotional content of what I had just said was suddenly
extraordinarily soothing.

"Yes," I said feeling relaxed, unguilty, somehow safe.
(What an odd word for me to use! I hardly know what I
mean by it. I *think* I mean safe from exploitation. I still am
irritated by and don't particularly care for Zold. I can't put
a shape to his personality. But already I know this much;
he will not ever use my circumstances or anything I may
say of myself against me.)

"About what I was saying before," he said suddenly in an
abrupt tone, "about understanding people."

"Yes?"

He started prowling up and down once more, pausing at

each turn, one knee vibrating, before taking a hesitating, tiptoed stride forward again.

"The fact is," he said, "if you go over the limits of ordinary understanding, ordinary forbearance, people don't know where they are. They don't know how to behave back, you see. They feel too much understanding is being asked of *them*. And then they get angry."

I flushed slightly but this time, obviously thinking of something quite different, he didn't notice.

"The fact is," he said again, his tone—decisively, as if making up his mind at last—changing from the analytical to the purely personal: "I have a problem here, Mrs. Holland, and I'd be glad to have your help."

I started to say something politely on the lines of "Anything I can do—" but he said quickly, overtaking my murmuring: "What I want to ask you, while this opportunity pre-sents itself, is just to . . . well to do whatever you can, put up with . . . I mean help my mother settle down here. I mean, no matter how grumpy or whatever. . . ."

He suddenly stopped talking, stopped walking, stood with his head bent; not supplicating but with a kind of impatient, harassed stance. Then he said, sighing: "It's difficult for her. The change comes hard you know at her age . . . away from her own bed and routine and all. If I could have . . . well I hadn't any alternative—short of giving up the whole idea. Perhaps I should have." He sighed again, his face shiny, his lips feminine and soft. "Perhaps I should have; given up Europe, the dream . . . I'm not that sure it's going to work anyway. Oh well! early days I guess. But I couldn't have left her on her own for a whole year either."

"It depends on the kind of person—"

"Yes. Exactly. It depends on the person. Jessica now, you could put her down in an igloo and she'd hardly notice it just so she's got other igloos around she can go visit."

"I must say," I said, slightly nettled by an insubstantial

feeling of criticism in the air, "I've seldom met anyone with more charm."

"Yes. Charm," he said. "The all-important quality. The great ingredient; conspicuously missing in those of us knocked silly by the blows of life."

"Is that what has happened to your mother?" I said.

"Putting it briefly, that is to say falsely—you can't express complicated truths in a nutshell—yes. Her life, her life—" he began, inspecting his finger-nails, but suddenly feeling I could not bear to hear anything more about Mrs. Zold's life I interrupted, saying: "I've had no opportunity to see or read any of your work but I should imagine from what you say that it must be largely concerned with people being 'knocked silly'?"

He hesitated, gave me a look at once sad and quizzical as if to say All right, I won't bore you, then he said: "No. Nothing so concrete, I'm afraid. My work would probably be more successful if it *was* concerned with. . . . No, in fact—" He stopped and looked indifferently away. "My plays," he said getting the words out with a stiffly dissociated expression, "are not . . . do not start with 'situations.' Or at least they finish before the final 'knocking' happens. Most plays," he said, beginning, as it were, his "lecture," "most plays as you know like most novels, start with ready made situations. Simple example: A is in love with B who is C's wife. Enter complications, suffering, perhaps tragedy. But my plays are not like that at all. What, to begin with, made A fall in love with B? What is the sum total of A's psychological history which brought him to that point? My plays end where others begin, with each character left with a long, embroidered train of personal history hanging from his shoulders. Some dramatists, you know, try to cope with this accumulated psychological *motive* by writing from oblique angles; or by depersonalizing into allegory; or by inefficient flashbacks; or by putting into poetry or music what they

47

think unsayable in ordinary words. I do not think *anything* unsayable in ordinary words. What is lacking is the bravery to confess in simple language. There's always this fear of ridicule. Life and pain and feeling, even joy, even pleasure . . . they are all *ridiculous.* So we have to put them at one remove. I am trying to remove that . . . remove. But then you see this means I have to attack the conditioned norm, the norm of 'situation' the way other playwrights attack the proscenium arch—or language. I'm going to shock you, Mrs. Holland! I don't care about language! I use simple words, ordinary sentences. All this over-concentration on *language.* Ach!" He made an impatient gesture. His mouth lifted at one side. He looked suddenly very Jewish. "Crossword puzzles! All these precious finickers over words . . . they make literature into a crossword puzzle. Particularly in my country where they think they can learn to write by manipulating words. *What matters are feelings;* feelings irradiated by *ideas* about feelings.

"But to revert to my own problems. To put over my kind of play . . ." (he sighed) "to have to abandon the norm—which gives authority . . . Have you any idea how difficult this is? To do quietly, reasonably. Oh you can get away with murder—if you do it with a Salvador Dali moustache! But to say something true and new and *quiet* . . . it is the quietness that flummoxes people. They become so uneasy that they release themselves in ridicule. They don't see that it is life, not the recorder of it, that is ridiculous. Or at least, even if *I* am ridiculous, my work is not. Very often my work is confused with my personality, you know," he said, giving me one of his sudden, shy, hooded looks, a black and white flash before a quick veiling of his dark, brooding stare, "They judge it by *me.*"

(I should have said something pleasant at this point. I *know.* But I felt a curious, guilty embarrassment at his—I could not help feeling—foreign frankness. I found myself wishing he would stop. I did not want to hear his truths about himself.)

"But the critics," I said at last, "they seem to have understood you very well, I gather. You can't complain there."

He lunged one shoulder up and down, looked sceptical and said nothing for a moment. Then he said: "Really only God's darlings should attempt this job. No one else stands a chance of being listened to."

"Then why not leave it to them?"

"Do you think I did the choosing?" he said impatiently. "I sometimes wonder myself at the lack of discrimination which would select *me* as a vehicle of vision! Oh but that's putting things too high! You will think me a monster of vanity!" He laughed then gave me a sideways, knowing look as if to say "Yes! You did think that!"

A kind of rough, patronizing laugh had in fact risen in my throat at the thought of Bernard Zold as a "vehicle of vision" but at his words I felt myself give a soft wriggle of irritation. I found I knew exactly what he meant about people not liking to be understood too well. I suppose this has often happened to him. The fact is, we don't mind being understood by *some* people but for some reason I can't make out, I feel it an imposition from someone like him. I have an irritable feeling that he has no right to see through anyone. He is quite right about himself. He has not the authority, the bearing. (Yet even his self-knowledge annoys. Why?) I was half inclined to make a flippant or perhaps even snappish retort—a desire enhanced by the sight in my line of vision of the baggy, vulnerable-looking knees of his trousers —but for some reason found I could not. Instead, I looked up in silence and tilted my head in a listening position. He bent his own head towards me with a very slight, tender movement of his mouth, forgave me, so to speak, for the rejoinder I hadn't made, and went on.

"You know," he said conversationally, "you know something, Mrs. Holland . . . when I look back at myself as a boy I cannot believe I existed, that anyone so blind could have lived. All through my youth, my twenties, my early thirties, I knew *nothing*. Nearly every one of my acquaintance knew more than I did, conducted their lives, their actions, their conversations with more sheer sense and knowledge than I did. And yet I felt—and I suppose unconsciously showed—always a kind of arrogance to everyone else. I can hardly describe, let alone explain it . . . this deep sense of *knowing* when, by any possible standards of measurements, I was naïve and ignorant to the point of idiocy. And yet"—he suddenly moved forwards to the sink, turned on the cold tap, strode to the cupboard for a glass then walked back to the sink and stood there filling it, his back to me, still talking—"and yet, you know, I *did* know. After all. Under the stupidity, the blankness, the unbelievable naïveté, the incomprehension there was after all . . . Bernard Zold, dramatist, innovator—of a kind, anyway!" He drank some water quickly and turned round.

"But who was there to see beneath my skin? There wasn't a perceptive eye in the place. D'you know what American small town life can be like? On our level anyway. D'you know we never had a book in our house till I began bringing them home from the library. *Even now* I feel kind of surprised when I hear of someone actually buying a book. Books! The only books we bought were for kids as presents. Occasionally we'd buy a story or picture book for some kids we knew. But to *buy* one—for oneself or for any grown-up person . . . that was an idea which never entered anyone's head. *That* was the kind of society I lived in."

"That was the kind of society I lived in too," I said.

He gave an astonished jerk of his head. "Oh now!" he said. "You here in Europe . . . you don't know just what an uncultured society can be like. Your country's too small to get very far away—"

"Mr. Zold! you are talking, if I may say so, absolute nonsense!"

I paused to laugh at his expression which was delighted. (An intelligent, heated argument seems to toughen and straighten him physically.) "There is as much sheer, coarse-fibred, ignorant . . . *loutishness* of the intellect in any English city—in many a London suburb even—as there is in any small town in the middle of the Middle West of America. I am convinced of this. The fact is"—I paused because it was only occurring to me myself as I was talking, what the fact was—"what counts anywhere are the people one *knows*. How tied we are," I suddenly burst out, "by the limits of our acquaintance." (And as I said the words a scalding, bitter grievance seemed to break and echo about my head and I remembered in brief, furious detail all the holidays you and I ever spent together; my blind search year after year for something between the lower middle-class monotony of beach and front and the upper middle-class golf and smart-bar. The panic change from England to abroad. The third-class hotels in Brittany and Majorca and Paris, the maps across the breakfast table, the other English schoolmasters, the Civil Servants. . . . The blue skies, the soft evenings, the conversations everlastingly on food and currency, the "people at the next table," their recommendations of little bars with "loads of atmosphere." I recalled the embarrassed drinks at the top hotels, feeling like trespassers; my wild, sorrowful envy watching and listening there, the meetings between the rich and distinguished and famous faces. . . . "Mother will be down directly, Sir Edward. What'll you have, sir? Waiter!" Yes! I *know* you were willing for us to have dinner there. To what purpose? To talk? With each other? Ah! how insupportable! To know no one but dull reflections of ourselves.)

He was watching me. And suddenly I remembered that— in a limited way of course—*he* was famous; or very nearly so. Yet I could not see him at any Ritz-Carlton. He would have been as out of place as we were.

"You really mustn't," I said at last, "romanticize English life. Especially in the provinces."

He looked unconvinced. Then he said with a shade of embarrassment (I see that he finds self-justification difficult, even indelicate): "Perhaps . . . my experience . . . in my kind of small-town society, you see, I was, I am, doubly out of place. It isn't that my kind of temperament is misunderstood. It isn't that my character isn't liked. I guess I wouldn't mind that so much. It is that it is *not allowed for*. In American life conformity has become a drug-addiction; the kind that carries with it a wilful, blind oblivion to anything but surfaces. The interesting contradictions of behaviour . . . people in my country fight like tigers to avoid all knowledge of them. As for *tolerance* of contradictions . . . Mrs. Holland, this does not exist in small-town America!"

"But surely . . ." I was beginning when we both heard a noise upstairs and then the sound of the lock in the bathroom. I rose with a kind of controlled rush and he too moved—though casually—to the door. With his hand on the knob he said quickly: "You'll be patient with my mother, Mrs. Holland? It's . . . kind of important to me that you and she should get along."

"Of course," I said, and with that he was gone, the basic intention of all his talk not forgotten, a plea to me to be kind to his mother.

An instinct of caution kept me there in the kitchen till whoever had been in the bathroom had gone back to their room, then I too went to bed where I am writing now. That is—I am writing between long thoughts. For something of what Zold said has sent me back; back to a time long before our marriage, to the hungry, painful years of my adolescence.

Only a few days ago I happened to turn on my radio, here in this room, and heard a Maurice Chevalier recording of some of his old songs and immediately a kind of agonized nostalgia for my youth swept across me with an effect of most terrible, sad joy. You would never listen (for some reason it always made you impatient and bad tempered) whenever I tried to explain the "magical" part of my early imaginings, the adolescent identifications with Paris in the spring, with American college life, or, most particularly, with "theatre." (You could not in the least understand me when I once told you that in a way an evening at the theatre was over for me before the curtain went up. That the very entering the foyer was almost marvel enough.) You did not understand—you still don't—what it is to have a romantic imagination, a constant vision of other and more wonderful lives—and to have been living at the same time a lower middle-class life in a drab Liverpool neighbourhood. You cannot imagine what the Chevalier films did for me in my teens; damage, I suppose you would say and in one sense you would be right. But consider my realities at that time. The complete lack of grace; and worse (I know exactly what Zold meant just now) the unawareness that it existed.

Oh there were *rudiments* of culture in our society. This is where social observers, even sensitive ones, go wrong. They judge optimistically by these rudiments. It was it is true the "thing" for me and my friends to go to the Repertory Theatre, to go to Philharmonic concerts. But there was never any informed *talk* about what we had seen or heard. When people talk about culture in the provinces they nearly always mean performances of Schubert, of Shaw. But that isn't what *I* mean by culture at all. What happened in those days was that if I brought friends in to listen to my gramophone records they were willing, indeed eager, to hear opera —because you see, that was O.K. They'd been told that was culture, opera was. (No, perhaps I am being unfair, they

53

really did enjoy opera in a loose, sentimental way.) But
when I tried them with my French and German cabaret
songs they wouldn't listen at all. Those racked, unquiet,
melancholy sounds, that sensual and harsh despair . . . it all
passed them by. "But *listen*," I used to say, desperate to
convey. "Listen! you can hear the ruin of Europe. . . ." But
bored, uncomprehending, provincial, it all passed them by.

If we read books we didn't understand them; but we always said they were "very good." But only my generation even
attempted a book. The older ones, our mentors, if they read
it was *Tit Bits* for the men and *Home Notes* for the women.
(Not *Peg's Paper*, mark you! That was for servant girls. We,
God help us, were a cut above.)

One of my arguments with you all through our life together was continually provoked by my insistence on buying
all our provisions at Selby & Downes. "It's unnecessary—
and expensive," you used to say. And of course you were
quite right. But I found it impossible, I was too self-conscious
and tender and shy about my early *naïvetés*, to tell you about
my youthful fascinated hauntings of Selby's counters, my
long lookings at bottles of peaches in brandy, *pâté de fois
gras*, gruyère cheese. . . . They were not foods, they were
symbols. Above all they were the opposite of assorted
biscuits. Ah, those provincial biscuits! To the dull tea-times
of my youth they were a kind of trivial adventure, the select-
ing of a custard cream, a ginger nut, last and luxuriously,
a wafer. They gave variety to a dull life. But when I think
of them now it is with hatred. (Now you know—it has
taken you sixteen years to find out!—why I would never
have them in the house. What a *lot* you have never known
about me.)

I am of course à freak! No wonder you have been uneasy
all these years! A lower middle-class, provincial English-
woman with immortal longings . . . who ever heard of such
a creature? Many women of my class long for wealth or

excitement or—above all—for romantic love. But to desire style and oddity and brilliance. . . . I will tell you something, Francis, something very important. *I am a new kind of woman.* I am a type of intellectual Englishwoman who has hitherto never been found outside the upper classes. Oh they abound there . . . intense, unconventional, restless, intelligent; so many Caroline Lambs in every generation. But *I'm new*; a new kind of provincial-urban, intellectual Bovary from the sooty-brick, mean streets and the sweet shop on the corner.

Can you see yourself as Monsieur Bovary? No. For the simple reason that you have never read the book. This is another example of what I mean about provincial "culture." Yes, you know a bit about art and architecture. You go to concerts. You even enjoy them in a stiff and limited way. But talk to you about Bovaryism . . . and you would not know (you wouldn't know even if you'd read the book) what the term meant. It would be a reference to areas of thought where you are a stranger.

If only there were someone alive in England to understand me! But there was only Orwell who might have done; and he is dead.

Zold of course is no Orwell. But I am beginning to believe, to hope, that he will prove perceptive about me. You need not be jealous! My only use for Zold is to *use* him. Would you deny me the luxury of being understood? A luxury *you* never gave me. Partly because you couldn't, you were born without certain faculties of the spirit (this—like your scanty, sandy eyebrows—you cannot help) but partly also because you were frightened. Yes, you were too frightened to admit the existence of other worlds. You thought by denying them that I would disbelieve in their existence too. You even wanted to reduce your little talent for art still further, to confine it within safe boundaries. All that line and colour talk! Heavens, what a fraud you are! Yes, a fraud! To think how I was taken in at first. A wave of impatience with you seizes me. I can hardly write. . . .

Ruth

ΦΘΙΦΘΙΦΘΙΦΘΙΦΘΙΦΘΙΦΘΙΦΘΙΦΘΙΦΘΙΦΘΙΦΘ

4th June

WELL, Ginny's pictures have come at last and there has been a great deal of fuss and talk—not, to do him justice, from her father but from the two women and of course Ginny herself—about where to display them. At present they are ranged, all fourteen of them, in an unpleasing, straight line along the top of the bookcases in the dining-room. In fact—in surprising fact—they are not *too* bad; certainly better than I'd have thought that little bowl of porridge would turn out. But they are not good either. The interesting thing about them is their colour. This is uniformly dark, only relieved by heavy, hellish reds and big splotches of her favourite sulphur yellow. I wonder what a psychoanalyst would make of them?

The pictures arrived, it was decided to get on at last with the final arrangements for a tutor to give her private lessons at home. These will almost certainly have to be given in the dining-room with newspapers on the table and all over the carpet. I foresee endless clearing up after them and this has put me in not too good a mood.

At least . . . I say it is that; the prospect of extra work. But if I am to be truthful I must admit to a very curious feeling which is disturbing me. This family which has been my exclusive property for some weeks, which has had only me as a link of any size at all with the world of English life, is now about to admit someone else. And—though it is I who have told them how to do it, put them in touch with the agency and have been spending the last hour helping them to choose from the letters of application—I feel apprehensive and resentful. In a word—possessive!

Something very odd, I must say, has come out of this tutor-choosing business and that is the amount of snobbery I have suddenly discovered in this very-ordinary-class, American family. I am beginning to find it very hard to believe—as we are so often told is the case—that there is so much less class-distinction over there than here.

Three letters of application from private art tutors were sent on here by the agency. One was from a man, a teacher of Art in a Secondary Modern School. Telling them what this meant I let slip that my husband was art master in a *Grammar* school—but without further details though I can see the old woman is dying to know more. However, as soon as I had explained the difference, though Bernard maintained a patient "Well let's see," attitude, I saw that this applicant was out.

The other two were both women. The choice took place over lunch today.

"I just feel, Bernie" (this was old Mrs. Zold), "that this Miss What's is—Dickinson is it?—wouldn't be right. Maybe I'm wrong; but I have that feeling."

"D'you think, Mama, you could just once call me Bernard?" (He pronounces his name in the American way: Ber*nard.*)

"Bernard!" she said impatiently.

I have heard this argument before. And I must say that Zold is quite right to object to "Bernie." There is a kind of sensitivity in his objection, an intuitive feeling or knowledge that not only is "Bernie" wrong for him in general but that it is doubly wrong and indeed absurd (in a peculiar, Yankee way) to European ears.

"Good girl!" he said lightly.

The old woman pulled her chair to the table—they were

57

just about to start their meal—and helped herself to hors-d'-oeuvres, putting them, however, not on the centre plate I had set for her but on her bread plate and eating them sideways from there. This assertion of individuality (purely instinctive, she doesn't know she's doing it) is by way of protest at being made to say "Bernard." She remained silent for a few moments, eating away, doggedly sideways, while Jessica took up the discussion.

"Miss Dickinson *sounds* all right," she said, "I don't quite see what it is you don't like about her. Only I somehow feel myself that perhaps Miss Thomas would be more suitable. Oh my! I don't know. What do you think?" she said to her husband.

"Let's ask Mrs. Holland," he said taking a spoon to his soup.

His mother flashed him a look but taking no notice he handed me the three letters. I read them through quickly, standing by the sideboard. It was perfectly obvious that the unknown Miss Dickinson had by far the best qualifications. Apart from the somewhat ingratiating tone of the man's letter—a tone which instantly brought an image to my mind of failure, of evening work undertaken exhaustedly and reluctantly to help pay off the mortgage—he lived in a far-too-distant suburb of South London. I looked at Miss Dickinson's letter again. She taught art in a school in Ealing. She had given private tuition to children for many years. She was well recommended by all her parents. Her letter was short and business-like. I had the feeling that she would be bossy and full of advice . . . the sort of advice they were now coming to me for. Again I felt that shockingly ignoble, even idiotic, twinge of jealousy. (See what claims *dependency* places upon us! Quite unknowingly I have begun to like the idea that I am the only friend they have, that they rely on me. But do not build on this where you are concerned, Francis. I have an idea dependency only works when it is unconscious.)

All the same, when I re-read the third letter, from Miss Bridget Thomas, aged twenty-seven, who recommended herself as having no actual experience with children, that she had a job in advertising, but that her father was Lieutenant-Colonel Thomas and she could furnish references from Lord Boniface, I could not help dutifully but tepidly coming out for Miss Dickinson.

"You're probably right at that," said Bernard absently, helping himself to salad. He sat back and wearily regarded his plate. He yawned and I saw that he was thoroughly bored by the whole business and that he did not (I think rightly) take Ginny's possible talent in the least seriously. (I have had another look at the pictures. They are *not* good; save for the colours—which make one slightly uneasy—they are the pictorial equivalent of the soap operas she has spent so much time listening to.)

"Mrs. Holland," said old Mrs. Zold, breaking back into the conversation with a sort of flurry. "Would you mind, Mrs. Holland?" She pointed to the salad bowl with her chin. I looked at her inquiringly.

"The tomatoes," she said.

"The tomatoes?"

"We . . . don't like them like that. Don't eat the tomatoes, Bernie," she said hastily.

"I washed them you know."

"Oh yes, I'm sure you. . . . But we did mention. . . ."

"Oh Lord!" I said clutching my forehead. "I'm awfully sorry. I forgot."

"We, er, we pre*fer* them skinned," said Jessica in a—for her—slightly embarrassed voice.

I whipped the salad bowl off the table and into the kitchen, took out the sliced tomatoes, poured boiling water on some others and skinned them . . . all in a slightly irritated rush. I had completely forgotten their typically American fuss over food and health. Years ago, I remember, the same rumour went round this country: that tomato skins are unhealthy.

Whether it's ever been proved or not I don't know. But the Zolds are absolutely bedevilled with fads of this kind, all of which they follow scrupulously. The odd thing is they won't admit it, just give thin reasons. I imagine they sense the European view of American hypochondria. They know they're absurd. But my goodness, what a people! (You'd get on well with them over this, though, wouldn't you? You and your endless scrubbing yourself, your hands always raw and pink. *I like dirt.* But you. . . . You'd keep everything in cellophane bags if you could: heart, soul, love, longing, grief . . . yes, even your grief is clean.)

I took the salad back into the dining room. Bernard was re-reading the Bridget Thomas letter, lifting his eyebrows satirically and saying: "Loo-tenant Colonel . . . Lord Boniface . . . sounds pretty good!"

"Well I just think that a younger person would be better anyway," said Jessica, her clear brownness slightly flushed.

"Family's family," said Mrs. Zold delphically.

"Are you deciding against Miss Dickinson then?" I asked feeling relieved yet apprehensive. Miss D. I felt I knew. But a recommendee of Lord Boniface. . . .

"Well what do you think, Bernie?" said Jessica.

"We-ell . . . what's good enough for Lord Boniface should be good enough for us I guess."

He spoke in a still satirical voice but I saw that he nevertheless could not restrain himself from a highly pleased frown and I realized that he too was both tickled and attracted by the idea of an aristocratic connection in his home. He was no snob. It was the *romance* of the notion which pleased him. The romance and—for in a way I felt it too, I knew exactly what his feelings were—the strangeness. He was *curious* about the English upper classes.

"Maybe if she comes she'd bring this lord to visit sometime," said old Mrs. Zold giving the game away completely. Bernard broke into a genuine but irritated laugh but Jessica taking her mother-in-law's side (surprising me but I see that it shouldn't have done, she is almost as naïve as the old woman) said in perfect, gay seriousness: "I bet he'd just love to come!"

I could not repress the smile in my eyes as I looked over at Zold and he in his turn gave me a cautious, amused flicker of a glance which was still not quite cautious enough to escape his mother's attention. With a kind of snap she put down her spoon and leaving her pudding three quarters uneaten said: "Well you'd better decide amongst yourselves. Don't ask me. I don't want any part of it."

The logical behaviour after this would of course have been for her to get up and walk out. But—with what I am beginning to recognise as her curiously unpredictable reaction to any situation whatever—she stayed where she was, rigidly *not*-eating.

I collected some plates, put them through the service hatch and went out to the kitchen. As I reached through the hatch for the dishes the sliding door on the dining room side was slammed by Zold . . . with so much force however that it bounced back again leaving a slit about one eighth of an inch wide. Enough for me to listen and get an occasional glimpse of Bernard who had it seemed jumped up from the table in fury and was now pacing up and down.

"Look, Mama," he was saying. "D'you think **you** could be a bit reasonable once in a while? What's anybody done or said that you've got to start creating atmospheres all of a sudden?"

"Who's creating anything?" she said in a suddenly sharp voice.

There was a pause as if for him to get a grip on his self-control. Then he said more quietly: "Mama, this is not the time to start one of those dragging quarrels with me. I can't take it just now. I wasn't going to tell you this but there's been some trouble over the play. I heard from Braithwaite" (his agent) "this morning. The Vauxhall are asking for a lot of changes that I don't want to make."

"Well of all the so-and-so's," said Jessica with a kind of serene annoyance in her voice. "They liked it well enough when they read it, didn't they?"

"So what's wrong with making a few changes?" his mother said, wilful and peevish, unwilling to abandon her ill-temper even in the face of his need. "Maybe it's better if you give the public something they can understand. Who wants—?" She stopped short.

"Yes," he said in a determinedly light voice. "Like put a bit of sex into it for instance. Is that what you recommend I do?"

"Well . . ." she said uncertainly.

"Mama! That I should live to hear—"

"D'you think me crazy?" she said, her voice rising with an edge of hysteria. "You don't know how it makes me *sick* that sort of . . . ? But you say yourself people won't go and see any good stuff these days. So if it's tripe they like then why not give it to them? At least you'll have a long run. Your name'll get known."

"My name isn't known enough for you? Is that it?"

"Did I say . . . ? Stop trying to trap me, Bernie. You know very well what I mean."

"Oh sure. I know. You want me to make a name. So old Mrs. Glickman down at the Sisterhood will know who Bernard Zold is. If Mrs. Glickman's heard of me like she's heard of Mickey Spillane, *then* I've got a name."

"I don't think you ought to say what you said just now, Ma. Look at all those wonderful notices. You can't say Bernie's name's not known to a whole lot of important people in America."

"After all my talk," he said softly. "*After all my talk.* Does it matter, *does it matter* if I don't run like *Tobacco Road*? Does it matter if I don't make ten thousand dollars a week?

We've got enough to live on right now haven't we? I can always go back to my job. *Jessica can go back to work* if we look like we're starving!"

He had spoken satirically but I heard Jessica say immediately with that girlish, sporty animation of hers: "Sure. Any time."

There was a curious pause.

"Back in Philadelphia?" said her mother-in-law at last.

"I'm not saying I wouldn't like to be there for a while," said Jessica musically. "You know my family! All for one and one for all. We were brought up to be loyal and we've just naturally stayed that way. I don't see anything anywhere better than what I have back home. We have such a lot of fun together. We just enjoy each other's *company.*"

"To change the subject—" began Bernard but it was too late. Jessica, overtalking him with a kind of silvery insensitivity went on: "I've never known a time when our family wasn't absolutely united."

Even I, who knew so little about the Zold family history, would have known better than to thrust them so carelessly with that sword. I was wondering in a vague way if it *was* carelessness (perhaps Jessica, for all her sweetness, isn't above a bit of Lifemanship?) when I heard Bernard say to his mother, the more roughly since he was angered by Jessica: "Look, Mama, once and for all . . . I've told you this a million times. A. it isn't money I'm out for. B. it isn't what you call 'a name' either. Not that kind of name anyway. But even if I wanted them, I can't even try for those things—because I wouldn't get them that way. Don't you see . . . ? *try* to see . . . my only chance is to be *me.* I've got to follow what lives and burns in *me.* That way the other things might come too. Or perhaps not. But to ask me to *plan* corruption. . . ." (He was working himself up, a note of desperation almost of weeping in his voice) "I'm not going to use cheapened, disgraced words like integrity, a word

that means nothing any more, but what you don't understand . . . I've told you how many times? . . . *I've no talent for
compromise.* It isn't even that I won't. It's that I can't. I don't
know how. You need a special talent for it. If I tried I'd
fail. At least, going my own way, if I fail I won't be dishonoured by my own idiocy."

"Dishonoured?" she said doubtfully as if she'd never heard
the word before.

"Yes. Dishonoured. Without honour. So now you don't
understand English any more! Well see if you understand
this. I believe in the *good.* In the end *quality* prevails. *Quality
is all.* That is what I believe. That is the belief my heart
bursts with."

There was a silence. Then he said: "So don't push it,
Mama, will you? Don't push it."

"Who's pushing anybody?" she cried out in a violent,
strangled voice. "I don't know what you're talking about."

"Now Ma," said Jessica pleasantly, "you mustn't let yourself get so upset. Bernie didn't mean anything. . . ."

"Upset! Who's upset? I shouldn't be upset—?"

"Ma! Will you try not to get yourself so excited? This
isn't going to do you any good at all. Now calm down, *please.*
Just calm yourself down. Please, Ma. For my sake."

"What d'you mean, 'for your sake'?" the old woman suddenly interjected in a loud, scornful voice. "What for, for
your sake? What more rubbish? Why for *your* sake?"

Still listening from the other side of the hatch, I brought
my hands together in a silent clap of applause. This stupid
"for my sake" ploy; how I detest it. And now, from all the
people in the world, I have at last heard it put in its place by
a perverse, suspicious, obstinate, difficult, old woman.

Yes; she is all these things. And yet I am beginning to see
why he spends so much time reasoning with her. I see that
in some strange way she is not only a person to him, his
mother, his charge. She is a person in her own right. In

some ways she is more worldly than he is. She notices. She is logical. Her opinions count. It is only their expression that is ill-judged sometimes; and wrongly timed.

He gave her a minute. Then I heard him say: "I've got a lot on my plate just now. I've got to have a clear head, Mama. I've got to have peace right here in my own home while I work this out. . . ."

"But you're *not in* your own home," she brought out almost triumphantly. "Maybe it would have been better if you were. All this travelling and picking ourselves up . . . and all for what? You did all right without, didn't you? Europe! So you were crazy for Europe. So what is there in this Europe now we're here? Streets! like any other place. So we've *seen* the Tower of London. Better if we saw a few people. Like living on a desert island all these weeks. Who've we got here? Does a soul come in? You and you and me. And Ginny when she comes home from school. That's all! Not a friend. Not one person to come and visit. I was better off at home with one room. At least I had the customers. I had fittings; I had *people*. What have I here? Enemies in the kitchen. That's all I have here." Her voice, which had risen, dropped on the last two sentences but I heard them.

Bernard said even more quietly so that I had to strain to hear: "*There* you're wrong—" (But she wasn't! As I have just told you . . . in some ways she is cleverer than he), "you're being ridiculous. She wants to help you. She *wants* to be nice. You don't give her a chance."

The old woman muttered something in what I guessed to be Yiddish and he said sharply: "Nonsense. For God's sake, Mama, will you have some sense. You come away on a twelve month trip, you can't count in dimes. So who's going to do everything? You're not fit, you're hardly over that last attack. And Jessica—" he heaved a sigh and said tiredly: "Yes, well. . . ."

"Why you know very well, Ma," said Jessica, "we've got to

have somebody. There's a lot of work in this house. Frankly I don't think we pay Mrs. Holland enough. I wouldn't blame her one little bit if she left. I only hope she doesn't, that's all. I like her. She's company. Ma's right one way though, Bernie. I wish . . . well, I wish we knew just a few people in this town. It *is* lonesome with just us. I wouldn't have mentioned it—you wanted to come to Europe, you wanted to live in London . . . well all right, well O.K.—but it's a little tough on us. *You've* got your work to think about. You're all right. But it's not that easy—"

"Yes," he said in a different kind of low voice. "Yes. I see what you mean. Think I didn't know? I knew. I knew. I just wanted to get things swinging down at the theatre before letting myself think about anything else, that's all. I thought you might get yourselves organised without me for a while. Just. . . . Look, I'll do something. I'll ask Braithwaite and his wife over; maybe one or two others. Just give me a few days to straighten out with the Vauxhall and start casting. We'll have people around."

"What kind of people?" said old Mrs. Zold.

There was an absolute silence. And I realized what I should have realized long before: the extent of his problem. For who, in fact, was going to be suitable company for the Zolds? From what I know of theatre people generally, Braithwaite and any possible wife Braithwaite may have would be as fitted to make friends with Zold's family as . . . as the Vice-Chancellor of London University. Even Jessica—though she would possibly get by on her pleasant manner—would be hopelessly out of her cosy, gossipy element with people like them. (You will think, as many people do shortsightedly when confronted with this kind of situation, that I am denigrating the small-town Zolds as against the sophisticated Londoners, but this is a false antithesis. I am *not* on the side of the smart. Where my personal, emotional affairs are not concerned—as they were with

Danny for instance—I detest the smart, the "amusing," the shallowly sophisticated. But I wince and burn against provincial narrowness too. The choice is not just between simple and worthy versus stylish and shallow . . . nothing so uncomplicated. It is between two kinds of lack. How, incidentally, it occurs to me to wonder, does Bernard himself—let alone his family—fit with the Braithwaite world?)

"Don't *please* let's go into all that *now*," he was saying. "Let it ride, will you. Just let it ride. Let me get the next week or two over and then we'll see. Meanwhile—about Ginny. I *suppose* this Miss Thomas. I'll write and ask her to come. I guess she'll do—for Ginny's great talents!"

"She's *your* child, Bernie. I'm only a grandmother. But talk like that is more than I can bear. If a child shows so much promise shouldn't a parent encourage—"

She stopped dead suddenly.

"Yes," he said very quietly.

"Well? so what're you looking at me like that for? Didn't I encourage *you* as a child? Haven't you always had your own way? Ruled everything? Ruled and over-ruled. Don't I always listen to you?"

"Except when Jakie's around."

"Jakie! Oh, so that's it," she cried, her voice shaking a little. "If I happen to listen to your brother—who is after all ten years older than you—once in a while . . . that's no good?"

"For *years* he didn't bother about you or me or any of us," he said in a very strong voice, his attempt at self-control fading. "And when he comes back into our lives and wants to take over, not because he's ten years older but purely on account of he's ten times richer than I am . . . that's all right? *That's all right*? Eh, Mama?"

"He's your brother. He's got a right—"

"And not only take over," (he was fast weakening into

67

rage), "demand. Boss around. And despise me because I'm
not rich, because I don't twist myself into knots for a dollar.
And with it all . . . did he give you a red cent till quite
recently? *You* worked all your days till now. *I've* worked.
I'm keeping you—not him. But let him come into the room
this minute—and you're on your knees. Why? D'you think
three hundred thousand dollars in gilt-edged securities
makes your son God Almighty? Have *I* achieved nothing
in your eyes?"

"I come thousands of miles from my home," she said, her
voice tearful, "to have my son throw in my face that he's
keeping me."

"Oh, Ma . . ." said Jessica without either of them taking
any notice.

"Jakie's also your son," he said in a grim, determined
voice, "he's thrown far worse than that in your face without
one word of reproach from you. He's come in to hurl dirt in
my face—and what happened? Did it ever by any chance
occur to you to defend me? Mama! is there *nothing* of me
that you value?"

She began to cry in earnest but with such a belligerent
note to her weeping that I found myself in a sort of hysterical
impatience with her. But Bernard instantly—whatever
similar reaction he may have had—suppressing everything
from his voice save a reasonable concern said (and I guessed
he had gone over to her): "I'm sorry, Mama, I'm sorry. I'm
worried and I'm worried. About you and myself and my
work. You're right about some things. You're right. I admit it.
I don't know what it is. . . . We've been here—how long?
five, six weeks? And what's happened? Nothing. Nothing
at all. We've just changed dollars for pounds, familiar walls
for unfamiliar walls . . . and that's all. I feel like we're becalmed. I feel we're on a raft just swinging slowly round
and round in an empty, grey sea. There's no tide, no move.
Maybe I made an enormous mistake coming here. *May be.*

But now we're stuck. We can't get off the raft. All we can
do is wait. Have patience, Mama. I beg you, have patience.
Things'll start moving soon. We'll adjust."

"I don't mind for myself," I heard the old woman mutter,
"it's Ginny. That child's got no one to talk with, no one to
play with. . . . That school's no good. She hasn't made a
friend."

"Ah, drop it, Mama," he said with a slight return to irritation. "What did Ginny do at home when she wasn't in school?
Watch television like she does here. Thank God she'll be
starting her painting again. At least that'll keep her away
from that damned screen."

"Anyone would think you didn't love your own daughter,
the way you talk sometimes."

"Oh now, c'mon! I'm not going to have any more of this,"
he said quickly, adding: "Look, I'll tell you what we'll do.
Let's all go out this evening. Ginny too. We'll have dinner
out and go look at London. This beautiful June weather, we
ought not to be indoors so much. I tell you what . . . we'll
take one of those steamer trips down the Thames."

Jessica, who had remained on the whole remarkably
quiet and (I guess) mostly inattentive during the argument,
came alive at this—she adores excursions of any kind—
and between them they persuaded the old woman, grumbling
to the last, into acquiescence.

I watched the four of them go out later that day, leaving
me alone in the house. Though they make me free of it, urge
me to watch the television and so on, I found myself wishing that they had asked me to go along with them. It is not
that I enjoy their company particularly. Indeed, as I saw
them go and noticed Bernard taking Ginny's hand, his
mother's arm, trying (it seemed to me) to make of them as
they all walked along, a cohesive, family unit, casting himself as the authoritative, responsible, male centre of his
three women, I felt a kind of . . . not pity, not contempt . . .

something between the two. And yet I would like to have been with them not left behind. I find it very strange, this sense of being *intermittently* a part of other people's lives. I suppose all servants must feel like this.

There was something else I noticed—for the first time—as they walked off down our sunny, flowery, little street. And that was that where the female Zolds *looked* American in some quite undefinable way, Bernard didn't look so at all. Indeed, as I watched him I began to see an element of something strange, some discord in his physical make up, which, obscurely, has I think bothered me for some time. I have only just realized what it is. He has the body, the hold and turn of the limbs, of a European. There is physically absolutely nothing American about him; neither the pink-pig fleshiness, nor the rangy boniness nor any of the other transatlantic characteristics which are difficult to define and yet so unmistakable. This discovery has made me wonder whether his whole temperament, the very fibre of his nature is not perhaps European; that on top of his other troubles, he may have been truly and genuinely an expatriate all his life from the continent which would best have suited him.

I find myself wishing that things should change for them. Not through any generous impulse on my part. It is just that the pall of their loneliness is beginning to settle on me too. If only they could have some company. I hate this obligation they are laying on me to pity them. Worse! I am beginning to feel guilty—as though everything's my fault!

Ruth

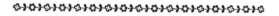

19th June

TWO good things have happened! One: Bernard has settled his difficulties with the Vauxhall director and they are to start casting immediately. Two: Bridget Thomas has appeared, given Ginny her first lessons and put us all in a cheerful mood. We have all taken to her.

She doesn't look twenty-seven. It is not that she is particularly good looking. She's not pretty at all. But there is something extraordinarily youthful about her, a combination of *naïveté* with a sort of comical sophistication which makes one feel gaily that the world is young.

I suppose we all had our private images of what the "Loo-tenant-colonel's daughter" would look like. I expected myself a slightly long-toothed deb with a deb voice from Harrods and—for some reason—tall. Bridget is not even medium height but almost if not quite small. She is also roundly plump, has reddish-brown hair which grows, as on some small boys, in a sort of whirling circle from the top of her head. It is straight but frizzy in texture. She has also popping, warm-brown eyes, a flattened little button of a nose, a very wide mouth and a chin like a little bump in the middle of a square jaw.

She is enchanted to be working for Americans since it is the dream of her life to go to the U.S. She has had a very unhappy life because her parents divorced when she was nine. Her mother's neurotic and her father's a gentle lamb but this is balanced by her stepfather being an angel and her stepmother a "worthy" (a "worthy" is, I see already, Bridget's blackest reproach against any human being) . . . all this in the first twenty minutes!

The lessons, as I foresaw, are given in the dining-room but I don't mind since Bridget cheerfully opens the service hatch (she is the kind of creature who will walk straight into your kitchen or curl her legs up on your settee the first time she visits) and chatters through it to whoever is at the sink. Though she has not taught children before, she took the trouble to mug up some of the techniques (perhaps she is not quite as scatterbrained as she seems?) and she and Ginny have been enjoying themselves cutting out shapes of coloured paper and making patterns by some complicated system. I had to laugh yesterday when she came into the kitchen to tell me she was barely one step ahead of Ginny in knowing about the process. "Still, as long as I'm a page in front of me lesson I guess I'll get by," she said in her pleasant gurgle of a voice, just touched with the Irish. (She comes originally from somewhere near Cork, it appears.)

I asked her about her regular job and if she was as precariously balanced on that. "My Lord, no!" she said. "I don't illustrate or anything. My special is lettering. Next time you're in the Tube look out for the Jenny Jones Toothpaste ads. I did the lettering for that. My best effort to date."

"You must get a kick out of seeing your work bang in front of the public eye every day."

"We-ell. I've done a bit more here and there you know. It isn't a new experience. The first time it felt pretty good. But you get so damn blasé. Hugo says," she added with what I have found to be her usual, inconsequential change of subject, "I've a very curious split in my basic personality. I'm half naïve and half knowing as hell. *He's* an artist if you like. The real thing."

"Hugo being your boy friend, I gather?"

"I gather too. Whether Hugo gathers is a moot point."

"Oh dear," I said. "Is it one of *those* relationships?"

"It's *the original one*," she said and, babbling at top speed, gave me a play by play description of her "affair" with Hugo—though I don't think that word technically applies. Not that the lady isn't willing but that the dear boy (her expression) is mixed up with a married woman and Bridget's shoulder (for weeping on) is about the only part of her that's any use to him at the moment.

Old Mrs. Zold came in in the middle of these revelations but Bridget quite undeterred (as I might have been) chattered on about Hugo's sexual and psychological needs and exercises, addressing her remarks indiscriminately to both of us. Again I had to laugh both to and at myself when I discovered that while I was feeling embarrassed for the old woman she was vividly enjoying herself—though you would have to be used to her to know this. Enjoyment with her shows itself in quick, sideways glances, a guilty, creased, cunning laugh round the eyes rather than on the lips, an extended lift of her thin shoulders. Anyway, she gets on well with Bridget whom she does not—quite unlike her attitude to me—seem to regard as a menace. She isn't of course . . . but then, neither am I! However, I do not resent her having called me an enemy. I see that my attitude to her, which she senses with absolute accuracy, is inimical; that I am by turns impatient, resentful, scornful; that because of her I am sometimes near to despising her son. All this she knows with her blood. But where she goes wrong is in thinking I represent danger. I doubt if she has any affection for Jessica though superficially relations are fairly amicable between them. But the idea that I may constitute a threat to their structure *as a family* rouses her to behaviour of a frantic and devastating idiocy, mixed—as always—with shrewd, peasant sense.

Take yesterday morning, for instance. I overslept and, not wanting to be late with Ginny's breakfast, I went down to the kitchen in my dark blue dressing-gown with white lace edgings. It is a nice one which I bought recently. (You wouldn't like it. It gives my person a flavour of . . . what is it? Fatality? *Fin de siècle*? Mimi in her garret . . . ? Anyway, something which you fear. Do you understand what I am trying to say? Well, it doesn't matter.)

Old Mrs. Zold came down as I was in the middle of squeezing the orange juice. She hovered round for a few minutes though there was absolutely nothing for her to do, casting sharp, quick looks at the dressing-gown but saying nothing until we both heard Bernard's step in the bathroom directly overhead. With a remarkable and immediate resource (really I didn't know she had it in her!) she jerked an overall off the hook on the kitchen door and held it out to me back to front, saying: "That's such a pretty robe, Mrs. Holland, you want to mind it doesn't get dirty working around here. I suggest you put this in front of you." And before I knew where I was I had put my arms through the sleeves of the gaudy, shapeless, cotton thing and she was buttoning it down my back!

She was so clever and quick that I have found myself unable to be annoyed. Besides . . . she was *right* to do what she did. (Though Bernard didn't come downstairs for hours, after all, and I was washed and dressed long before.) Yes, she was right, according to her lights, as they say; quite right. Anyone who might distract *him* from *them* is a menace. The fact that she has misread the situation completely, that he no more regards me as a female than I him as a male, the fact that to the best of my belief we wouldn't touch each other with a barge pole, both escapes her and is in any case irrelevant. I am a possible chink in the wall of his attention, of his entire concern—which is, or ought to be, his family. Grudgingly she allows a small part of this wall to be separated off by his work. But that is all. The man is as imprisoned as in some Château D'If. I wonder if he knows this, sees this as clearly as I do? I have a feeling not. I doubt if even he realizes the strength and sharpness of the barbed wire.

I have no time to finish this—

Next day

I had to break off quickly last night as Bernard came into the kitchen (where I was writing) to say that he was hungry and would I make him a sandwich? He adores sandwiches for some reason (memories of youth? picnics? hereditary dislike of formal meals? . . . cf. his mother!).

He was in a genial mood and talkative. This, I have discovered, is not really an advantage to his personality. Talkative, he is not interesting; talkative in the loose, flowing sense, I mean. When this happens his face becomes expressive and mobile—and all wrong! It is a ridiculous thought-cliché to imagine that expressiveness is a good thing on every human face. It is absolutely wrong for Zold since it impairs the only personable advantage he has; a kind of heavy, hooded restraint, an impression of spiritual *weight*, which is ruined when he becomes lively. But I can see why—unconsciously—he lends himself to this unseemly attitude. He has been affected to a certain degree by the contemporary fashion in manner; which is to be alive, vivacious, amusing . . . all the adjectives which spell "life." Only (I began to discover this through Danny and his friends) the more we chase after this elusive "life" in talk, the more it eludes us. That's the irony of it. Everyone flogging themselves into sparks only to find their interchanges more and more dead ash. But—*again* I must tell you—the answer does not lie in Eversley Road either. Narrow, blind dullness is just as bad as forced aliveness. A serious, full delicacy, flexible, sweet and candid; knowledgeable and intuitive; forgiving and upright; *that* is my dream of social intercourse.

(You don't understand a word of this do you? All you will do—so much better educated than I—will be to parse the sentences and define in dictionary terms each adjective. What good was it for you to say Tell, tell? You can't comprehend the lie of my thoughts. You are educated only to *facts*.)

Well. . . . to go back to the surface *details* you so curiously value so much . . . I was making the sandwiches—I know by now how he likes them; big, stuffed, untidy with meat hanging over the edges, he loathes prissy, neat, little tri-angles—when he said: "Well, these ought to give me strength for any further battles!"

"What particular battles?" I said.

"Over the play." (He has an odd habit—engendered, I think, by modesty—of hardly ever referring to his plays by name or even with the possessive pronoun; *the* play, he will say, never *my* play.) "Thank the Lord I'm getting used by now to the necessity of having to fight. It doesn't throw me quite the way it did at first. My! when I think of those early days . . . only three years ago in time but a century in experience . . . I wonder how I lived through them! *Writing* a play is hard enough—"

"How did you come . . . in the first place . . . ?" I asked, genuinely interested.

Sitting down in my easy chair he took the plate of sand-wiches and, snatching large, clumsy bites said through his, I must say, unaesthetic, not very well mannered chewing: "How did I come to write at all? Does that interest you? Those mysterious, tender beginnings of artistic creation . . . like the roots of one's finger nails. I don't really know my-self. I can only say that after what seems like a lifelong pregnancy (looking back now) the first play suddenly—though not without labour pains!—pushed itself out of the womb!"

Automatically, it was only a reflex action, I began at that moment brushing the crumbs together on the table; which was a mistake. Changing the subject slightly from what really interested me to what he thought *socially* interesting (I can only suppose that he has been conditioned to re-

garding his own thought-processes as boring) he proceeded
to relate, with that heavy gaiety which does not suit him,
some of his brushes with theatrical managements. He tore
into his sandwiches, talked, made modish gestures, gave at
one point a slight imitation not too badly done . . . and
bored me! "Yes," I said and again, "Yes," and "Then what
happened?"

"This guy . . . you should have seen him! Deep grooves
down his cheeks," he ran his thumb and middle finger down
his own, "shaggy, dyed hair . . . junkie almost certainly . . .
he *minces* on to the stage . . ."

I cannot imagine why, though normally avid for theatre
talk of any kind, I couldn't bear him in this strain, but I
couldn't. It seems to me that the moment he talks like other
people he becomes nothing. As soon as I could I got him off
it. This was not very difficult. He is not *insistent* in conversation. And I suppose that the shallow-rootedness of this social
bonhomie manner he tries occasionally is so wrong that it
is not only a source of impatience and strain for me; it is a
strain for him also. Yet, when I think it over, I see that, as
I have mentioned before, there are great difficulties for him
in behaviour; difficulties which are not *usual*. (Or, if usual,
never admitted to.) What, in fact, is anyone to do if liveli-
ness (or enjoyment . . . or expansiveness) does not suit
them? If they have not the personality—apparatus to express it? Yet he can't be strong and silent either, since for
this he would need to be either sardonic or lean-jawed. Zold,
silent, looks only melancholy and fat.

(A thought strikes me! Have you the same disability? Yes,
in your stiff, chunky way you have. But you see you differ
from Zold in *thick*-ness. In you there is not much conflict
because the stuff of you is thin. But *he* lives, this fattish,
pale, ugly man, with what I sense more and more to be a
profound intensity of spirit. Yes; that is all I can call it
however pretentious it may sound. And that is the difference

between you. But how is he to express this quality—the only one he has—within the boundaries of social intercourse? After all, who wants spiritual intensity in conversation? The problem seems to me insoluble.)

Zold was saying: "You know, I doubt if I'll ever get used to theatrical life. For one thing it takes a special kind of temperament to be at home in it."

"For instance?" I said thinking of Danny who was certainly at home.

He pressed his four left fingers flat against his mouth for a moment, pondered, then said: "One needs one of two things. *Either* a tough-skinned, absolutely undauntable ambition or else a sort of twinkling, good-natured sophistication without too much consciousness of moral issues. I haven't either."

"Well you must evidently have *something*," I said cheerfully.

"My best asset—as a *writer* for the theatre—is that I've gotten the business of living over with."

I looked a query and he said: "Does that surprise you? Well, perhaps other writers can 'live' while they're writing. But in my case I had to get 'living' out of the way before I could start. Everything had to be gone through and laid aside before I was free to write. If I'd started—or tried to start—earlier I'd have gotten nowhere. Because I *was* nothing. Experience manufactured me; not thought, not education."

"But experience can only take you so far. After all, experience happens to everybody, not only artists. What matters, I should have thought, is the you it happens to. You were still you even when you were much younger. All you had to do was be yourself."

He threw a crust down on his plate with some violence, ran his tongue round inside his mouth, swallowed with an irritated, sucking noise and said: "Be yourself! The biggest damned half-truth in the pack. Nothing annoys me more than that kind of remark. People say: 'Be natural. Don't worry about the impression you're making. Be yourself.' This is," he picked up a crust and pointed it accusingly at me, "a tremendous fallacy. Shall I tell you what would happen if I were to 'be myself' as you call it; not my deepest self which is something else again, which is something no one shows except obliquely . . . but the second-layer self which most of us are, which is grafted on to us from the experiences of our every day? I'll tell you. I should cringe, be frightened, wait always for a lead from others, keep my mind in chains till others tell me what to think. . . . This is what would happen (*did* happen in fact for long years) if I were to 'be myself.' That is, the self which circumstances flogged me into being. The real self, in the dark centre, that's a different thing again."

"But how did you manage to release that?"

Looking all at once very self-conscious—he has this habit of speaking frankly then suddenly realizing that he is and drawing in again (I suppose he still doesn't quite trust me) —he swerved away from a direct answer. "One doesn't really," he muttered staring down at his tie. "All one does is peel away some of the false: very gradually. It's very painful. And then rebuild around the . . . holy core."

"That's all right for you," I said unable to keep a strength of bitterness out of my voice, "you have a resource, a means of expression—however late it has to come to you. Whatever your life, however terrible you can build something else. You can escape. But what about the non-artists, the rest of us? How can I?"

He gave me a hesitant look as if to ascertain whether I desired to speak more freely of myself and said: "That depends. That depends. To a certain extent you are right. I am dodging the issue. But there are other. . . ." He paused then said, without any embarrassment: "Why have you left your husband?"

"I didn't just leave him. I ran away with another man. A

not very successful actor who treated me rather badly and who ran away from *me*."

"Yes." He looked away from me. "But why *did* you leave him?"

At this comprehension a great sigh of relief went through me like a warm, liquid flooding. And with the flowing came the image, the remembrance of the crystallizing moment which first set my thoughts towards serious escape from you. It happened even before I knew Danny. About a year before.

It was summer; a bright, weekday afternoon. All the housework was done. Your dinner was ready on the stove. I was sitting reading in that sunny, tiny, bay-windowed "front room" of ours in Eversley Road. (Perhaps you are sitting there now?) The book was a good one. I was enjoying it sitting there in the red armchair we bought at Webb's. (Should I cross that out, I wonder? Perhaps this one small remembered detail from our dead life together may hurt you more than any barb or revelation? I will leave it. It can make no difference.) Then I looked up for a moment and saw through the window our neighbour, Mrs. Palmer, passing with two weekly women's papers newly bought under her arm. She had been shopping and I saw in her string bag a packet of detergent and a packet of cornflakes and a chain store Swiss roll wrapped in cellophane.

And all at once, without warning, a furious, cramped agony of temperament flared and roared and beat inside me as if a great flame were trying to find room to burn. I became aware of my whole nature, suffocating, demanding, desperate, lashing out against the limits of the circumstances to which I had been born. I found myself beset by plashing images, absurd, cool pictures which kept tormenting me; pictures of myself still reading but in a long, green drawing room somewhere in France with outside a blazing blue sky and sea. I saw myself in a *château* with huge, pale rooms, among satinwood and malachite and gilt, soft voices and marvellous dogs, unhappily married (you see! the image was not one of romantic *happiness*) to an elegant, indifferent husband with a beautiful mistress. Style! Style! I thirsted for it, lusted for it. My whole existence in Eversley Road seemed like a mortal insult. . . .

All this I told him. When I had finished he said nothing for a few moments, only looked down at the plate he was still holding, fingered the crusts he had left and, looking patient, sad and curiously embarrassed, said at last: "And *we* are no use either. What a disappointment for you."

His accuracy was so deadly and unexpected that it left me completely without words for a moment. Then, though I am not a kind creature, I felt an impulse of soft pity. Inadvertently, underestimating him, not making proper allowance for his subtle understanding (which indeed I find myself continually forgetting he possesses) I had pained him with the knowledge of his own inadequacy. I said: "You are quite wrong, Mr. Zold. I am very happy here."

"That is not what I meant," he said.

"No," I said quickly, "you are quite right . . . I *know* what you meant; and I should have answered you properly. But I am often affected by a kind of laziness in argument. I don't *bother*, I become impatient with having to explain . . . so I let things go; fatally sometimes. But even in the sense you meant . . . you were still quite wrong."

I spoke those words again (though with flurry and confusion) from pity. And yet, even as I spoke them they appeared to change, as my breath expelled them on the air, into a kind of truth. What I was looking for, as he and I both knew, I would never find here. But what I was looking for was no longer so clear to me as before. I hardly know how to express it but . . . it was as though the delicate, ivory figurine of my longing which I had held always before my mind's eye was taking on the strong, flushed, metal look of bronze, the precious, secret image changing before my eyes.

Tiredness beginning to fall over us both, he left me then, saying goodnight with care and repetition, trying to indicate that no hurt had been intended or done by either of us. But I am still sitting here, still I cannot bring myself to go to bed. I am thinking of a phrase I used to him . . . "I let things go—fatally sometimes." I am thinking of what was at the back of my mind when I said those words. . . .

I was remembering the night after I had accepted you, at last promised to marry you. (Ah, those nights after deep decisions! How do we live through them?) I slept, I remember, and woke and slept and woke again. There was a terrifying feeling all through those hours of darkness as if some heavy bird were trapped inside my breast. I could feel its constricted, weighted wings beating, beating. . . . Reason would not calm it. I endured only because with the morning would come, I thought, release. I would ask you to release me from my promise.

And then, with the light, I felt abashed and foolish. It seemed so silly, so tiresome to say No when I had said Yes. I knew you would wish to argue the matter. And in the end I let it go on because I shrank from long discussion. Can human behaviour be so silly! To let one's whole life be shaped for the sake of an hour's talking.

But no, that is simplifying everything far too much. The fact is there was also miscalculation, a gross miscalculation on my part. *I did not know* what living with another person meant. That is—I did not know it could mean in some ways so little. I thought the state of marriage to be somehow mystical. I thought it would transform the mundane; that washing dishes within marriage would be quite different from washing dishes without; that getting up in the morning would be done with joy. Yes; though I did not love you I expected joy. I was in a state of primeval stupidity over the whole business which any woman's magazine writer would have reproved me for. And yet, I am an intelligent woman, I was a reasoning, intelligent girl. And look where intelligence takes us. Intelligence! It is nothing but a tin can tied to the tail. We no more properly direct our lives by it than by the signs of the Zodiac.

It was not your intelligence, which I respected at that time (I admired you from the depths of my lower middle class conservatism for being Left and academic—the pompous, pedagogue pink so typical of your class) which finally decided me to marry you. It was not your good qualities—of which you have many. (Oh don't think I don't know this.) It was not your considerably higher social position (relatively speaking of course). Though I was not free from snobbery then—nor am I now. No one is who is not well born. It was not even that fever for marriage which surrounds every lower class woman. It was none of those things. It was the weather that evening.

We had been for a walk in the park. How I loathe parks anywhere but especially in provincial cities. Melancholy horrors! We sat down on a bench to smoke and talk a little. It had been a mild, late-spring day. I had unbuttoned the jacket of my suit. But when we stood up to go a small, chill wind unexpectedly blew round us and so, before walking on, you stood me before you and carefully, gently, buttoned up my jacket, straightened the lapels and taking your scarf from your pocket put it round me. Then you asked me again to marry you. And . . . softened by the twilight and the gentleness and the romantic image of knightly care which, by that accident of gesture, you gave my imagination to feed on . . . I said Yes.

A sudden, small, cold wind on a spring evening; that was all.

Ruth

❀❀❀❀❀❀❀❀❀❀❀❀❀❀❀❀❀

Next day

(I AM reopening this letter to add an account of today.)

That child! There is certainly a kind of geological fault in this family; deep, riven chasms of the psyche deeply affecting them all—except perhaps Jessica. And even her I am beginning not to be sure about. But before I tell you about Ginny's behaviour this afternoon, let me relate what preceded it this morning.

I was preparing breakfast (fully clothed this time!) with old Mrs. Zold fussing about as usual doing nothing—except keeping a sharp eye on me to see I wasn't being wasteful over anything—when Ginny came down and over her orange juice proceeded to give us her usual résumé of some soap opera instalment she'd once heard. The child's memory is good and she was giving a passable regurgitation of the corny dialogue with long, syrupy pauses when at some point she came out with the sentences: "But Harry . . ." (long pause), "I don't want a pay cheque for a husband . . . I want *you* . . . your arms about me, your warm kisses on my lips—" when her grandmother said very sharply: "Now just you stop repeating all that nonsense, Ginny. That's *enough*. We don't want to hear any more of it."

With a look both bewildered and sly she asked why.

"That kind of talk isn't nice for little girls to repeat."

"You mean about *kissing*?" she said in an upward voice of sly innocence, her creamy, heavy-jawed look turned to her grandmother. The old woman flushing a bit said: "Now that's enough of that. You just take heed of what you're told and stop asking so many questions."

"Well people *kiss* don't they?" said Ginny. She was half sprawling on the kitchen table, one shiny, stolid, pink thigh

84

exposed right up to the elastic of her knickers. "I bet Daddy kisses Mommy—"

The old woman with a quick, wresting movement snatched Ginny's almost empty glass from her. Bustling over to the sink and making a great splashing to-do about washing it she was saying over her shoulder: "You just go and prepare for school now or else you'll be late. Go on now," when Jessica came into the kitchen. Or to be more precise she almost waltzed into the room and, moving around on light feet, began lifting lids, swinging kettles under taps, humming . . . her rather heavy, deliberate way of moving quickened and lightened.

"My, what a lovely morning," she said—though in fact it was rather dull. Fetching up against the china cupboard she turned and faced us, one arm spread across the glass door, the other holding up the skirt of her long, red dressing-gown in an actressy gesture so that she looked, with her full figure, like some Edwardian leading lady. "Aren't I the lazy one this morning?" she said. "My! just *look* at the time! I haven't even taken my bath yet. That reminds me!" With a large, graceful twirl she went out of the kitchen to reappear with a bottle of toilet water. "I got this yesterday," she said, "and I can't wait to try it out." Unscrewing the stopper she held it high under my nose with an airy gesture, the wide sleeves of her dressing-gown slipping away from her long arms.

"Isn't it gorgeous?" she said gaily, waving the bottle in front of my face. We were both laughing at nothing but her high spirits when old Mrs. Zold made a kind of impatient movement with her hands. Jessica immediately broke over to her, continuing her joking insistence on the beauty of the scent. Taking out the stopper again she attempted to dab Mrs. Zold with it, playfully telling her it would increase her sex appeal.

That did it! Both for the old woman and myself who

realized simultaneously and immediately what had happened. Jessica had slept with her husband the previous night. I had no sooner realized this than I understood what I had only vaguely perceived before; that this was by now an extremely rare occurrence.

She was teasingly dabbing Ginny—who was all for it!—behind the ears when there was a sudden clangour at the stove and I turned to see that her mother-in-law had managed to spill a kettle of boiling water all over the place. Though the water had not touched her her face had gone greenish and sallow, her body was trembling. And then I saw—as I rushed to mop up the flood—that she was in a torment of jealous misery. She could not *bear* the thought of their night together.

There is something terrible, tragic, nauseating about sexual rage in the old. And yet . . . I catch myself back from that easy, too easy, too fashionable interpretation. It was *not* sexual jealousy in its raw sense that was filling her with agony so that the spasmodic, aimless jerking of her hands, her rigid neck muscles, the grimacing upper lip she could not control were ugly and painful to see. It was a jealousy of *joy*, of inclusion. She had not been invited to a party, had been left alone while others were together.

I saw Ginny looking at her and then at her mother and, in the midst of my own impatience, wished I could protect the old woman from both of them. Jessica, after some useless passes with a dishcloth, had retreated to her customary position of quietly doing nothing with an expression of mild concern, perfectly ready of course to make some gentle, ineffectual move should anyone ask her to do so. For the second time since I have been with them I felt a sort of suspicious impatience with her. After so many years of living with her mother-in-law surely she should have known better than to flaunt her marriage bed before the old woman's eyes. Could she have been feeding her vanity at the other's expense? Did she enjoy vaunting, only half-

innocently, her large, smiling girlishness against the graceless resentments of age?

I had been using the long-handled mop on the floor and
had just finished when a protruding nail-head on it caught
my leg and laddered my stocking. I exclaimed in vexation
and Jessica was immediately full of concern. Was it my
last pair? Wasn't that just too annoying? She would go and
get me a pair of hers; she had lots.

"No, thank you. Really," I said. "They were old and
snagged anyway. But thank you, all the same."

I said this with real warmth since I have noticed before
that she is always generous with her personal possessions.
And then . . . she looked so *nice*, her clear brown cheeks
slightly pink, her hair hanging in a thick, sleek plait, so
that she looked more Red Indian than ever.

Impulsively I said to her: "How nice to see long hair like
yours."

"It was much longer when I was a girl," she said. "When
I was first married Bernie used to insist I wore it down
around the house. He liked to see it all loose. He was furious
when I had it cut."

"Oh, you didn't!" I said.

"Well it was so *unfashionable*. Of course when long hair
started coming in again I grew it but it's never reached the
same length since. I don't believe Bernie's ever really for-
given me. My, he was wild at the time!"

Bernard himself came in at that moment in a scowling,
ripe, bad temper and, though saying very little, sent us all
scattering.

A curious suspicion has since awakened in me: that I
felt that touch of anger against Jessica not on the old
woman's behalf but on my own. So that though it might
disturb you I feel I must now examine and lay down my
conclusions. You see, as I write I discover. There! I have
found a use for you at last! Are you pleased?

Though sensual I am not prurient. You would admit this,

I think, even in your bitterest moments. Yet I find myself pausing, even as I write, to dwell inquisitively on the facts of last night. Why did Bernard wish to embrace his wife after (I do not speak without reason; there have been obvious signs) so long an abstinence? That he regards last night with a disgust at his own weakness is glaringly obvious from his temper this morning, his harsh voice, his averted, almost sickened gaze away from his wife. . . . Why then? Am I being fanciful in supposing it something to do with our conversation before he went to bed? That, feeling himself a failure in the providing of that Style for which I (and perhaps he too?) hungered, he took refuge in the conventional recompense (the very conventionality would have chagrined him more) which—save for the one blinding instant—would be no recompense at all? Or could it have been that I provoked in him some pity—for the easement of which he took pity on *her*? Or is it possible that . . . well, yes, I *will* say it . . . that I have provoked in him (though unwittingly I swear it) the kind of vicious, sensual feeling for one person which is only assuaged by the revenge of making love to someone else. *I* have known this, Francis. I have known myself to sleep with you deliberately out of triumph over some other whom I roared to possess. (You have *asked* for this knowledge. Remember that!)

Any or all of these are possible. What is *not* possible is that he still regards his wife with any affection whatever. I see this clearly though the reasons are obscure. Perhaps for her sheer, sexual stupidity, or for such sheer lack of imagination as caused her—for fashion!—to cut short her hair when he liked to see it long and flowing. I have an idea based on nothing but a hunch that that incident had some final, straw-weight, traumatic effect on their marriage.

Do not, by the way, read into any of this the possibility of my being interested in him. My anger—if it was anger—was at the idea of being *used* as a spark to ignite other people's fires. In fact I am greatly interested in him as a human being. But as a man I can assure you he does not exist. The men who feed my fires are dark; the dark-faced men, the confident wreckers, the demolition experts. As lovers the builders bore me.

But the repercussions of the morning did not end there. When I went to bring the child home that afternoon we made a detour, as we often do, to a local playground where she likes a few minutes on the swings before going home. Leaving the playground she still seemed normal enough. But when I suggested that we stop to buy ice cream to my surprise she said no. Suddenly she was in a great hurry to get home, slapping up and down on her heels at the bus stop till it came, almost kicking me in her frenzy to get on to it. We climbed to the top deck only to find that her favourite seat, top front right, was occupied. "Never mind," I said, "it can't be helped." Making no answer she sat down, though there were others vacant, on the seat she most dislikes, the one immediately adjacent to the stairs, turned her shoulder to me and stared out of the window. Suddenly I felt the solid, little body touching mine give a great tremor. "What's the matter, Ginny?" I said rather anxiously. She said nothing. I put my hand round under her chin and forcibly turning her face towards me I saw it convulsed with tears.

I will admit without shame to being for one long moment more panicky, more concerned for myself than for her. Other people's children . . . I would not have the full care of them for a fortune. The responsibilities are too appalling. "What's the matter, Ginny?" I said again. "Did anything happen in school today?"

She shook her head, wrenched her chin from my hand and began to sob: "I want to go home. I want to go home."

"We'll *be* home in just a few minutes," I said reassuringly.

"*No,*" she said, the tears still pouring over her wet, clenched face. "No. I want to go *home.*"

"Do you mean to America?"

"*No,*" she said on a louder, more hysterical wail.

I put my arm round her shoulders. "Ginny dear, don't cry. Don't cry, tell me what it is."

She shook her head.

"Well never mind, we're nearly there. You can tell your mommy—" but at this she wailed aloud again.

"Are you feeling sick?" I asked. "Have you got a pain anywhere?"

I put my hand to her forehead which was hot. (The motherly gesture felt strange to me. You never wanted children and I . . . I was afraid of having dull ones.)

She did not speak for a moment, only sobbed. Then she said: "I got scalded."

"Scalded? Where? At school?"

She shook her head.

"When then?"

"S'morning."

"This morning? But the water didn't go anywhere near you! Where did you get scalded? Show me."

She held out her hand. On the joint of her thumb there was a minute, pink mark.

"That's not a scald, Ginny. You've probably pricked yourself with the point of a leaf or something. You're not scalded." I gave her shoulder a sort of "silly girl!" shake. Her tears came thicker than ever.

"I *am* scalded. I am too."

She lifted up her other hand and pressed the window as if trying to break through it. The nails went white on the stubby little spread fingers against the glass. Suddenly she doubled her small fist and, banging it against the window, said in a wholly adult voice with a hard, taunting slap to it: "I hate you! So does Gran. So does Mommy. We all hate you."

I do not know what shocked me more; the child's malevolence or my own feeling of utter inadequacy to deal with it. Apart from the sheer *hurt* (yes, yes, I know it was ridiculous to feel seriously hurt by a hysterical child) I was made deeply uneasy by the notion that she was only coming out with what they all felt—perhaps had even discussed. I see that this cannot really be so, Jessica I am sure does not hate me and neither does he, but the idea remains.

With a sigh of relief I saw that we were approaching our stop. I managed to get her off the bus, still sobbing desperately, and hurrying her to the house turned her over to her mother and grandmother, apologizing guiltily for her tears. Of her remarks I said nothing. The funny thing was that they immediately started apologizing to *me*. Even the old woman, normally pleased to have something to complain about was for her strangely, uneasily apologetic.

"She just gets like this sometimes," she kept saying. "I'm real sorry it's happened while we've been here, Mrs. Holland."

"Please don't worry about me," I kept saying, much disturbed by their evident shame. "It's Ginny I'm worried about. I mean I could understand a child crying if something had *happened*. But so far as I can tell, nothing *has*."

"No, I guess nothing has. She's just a very highly strung child that's all. She's been like this before."

I thought of all the adjectives I have been using about her to you; lumpy, solid, cheese, porridge. I see that I have been quite wrong. I see that Bernard has more burdens than I thought. I see that there are dreadful complexities everywhere.

It was Jessica who told me later that the child had been having psychiatric treatment for over a year before they left home. In America of course, as I know very well, this is almost as commonplace as taking one's child to a dentist. Yet I cannot resist a feeling of great disturbance. Apart from anything else no one likes to be told: "I hate you."

Ruth

❀❀❀❀❀❀❀❀❀❀❀❀❀❀❀❀❀❀❀❀

30th June

MORE revelations from Bridget! This time made in her bed-sitter to which I was invited to tea. (The invitation has —by some unspoken agreement between us—been kept secret from the Zolds—for the life of me I can't quite say why. Perhaps because it would hurt them to find that they had been excluded? I don't know.)

She lives on the Fulham-Chelsea border in one of those seedy-looking semi-hotel, semi-flatlet houses where one feels, as the old joke has it, that a bell rings at six o'clock every morning to enable everyone to get back to their own rooms (or out of the place altogether) in discreet order. Her semi-basement is only just short of squalid, large but dark and furnished with the glum, light oak throw-outs of thirty years ago, but she does not appear to notice it. For the first few minutes her manner was pronounced Kensington-hostess with many little politenesses. . . . "It's *awfully* nice of you to come. Would you prefer milk or lemon? I've *got* a lemon. Would you like the fire lit? I hope you're not cold. . . ." I tried not to notice that the tea cakes were buttered with margarine.

We talked of course about Hugo. The poor girl is certainly much in love with him; or perhaps I should say obsessed. Three times while I was there we heard the house telephone ringing. Each time she tensed, making no attempt (the Kensington, well-bred act fell down badly here) to continue our conversation until it became plain that the calls were not for her. So far as I can tell, Hugo is yet another Danny, only—as we used to say in Liverpool—with knobs on. He too is a Jew—full not half—and his real name is Harvey; Harvey Lehman, now Hugo Lee. This changing of name tells me quite a lot about him. What is unexpected is that Bridget sees quite a lot too. I don't know whether it's natural perception or the fact that she mixes in circles where a certain degree of analysis is common, but she talks about him in a disconcertingly shrewd way—though mixed, I must say, with much nonsense and sighs of love!

"It isn't that his parents didn't understand him wanting to be an *artist*," she said standing, small and comical, in the middle of her room clutching the teapot, her centrifugal hair circling wildly round her head. "It's that they don't understand *any* difference from their own opinions. If his father has an idea about banking for instance—he's stinking rich but *pure* working class in origin—he doesn't believe there could be any alternative idea. A completely closed mind you see. And when he finds he's got a son with completely alien ambitions, somebody with very sensitive feelings and yet sort of alert and tough at the same time . . . he's foxed. Sure, it's a new idea to him that people are *different* from each other. I guess the only differences he can admit are those between men and women. He knows about those all right. Hugo knows for a fact he's been an absolute rip in his time; but never let himself know it of course. Absolute watertight compartments. I told Hugo some chips from the old block fell on him from that direction anyway! He was furious. He's got his own watertight compartments, d'you see. I didn't lay eyes on him for nearly a week after that expensive crack. I'll be having to learn to hold my tongue I guess. It costs me too much when I don't."

"Frankly, Bridget," I said, looking over at her and smiling, "I can't see you belting up in any circumstances whatever."

"Sure I talk too much and too quickly. I just *cas-cade*. I know! All the Irish are great talkers. But that's part of me charm!" she said putting on the accent very strongly and giving me a grin. "Me father's just the same."

93

"The 'Loo-tenant-Colonel' as the Zolds would say."

"Ah now," she said with a slanting look, "you mustn't tell them in Honeysuckle Road but I sort of stepped up his rank a bit . . . just for purposes of reference of course. Sure me dad's been in the army but he was no more than 2nd lieutenant jumped up from the ranks. He's an accountant now. Chartered of course," she added hastily with typical provincial snobbery.

"You *naughty* girl," I said, feeling Bridget would only dismiss me as "worthy" if I showed as much disapproval as I felt.

"Aren't I?" she said delightedly and with pride.

(Undergraduates often display this same pride at having "wangled," on the most dubious claims, some grant or other, or outwitted, by some equally dubious cheat, an examiner. They are usually Leftish and very high principled and hold long, heated arguments on how to make a better world.)

"And what about Lord Boniface? Don't tell me. . . ."

"Oh, he exists all right. But he's living over in Ireland way down at the southern tip. Me grandfather worked on his estate for a while. He's ninety if a day. He wouldn't mind being used for referee if he knew about it. But who's to tell him, anyway? To be truthful I wouldn't have thought of him. It was Hugo and Erik worked it out between them."

"And *who* is Erik?"

"Erik? Why he's this hulking, great Swede who's a great friend of Hugo's. He's a sculptor. A genius. *Really*. And terribly good fun. He spins these *marvellous* stories" (she has a way of saying "mah-vellous" in a sort of innocent-sophisticate, pastiche-Twenties way. In fact, now I come to think of it, there is something extremely Twenties-ish about Bridget. Her figure seems made for long waists and short skirts, her small-boy's head cries out to be Eton-cropped) "that go on and on you think they're all lies but terribly amusing and then you discover they're all *absolutely true*. He's *marvel*lous. I adore him."

A little dizzy with Bridget's switches from Kensington hostess to Irish gamine to early Sally Bowles all within twenty minutes, I changed the subject and asked her what she thought of the Zolds.

"*She's* sweet, isn't she? The old girl's a bit of a bind, though. The kid's nervy as hell."

I couldn't help sitting up at this since I knew she had been told nothing about Ginny's behaviour the other day.

"What makes you think so?" I asked cautiously.

"Those grim paintings for one thing. Those colours! My dear. . . . Hugo says from what I told him that they're definitely neurosis-potential."

"Oh come off it, Bridget! The child's a bit temperamental, that's all."

"Have you noticed those *triangles*?" she said, her popping brown eyes opening wide.

"Triangles? What are you talking about?"

"All her shapes are *triangular in essence*," she said solemnly.

"Are they? I hadn't noticed. But anyway, so what?"

"Hugo says the triangle is *the* sex symbol of the un-conscious—"

"Brid-get!" I said, laughing.

"It's true," she said seriously.

"Oh, come on, come on, come on . . . so is the circle— even more so I should think!"

"Hugo says—"

"One more quote from Hugo and I shall hit you over the head. He's becoming a bore."

Terrified immediately by this word she said: "Oh my Lord! I shall have to watch it! Love does make people boring though, doesn't it? I don't know how I've let myself get into this state. Or at least I do. Sure, the fact is," she said giving me a sideways, rather pathetic look, "I love this boy."

"Yes but he's no use to you, is he? You've already told me he's in love with someone else."

"He does love Barbara. But that can't go on for ever can it? After all, she's married."

"I don't suppose *that* makes much difference."

"But she's in love with her *husband.*"

"I thought you told me she was having an affair with Hugo?"

"Well so she is. But it's really her husband she's in love with."

At my look she said: "It's all perfectly clear when Hugo explains . . ." but her voice tailed off on so desolate a note that I felt a moment's pure, murderous rage towards this Danny-surrogate. How well I know those "explanations," those long, enjoyed, logic-twisting confessionals, using women as priests, then off, purged, to the next round.

"Why don't you chuck him?" I said impatiently. "You know perfectly well—you must know—he's no use to you at all."

"Oh I *couldn't,*" she said. "He needs me."

"For what?"

"Well I need him anyway."

"Again—for what?"

"For fun," she said sounding again so forlorn that my impatience and censure died in a sudden surge of sympathy and fellow feeling. Who, after all, was I to talk? Except that I was older and married she was not so very different from myself; one of the great, unhappy army of provincial girls who come to London for "life."

Society is curiously cruel to such girls, I think; indifferent, unimaginative, quite blind to the impulses which impel them sometimes to silly Bohemianism as with Bridget, sometimes more seriously, to prostitution. The impulses are good not bad. They are drives towards splendour and wideness in living. Why does responsible society never ask itself: But what are they to *do*, these girls with their fumbling imaginations, their obscure longings for some gripping joy?

Do they *know*, the interested, anxious researchers sitting in Oxbridge and Fleet Street and the House of Lords, what lower class provincialism can be like for so many? Are the dull homes in dull towns, the dull talk and dull jobs, above all, the dull men and women . . . is this all they are to know of what life can be?

What are they to do? What are they to *do*? I asked myself frantically while Bridget went to boil more water. And, by transition, what am *I* to do? Where is the answer?

When Bridget came back I said casually: "And what do you think of Mr. Zold, our 'famous playwright'?"

"Mama's boy? Oh, positively a text book Oedipus don't you think?" she said with a resumption of her Kensington manner (since she was pouring out more tea).

"Certainly not," I said in a tone of quite incautious fury. (Incautious because Bridget in her naïve, gossipy way is both shrewd and incontinent in talk.)

"But it *leaps* to the *eye*," she said.

Up till two minutes before I would have agreed with her. And I cannot even now explain the feeling of drastic outrage with which I heard this half-baked, easy explanation of Zold's character or why I should have felt that I suddenly detested her words. Perhaps it was the shallow catchphrase, reminding me again of Danny and his circle, which touched off some deep-seated anger which had nothing to do with Zold.

"I think myself," I said, choosing my words with some care, "that our Bernard is a man of . . . considerable principle. I don't think you can dismiss him with a phrase, just like that."

"Hugo—"

I lifted my teacup with a threatening gesture as if to throw it at her and she laughed.

"*My friend . . .*" she said, "thinks he's obviously a super wet."

"*Your friend,*" I retorted, "is obviously talking through his hat. For one thing, *your friend* does not appear to have gone as far in *his* field as Zold has in his. Perhaps it's escaped *your friend's* notice that Zold is an already established dramatist in his own country and will probably become one over here too."

"I *suppose* . . ." she said dubiously, "only—sure and I don't know why at all but I can never think of him as a highbrow; *or* a playwright. Can you? The truth now? I mean, you'd expect to meet someone quite different wouldn't you? I mean I keep *forgetting* who he is. He's more like an over-worked doctor on the National Health if you know what I mean."

Finding it impossible to deny this—she had hit off with perfect accuracy his air of abstracted, harried patience—I said: "I expect we shall all have heart attacks before the first night at the Vauxhall."

"I'm wishing he'd commission Hugo to do the decor," she said thoughtfully.

"It's almost certainly not in his hands."

"Maybe I could just ask—"

"Oh no," I said. "For goodness sake don't, Bridget."

"I don't see why not," she said with a sort of closed obstinacy to anything but what *she* wanted which surprised me. Dizzy and silly she may be but there is a hard core there. I found it difficult to answer her since I had no reason save a strong feeling that I didn't want Bernard to feel that the Bridget who amused him with her chatter wanted to *use* him for something or other. Though I could not say this to her the train of thought reminded me of something else and I said impulsively: "By the way . . . there's something I really do hope you won't tell him or any of the Zolds . . ."

"What's that?" she said inattentively.

"*Don't* tell them what you've told me—about your father and Lord B. and so on. I have an idea . . ." I hesitated, not knowing quite how to put it without betraying the Zolds in some indefinable way, "I think they might feel a bit let down that you're not a member of the aristocracy after all!" I finished with a laugh.

"O.K.," she said absently and, afraid to give them away further by pressing the point, I left it at that. And shortly afterwards I left Bridget too, still waiting, babbling and in-attentive, for the telephone to ring.

Ruth

✿)✿)✿)✿)✿)✿)✿)✿)✿)✿)✿)✿)✿)✿)✿)✿)✿)✿

4th July

WE HAVE HAD visitors at last! Today being Independence Day the Zolds were invited to a cocktail party given by some Anglo-American organization. Jessica was in ecstasy; Bernard less so. The old woman was sent into a flurry of last-minute dressmaking from which she emerged exhausted. Also she wanted to know why they hadn't been invited to one of the big dinners!

"For pity's sake, Mama, not every American in London is invited to those. Just the inside big wheels. We're outside those circles, don't forget."

"It's you that's forgetting. You're not just an ordinary tourist either," she said shifting her usual ground to suit her grievance. "Your name's already known to a lot of people in the theatre anyway. You say what you like, Bernie, you should have been asked to one of the big private parties. . . ."

He gave an impatient exclamation but I caught a look in his eye of rueful, unacknowledged agreement with her. As usual, tactless and hurtful and peasant-shrewd, she had put her finger on a sore spot.

All the same the cocktail party went off successfully since

they actually brought people back with them for a scratch supper! A woman Jessica had known in Philadelphia; a married couple connected with the literary world (I think he's an agent); an oldish man who turned out to be another playwright, and his wife; and—the prize capture—a quite well-known literary critic on a New York journal. Coming back from the corner pub with the collection of bottles that Bernard had hastily and apologetically asked me to run out for, it gave me a sensation of almost disproportionate surprise and pleasure to see all the lights on and hear a chatter of conversation coming from the house as I walked up the street. I realized once again how appallingly narrowed down, how claustrophobic, their lives have been all these weeks.

Busy in the kitchen preparing food and opening tins I didn't have much time for listening at first, though the double doors and the service hatch were both wide open. Besides, old Mrs. Zold, useless as ever in a kitchen, was there, fussing more about cutting up a few slices of bread than I would have thought possible in any adult human being. Irritated beyond measure at one point I said almost sharply: "Do go in to the company, Mrs. Zold. I can manage perfectly well." But she wouldn't. And after a few more useless urgings I realized why. She was, quite simply, terrified. The cocktail party had been bearable since, with hundreds of people milling round her she had had no demands made upon her beyond standing with her son and daughter-in-law in whatever group they found themselves. But half a dozen people in their own drawing-room was quite a different proposition. Not until Bernard came in and forcibly led her out and into the big room would she move, protesting with every step.

"Just you go on in. I'll join you just as soon as we've got the food ready. Mrs. Holland can't manage everything on her own."

"Yes I can," I said quickly—and could have kicked myself the next moment. I should have helped her in her fear; but I saw this just too late. And for once Bernard seemed insensitive to it too and insisted on leading her, petrified with shyness, out of the kitchen.

I sympathized with her all the more when it was my turn to go in and help serve out since, totally uncertain what attitude to adopt, whether to attempt invisibility or not, I became nervous myself and retreated as quickly as possible to the kitchen where I sorted out my impressions.

The predominant one I think was of feminine *shrillness.* I do not think English women of that class have such penetratingly shrill voices. Even Jessica who speaks normally in soft tones sounded strained and forced, her laugh far too loud and piercing. As for the male American voice, this seems to me to present them with certain difficulties since what they have to say, which is often grave and European, is frequently made pallid by the curious, feminine timbre of their speech.

Bessie Levitt, the single woman friend from Philadelphia, turned out to be, from what I could gather of the conversation, a Career Woman with a high executive post in one of Philadelphia's biggest shops. "The store" figured largely in her remarks. She is Jewish, fortyish, rather small with a plump, tailored, compact figure. Her presence was a delight to Jessica and a relief to the old woman since, clustered round her, they did not have to tense themselves to the conversation of the others. This was in its turn mostly geared to that of the literary critic, Debenham Bleu, who was letting off a series of slow smartnesses to Bernard, the literary agent Gordon, and his wife, and the other playwright, a man called De Toke. (This name will probably not convey anything to you but I have seen two of his plays on the stage and one of them was made into a big film in the 'thirties.)

As soon as I had recovered my nerve a little my curiosity revived and after a time I went back into the drawing-room and unobtrusively began taking away the dirty plates they had been balancing on their knees and collecting used glasses for re-washing, stacking them first on the dining-room table and then removing them slowly to the hatch. This gave me splendid opportunities for listening and looking.

Debenham Bleu was sprawling loosely in one corner of the oatmeal silk settee. He has a curious figure, tallish, slim, but his long legs seem to run straight into his stomach which, a high, oval paunch, gives him a period, decadent air. He was wearing a dark blue suit of some extremely expensive-looking material (like heavy, silk cashmere), short silk socks and black suede shoes. He has a long head, a small, cherry mouth and a high colour. He could be a king in some historical portrait.

De Toke was as complete a contrast as one could imagine. A good twenty years older than Bleu, who is I imagine in his middle forties, he looks like the suburban daddy to end all daddies. His face is so completely ordinary that it is indescribable save in Police Poster terms; grey hair, hazel eyes, slightly ragged moustache . . . how *describe* a face like that? . . . let alone reconcile it with the tough little studies of small town American life he made his (slightly passé) name with. *He* wore, if anyone can believe it of a former Hollywood figure, one of those shapeless, old-fashioned, pin-striped, navy suits with a loose waistcoat bagging across his narrow chest. I found myself glancing several times at his feet under the strong illusion that he was wearing carpet slippers. His wife was as unremarkable looking as he; Mr. and Mrs. Fuddy-duddy Everyman, rocking on the front porch.

(I remember my girlhood, years ago . . . the huge, garish, coloured posters outside the cinemas in Lime Street, the name beneath the Stars . . . "From the play by S. R. De Toke." I remember the polished and englamoured dream, to my provincial young girl's mind, of a Hollywood life, strange-lighted, extravagant, extreme . . . could this shabby pantaloon be a man who had been part of it?)

The agent, Gordon, was short, purposeful, solid, easily the most American looking of the four men save for an unexpected dab of circular, white beard like a small powder-puff stuck to his chin, giving a look as of a Swiss professor. His wife in her turn was by far the smartest of the women, youngish, dark, rather haggard; very eye-catching with her scarlet frock and thin, good figure.

Jessica, though she wore far too much chunky jewellery, looked, with her slow movements and brown skin, nice but dairy maid in green taffeta. Old Mrs. Zold, running characteristically to fuss, wore a flowered dress and jacket in a tasteless combination of red and lavender. Bessie Levitt— of course—wore a navy silk suit; standard wear for travelling American women.

I found it a little odd, even if I wasn't part of the party (though Bernard had scrupulously introduced me to everyone as their prop and stand by, exaggerating my position in the household) to find myself the only English person in a room full of Americans. Indeed I felt, after a time, despite our common language, an absolute, almost shocking feeling of alienness. I felt they were *foreigners*. It was not a question of difference in accent or in class. What I received was the deep impression that their rhythm was somehow strange. The circulation pace of American blood (not quicker—sometimes they are slower than we are) is somehow altogether different from ours. Their temperaments seem to march to quite other music.

Alone with the Zolds, particularly Bernard, I had not noticed this so much. Now, amongst the others, his European quality receded; but with it went also, it seemed to me, much of that sole asset of his, the spiritual weight I have mentioned before.

Part of this loss may have been due to his special diffi- culties as host. These included the fact that Jessica in her usual helpless way had drifted about for a few minutes with a bowl of salad and then, giving up, had become a guest at her own party, settling into absorbed Philadelphia gossip with Miss Levitt. For all the notice she took of the sprinkling of artistic "names" in the room or the fact that spurts of smartish, intellectual talk were at hand to be heard, they might not have been there at all. It was not shyness, it was profound disinterest. Minna's marriage to an old bachelor with a hardware store on Fenwick was what really held her. I have an idea that even her friend had other ideas and was itching to join in with what she could overhear in other parts of the room. But Jessica had wrapped her round so securely with so adhesive and unending a flypaper of home town gossip that she couldn't escape. I must say I sympa- thized with Miss Levitt who hadn't come to Europe to talk about old school friends. So, I fancy, did the old woman who, tormented with nerves and shyness, stuck grimly to Jessica and her friend though all the while her eyes and ears flicked and strained to hear what Bleu and the others were saying. I have an idea that beneath that thin and fussed exterior a kind of embryonic social ambition lurks. Perhaps this accounts for her impatience with her son? I must admit that in company he does not shine.

One of the reasons for this, it seems to me, is the lack of either oil or vinegar in his temperament, those special in- gredients which either bind or touch up a group of people. He was a *kind* host, generous and peripatetic, walking about with plates and bottles, but with something too self-effacing about him so that for a time he became a sort of super- butler, not taken too much notice of by his guests. This changed a little when he sat down. After all a host, however

shy, always feels a kind of ease about breaking into a conversation: his own walls about him gave him *rights*.

He sat in the opposite corner of the settee to Bleu, looking podgy, his full, pear-shape face pale and swarthy at the
same time. Debenham Bleu looked quite impossibly elegant
in the other corner. As I watched I saw him cross one long,
blue-cashmered leg over the other and with a slow, sensual
movement gently flex his foot in its narrow, Italian-looking,
black suede shoe to and fro in the air; his ankle, looking
extraordinarily slim and loose in its short, silk sock, giving
me, all at once, an impression of deep corruption. This
sounds, perhaps, fanciful. Yet I can only repeat that that
narrow, loose-jointed, silken ankle conveyed to me an impression of exhausted, mannered vice.

It is of course entirely possible that some flavour from
his conversation was colouring my feelings about his personality since I heard him say to Bernard: "That's all very
fine as an abstract conception. But let's face it. Racine
was a great bore. For my money I'll take Molière. Now
there's a dramatist who was *live*. I could spend an evening
on the town with that guy and feel I'd spent it good . . .
but *good*. Maybe this is a matter of temperament. It may
be we shouldn't use subjective, personal criteria . . . though
why in hell these should be less respectable than any
other. . . . Maybe the Aristotelian unities count to the dry
mind. Me, I prefer lung and liver—and all parts south."

I saw him look down fleetingly at his own paunch which
he was slowly stroking up and down with a slim-wristed
hand.

"It depends what you call life," said Bernard. "The dry
mind, as you call it, has its own life. And a much more
exciting. . . ." He leaned forward, a little excited himself,
to put forward what was obviously a dear theory to him.
"For instance, people talk about the Bomb as if it's the
most important thing in the century. To me that's nonsense

—and highly immoral nonsense since numbers don't deepen sin. One man's murder or one million men . . . what the hell difference? Individual guilt is what counts. Not weapons. The club, the bow and arrow, gunpowder, the wicked, wrong decision . . . the Charge of the Light Brigade, the massacre of Passchendaele . . . to me there is no difference. The Bomb won't destroy the world. At worst there'll be a Noah. But the big thing, the truly big thing of our time is the toe we've dipped into the unknown waters of the mind. . . ."

He paused there, feeling delicately that he was monopolising the talk and hoping that the others would take it from there, but De Toke said nothing and Bleu said "Maybe," rather indifferently. Attempting to strike a response he went on: "Just about the most exciting lines in the whole of literature to me are Hopkins's: Oh, the mind, mind has mountains; Cliffs of fall—" but this was almost too successful and the rest of his words were drowned since De Toke and Bleu both immediately rushed upon the opportunity to relieve *their* minds of a load of quotes.

"Of course," began Bleu, "literature stacks bigger and more explosive balls of fire than any we can stockpile at—"

"I remember," said De Toke, his high, Yankee quack winning out above Bleu's drawl through sheer persistence, "I recall my professor in my first Harvard semester telling the class that the most morally" (he pronounced it more-allee) "incendiary line in the language was: 'I need no assurances—I am a man who is preoccupied of his own Soul.' . . ."

"Old Walt did better than that in the *Je m'en fiche* stakes," Bleu cut in with a smoothly conversational skater's glide. "How about 'I heed not and have never heeded either experience, cautions, majorities or ridicule.' "

"Young men's sentiments really," said Bernard.

"Are they?" said Bleu, smiling his high-coloured, kingly, destroying smile. "A fair statement of my own position I like to think."

Mrs. De Toke who had been sitting near got up and went to join the other women. Mrs. Gordon, who had been sitting doing nothing with an expression of boredom—I got the impression she felt the evening was being a waste of time—followed her. Old Mrs. Zold, seeing their positions vacated, made a sudden, quick, defiant decision and moved herself across into Mrs. De Toke's chair. Bernard leaned forward and gave her a smile. Her fingers moved a little for a few moments then, as the men went on talking, her nervousness subsided and she sat on with quiet attention.

" 'What is called hell'? Well? What *is* called hell?" said De Toke. He put his whole hand inside the front of his loose waistcoat (or vest as I suppose he would call it) and massaged his ribs. "For my part I agree with the verdict of the great writers in all languages." (His voice suddenly turned parsonical, giving each word a clergyman's tremolo in the middle.) "Hell is the absence of love. 'If I live yet it is for good, more love through me to men.' " Rolling out the words with his forefinger uplifted and in his preachy twang he gave an impression of a Los Angeles faith healer.

While talking he had moved a foot sideways and kicked over some empty glasses which were standing beside his chair. I had crossed the room unobtrusively and was bending down to collect them when, making a somewhat elaborate, fussy demonstration of picking them up for me without actually bothering to do so, he said: "That was said by one of your great English poets, Mrs. Holland."

"Yes I know," I said without thinking as I straightened up clutching the glasses.

"Do you know which one?"

I hesitated. Old Mrs. Zold in whom suspicion of me
was never far below the skin had, I saw, physically jerked
with resentment. Again I hesitated. It would be kinder to
her, to Bernard, to myself even, if I wanted to go on
working there in peace, if I said I didn't know. She would
be pacified by my ignorance, her own sense of inadequacy untormented. It was one of those moments of tiny,
delicate decisions, to be kind or to be selfish, by which
I think God must judge us. And yet . . . "Browning," I said
. . . for defiance, for vanity.

"Say! this is quite some helper you've got in your household," he said to Bernard who pleasantly but unsmilingly
agreed. I moved quickly away to the kitchen, pleased to
have had an opportunity to impress my minuscule knowledge on the company, pleased to have shown the old
woman I was more than servant, pleased, *pleased* with
myself. And even now I am still pleased; even now while
I blush with shame at so mean a victory.

When I came back into the room with some ice cubes
old Mrs. Zold had changed her seat again and was now
talking or rather being talked to by Mrs. De Toke who
appeared to be one of those women who can squeak on
for hours regardless of any quality of attention in her
hearer. The old woman, still deeply agitated, was making
a pretence of listening.

Bernard was saying: "No, I don't long for *my* youth
again—"

"Youth's a stuff will not endure," trolled out De Toke,
still hell-bent on quotation.

I saw Bernard give him a fleeting look of some impatience. It was evident that he still wished for *talk* not
the exchange of tags, the lees of education or memory.
He had quoted Hopkins to prove a *point,* not himself.

"But seriously," he said (but in trying to swing the
conversation back to a level where he would feel more

at home his tone became ponderous and I saw Debenham Bleu beginning to tap his middle finger on the arm
of the settee) "why we as a nation worship youth so
much is because we confuse it with innocence. We long
for the irresponsibility of not knowing. I would not myself
be young again for anything you could offer me. But I
long, I must admit it, for innocence. To be ignorant of
the pain of the world . . . not to be haunted by knowledge
of the pain, the suffering, the injustice and horror that's
going on all the time everywhere . . . If I could have unawareness back again . . . *that* would be happiness."

"You think so," said Bleu, his eyes resting on Mrs.
Gordon's shoulders which had almost slipped out of her
scarlet dress. She gave him a long look back. "But in
fact you've touched on the classic dilemma. Because of
course you can't know happiness, full happiness, if you're
unaware." He looked away and down the length of the
room towards where I was standing, his eyes cold and
absent. "I recall from the remnants of my own education in Philosophy some discussion with my professor
(Ballard, you probably read some of his books) on this
same point. How experience the ultimate possibilities of
happiness—or ecstasy; say sexual ecstasy—" (his eyes
flickered towards Mrs. Gordon again) "without an en-
larged perception? Yet the more extreme the perception,
the more you're able to perceive joy, the *less* you're able
to experience it since then you're more awake to pain
also. Yes, sure, we talked a lot about that little problem.
You ever meet Ballard?"

Bernard shook his head.

"Say, I know this Ballard," said Gordon. "I remember
now. Came to us when he had a fight with his publisher.
Didn't want to leave him but didn't want the indignity
of fighting with him over sordid little details like money.
We offered to place him elsewhere but he said no, no,

he didn't want that, he'd always carry a feeling of divided loyalties if he left Harrison Lewis."

"More likely divided royalties," said Bleu. "I happen to know he's got a firm contract three books ahead with Lewis."

"That reminds me," said Gordon, "what about offering us something yourself? You tied up with anyone?"

I was standing by the drinks tray and Bleu, catching my eye, held up his empty glass. I came over and he said with a look at Bernard: "If I may . . . ? Scotch please. Well now . . ." to Gordon, "as you probably know, *Value Judgments in Orbit* did pretty well. I guess it's one of the few works of purely literary criticism that sold like ice cream in August—back home *and* right here in Europe . . . thank you," he said taking his Scotch with an upward, considering look at me from where he sat like some slack potentate.

"Sure. I know," said Gordon firmly. The round, silvery powder puff of beard on his chin seemed to bristle with confidence.

"*But,*" said Bleu, his eyes narrow and autocratic, "I don't know that Mommsen is quite the right house for me nevertheless. All publishers suffer from a curious disease called Memory Lag. Anything out more than twenty-five weeks gets expunged from those ivory tablets they use for minds. They've got to keep them clear for the next title."

"Ah, come on now," said Bernard. Baulked of the discussion which would really interest him and obliged to go along with the others, he was falling back—as usual when he was ill at ease—on the heavy-playful manner which suited him least of all. "I'm always hearing horror stories about publishers. I haven't had all that experience but my first play has been treated pretty well in print. Damn it, I *like* my publisher. He's a nice guy."

"You're with Frock & Scholes?" said Gordon knowledgeably.

"They still around?" said Bleu lazily. "It's a miracle. They've been on the skids for years."

"They're not a bad little firm," said Gordon with brisk, professional summing up. "You underestimate them, Bleu. They're modest, they don't splash around, but they're sound. You could do a lot worse," he said to Bernard.

"You're darn right I could," Bernard said rather angrily. "Because Scholes is a nice guy that doesn't mean he doesn't know how to run his business. Isn't that just what's wrong with us, with America, with civilization come to that . . . always equating integrity with being soft in the head."

Though he sounded suddenly contentious it was not because he wished to be offensive to Bleu. It was rather that he was offering intimacy, as if he were saying: "I know you so well that I can be blunt and quarrelsome with you. Only friends can hector each other." *I* saw this, but Bleu didn't. Along with that look of dissipated monarchy there was a touchy arrogance of kings to match it. He did not like Bernard's tone. I saw him give his host a glance, frown slightly, seem to debate within himself whether Bernard was anyway a big enough name as yet to be worth the trouble of arguing with, decide that the kind of party talk and definitive proclamations which suited *him* best were continually being dragged towards serious comment by a man who actually expected conversation about *ideas*—and that it was time for him to go. In any case, he explained as he lazily prepared himself to get up, he was due at a supper party and was terribly late.

(I had already been wondering why he had come at all since he was not the man to be without an invitation for the 4th July. My guess was that he wanted to keep a light tab on Bernard just in case he had a smash hit in the near future.)

Yet when he had gone I must admit that a quality of Style—made even more potent by the sheen of corruption on it—went with him. The atmosphere became easier but dulled.

"You want my opinion," De Toke was quacking, "we're in the wrong racket, Zold. Unless you make the big time a dramatist might as well shut up shop. Know what percentage I pulled down these last five years—?" He stopped short, suddenly aware that the Scotch of which he'd taken a considerable amount, was loosening his tongue almost to confession-of-failure point. "Well . . . it wasn't peanuts but it wasn't coconuts either. You want to get out of it like I'm doin'. Write a novel. Leastways there it is in a hard cover. Always a chance it'll catch sooner or later. And by golly it's easier to sell the movie rights of a novel than a play these days. What you want to do is write a whaddyacallit? a *bildungsroman*. That's it! A *bildungsroman*. Know what that is?

"Yes," said Bernard. He was sitting in a hunched position and looked very tired but I think it was the tiredness of disappointment. The pleasure of intelligent talk which, surrounded by so much womanishness he must have been longing for, had been largely denied him. Bleu had made him feel both oafish and dissatisfied.

"It means," said De Toke determined to explain, "the novel of education. Goethe, Werther . . . all that malarkey. The young man's apprenticeship, the facts of life. . . ."

I was still standing by the drinks tray, ostensibly in case anyone wanted another drink. No one, not even old Mrs. Zold was taking any notice of me. I was free to watch and listen. The women were talking amongst themselves. Gordon, firm, compact and fleshy, seemed alert but was beginning to take quick looks at his watch. He, too, felt diminished by Bleu's going.

"That's where the dough is. Take my word. A young man's education in bed, outa bed . . . in not less than 150,000 words. You'll clean up. Isn't that so, Gordon?"

"You may be right. Size . . . that's the criteria. Sheer, physical bulk. Makes the customers feel that they're getting value for money. But it's more than that, mind. They kinda like the psychological feeling that they're not going to be caught short on a long journey with nothing left to read. Like even a winter week-end at home, even a rainy Saturday afternoon, is a lo-orng journey."

I saw Bernard look up with interest—as I did myself—at this remark. I had not thought Gordon so capable of penetration. But what he had just said was not only penetrating; it was so in a peculiarly American way . . . in its slant, in its recognition of what must be the facts of everyday American life, its special brand of boredom, its need to fill the hours with a feeling (as against the British sittingdownness) of travel and movement . . . even from, through and to a vacuum.

"Size!" said Bernard. "It's a damned national neurosis. Like freedom. Freedom to do what? Be trivial?"

"You can't talk about freedom," said Gordon, "in that dismissing way since you don't know, none of us know, what life can be like without it. You go live in Vladivostok or some place—"

"O.K.!" said Bernard. "O.K.! I know the argument by heart. Granted that life in Russia is a terrifying thought to any American. It is to *me*. And yet, terrifying or no, the idea has one enormous attraction."

"Yeah," said De Toke rousing himself. "Cheap Vodka. Say, you guys wanna avoid a hangover anytime lemme recommend a lil tip I got from a naval orficer I met in Minneapolis time I lectured out there. Vodka and pineapple juice! Whee . . . ! High as you like at night and fresh as a baby's eyes in the morning."

"Vodka and pineapple juice?" said Gordon thoughtfully.

Bernard, still stubbornly trying to save the evening for himself, to discuss an idea intelligently for more than two consecutive sentences, said irritably: "At least the Commies have one great virtue. They're *serious*. Living beyond the Curtain you'd at least be in a serious environment, you'd be free of this . . . this poisonous *flippancy* that's destroying the Western world, this social refusal that's going on all the time to be serious about anything but money."

"What else is there to be serious about?" said De Toke looking peculiarly infantile with his little, reddened face and straggling grey curls. He was almost completely tight.

"To find a society not absorbed in dollars and drink and sex and being amusing," said Bernard addressing himself entirely to Gordon, "*not smart,* a society where it isn't smug or boring or pious or naïve to be *interested. . . .* To be able to be *serious . . . that* is the Russian secret weapon; the most powerful they possess. That is their magnetic strength, the point at which they make their converts from our own sickening, sick, shirking triviality."

"I don't know about you, Gordon," said De Toke wagging his head, "but I feel we've gotten ourselves into dangerous company this evening."

"Don't you worry," said Gordon looking at his watch again. "I don't think our friend here is a Red. Fact there's quite a lot in what he says. Quite a lot. But . . ." he rose as he was speaking, "time goes on. It goes on."

"It certainly does," said De Toke rising himself though not without difficulty.

"You and your wife must come over to us soon," said Gordon as they all moved over towards the women.

"I'd be glad to," said Bernard.

The two men collected their wives and offered Bessie Levitt a lift back to her hotel, Jessica, gossipy to the last, insisting that she spend a whole day with them before her Tour moved on.

Bernard stayed out on the front door step for a few minutes after they had all gone. Then he came back and into the kitchen where the two women were drinking glasses of cold milk while I was emptying and washing out ashtrays.

"Don't do any more tonight, Ruth," he said, too tired to notice that he was using my first name, though since Bridget's arrival on the scene Jessica had been doing it too. (Their formality in sticking to Mrs. Holland had surprised me a little though I know now that Americans can be much more formal in social usages than we are.) "You must be whacked. I know I am. We all are," he added hastily. "Mama, you're to go to bed this instant. And you'd best stay in bed tomorrow—till lunchtime at least."

"I'm perfectly all right, Bernie," she said in an irritable, sprightly way. And indeed, though I had seen her yawning her head off earlier, as soon as they were free of their visitors she seemed to have picked up her second wind since she looked and obviously felt extremely lively and ready to go on talking over the party till all hours. Jessica's flow too seemed quite unbelievably unabated. She was quite ready to talk all the Philadelphia news all over again. Bernard, much more tired than either of them, was trying vainly and exhaustedly to get them both off when I said to Jessica: "I wonder if you'd mind my finishing a little earlier tomorrow evening. I have somewhere to go. If it isn't inconvenient?"

"Of course you can," said Bernard speaking abruptly from sheer weariness. "Your evenings are your own, you know that. You go out any time you want."

"Why of course," said Jessica in her most delightful way. "Don't you give another thought to it. We'll manage fine."

"I'll leave everything ready."

"Don't give it another thought," she repeated. "What time do you want to go?"

"About six thirty."

Mrs. Zold was eyeing me, dying to ask where I was going but not daring to. And eventually we all went to bed.

I suppose curiosity has leaped like wild-fire in you too? Well, I shall be kinder to you than I was to them and tell you. For what I didn't mention before was that at one point in the evening, just before he left, Debenham Bleu, who had gone upstairs to the bathroom, came down again very quietly and into the kitchen where I was tidying up. He stood unconcernedly watching me for a whole minute. I noticed that he had a curious double fold in his right eyelid, making that eye appear down-slant, almost squinting . . . and deeply sexual. Then he said: "I'm staying at the Hotel Brazil. Would you care to have dinner with me tomorrow evening? Seven o'clock?"

I polished a tumbler and reaching up put it carefully away on a high shelf. I pushed it further back from the edge to make sure it wouldn't fall. Then I said: "All right."

Ruth

❖❖❖❖❖❖❖❖❖❖❖❖❖❖❖❖❖❖

6th July

Do not read this letter. It will give you pain.

DEBENHAM made a curious lover. It was like going to bed with . . . to what or to whom can I compare him? Someone in literature or history perhaps, since there is no counterpart to him in the English society I know or know about. But I can't think of anyone. A late Roman Emperor perhaps, obese, imperious, decaying. But no, that will not do since he is not obese and his imperial quality is only enamel deep. In what period would he have found himself at home? The answer to that is that he belongs to no period but his own, to no country other than his own. Only America *now* could have spawned him; and his like. For I realize that there are many Bleus, sheening the skin of American intellectual life with their phosphorescent, shifting, rotting colours.

He does not kiss. His head, quite separate from his body, goes on thinking, even talking, all through. He likes the light on. If it were possible he would like a glass in one hand and a cigarette in the other. He whips himself with words. I was mistaken when I called him decadent since this implies decline. Bleu has no peak from which it would be possible to decline. He is a round bubble on a muddy lake. At one point he found it appropriate to tell me of his experiences in a New Orleans brothel. He had to try four girls before he found one the right size. He told me about the New York party game . . . already, I gather, a commonplace. You play over a tape recorder you've had under the bed the night before. On one such recording a girl he had there became suspicious. "What's going on?" she wanted to know. "What've you got under there?" "She was wild" (he said), "when she found out. But she didn't go. I guess she needed it for complexion." (In the end it was the *infantilism* I minded; the sense of a whole layer of society soaked in childish perversion.) "Anyway it was Saturday night. What was she going to do with herself if she walked out? That's what she said to me. 'What'll my friends think if they find out I'm home by nine-thirty, Saturday night?' "

He told me about a married couple he knew, the man handsome and rich and talented; the woman beautiful. "He's no sooner away in the morning his sheets still warm, and her lover's climbing in. Know why? Oh she loves her husband, sure, but they got a trouble, see. Know what they're worried about? Scared to death their little seven-year-old girl isn't going to make it. She's not popular enough with the other kids." He raised a naked foot and flexed his ankle.

"To look in a mirror and see themselves whole and beautiful and healthy. To be able to use a talent. To be rich as well. To be married rightly. In heaven's name how do they come by *fear?*"

"We're losing the sense of entitlement," he said. "We're becoming aware. But we're not yet prepared to believe it. We're awake but we won't open our eyes. We want to go back to sleep. Once we're awake we'll have to do something then, see. Share out. Lead. Take responsibility. Admit that pain exists; something we're not doing right now. Your Mr. Zold put his finger on it," he said, turning and giving me a look from under that debauched, double eyelid.

Through all my strange evening with him I had so far felt no shock; nor pleasure either. Only a cold intensity. All my shock came later. But at mention of Bernard I all at once felt a sudden realization of my physical self. I pulled up the sheet. Debenham squinted, and smiled with his small, red lips. Reaching out a lazy hand he placed it on my sheeted waist, spreading his fingers. Then he turned his hand sideways and moved it up and down as if hatcheting me in half.

"Chop. Chop. Chop," he said, his eyes half closed watching his hand. "Poor, little rich girl America never had a chance to grow up like ordinary girls. What does she know? She hears the cries all right, the warnings. She hears the screams outside the palace. But she doesn't know what to do. She hugs her dolly closer. Guilty, guilty. . . . Besides . . . what's mine is mine. And yet, for all the alms at the gates, guilty, guilty. . . . Ah! America; you naïve, hard-eyed, blonde-curled, little crown princess. Your father died too soon. You are too young for that gold-crusted throne. Too young to rule. You know so little. And anyway the time has gone for thrones. You were born too late you sad, little, upstart bitch."

He offered me a drink before I left. Courteous and cold we drank, standing up facing each other, both leaning lightly against the mantelpiece.

"Where do you live," I said, "in New York?"

"I gave up my apartment some time back. I have a room in a hotel in the Seventies."

"A room like this?"

"Pretty much."

"What do you do about all your things?"

"In your sense I haven't any 'things.' Just what you see here."

"Just what you carry in your suitcases?"

"Yes."

"Just clothes?"

"Clothes, books . . . odds and ends."

"Did you never marry?"

"Once. Didn't take, though."

"Why?"

He spread out his hands. "Why? Why? That's kind of a naïve question isn't it?"

"Have you a photograph of her?" I said on impulse.

He raised his eyebrows then said with a shrug: "I guess so. Want to see it?"

He swung a case off the top of the wardrobe, opened it, and after some rummaging took out an ancient, leather folder. It was full of photographs and old snapshots. It did not seem to me in character that he should carry them around and I still think it strange. He showed me a photograph of his wife. She looked fierce and Continental with thick, black eyebrows.

"She doesn't look American."

"She's Greek."

"I suppose you thought you were marrying Demeter?" I said cheerfully.

He laughed for the first time that evening. "Could be," he said.

I sat down on the bed to study it. He picked up another photograph and handed it to me. It was a group snapshot taken, he explained, at a picnic in his Sophomore year at Harvard. "Twenty-seven years ago," he said. His double eyelid came down and he looked at me for a moment with an expression I did not understand. I looked back at the picture. The young men and women beamed out from it, dowdy and gay, a big, cumbersome Buick behind them. Debenham had his arms round two girls, pretty even with their rigidly waved hair, military shoulders and long, flopping skirts. He looked like the young, high-nosed son of a sheik.

Tears came suddenly to my eyes. "And is this all?" I said looking up at him and then round the room. He looked at me angrily. He knew at once what I meant. (And, beneath the ice of my still frozen reaction to the evening, stirring in the slow waters of shock and distaste which were beginning to melt and flow from it, there was all the same a current of pleasure at the quick intelligence, a gratitude for the sophisticated mind which needed no explanations.) "Is this all that is left from that?" I said, insistent in spite of myself. "All that you had *then* to come to three suitcases in a hotel room?"

"Ah, you don't know what in hell you're talking about," he said with cold violence. "What is this? Nostalgia night? What I have is what I want. Get that into your sentimental, British head." He began to pace about the room.

Hunching my shoulders forward I brought the pictures up again before my eyes. Oh the years, the years, I thought with an inward scalding. Twenty-seven years for that bright moment on the grass to come to my eyes and hands. The contiguity, the joining of me to those unknown lives, that vanished point of time, made my heart move with anguish.

"What happened to them all?"

"Yes. I thought that was the next question. No better than what's happened to me. Worse in most cases." He bent over me moving his finger along the row of heads. "Divorced, divorced, dead, better dead (he's been in mental hospital five years), married but might as well be stuffed, don't know, a whore on three continents, married but works like a slave on account of her husband's bone lazy, dead in the war, famous doctor hates his wife. . . ."

"Oh stop it. *Stop it.* Not one happy life? I don't believe you. It suits you not to believe anyone is happy."

"It suits you not to believe what life is. Are *you* happy? How come you left your husband? No, no one told me; it just shows. What are you doing but hacking down the days? Chop! Chop! Another one gone. Another piece of time over. Who're you to dish out poignant, little remarks about three suitcases in a hotel room?"

"There *is* a difference between us," I said after a pause. I pressed my hand against my forehead trying to isolate it out. "The difference is that you want to believe—perhaps you do believe—that there is *no* good—"

"You're darn right—"

"While I believe that there *is* good; even if I've never seen it."

"You keep right on looking, honey. It passes the time. If you've got any left over after coping with that family you've latched yourself on to."

"They're not hard to work for."

He looked sideways at me under his double eyelid. "I guess the master makes sure *personally* that you get enough sleep."

"You may be a good, literary critic, Debenham Bleu,"

I said equably, "but you're a bloody, lousy guesser. It's even laughable to think how wrong you are."

"Not wrong. Premature maybe," he said with equal equanimity.

I smiled and shook my head slowly. At that moment I felt a queer, almost cosy pleasantness with him, a desire to sit on and gossip. With a kind of corrupt, intuitive benevolence he, sensing this, took my empty glass, gave me another drink, took one himself and sat down.

"Maybe when he's dead," he said.

"What?"

"Zold. He's probably—though I wouldn't say for certain—got the demon. A small genius perhaps, but the genuine article. Trouble with him is he doesn't know how to put a saddle on it. You've got to learn to ride in this world. That guy takes a toss every time. His plays are going to make a lot of money—about 1994. But I doubt if he'll live to bask in his fame . . . *or* get his hands on the dough."

"Don't you think he's going to make a success over here?" I said unable to conceal my alarm.

"That worry you? Why?"

"I'd just like things to go well for him, that's all. It isn't *personal* feeling . . . not that I expect you to believe that. I just . . ." I sighed, "I don't know. I'd like things to work out for him. It would . . . restore belief . . . if I could see them doing so."

"So you're making him a test case for 'good'? You'd better not tell him so. You'd only be putting another burden on those heavy laden shoulders."

I looked startled and he laughed again. Then he said: "Drink up. And then I'm going to have to let you go." His tone was genial but his manner had become monarchical once more. It was a royal dismissal. The impersonation was perfect. For a moment I was almost taken in. Then

I remembered what lay inside it. Not the spirit, bone or blood of a king but a rotted intellectual, morally arrested at the age of twelve.

We bade each other a casually formal goodbye. I might have been a temporary secretary finished with the typing. He waved casually from the door then turned and went inside his room.

Ruth

☼☀☼☀☼☀☼☀☼☀☼☀☼☀☼☀☼☀☼☀☼☀☼

10th July

YOU cannot complain! This is my third letter to you within a week. How kind I am to keep your thoughts and feelings so much occupied!

Bessie Levitt came to lunch yesterday and afterwards the three women spent the afternoon in the West End. She dropped one curious piece of information while she was in the house. Chatting to me in the kitchen while the other two were dressing to go out after lunch I said something about Jessica missing her hospital work very much when she got married.

"Her hospital work?" she said.

"Yes," I said, rather surprised she didn't know. "Mrs. Zold was visiting physiotherapist to a number of hospitals in Philadelphia before she was married."

"Not to my knowledge," she said.

"But—I'm sure you're making a mistake. . . ." I began.

"Not me," she said. "I've known Jessica for twenty years. Oh now wait a minute. I know what's confusing you. She worked *for* a physiotherapist for a while as sort of, well, clerk, receptionist I guess you'd call it. That's where she met Bernard. Or was it at the X-ray clinic? She worked in one of those for a time too. Same kind of job. Now it's funny about folks, isn't it? Me, I can't bear going *near* a hospital—or any kind of medical institution. My friends all know if they're sick or anything I'll just move heaven and earth to help them. But visit in hospital I *will not* do. They're all used to me by now. But Jessica now, she just adores anything to do with the medical world. God knows why, with doctors coming a dime a dozen these days. But that's her little foible, I guess we've all got one. Between you and me I'd say if she's had a disappointment in life it's that she didn't marry a doctor. Not that she didn't do a whole lot better as it's turned out. But there you are. We none of us get what we want, do we? Me, I'd settle for a good husband, regardless!"

"You never know. You might find yourself marrying a doctor, one of these days!"

"Confidentially I'd settle for a plumber with a kind heart!" she said. Then the two women came down and they all went out.

But it's strange, isn't it? I had not thought of Jessica as a liar though thinking back I see that she often not so much deliberately lies as slips gently over the truth, leaving you, until you've grasped the gentle trick of it, with an entirely false impression. There is, I suppose, no harm in her harmless little snobbery. As Miss Levitt said, we all have our foibles. But there seems to me to be something disquieting, some obstinate, shallow vanity behind such constant, unobtrusive re-modellings. It must irritate Bernard to distraction.

He came into the kitchen soon after the women had gone, just as I was going out to do some household shopping.

"I'll walk up to the stores with you," he said. "I need some carbons."

"I don't think you'll get them round here. You'll have to go to Swiss Cottage."

"O.K. So I'll go to Swiss Cottage! Can you do your shopping there too? If so we can walk up together. It'll do me good to walk around a bit and get some air. I sit too much. And you don't get out too much either, do you?"

"I'm not complaining," I said as we let ourselves out and walked down the path.

It was a very fine, sunny day. Our little street looked very pretty, the St. John's Wood women out in numbers. These are a certain type. They differ from the Edwardians since there is no element of charming disrepute about them. They are mostly youngish middle-aged, respectably married into professions with artistic connexions; publishers, architects, some genuine (if Royal Academy) painters, well-bred theatre people, antique dealers. . . . They are too old for jeans but usually shop in slacks. Passing their windows at night one sees filled bookcases, wrought iron tables, pale green walls and light, natural woods, dead-white and scarlet lampshades. They are very civilized and open-minded and keep bottles of good Graves and vodka amongst the drinks.

There was a time when I thought such lives entirely enviable. Even today, compared with Eversley Road, they *are* so. And yet there is something which now appears to me intolerably snug and smug and in some way unreal about them. Their good taste is only one step ahead of the women's magazines. They are ensconced in their little circles. They are intelligent and often intellectual, they have opinions and vocabularies, they are sometimes gay and usually modish, they even allow themselves a careful ration of eccentricity . . . but . . . their lives are not *living*. The deep, rocky sweats and humiliations, the madnesses, leaps, fruitful melancholies of less privileged people which in the end push up true art, great reformation . . . these they do not know.

"I do get out," I said as we walked along. "Besides, I collect Ginny every day from school."

"What time d'you have to be at the school this afternoon?"

"As a matter of fact, Bridget's calling for her today. They've got some end-of-term exhibition of drawings by the Art Class that Ginny's nagged her into going to see! So I'm *really* off duty this afternoon."

"Sort of half-day holiday! Say! You know something? I could use an afternoon off too. Anyway it's a desecration and a waste to spend a day like this indoors. Perhaps when we've both finished shopping we could take a walk, maybe on the Heath. Have tea somewheres. How about that?" He swung along beside me, lumbering and awkward and enthusiastic.

I was not, to be truthful, over-anxious for him to accompany me. I had been looking forward to strolling, with no necessity for haste, through the shops; window gazing; enjoying the Finchley Road on this bright, busy, sunny afternoon. I didn't feel like talking. I didn't particularly fancy his company. But it was impossible to refuse. Especially as he has been very kind to me the last few days. I would use the word tender if it did not carry lover-like overtones. He seems to have sensed that I have recently undergone some kind of psychological tremor and has taken pains to talk to me on the principle, I suppose, of distracting my mind. (And God knows, it has needed distraction from the huge, crawling distaste which has been the aftermath of my hours with Bleu.)

I asked him, as we walked on, how things were going with the play.

"Reasonably," he said. "We've been lucky over the casting anyway. We've signed Lorraine Clark for the lead. I saw her on Broadway two seasons ago and she's damned good. Wallace Grey, my producer, has been angling for her for months."

"She must think your play's damned good if she's willing

to appear in it. I should think she's about the most sought after actress in London just now."

"I guess it's the Vauxhall prestige more than the play—" he said then stopped and laughed a little self-consciously, seeing that, however modestly he tried to put it, it was still a compliment to himself since the Vauxhall was putting *him* on.

"And the other four parts are practically settled. We start rehearsing soon. *All being well!*" He crossed his fingers.

"D'you find actors easy to get on with?"

"Fairly easy on the whole, I would say. (When I'd gotten over being petrified at the idea of me, Bernard Zold, mixing on equal terms with that kind of company!) Y'know, there's a sort of idea around that actors and actresses are wholly absorbed by 'theatre,' that they talk nothing but shop. I don't think this is true; or leastways, it may have been true but it isn't any more. I find the younger ones anyway, on the whole intelligent, interested in what the world's doing and thinking. . . . Say, a lot of them are religious! Did you know that? There's a lot of Catholic converts in the profession."

We had reached the shops and our conversation stopped there. But when we had finished and were walking up Fitzjohn's Avenue we found ourselves touching the subject of religion again.

"You're not particularly religious yourself, are you?" I said.

He hesitated, his walk slowing down. He put out his tongue over his lower lip then withdrawing it said: "Believe it or not I *was*—until my fourteenth year. With no encouragement to be so. Neither my father nor my mother cared to think about belief. I guess they were too busy, too involved in their separate hells, to think much about possible heavens. They were born Jews and they weren't going to go away from that, but that was all. But I . . . I even insisted on confirmation when I was thirteen. Mind you, my mother was pleased when she thought about it. She had sort of instinctive leanings that way. With another kind of marriage I've often thought she herself would have been of the practising kind. Maybe it would even have lasted with me, maybe not, maybe it was something I'd have grown out of anyway—teenage stuff. We all get it, like measles. But something particularly disrupting happened to me . . . one of those traumatic incidents that create a block in the spirit. (How wrong the psychiatrists sometimes are, incidentally. I don't have to dig down into my subconscious memories to find out a causal incident in this case. I *remember* it. But I still have the block!)"

We reached the top of the Heath and turned into one of the coffee bars for tea. It was, in contrast with the brightness outside, very cool and dark in there. He sat down rather heavily at a table right at the back. His full face was pale and shiny and perspiring, his body clumsy in the grey, baggy suit. He mopped his face, breathing rather stertorously. "Tell you the truth, the heat doesn't suit me all that much," he said. "For some reason it makes my catarrh worse instead of better. Feel myself dizzy with it sometimes." He sniffed deeply through his nose and cleared his throat several times. If I hadn't been there he would have spat into his handkerchief. I find it odd to record that this idea did not disgust me. Indeed I felt like telling him to go ahead and not mind me. I almost did but the thought that *he* would be shocked held me back. I must have been looking rather white (you know I always do in the heat) and wan, and even more gentle-browed than usual. It would have been a shame to break the image! Instead I led him back, once our tea had arrived, to what he had been talking about.

"The religious block I can't get over or under? Yes. What caused it?" I stirred my tea. As he began to talk I found myself listening with absorbed attention. Serious, relaxed, away from his family, all his nervous, embarrassing attempts at joviality discarded, he became a wholly articulated personality for the first time. The assurance of intelligent attention—that was all he really needed to be interesting. The more I *listened*, the more he became worth listening to.

"I was a month under fourteen," he began, "and I was coming home from somewhere one night when I met a guy I knew. He walked along with me. The night was dark but sort of sparkling with frost, the neighbourhood quiet. We were fooling around the way boys do (he was older than me, sixteen; a big beefy guy) when he suddenly got me in front of him with my back to him, placed his two, heavy, brutal, scoffing hands on my shoulders and began to run me to and fro across the road. As we jerked about he made homosexual gestures with his body towards my wriggling back. I remember how our shouts echoed in that dark, frost-white street. I twisted in his hands, took short, dabbing, ridiculous steps in the air, tried to keep the thing a joke by letting out loud, shrieking, mock-yells until at last he let me go. There was nothing cruel physically or even mentally in what he did. It was only stupid horseplay with a touch of schoolboy dirt. And yet the effect of it was terrible, terrible, terrible. That feeling of ridiculed helplessness, the forced indignity that was being laid upon me by a lout's stupid brutishness, the knowledge that in a possible moral situation only sheer, physical strength would have been any good—and that I did not have . . . all this frightened me. Nothing had happened. But some God or other was destroyed that night in that empty, ringing, black and silver street; and I've never been able to get Him back. Oh I think about Him. I even find myself speaking to Him, arguing with Him at odd moments. Swinging off a bus I find myself suddenly telling Him something. I might be licking a crumb of cake off my thumb joint—as I'm doing now—and find myself in urgent explanation of some thought to Him. But I guess it's just the desperate need to tell, to explain, to argue with Someone.

No one ever listens to me, you see. No one—till I wrote the plays—ever listened to anything I had to say. And even now. . . ."

"Oh surely *now*," I said.

He gave me a heavy, rueful glance and said: "You too! the same universal delusion. Write a book, get a play staged . . . you're made, you're famous, you're *respected*. Let me tell you what *actually* happens. One man's experience . . . maybe aggravated by my special faults . . . but not unique. Oh no. Not unique.

"There's friends and neighbours. (There's your immediate family of course but I guess that's a saga in itself. We'll skip it for today!) Friends and neighbours . . . yeah. That reminds me of something . . . We have a neighbour back home, in the top apartment above ours. She has a little boy, a sullen little bastard; bad-tempered, bad-mannered. Try to make friends with him, talk with him, tell him things he ought to know like he'll hurt himself doing what he's doing, and he'll scowl and not answer in an insulting sort of way and sidle off quickly. I sometimes think all artists try to make friends with this boy, with ordinary life, and life behaves like he does; indifferent or hostile or both. But let me tell you in actual fact, without any fancy decorations, no symbols, just plain, related fact—" He stopped short, looked over at me with a short-sighted screwing up of his eyes and said: "Maybe I'm talking too much."

"No you're not," I said quickly.

He stroked his forehead looking still unsatisfied, eyeing me. "I wouldn't want," he began, "to take advantage of your being here to bore you. . . ."

"Oh for goodness' sake," I said, "for *goodness'* sake you're not. Truly Mr. Zold. I can't put it emphatically enough that you never bore me."

(This was not true. Yet it was. I don't know how to explain this double-layered response.)

"O.K.," he said very quickly and shortly. And, smiling at me (he has this trick of being about to fall into clumsiness and embarrassment and then walking with an open simplicity out of his danger) he went on with what he had been saying.

"You know," he said, "you know, there's an awful lot of talk going on these days about the isolated position of the artist in society. One of the words I for one am sick to death hearing is 'split'—as of our culture. All the artists huddled together in one small group heading one way; all the 'people' in one big, blind mass heading another. Though I guess by and large it's a true picture. Anyway, though I'm *for* the artist I just want to say this much for 'the people' . . . before I proceed to knock 'em! And that is this. No writer—I wouldn't know about painters or musicians, but no *writer*—has the right to knock the people unless he's living with them, right in there, on Main Street, on Suburban Avenue . . . living in terms of day to day coming and going amongst them. Any writer lecturing people on how to live in Hicksville when he's perched on the branches of some expatriate tree in Paris or San Francisco or even on some cosy, campus shrub, *anyone* who lives in some kind of intellectually wakened-up group is cheating when they say Do this, Think that. If they really want to teach the 'people' how to live let them settle in some exurbanite neighbourhood, some small town mid-west, some Pittsburgh factory district . . . and let them start converting from there. Because if our society is going to change its attitude to the artist, that's where the change has got to start. That's where the yeast has to be . . . in the dough not thrown at the loaf."

"I suppose that's why you're in London this minute?" I said lifting my eyebrows and satirically but gently laughing at him.

"I warned you I'd be changing sides!" he said. "Now I'll tell you what happens to the artist when he *stays* in Hicksville.

First you've got to remember that what we call normal life is pretty dull anyway, even to the average Mr. Citizen. Oh he gets by—from a birth to a death—but life grinds slow. There's little tragedy and less joy. That's why keeping up with the Joneses isn't quite so bad a thing as the thinkers say it is. That is—it isn't a cure for Average Citizen's disease, but it's a partial remedy. It gives him something to do, something to live for. *But . . .* like everybody else he don't like being made to feel his life's targets are so much cardboard, that he's living in a shallow, muddy pool. Americans above all resent this. And above all they don't like it being implied by a man that's taken one step out from the local mud. It's a criticism from inside, see. It's saying they're not good enough for him, the people he's known all his life, the thoughts they think, the kind of living they've all put up with. And the first thing you stir up from that muddy place you've put one foot out of is a resentful ignoring. Take one step upwards and *they* don't want to know *you.*"

"They can't be that blind, even in Hicksville, to an artistic achievement," I said rather impatiently, feeling he was rather fabricating a grievance. "You surely can't be saying that Local Boy Makes Good isn't a slogan with any pride to it any more?"

"It depends on the splash," he said, "leave alone the field. Baseball hero, movie star, cosmonaut . . . sure, they're O.K. They're fields within the grasp of Hicksville imagination. They're *technical.* But write an egghead play—or novel—and see what happens. Shall I tell you what happened to me?

"My first play was put on in New York by something equivalent to your Vauxhall Theatre here. A small playhouse, a highbrow audience. It . . ." (he looked shy and heavily embarrassed having to say this) "it got . . . pretty good notices. You know. It even did pretty well financially for that kind of theatre. Comes summer and it's being played out of

town by a famous little summer stock company just a few
miles out from my home town. Again it's doing darn well,
for that time, for that place. Week it opens near Allegra a
kind of a third cousin of mine, guy I've known all my life,
shows up at my home one evening. Brings his wife along too.
Nice, quiet girl. So this Melvyn and his wife are sitting there
in my living room, fidgeting around. Neither of them
mention (or come to that have *ever* mentioned) the play.
No congratulations, no questions, no curiosity . . . nothing.
Blank. I get my name, the *family* name, in the papers, I'm
interviewed on television, New York critics say nice words
about Bernard *Zold*. Mr. and Mrs. Small-town Melvyn Zold
sit there talking about their vacation. Finally Jessica can't
stand it any more and mentions the play. 'Yes, we heard,'
they say. Mrs. Melvyn has the grace to add, 'Very nice.'
Jessica tells them it's playing at the Fountain Theatre that
very week. 'Used to be a movie house,' says Melvyn. 'I remember that fleapit when I was in short pants. Hope they
cleaned it up a bit since then.' 'You want to see it now,' says
Jessica, 'it's a beautiful, little theatre.' (It is too.) 'Haven't
you ever been?' 'Got more to do with my time,' says Melvyn
(he's a chemist in a textile mill) 'than tear around taking in
every arty, long-haired, off-Broadway throw-out.' He's got a
bitterness on that long, chunky, sand-coloured face of
his that when I looked at it I couldn't believe I was seeing.
Apart from anything else I couldn't believe in the bad
manners. I couldn't believe that any civilized human being
over the age of ten could expose his nature with so little
shame. And above all I couldn't believe in the hatred. . . .

"His wife says in a tiny voice she hopes it'll do all right.
Melvyn gets right into his stride at this since measuring by
money's what he's good at. 'Do all right! Sell every seat in
the house and he makes enough for buttons. Don't tell me
about the theatre game. Unless you make the big time—and
don't let's kid ourselves,' he says narrowing his eyes and

A *slanting* ʟɪɢʜᴛ

nodding his head with that contemptuous *viciousness* still on
his face, 'Bernard's not in *that* league . . . what d'you make
out of it? Peanuts!'

" 'It's not quite peanuts,' I said . . . mildly. (In fact I was
in the middle of negotiating the movie rights but I didn't
dare tell him. I had a superstitious feeling that he'd ill-will
the whole thing and it wouldn't come off.) 'But in any case
there's more to it than money.' 'Like what? For instance?
Like fancy-pants ideas that won't buy a pair of shoes? You
can put them down the toilet?' says Melvyn getting up from
his chair as if the spite boiling inside wouldn't let him sit."
(He stood up himself as if he had to do something physical
to take away the tension of memory. Calling the waitress
over he ordered more tea.)

"But I can't believe it even now," he said sitting down
again. "So much hatred—from a guy I'd never done any
harm to. Why? Why? What *is* it about art, intellect, insight
into the nature of things . . . what have we *done* to these
superb springs of pleasure to foul their names? How have we
managed to make what is desirable and golden into what is
pelted and despised? That men like Melvyn should become
Goerings before our eyes? Why, at the very word Art, must
average men reach for their hate as if faced by an enemy?"

"They are," I said. "Art is an enemy. It takes away illusion."

"Yes of course," he said. "I know that answer. But it won't
do, it doesn't altogether satisfy. There's some other level on
which Art terrifies. It's not losing their illusions about the
nature of life, not even so much the loss of illusion about
themselves. After all, even the Melvyns have moments here
and there of confrontation with their own realities. No, no
. . . it is something more like that deservedly deadly sin,
Sloth, which I believe lies at the heart of such bitter enmity.
It is their spirit's torpor which they cannot bear to have
disturbed. If they allowed themselves to wake they'd have

to take steps, be better than they are. And so they refuse to know and hate the one who forces knowledge. And of course there's inability too. Men live their inner lives with such vast incompetence. Whereas Art is able, Art *can*. But ultimately artists are abominated because they are energy, because they are enemies to the sleepy death wish of the heart, the 'Let us alone' murmurs from the hollow Lotos-land. No wonder the artist, that nagger, that damned reveille man is hated."

"There's also plain, old-fashioned, uncomplicated jealousy."

Looking extremely perplexed he shook his head. His bumpy, baby's forehead shone with puzzlement. "I've heard that before, too," he said. "To me, in my circumstances, it seems an incredible explanation. Darn it, who in their senses would be jealous, for instance, of *me*? Here I am, forty-one years old, and for thirty-eight of those years nothing but failure. What was I for thirty-eight years? Poor, unsuccessful, undistinguished. . . ." He hesitated, then added, "Ugly." (I saw that this word pained him but it was true and so must be said.) "No class, no education to speak of, an ordinary guy married in an ordinary way with an ordinary child. A daughter. I didn't even achieve a son!"

"Does that matter to you?" I asked with some interest.

He laughed on a sort of deprecating snort.

"Yes it does! Are you shocked? Yes, I guess you are! Well . . . that's one disadvantage to being the perfect listener—" (I—who very seldom colour—went pink at this!) "you hear a lot you never bargained for. Yes, I wanted a son. Not for any worked-out reason. It's just that a son is the acknowledged perfection of fatherhood. Acknowledged! that's the important thing. I'm neither saint nor philosopher nor anything but unadmirably human. I wanted what to other people seems the 'Best.' I wanted Fate to call Heads for me. And when Ginny was born I endured as sharp a pang

135

as any I have ever known. Instead of joy I felt only—may God forgive me!—that, as in everything else in life, I was being fobbed off with second best. I had to keep telling myself that I must be grateful to be a father at all, how many childless men and women would envy me. I must be thankful my child is healthy and uncrippled. . . ."

He caught a faint tremor of expression on my face and said more quietly: "Yes. I know. I got a problem with Ginny. She gets these hysterical fits. She's. . . ." He paused then burst out: "That's my fault. It's my punishment for wanting a son too much . . ."

"That is quite wrong, Mr. Zold, truly it is. My goodness, if every parent with a sick or temperamental child. . . ." My voice tailed off. He was repeatedly lifting the lid off the teapot and fitting it on again with close, agonized attention. And he was saying in a soft voice: *"I don't like her.* I don't like my own child, Ruth. What am I to do about this? What can I *do?* There is nothing of *me* in her." He shook his head slightly. "But that wouldn't matter. But there's nothing admirable there. She's just Levy through and through; like the whole bunch of them back there in Philadelphia. All she's got from my side is the bad thing, the nervous instability, the hysteria. Otherwise she's dull. She's a dull little girl," he said softly and flatly. I found it impossible to contradict him. But in trying to say something of comfort I said the wrong thing altogether.

"Mrs. Zold isn't dull," I said.

"Jessica you mean? Underneath that pleasant, charming —oh so *charming,*" he said in a bitter voice, "manner, she's the most trivial woman in North America. *I* live with her. *I know.* And I'll tell you something. The charm doesn't even travel. Outside her own little circle of family and 'girls' she's nowhere. Think I didn't know how much she fell short, Independence Day? Home town gossip! That's her life's blood."

"She has a sweet nature," I said feeling somehow obstinate on this point.

"Sweet!" he said giving me an angry, impatient glance. "I expect better than that from you! I suppose you mean sympathetic? Yeah, well, let me be fair, Jessica can be very sympathetic. But even at its best what she's got is suburban sympathy. And what the hell good's that nine tenths of the time? There's a difference you know between suburban and sophisticated sympathy that we don't take enough account of. The difference lies in the areas of suffering we feel for. Suburban, provincial, bourgeois—call it what you like— sympathy is directed solely towards physical pain and conventional loss; of a child, a relative, a friend, a job. Sophisticated sympathy reaches out to quite other anguishes, to mental pain, moral torment, the shifts and stresses and guilts, the inadequacies under our skins. . . ."

His wording, his expression, his manner as he was speaking suddenly became, though his words were "literary," full of authority and force; something apart from the truth of his words—though these I recognized as being instantly true and illuminating to my own feelings.

"How well you speak!" I exclaimed impulsively.

He turned to look at me in a most affronted manner.

"Rubbish!" he said. "I talk like Poor Poll. I always did."

I attempted to deny this but he said, over-riding me: "I do believe I married Jessica solely because I hoped to learn her secret of 'how to talk to people'! I admired her tiny talent for that very much. (That'll tell you how stupid I was then!) I used to watch her in conversation, smiling, gentle, pleasant, words always ready, quite unstrained even in moments of silence. And I so envied this talent I thought I could learn it from her. Idiotic, hah?

"Yes, well," he said lifting his hands outwards at shoulder level and flapping them like wings, "all right, I know. I'm being unfair. She passes more or less. At first acquaintance anyway. But must everything in my life be just a matter of 'passing,' of getting by? All my life all I've ever had are the negative benefits of a life, the saying to myself continually: 'I haven't . . . this or that terror or worry or shame. *Therefore* I should be happy.' *This was not enough.* I wanted a positive; something more than health and modest living and not being a refugee in flight or a Chinese peasant in a paddy field. I wanted something more. And then, miracle of miracles, I got it! Or began to. And straight away I found I had to pay. The Melvyns pulled their guns. Perhaps to others this might not matter. 'To hell with Melvyn' is their motto. But me . . . I've a lower class, small-town, naïve wish to see men as brothers. I have a child's longing for everybody to be friends. An image of hands joining comes continually before my mind's eye."

"You have a brother, haven't you?" I said casually.

"Yes," he said. "I have." And suddenly silent said no more for a few moments only sat looking bulky and shapeless and hunched, looming over the small table. "And that's a story too," he added at last. He laughed and said coldly: "You may be seeing him one of these days. He's talking of coming to Europe for a trip. Or so I gather from Mama, he doesn't write to me." Then he fell quiet again. I was beginning to want to go. We had sat there too long already. But he suddenly started talking again.

"There was a Melvyn at the library too," he said. "Where I worked. Guy named Penn. This Penn, he didn't even have a Melvyn excuse like being a blunt materialist. This Penn; he counted himself a culture-boy. *He* . . . had it on the line. *He* . . . knew the score in Greenwich Village. Well . . . you heard of Nuttall Blake?"

"Of course."

"Yes of course," he said quickly and apologetically. "Of course you would have. Perhaps the greatest American literary and dramatic critic of our time. All of a sudden, Penn thinks *the least* of Nuttall Blake. Mr. Penn, small time library assistant in small town Allegra thinks Mr. Blake nothing. But nothing! A dead-beat never was. And I was such an innocent, I was such a Goddam, innocent *idiot* I never realized for months that our Mr. Penn was crabbing Blake because he'd written a long and . . . and . . . well it was so I might as well say it . . . rave review of the first play. And believe me, Ruth, it wasn't that I was throwing it around; what he'd said, what I'd done. I didn't throw it around."

"You don't have to tell me that," I said. "You're far, far too modest about the whole—"

"No!" he said with a snap. He heaved his body out of its huddled sprawl and sat up. "You're making it simple—and I'm not sure you're not being insulting! I'm as complex as the next man, I'd have you know! Think I didn't want to get out on the roof and have a tape of that review played out loud over the whole neighbourhood?"

"What stopped you . . . doing the equivalent?"

"A . . . whole complex of fears—and difficulties. There was, apart from anything else, the sheer difficulty over . . . over ways of measurement. What I meant when I used the word 'splash' before. All right, I made a small splash in a rather distinguished pool. Think the ordinary man has any use for that particular pool? A splash in that particular place doesn't even register with him. He simply doesn't understand what it takes in terms of mind and luck and talent to displace just a few of those sacred drops of water. Only if the displacement is enormous, the intellectual, the artistic achievement of that rare, miraculous kind which is publicly spectacular as well, the kind which brings enormous publicity—as well as a whole lot of dough!—with it, is the true artist helped one inch towards the respect of average men. Anything less only increases the alienation, the isolation, the suspicious resentments which he knows only too Goddam well already.

"Too many artists have not had the spectacular experience. And so we get the desperate attempts from fundamentally good, profound, unassuming, serious artists after novelty and shock. They don't *want*—at least most of them don't—to inject what's meretricious into their work. And of course there's always the one artist in a hundred who really has got sensationalism in his vision. But for the others . . . well, the less scrupulous, the more childish 'put it in' with a kind of idiotic, forgivable hope that the rest of their work will then be noticed and so they *themselves* will exist in the common consciousness. And the rest of us . . . we leave it out and take a chance on our work (if we're writers) making the long, slow journey into 'literature.' 'Posterity' is the word which haunts us; our fragile, husbanded comfort in the terrible hours. For that is when we know the other great fear. How does one keep this gift from God alive? One dare not expose it, boast of it, tell too much . . . or it might die. How often have I wondered by what miracle of dropped seed from heaven was it brought to birth at all in *me*! this small, pale bloom of my talent growing, incredibly, from the cracked stones of this, my grinding, paltry life? How will it live? How can it flourish? How can I protect it from the grudging winds of my society, my own immeasurable fallings short, my few defences, my mean enemies? *I dare not boast.* I dare not hold it high, revel in it, *use* it for anything but its own beautiful and holy usage."

He paused and I thought for one moment that he was going to be so wrong as to apologize again for talking so much. But—as always—I underestimated his delicacy and sense. He had no intention of cheapening what he had just said with vulgar niceties. Instead he said: "That is why I must take care. That is why I came to Europe. Only I cannot make my family see it. I have not the gift of making other people care about my fate. It's a great talent that . . . to be able to make others feel concerned (Jessica's got it) but it's not one I possess."

He took a gulp of tea which had been stone cold for some time and went on: "This sounds like the most dislikable self-pity. But I truly do not think it is. I am only making a statement about a condition which occurs with some people and not with others. Attitudes of loyalty have always fascinated me. Looking around at ordinary life you know you find it difficult to believe that loyalties exist at all. And yet they do. I read somewheres once about your first Jewish Member of Parliament here in Britain; how his constituents kept on electing him even though the House wouldn't accept him. Now just what made those voters keep on doing this—again and again? There must have been something . . . something in the make-up of the man himself, some kind of charm—in the witchcraft sense almost. . . ."

He sat back rather wearily and folded his hands and we sat like that silently, for a few minutes. Then he lifted his eyebrows at me to see if I was ready to go. He paid the bill and we left.

When we reached Swiss Cottage I said: "By the way, I've just remembered . . . there's something else I've got to get before the shops close. But don't you wait. I'll follow on."

He stood looking down at me for a moment, understanding very well what I was really saying which was that we'd better not let our afternoon out together be known, and said with a quirk of a smile: "O.K. Thanks a lot, Ruth."

"For what?" I said as I turned to go.

"For . . . !"

"Think nothing of it," I said.

And then we parted.

Ruth

❖❘❖❘❖❘❖❘❖❘❖❘❖❘❖❘❖❘❖❘❖❘❖❘❖❘❖❘❖❘❖

21st July

I KNOW very well in my quieter moments that my letters to you are a cheerful cruelty. They are self-indulgence carried to the nth degree. Yet if I stopped them I would be still crueller. They are the hurts by which you live, by which you know you are alive.

Perhaps I am being more cruel to you in not allowing *you* to write to *me* than in any other way. But somehow I cannot bear the mental picture of you sitting down at that oak bureau in the living-room and *writing*. You are, I remember, always writing letters; to distant cousins, old associates . . . for one thing because that is the kind of remote contact you like best. But the other reason is the one that irritates me. You don't write because you like the mental part of writing, the act of communication. You write because you enjoy the *act* of writing. You write as other men kick a ball about—or make love. You enjoy your own handwriting—which is, I admit, very beautiful. It is of course wrong of me to despise you for this which is, after all, a true artist's pleasure. But I cannot bear the small and finicking *scale* of it.

Bernard went away yesterday for a day or two. He has gone up to Yorkshire to see an actress in a repertory company whom they think will suit for a supporting part. Rehearsals are due to start soon and the one they had lined up has reneged and gone off to Italy on a film.

Something happened in the middle of last night. I was awakened—well after 2 a.m.—by Jessica who said apologetically that she was going half mad with itching from an insect bite on her leg and did I have any calamine? She lifted her nightdress and showed me a great, red swelling just above her right ankle.

"Yes, of course," I said getting out of bed, and fetching a bottle of calamine from my dressing-table gave it to her. Then I said: "Look, what you want to do is bathe it first. Go back to bed and I'll go and fetch some hot water. It looks as though it's festering."

I brought the basin of hot water into her room, fetched some cotton wool and, putting a towel on the bed, bathed her leg and then put a dressing on it while she lay back on her pillows looking, as usual, large and docile and gratefully helpless. And of course talking all the time in her soft, strangely *un*-boring way about all the circumstances of the bite and her blood group and blood counts and her sister's one-time encounter with a jelly-fish and the nurse she'd had when Ginny was born and her *personal* friendship with her doctor. . . .

"Thanks a lot, Ruth," she said when I'd finished. "That's fine. You surely are a treasure. How about making yourself some tea, seeing I've gotten you out of bed at this hour?"

"If you'll join me," I said.

"O.K. And help yourself to some of that fruit cake you like. Guess I'll have some too. It's pretty good."

I went down to the kitchen, brought a tray up to her room and we talked on over our tea. She had finished her cup before I finished mine and was leaning over, her back towards me to deposit it on the bedside table when I suddenly *noticed* (where before I had just *seen*) her bare, brown back, the smoothly moulded, matt-textured shoulder and the chalk-white, ribbon shoulder-strap of her nightdress against that smooth roundness. And, on the moment of this sudden *seeing* came a totally unexpected and extraordinary flash of jealousy. I was not—I *am* not—in the least in love with Bernard. But at the sight of those naked shoulders the realization shafted into me with a most piercing and startling thrust that this, this flesh was what he lived with, saw, slept with, had sometime caressed with his hands. It was this smooth, brown skin he knew; not mine.

Can one feel jealousy without love? Yes, yes, I am sure of it. What I resented was being left out of his experience. I was no part of it. It was not the thought that he did not love me that seemed suddenly to open a great wound. It was that he did not *know* me. That was all. It was no more than that.

But I will admit to you that the tiny episode has disturbed me. Yes, it was disturbing. It kept me awake long after I had gone back to bed. Partly because I see in it a misty, half-traced-out analogy to your feelings about me. Because that is your trouble, isn't it? You feel I do not know you. That you have never impressed yourself upon my consciousness. And, equally, that *you* do not know me. All that there was of sexual trouble between us was due to this; your longing to get inside my thoughts. That was it really, wasn't it? The other experience was a reflection, no, a substitute for the deep thrust you wished to make into the very marrow of my mind. Your agony was and is that I am a mystery to you . . . even now, after so much revelation. And, with the best will in the world (supposing I had it) I cannot help you there. My poor Francis, I cannot *give* you perception. You think the will to know, the desire to understand, should be enough; you think that these, properly used, will create the ability. Let me tell you something. *Ability* is the rarest thing in the world. It is also the most haphazard in its choice of sites. That afternoon I was in the Hampstead coffee-bar with Bernard. . . . While he was talking I was watching the bright young intelligences with whom the place swarmed . . . the clever, young men and vivid girls, so dashing and interesting and absorbed and alive, portfolios under arms, scripts in hands, manuscripts in briefcases. . . . Yes, yes, I thought . . . and remembered Bleu's words: "He's got the demon." Yes. Fattish, plain and unremarked Bernard Zold, sweating and catarrhal and harassed—when those boys and girls are dust . . . and all their works . . . *he* will live. *Ability*, the *gift* has struck; there in that unexpected, un-distinguished-looking ground.

Ruth

❀❀❀❀❀❀❀❀❀❀❀❀❀❀❀❀❀❀

4th August

I HAVE an idea I preached at you in my last letter. And what is worse I did so on very shaky grounds. I took a risk when I spoke of Bernard's work since after all I had neither seen nor read it. I might have been quite wrong. But I was not. Bernard telephoned from the Vauxhall Theatre this morning and asked Jessica to bring down a folder containing some manuscript notes he had forgotten and needed immediately. As she couldn't go—her leg has become quite troublesome and she is obliged to go to the hospital every day to have it dressed (I would say "Poor girl" were it not for the fact that she is enchanted by her daily excursions into the medical world and can scarcely tear herself away after treatment!) I took it instead.

The Vauxhall—as the name implies—is near Victoria. It is a very nice little theatre with a coffee-bar and club room attached. When I got there they were just in the middle of a run through of the first act. Rehearsals have now got to the point where everyone knows their lines and moves. Bernard, seeing my longing look when I handed over his folder in the foyer, said immediately: "Want to stay and watch, Ruth? O.K. I don't have to tell you to keep quiet! O.K.?" He installed me half-way up the empty auditorium and went to join Wallace Grey, his producer, in the third row.

Lorraine Clark was on stage. She is quite exceptionally

beautiful in the ice-maiden-with-long-moonlight-coloured-hair style. Like most actresses she is smaller than one expects her to be.

When I sat down she was in the middle of a long speech, talking to her reflection in a mirror. She was supposed to be a grown woman on the verge of making some profound decision and at the same time remembering, *being*, her adolescent self. Already, even at this early stage, it was evident that she was pulling it off. "When I was fourteen, fifteen, sixteen . . ." she was saying with a wonderful, soft, hopeful pathos, "those summers . . . those sunny, Sunday mornings, with a sort of distant dance at the end of the street. . . ." She went on, her head and body unmistakably that of a not very young woman, her face that of a very young girl.

At the end of the first act Wallace Grey said briskly: "Right. Into second everyone. Break later. O.K.?" He left Bernard and came up the aisle giving me a half glance as he passed. A little later his voice rang out from over my head. He had gone up to the dress circle to watch the action from there. "Hold it. Hold it. Let's take it back a bit. Henry" (this to the male lead, an elderly and very handsome man), "cue in from 'Not since the party . . .' And Henry . . . lighten it a bit on 'automobile' will you? That's meant to be funny, remember."

Bernard made a note on a pad then looking round beckoned me to come down to where he was sitting. Tiptoeing, I joined him.

"Think it's coming?" he whispered as I sat down.

"Yes, yes indeed," I whispered back. "I'm longing to see the rest of it. But I don't suppose . . . I mean I ought to be getting back. Mrs. Zold—"

"Forget it!" he said. "I'll make some excuse for you. Now shut up and listen!"

Fortuna Gonzalez, the Spanish actress who was playing

second lead, had made an entrance and was speaking from the top of a staircase. Suddenly she stopped and, calling across to Grey who was still in the circle, said: "Wall-aice; I cannot *do* this. There is not enough time to get from down zere to 'ere. Impossible!"

"Just get on with it, Fortuna dear," Grey called back.

"But . . . impossible!" she said wailing.

"Just *get on, darling*," he said, his voice echoing implacably in the empty theatre.

She stood there, muttering and throwing her hands about for a moment then picked up her lines again. I felt Bernard laughing beside me. "Fights every inch of the way," he said. "Quiet woman really. But somebody's told her the Spanish are *supposed* to be difficult. Wally'll handle her! She likes him."

"Do you?" I whispered.

"He's O.K.," he said rather shortly.

I turned my attention to the stage again.

Wallace Grey came down at the end of the second act and, going on stage, beckoned Bernard over to him. I watched them consulting together over the script. Henry joined them and I heard him say, spreading his hands: "I would if I could. But the words kind of fall over each other at that point. Know what I mean? I can't space them to the moves. I'm sorry, Wally. I've been trying all week. You know that."

Grey was standing poring over the script he was holding in his thin, clever hands. A tall, thin, young man he was wearing grey flannels and a woollen, checked shirt. His face is very English, the long, bony face of the English working classes—which is where he's sprung from. At twenty-six he's had two wives and half a dozen whacking theatrical successes behind him.

Bernard was making quick, marginal alterations on the script while Grey was talking to him in a rapid undertone.

Though his body, standing next to Grey's bony leanness, appeared shapeless and large as always, it seemed somehow to have lost its slack look. He wrote on in his manuscript—Grey still talking—with quiet, firm energy. He knew what he was doing and what was required and exactly how to do it. *Authority,* to my immense surprise, like a cloak of heavy velvet, was being carried on those large, soft shoulders. For once, in company, I was able to see him relax—perhaps because he was dealing with word and feeling in a place where these were important?—into the true power of his nature.

It distressed me all the more therefore to see this power slip from him as soon as he began to talk to the players at the end of the second act. At ease with Grey with whom he was doing a job, he became shambling and awkward the moment he tried to be social. All his unbecoming, forced joviality returned making the others uncomfortable and curiously bad tempered. When he praised Myra Merridew, a middle-aged character actress, for the way she had interpreted one of her scenes she said curtly: "I was plumb bad and you know it."

"I didn't think so," he said placatingly.

"Look, Mr. Zold," she said, "let's face it. I played that scene all wrong. But *wrong.* So don't go saying how good I am—"

"O.K., O.K.," he said moving away sideways and laughing embarrassedly over his shoulder. "So you're lousy! If that's what you want to hear!"

He moved over to where Grey was standing smoking and talking to the others. He made some unimportant remark to his producer. Grey replied civilly enough but went on talking to the bunch of actors. He seemed to have nothing to say to him outside their mutual interest in the script. Then Grey said, raising his voice: "Right, everyone! Break for tea before we go on. Fifteen minutes *only.* Johnnie! Tea up!"

"Coming, Wally." A young man with an impossibly slender body, his tiny behind so narrow that it looked ridiculous, whom I now realized to be the Assistant Stage Manager leaped off the stage and made off through the side door to the kitchen of the coffee bar. Bernard called after him: "Extra cup, Johnnie," with a gesture towards me where I was still sitting in the stalls. "Right, Mr. Zold."

Bernard came down to sit beside me again. Johnnie came back with a wooden, kitchen tray holding huge, earthenware cups of scalding hot tea. I took mine thankfully when he came over to us. Though it was hot in the street outside, the Vauxhall, like all empty theatres, was freezing cold inside.

Grey was standing drinking his tea in the middle of the stage which, with its minimum of scenery and bad lights, looked extremely wan. Most of the cast and Johnnie were sitting on the lower steps of the staircase. But right in the middle of the front row of the stalls, a little to the left of where we were sitting, Lorraine Clark had, with an air of remote disengagement from the rest of them, ensconced herself. She was drinking her tea slowly, as if lost in thought, when the young and robustly handsome second lead, Miles Draycott, came across the footlights in a bound and joined her. Continuing to drink in the same absent fashion she took no notice of him at all. I saw him put his arm over the back of her seat then, partly withdrawing it, put his hand on her nearer shoulder. But she only turned her head slightly away from him, her long, pale-gold, fairy-tale hair streaming in the dim light.

Bernard was watching them too. Simultaneously we smiled as we saw Draycott, disconcerted by her indifference, looking about him as if for the scattered pieces of his dignity. "That's a new experience for you, my boy," I thought just as Bernard whispered: "First time that's ever happened to *him* I bet!" I gave him a glance and saw that he was, after his own experience, human enough to be cheered by someone else's snub.

For a moment this shocked me. But I see now that I was stupid. Integrity is not an easy crown for warm natures to wear since we at once demand too much from those we have enhaloed. I forget, I forget—I am to anxious to see perfection quickly—that he is human. I am too romantic, too extreme. I feel his smallest lapse a betrayal.

Johnnie, springing to his feet with a ballet dancer's bound, began collecting the cups all round. Watching his narrow, melting slimness, the graceful flick of his blond hair I said to Bernard: "Where *do* these creatures live? I mean one never sees them around in ordinary places; streets or Tubes or shops. I suppose they must get at least from where they live to where they work? But one never sees them; only *inside,* in specialized places like this."

"I know what you mean," he said. "I had a feeling something like that about the cast and everybody when I was at rehearsals in New York. Only with them my feeling went further since *all* their lives seemed so extraordinary, so spent in mysterious places. Whatever they said they did—I never saw them outside the theatre—but whatever it was it always sounded quite different from the same thing when I did it. They always seemed to me—even when I really knew better —to contain such exciting lives within themselves. Nothing I ever heard about them, drunkenness, abortion, quarreling, seemed squalid when it occurred to them. I always imagined their Sunday afternoons as marvellous."

"How is it that you never saw them outside the theatre?" I said.

"Same way I never see this bunch outside the theatre."

"Yes but . . . after all, you're a stranger here. You've hardly warmed your feet in this country."

"I was a stranger *there.* My situation duplicates itself wherever I am," he said mildly, without complaint. "Take

Phil Owens, my director in America. He's done both my plays. Nice guy; not unlike Grey here, thin, clever . . . only he's well-bred. Top Boston drawer. But out of the theatre we were never even within touching distance. He genuinely understood my work—he *liked* it—but he'd sort of forget I was the author. I'd hear him discuss and explain it to friends, actors, people concerned in the production. But kind natured as he was he never had anything to say to *me* about my own ideas. People never do, you know. People never do," he said turning to me with a sudden movement as of anguish, then turning quickly away again. "I keep hoping," he said in a close mutter so that I had to bend to catch the words, "that someone will one day say to themselves, 'Those ideas in the plays . . . they must come from *somewhere* inside this unprepossessing guy who's written them. Maybe it's worth spending a little time digging into him. . . .' "

I saw Lorraine stand up, turn her back on Draycott who had remained beside her and walk with her slow, swinging step back on to the stage.

"Owens now . . . maybe he was shy himself—I don't know. But Groton, Harvard, son of a famous writer . . . he could never talk to me. He somehow couldn't get the hang of my personality. You know," he said, "people who talk about 'contacts' always puzzle me. I can't get the hang of *them*. Fact is, you can have 'contacts' till the cows come home but if you don't click *personally* . . . they're as much use as a sick headache. For all the lip-service that's paid to the idea of non-snobbery in the world of the arts there are in fact enormous snobberies of personality. And that's where I'm sunk. I don't know the behaviour, I can't talk the language. Somewhere, at some time in my life, I lost the social faculty. A sort of chasm has opened out between me and the social usages which come to sophisticated people as naturally as breathing."

"You could learn," I said.

"Learn! Sure, like a child learning that walking is the movement of putting one foot in front of another. Yes, by putting my mind to it I might learn a precarious balance, put up a shallow, aped performance. I've even tried it! But the real truth—" he paused as if in doubt whether to take so deep a plunge into candour. Then he said: "The real truth is I don't want to. I'm frightened to 'learn' the sophisticated clichés and the hopped-up social thing. I have this curious feeling that it is my gaucheness, my placelessness which keeps my talent unhardened. Almost—this sounds absurd since I am saddened by my failures in society—but almost I deliberately court them. Learning the world's tricks and polish would mean the loss, the smoothing away of every true comprehension I possess. Ah! how pompous I sound! How can you bear to listen to me with such patience always?"

"I'm interested," I said.

He turned his head and, in the dull light from the stage, looked at me consideringly, his whole hand, in his familiar gesture, spread hard against his mouth. "No," he said at last. "Not really. Not interested. Desolate. Very kind, too. But desolate. You are filling up space with us, with my confidences. . . ."

"I'm *interested*," I said obstinately.

He might have argued further but Johnnie came over for our cups at that point and stood talking to us for a few moments. "I'm giving this up after your play, Mr. Zold," he said in a rather aggrieved voice. "I mean . . . one can't *get on*, can one? I've just about *had* the Vauxhall."

"What will you do?" I said.

"Oh I'm going into television," he said proudly. He went away.

Bernard and I looked at each other, amused.

"Is that a step *up*?" he said at last, again echoing exactly my thought.

They were beginning the third act and I sat back to watch it intently.

So far I have described very little of the play—or about my feelings at being at a rehearsal again. But this is something I cannot write about. There is too much pain. My young self sits beside me. I feel at once her hope (which has never died) and my own bitter wonder at where the years can be. (I remember once in Eversley Road, desperate with this sense of time gone, speaking of it a little to one of our neighbours, a middle-aged, placid (I thought) spinster. Miss Dean; did you ever meet her? "My dear," she said in her full-bosomed, cheerful way, "you haven't enough to do." I felt half-ashamedly that she might be right, and made another effort to accept the suburban pattern. And then, a few months later her younger brother with whom she lived suddenly got married. And Miss Dean, all her deprivations roused and rampant, went at the marriage with a chopper and broke it in half. I have never seen such undisguised, vicious energy. All those years she hadn't had enough to do either.)

But the play. Let me now tell you that it is remarkable. There is a kind of talent here which I did not, no I did *not* expect: a strong, spun delicacy, a quality not of glass or gold but of finest silver. Can this, I kept asking myself, have come from *him*? I am, you see, for all I have perceived of his true texture, still influenced by the boundaries of his outward self. Relating his work to Bernard as it unfolded there before my eyes was like hearing a great pianist evoking marvellous sound, while watching his stubby, thick, workmanlike hands.

Through all the play a soft wind blows. The light is slow, transparent, darkening. It is spring twilight, apple green and full of heartbreak. What he has caught as an aspect of our condition, of our time, is the moment of busy, sad dusk in crowded streets, that moment just before the long evening falls when it seems just possible that some sparkling joy will come with the dark. We look back and forward at once; to the long patterns of our pasts and the cozening shapes of our deceptive futures . . . all poised on that delicate moment of green dusk.

The end of the play had a curious effect on the cast. There seemed tears in the air when at last they subduedly broke up and left the theatre. No one spoke to Bernard. Perhaps they resented being made to feel beyond their normal span.

We got back to Honeysuckle Road, however, to find an only too normal reaction to my absence. They were having lunch when we got in. Bernard, sensibly I think, attempted no silly, lying excuse for my absence but said straightaway and cheerily: "I gave Ruth a treat and allowed her in to watch rehearsal."

"I couldn't resist it," I said to Jessica, laughing a little, "but I'm awfully sorry I wasn't back in time to give you lunch."

"Oh we managed fine," she said and went on talking as usual, rising nobly to new heights of chat though her mouth looked a little strained. I guessed that her mother-in-law had been giving vent to a great many oblique thrusts against me. *She* was fuming. I felt extremely sorry. I would not have missed the rehearsal for anything but I saw that we were all going to have to pay for it with a vengeance. And indeed she opened fire right away.

The old woman has an infuriating habit which I have had to learn to accommodate myself to, of doling out provisions in the most curious way. Bernard is anything but mean and there is always plenty in the house, but the old woman insists on it all being left in the storage larder, hardly anything being actually put out to go on with. Two ounces of tea for instance and two ounces only at a time are put in the tea canister—by me, but on the old woman's instructions.

Packets of butter pile up but only a small slab is allowed out for any one meal.

Stupidly, when preparing the salad that morning, I had hardboiled more eggs than were needed; though this was not really so great a crime since Ginny, who still only picks at her meals, is in the habit of taking a hard egg whenever she feels hungry and eating it from her fingers like a lump of chocolate.

"Er . . . did Hammerson's send the order yesterday?" she began.

"Yes, I checked it. It's all there."

"I was just wondering," she said, looking down at her plate with that disengaged obstinacy of expression I am beginning to know very well. "I took a look in the larder this morning and there don't seem to be as many eggs—"

"I boiled half a dozen this morning," I said quickly.

"Half a dozen? You put half-a-dozen eggs in that salad?" she said in maddening, deliberate, mock-innocent mis-statement.

"No. There were *two* eggs in the salad," I said attempting to control my irritation. "I put the others in the fridge."

"Six eggs!" she said as if talking to herself. She gave a slight shrug, lifted her eyebrows and ostentatiously kept quiet.

"Ginny likes eating an egg just like that sometimes," I said. "She often does when she comes in from school."

"The kid wants taking in hand," said Bernard who was eating his own lunch with the great speed of temper. "She never eats a proper meal."

"You try arguing with your daughter," said Jessica. "I just don't know where she gets that obstinate nature from but I'm positive sure it's not from me!" she added lightly—and stupidly. (Or was it stupid? I have again the feeling that she sometimes gets back at her mother-in-law in ways more subtle than anyone bargains for. Does *he* know this?)

"From my side! From my side!" said the old woman flaming, with this excuse, into relieved rage. "Of course! Where else?"

"Did you settle Hammerson's account, by the way?" Bernard said impatiently to his wife, pushing his plate aside and motioning me to collect it with the others. He turned his shoulder against his mother as he spoke as if physically telling her not to try him any further.

"Oh, gee, Bernie," said Jessica, "I forgot! I just clean forgot it."

"For God's sakes!" cried old Mrs. Zold so passionately and suddenly that we all turned to look at her, "you've had that bill in the house *three days*. It should've been settled by now. What're you waiting for? What'll they think at the store? Why didn't you leave it with me?" she said to her son, trembling. "At least I'd have seen it got paid. To leave a bill unpaid—"

"Mama! Calm down will you! So it's waited three days. Three *days*. Not three months. You don't have to get hysterical about it. So go out and pay them this afternoon."

"It's early closing day," she snapped back at him, triumphant in this fact.

"So tomorrow."

"That's not the point. A bill must be paid. In the whole of my life I've never let a bill go unpaid." (She said this with a glance at me—the wicked begetter of her hysterics—to see if I were impressed.) "If there's one thing . . . all my life, if I've not had a rag to my back, I've been a quick payer. If you're born honest, Bernie, you're born honest."

My hands paused of their own volition on the tray and I gave her a stealthy glance of pure astonishment. Only a week before the laundry had sent back by mistake two extra and very good bath sheets belonging to someone else. I had been going to put them aside to return but she had said absently to keep them. "We might as well use them now they're here," she said. "Time enough to send them back when we go."

Had she forgotten this incident? Yes, I suddenly felt with an odd touch of understanding . . . she had. I knew her well enough by now to know that she was not deliberately lying, not wilfully falsifying. It is just that she has, in general, no overall conception of conduct. She was being perfectly sincere when she called herself honest since just then she was feeling so. Her vision, in fact, is only a taken-to-impossible-lengths, unconcealed version of everyone else's. Sometimes I think I see in this old woman a cross section of the whole human race. Like Harpo Marx, she is everybody's subconscious. Seeing each moment by itself with no relation to the next she lurches, so to speak, from one moral position to another, obeying not law but psychological need. She was not being dishonest even over the bath sheets, only mixed and bewildered out of her "honesty" post by a momentarily more attractive social role. The fact is I think she wanted to keep them out of a kind of blind ambition to be thought "smart" in household matters . . . since she is actually anything but so. She can hardly cook, orders wrongly, can't set a table . . . she is as hopeless as Jessica in every domestic chore. (Though this does not prevent her making a great fuss about cleanliness. To leave the dining room unhoovered is to provoke down-dipping glances at the floor till I take the hint and bring in the machine.)

Bernard was counting out some money and pushing it across to her. "There! go in and pay the bill yourself and leave me in peace," he said with good-natured bad temper.

Looking pacified she closed her hand on the money and put it carefully away in her bulging, plastic bag. "I'll go in first thing tomorrow," she said with so much genuine pleasure on her thin, knobbly face at being able to do this that again a strangely sympathetic flash of comprehension enlightened me and I realized that this insistence of hers on

immediate payment was a kind of boast, a childlike, rather
moving, naïve pride in being *able* to pay. She must have
suffered greatly from poverty at some time in her life.

I say "sympathetic." And yet I was entirely to blame for
what followed—though I didn't start it.

Bernard asked me to make some tea with which to finish
his lunch. He has developed a passion for tea though a
running fight with his mother ensues every time he asks for
it. She has taken it into her head, in an arbitrary, reasonless
way, to consider tea bad and coffee good for the health!

"So all right, there's a little tannin in tea," I heard him
arguing through the hatch while I was making it. "It won't
kill me. So listen! Mama! *I want a cup of tea.* So just for
once you leave me alone, hah?"

"D'you know what that tannin does to your stomach?" she
was saying when I came back. Jessica had left the room. To
do her justice she doesn't revel in their quarrels. They simply
gore her. When they start she sits like a mild glass of milk
between two fizzing ginger ales till she gets tired of them,
then leaves.

The old woman was muttering about doctor's bills if he
wasn't careful. Bernard, making the usual attempt to control
himself at least while I was there, said to me with a smile
and an attempted wink as I put the teapot down beside him:
"Thanks, Ruth." He looked over at his mother, winked again
and said: "Want a cup, Mama?"

"Of course you know better than me! Now you want me to
poison myself as well!" Her whole face began to work and
tremble with the beginnings of real hysteria. Burning inside
because I had been to the rehearsal and she hadn't, because
Bernard (in front of me) was not taking her seriously, she
burst out: "I won't go along with that, Bernie. You might as
well know it now. *Now!* Do you hear me?" Her voice rose.

Bernard gave an exaggerated sag of weariness which even
I could have told him was asking for trouble and, exhausted

into idiocy, capped it by saying would-be humorously: "Why don't I keep my big mouth shut?"

"Why? Why?" she gave him back in a hoarse scream. "That's all I get from you. Jokes! You'd sell your soul for a wisecrack," she screamed and went on into further grotesque and absurd accusations. Caught in the middle of clearing the table I was about to leave without finishing when her hand, flying out in a passionate, clumsy gesture, nearly tipped over her half-full coffee cup. "Careful!" I said involuntarily and went to get it. "Might have stained the cloth," I said trying to normalize the atmosphere out of embarrassment for him.

The narrow escape from the dire, tiny mishap of spoiling the cloth seemed to give her pause for a moment. Then she said in an angry mutter: "It wouldn't stain so much. So what if it *had* spilled?"

"Coffee not stain?" I said in astonishment.

"Not like tea," she said wildly losing what sense she had left.

"*Mrs.* Zold," I said really losing patience at last, "I've never heard such absolute nonsense!" And slamming my hand down furiously on the table I began brushing crumbs away with some violence. "And by the way," I said in a loud hard voice, "in case you didn't know it there's caffeine in coffee. Did no one ever tell you? That's a drug too. And a much stronger one than. . . . It's absolute nonsense to say—"

My harsh voice ceased suddenly. I took a step backwards.

Bernard was still sitting at the table, his left hand plucking at the table cloth, his lips sucked inside his teeth as though he were holding back a great sigh.

I looked over at his mother. Her head was bent.

"I . . . I'm sorry," I said at last. "I don't often lose my temper. I'm very sorry," I brought out in a very quick clipped voice.

The old woman raised her head. She was smiling but trying not to! Gleams of shrewd, hardly concealed triumph were escaping into the wrinkles round her eyes. Her mouth was stiff with suppressing a smile of delight. For the first time since I had come among them I had put myself in the wrong and her into a position of moral superiority. Now *I* could be blamed for something. Delighted almost into affection—I could not have pleased her more than by behaving badly—she took charge of the situation, grabbed at her advantage by becoming very soft, very pliable, very humble . . . and extremely happy. It was paradise for her to feel herself blameless. She kept repeating my name, while telling me, very humbly what they would have for supper, saying "Mrs. Ha-a-land" in long-drawn-out, soft tones . . . until finally she overdid it. Unused to triumph she drank too deep, got herself intoxicated and couldn't stop.

Bernard turned to her at last and with a face of thunder said: "That's enough now, Mama."

She gave him a sly look, still triumphant but frightened, ready to be slapped.

"Enough?" she said.

"I told you that's *enough*, Mama."

"What're you talking about?"

"You know," he said remorselessly and getting up moved nearer to her, looming over her chair.

She gave a kind of gasp, her eyes flickered, she put a hand and arm up as if to fend off a blow—an artificial, hysterical, maddening gesture—then as he attempted to take her arm saying: "Come on. You want to get some rest,"— she wrenched it away from him and began to scream in earnest. "Hound me! Hound me!" she tore out of her throat. "That's all you ever do. What have I done that I should be burdened with you? Murderer! Your father again, that's what you are. *He* wanted me dead; out of the way so he could have his women in the house. In my kitchen! In my own kitchen! The money he spent! *My* money. Money I made with my hands, with the very bones of my hands."

She held them out, pushing them with their big, milky nails to his face. He turned his head aside.

"No-o," she said in bitter scorn, her narrow lips thrust out, "no-o. My son doesn't want to see. Fourteen hours a day sewing to keep us alive . . . he doesn't want to know."

She began to sob, very loudly but without tears, beating one clenched fist on top of the other. "Murderer," she said again. "Murderer!"

Stirring myself from my frozen immobility I made to go but she called out: "You stay! You stay! You want to learn what sort of people you're living with. You pry around enough!"

"Mama!" he said, then in a quick aside to me: "Get some aspirin."

"Have sense," I heard him say when I was in the kitchen getting the pills, "Have sense. What have I done for you to get this way again? I thought this was all finished with."

"Murderer," she said mechanically. Through the hatch I saw her rocking herself backwards and forwards. "Your father!" She nodded her head. "Your father. Your father. *Your father!*" she suddenly screamed out at him. "Will I forget the shame to my dying day? In the same house. You in September and hers in— You got relations, Bernie. Close relations. Did you know? You got brothers and sisters all over the place."

I took in the aspirins and water and tried to give them to him. He took no notice. He had put his arm round her shoulders and was attempting to draw her towards him but she sat stiffly, resisting him.

"You promised me," he was saying. "You promised me you wouldn't think."

"Promised!" she said scornfully.

He suddenly sank down and squatted on his heels before her, looking up into her face. Then he gripped his left hand over his right wrist and stared intently into the palm of his right hand. "What can I do?" he muttered to himself examining the lines of his palm. "What more can I do? God in Heaven, what more can I do?"

"You! you don't have to do anything. I don't have to rely on you," she said spitefully. "Thank God you're not my only child."

He jumped up quickly.

"Is Jakie coming?" he said smacking the question at her like a wet towel. She shrugged.

"Well? Is he or isn't he?"

She licked her lips and looked sideways around her. She pushed at him as he stood in front of her indicating that she wanted to stand up.

He took no notice.

"When?" he said at last.

"Two or three weeks I figure," she said with sudden and astounding calm. "Maybe a month. If he can get berths. It's the vacation time right now."

"A few weeks," he said half to himself.

"He'll get them," she said, her face looking puffy and brooding but with a flash in the eye. "Trust Jakie. He can always get anything." She gave Bernard a look which said clearly enough, "Not like you!"

"Trust Jakie!" he said and hissed out a laugh. "Trust Jakie!"

"He's my son isn't he?" she said nodding her head, her lips tight.

He walked away from her and sat down. For the second time I held out the aspirins and water. Again he took no notice. Leaving them on the table I went back into the kitchen. But I left the hatch open.

"I want something from you, Mama," I heard through the hatch. "I want that you should do something for me that's important."

"Well?" she said hard-ly. "What is it?"

"I want you should write and put Jakie off (if you can)

till after this month—at least till after the twenty-fifth."

"What difference if he comes after, before . . . ? What's the twenty-fifth different from any other day?"

He said nothing for a moment, only narrowed his eyes at her with an expression of profound hurt which, try as he would, he could not keep off his face. "It's my premiere," he said at last. "We're opening on the twenty-fifth."

Her lower lip opened and she gazed at him with an expression of acute guilt. Then: "Why don't you say?" she cried out. "Is it my fault I forget? Do you talk to me, tell me? Couldn't you have told me? I'm your mother aren't I? I'm growing old I can't remember. . . ."

"Yes, well," he said getting up and putting his arm round her once more. This time she leaned against him. He held his arm firmly about her puny, gaunt shoulders for a few moments in silence. Then he said: "*Of course* I should have told you again. I thought you knew, we've discussed it so— You forgot that's all. It's all right Mama. Everybody forgets. I'm getting so I don't recall my own name half the time."

"I didn't mean to forget," she said in a tone accusing *him*. "I know it's important to you Bernie. You think it isn't important to me? You think I don't lie awake nights worrying? *You're my son.* I worry for you," she said lifting her head away from his chest and looking up into his face.

"I know you do," he said, "I know you do. Now stop reproaching yourself. It was my fault. It's my memory not yours that's going to pieces. Guess I'm wearing my brains out all this re-writing I'm having to do. Will I be glad when that first night is over! Now look, I want you should take some aspirin and go lie down for an hour. Will you do that? You're worn out." He removed his arm with a final squeeze, forced the aspirins down her and finally got her upstairs. But not before—with unexpected firmness—he had got her to promise she would try to put his brother off till after the twenty-fifth.

The house seemed very quiet after they left the dining room. Jessica had vanished; probably to the tea shop in the Finchley Road where she has lately picked up with a woman who runs a flatlet house in Swiss Cottage. Mrs. Capes, we gather, was a nurse once and can talk willingly about Jessica's leg and the medical world for hours.

I finished with the dining room at long last, washed up, and tidied the kitchen. The sun shifted into its afternoon position, flooding the front of the house and the hall with grainy, yellow light but leaving the kitchen dark. The rows of hanging cups, the refrigerator, the red formica surfaces looked all at once extraordinarily desolate, tidy and forlorn. I was about to flee from them when Bernard came in. Before I could speak he said abruptly: "I know exactly what you're going to say! You're going to apologize to me! Well you're not to. I'm apologizing to you for both of us: Mama and myself."

"Oh what for?" I said impatiently, turning away.

"For embarrassing you with a scene for one thing."

"That wasn't really an embarrassment," I said. "I'm not a well-bred middle class Englishwoman. I'm lower class and used to rows."

"Well. Thank God for that!" he said briskly. We smiled suddenly at each other.

"Is she asleep?" I asked.

"Yes." He hesitated then sat down in the easy chair. "Now you can make me a peaceful cup of tea!" he said.

We waited in pleasant, relaxed silence for the kettle to boil.

"All the same," he began when I eventually handed him his cup, "all the same—thanks!—all the same, certain things ought to be explained."

"You don't—"

"No, I know. I don't *have* to. But I want to! So pipe down will you and let me talk!"

I was a little taken aback by his cheerfulness. But, as I have noticed to be increasingly happening, he followed my thought, saying: "They're not so shattering as you might think, these scenes. I'm pretty well used to them by now. Once you learn to accept them as necessary, as a necessary medicine so to speak, they become bearable. At least . . . they're not so *un*-bearable as they were. They're therapy, see—like blood letting. If she didn't . . . if she. . . ."

To my own surprise (and indeed annoyance)—perhaps because we had just been mentioning "class" I found myself saying, using a crisp, upper class, social worker voice and manner: "Don't you think it's a bad thing to be constantly giving in to hysterics? One only encourages more."

"D'you suppose I could have one of those ginger cookies?" he said.

I reached up to the top of the kitchen cabinet and, taking down a packet of biscuits, gave him some on a plate.

"I'm sorry," I said abruptly. "I shouldn't have said that. But it seems to me that you are so enclosed in your . . . situation . . . that you don't know—"

"How undignified and grotesque it looks to others—"

"No—"

"Yes," he said with firm insistence. "In fact that's putting it mild. Other insinuations haven't been lacking either, particularly from the sub-Freud idiots tossing around their half-baked bits of jargon."

(I remembered Bridget and her prompt, parroted "Oedipus.")

"Look!" he said reasonably, stretching forward and taking another biscuit, "take a simple think like a physical gesture. I put my arm round my mother far more often than I do around . . . well, say, Ginny. The idiots, seeing this, are only too ready to spring in with some psychological hocus-pocus, bringing in Lawrence of course and heaven knows who or what else. And yet the real truth of it is simple. I put my arm across my mother's shoulders to make her feel less alone. I know that all her life she has had this feeling of standing alone in an empty, windy place, cold, unloved, isolated . . . above all, *unprotected*. And what's more, what she feels about herself is true. For much of her life she *has* stood alone, utterly without shelter, suffering greatly. That's why I put my arm round her. The weight of my arm (I *know* this) the weight of my arm across her back gives her a kind of physical sense as of a wall behind her. So I do it! I make a wall.

"And God knows, she needs one," he said after an appreciable pause. "You've gathered, I suppose, some idea of what my father was like."

"Yes I have," I burst out, feeling all of a sudden violently indignant. "But I don't see why you should have to suffer for it. Surely you don't believe all this 'sins of the fathers'—"

"Yes," he said, "I do." I looked sceptical and bad-tempered but taking no notice he went on, saying mildly: "You have to take notice of a fact when it's a *fact*. What my father did, what he was, marked me for life even before I was born. He was a weak, stupid man, with weak, corrupted blood in him from somewhere and he was a born philanderer. Jakie my brother was born when they'd been married a year and she was still comparatively happy but when he was about five my father was behaving so badly that they separated. He couldn't even make a living, apart from anything else. My mother had to work, to slave, to keep them. She had to hide her money so he couldn't get at it. But worst of all he was chronically unfaithful—though how he ever managed this (he was like a little weasel to look at . . . it is extraordinary how often these thin, sly little men contain inordinate sexual appetite) I've never understood.

"After four years apart—four years for her of being ashamed, of being despised, of being a failure at something so radical as marriage—they were brought together again by well-meaning interferers and a year after that I was born. They were renting out rooms in the house they'd taken after the reconciliation and he got one of the roomers pregnant almost simultaneously with my mother. So I was carried and born in misery and shame and betrayal . . . *all over again.* Can you blame her if at times she hates me? Can you blame her if she cannot face truth any more? Since the day I was born it has been necessary for her to lie to herself if she were to go on living at all. Ach! this college boy conception of 'truth' we meet up with so often, declared with such virtue. What childish, green nonsense it is. The fact was that in our level of society, betrayed and poor and vulnerable, she was open to every small-natured snub and sneer her world could give. The stock answer to women in her situation is that if people were unkind to her she should have dropped them. *Drop* people . . . in a small society! (For that matter we all live in small societies.) How could she drop her family, her few friends? We were only hanging on to social life by a thread anyway. So she took the only way out. She closed her eyes. She pretended not to see the amused, curious look, not to hear the insensitive, wounding remark, played a game of normal, happy families, lived the only way she could . . . *by illusion.* If now she lives by evasion it is because she has the habit. If on occasion she is demanding, it is a sign of spirit; a good thing not a bad. However hard it sometimes is to bear I take her scenes and fusses to be a proof of life.

"So there it is," he said rising. "The sins of the fathers. . . . Oh yes; I believe in that all right." He stood by the door. "He died in a madhouse by the way," he said. Then he flipped his hand, thanked me for the tea and was gone.

I suppose it is as well that more light has been thrown upon the old woman's attitude to me. The pattern, the feared parallels are obvious. But how convince her that she need not fear? One cannot help *him*. He is determined to immolate himself upon the fact of her suffering. He dare not even defend himself at any point since to put her further in the wrong is to increase his own agony . . . for she then takes still further revenge on him.

Oh, I am tired, tired. His problems are too appalling, too insoluble to be borne with. Almost worse than anything else, I think, is that they are *unfashionable*. The fact is, he is not only an expatriate in other ways, he is also one in time. His kind of situation, the attempt to behave well within narrow, domestic boundaries, the concept of sacrifice and patience with suffering which lies near to the hand . . . these are nineteenth century virtues. Charles Lamb for instance could devote his life to his mad sister without a sneer from the outside world, however wordly. Good behaviour was in tune with the times. Bernard requires twice the moral courage to behave half as well. The fashion of contemporary life is against admirable men. And when such qualities as his are coupled with creation, art, sensibility . . . then all our canons are upset and we hate the Bernards who bewilder us.

There is a melancholy restlessness inside me. It has been a long, disturbing, distressing day. I am glad it is over. I want something to change; *quickly*.

Ruth

❖❖❖❖❖❖❖❖❖❖❖❖❖❖❖❖❖❖❖❖

6th August

COMING AWAY after her lesson this evening Bridget caught up with me while I was going for an evening paper and we walked along together. She suggested we have coffee somewhere before she caught her bus home and we turned into a café. In the middle of her usual chatter she said:

"Look, Ruth, don't you think there's something wrong with that kid?"

"With Ginny? Why?" I said cautiously.

"You're being *cautious!*" she said immediately at which I couldn't help laughing though I knew she would at once and rightly take this as an admission.

"What about Ginny?"

"Sure and I wish I knew," she said doubtfully. "She's a fantasist if you ask me."

"A what?"

"You know . . . lives in a dream world. Look, I'll tell you. What d'you think I was catching her doing the other day?"

"Well? What?"

"You know that kitten they bought for her?"

"Binkie? It's sweet but I wish it was house trained already. What with Binkie and the barrels of disinfectant the old woman—Anyway. What about it?"

"When I came in on Tuesday I went straight into the kitchen for water. I don't know where you'd all got to but nobody else was around. I was just casually looking through the hatch when I saw Ginny. She was sitting in the dining-room, and she was holding that kitten in her lap, lying on its back. She was holding that kitten between her two hands and glaring into its eyes. And honest to God, what do you think she was trying to do with it? She was trying to hypnotize it! She wasn't playing either. She was . . . sure I know it sounds daft from a kid, but she was trying to *force her will* on that small animal."

"It's nothing," I said quickly. "Children often get the most extraordinary ideas."

Playing for a cast-iron certainty with which to divert her from the matter I asked Bridget what was the latest on the Hugo front.

"My *dear,*" she said, perking up at once and changing gear into Sally Bowles, "he's finished!"

169

"Finished what?"

"With Barbara! It's all over. Isn't it *mar*-vellous?"

I sighed, a tolerant, experienced sigh, and asked her if she thought she could handle the whole thing properly this time before—though I didn't put it quite that—he was off the hook again.

"Oh, I don't know," she said in that open, disconsolate way which I cannot help finding engaging. "I suppose all those women's magazines clichés are true really. Men *are* caught on the rebound very often. Aren't they?"

"Yes," I said with a judicious air. "I suppose they are."

"You see," she said rather wearily being momentarily no one at all, just miserable Bridget, "I keep wanting to please, to be the kind of woman he admires . . . but the kind he admires are the strong, firm personalities. Sure it's all bound up with this being completely dominated by his mother as a child—"

"Oh, Bridget, for heaven's sake," I said impatiently, "spare me the psychological junk."

"But it's *all true*," she said with the kind of opaque, silly obstinacy I have sometimes noticed in her. She is soft and open but much more impervious than one thinks. I looked over at her irritably then I saw with a slight shock that she was indeed unhappy. The popping, brown eyes had deep lines beneath them, her mouth, badly made up, had that hurt thrust of the lower lip, she had lost weight even during the short time I had known her. I felt extremely sorry.

"Look for someone else," I said, suddenly and urgently.

"To tell you the truth," she said in her candid way (I find myself often in danger of forgiving her calculation because of its candour, of letting myself fall into one of the stupider conventions of our time) "I would. I'm not so tied to Hugo—though I am terribly in love with him—that I wouldn't settle for someone else . . . if I could find that creature!"

A trifle shocked, I must say, by her immediate willingness

to transfer, I asked her why in that case she felt bound to expend her emotions on Hugo. "Wouldn't any other reasonably attractive young man do?" I said.

She looked forlorn again and said (quite rightly): "That's a silly thing to say now, isn't it? There aren't any queues battering me door down. And even if there were, it's a hundred to one they'd any of them be any fun to be with. Hugo's beautiful to look at, sure, but we have beautiful boys in Ireland. It's him being that much fun. Where else will I be finding someone I could have as much fun with?"

I was about to chide her but caught my reaction in mid air so to speak. For after all, I knew very well what she meant. Why after all have I left you? Because you are no fun. That is the cruel truth of it. This is something *you must face*. This is something everyone must face. Women can work their fingers to the bone, men can slave for their homes and families . . . if they are no fun to be with, in other words if for one reason or another they light no spark . . . then they are not loved.

Do not, by the way, confuse "fun" as Bridget means it with the stupid definitions of the travel poster. To do her justice she means nothing that can be bought with money. She is sometimes absurd, she has streaks of calculation and selfishness, I would not rely on her for *anything* . . . but she has a kind of cockeyed rightness in her values. She longs for personality, awareness, certain ways of thinking and talking, a degree of good sophistication. What she wants has nothing to do with night clubs or lavish parties or Monte Carlo; nor it is rich-little-girl-longs-to-escape-to-Coney-Island tripe either.

She lifted her wicker, model-girl basket (these are now "out" but that is typical of Bridget) on to her knee, rummaged in the mess inside and came up with several small sketches.

"Hugo's?" I said as she handed them to me.

"Yes. I begged him to let me have some. They're illustrations for a book by this animal man, the very famous one . . . what's his name? Foreign."

"Soulier?"

"Yes. Aren't they *mar*-vellous?"

"They're very good indeed," I said with some surprise looking through the bundle. They were really extremely good.

"The birds are wonderful," I said.

"Aren't they?" she said lovingly. "They were all done right here at the London Zoo, what's more. I went with him lots of times. We had an awful lot of fun. I should think they'd be worth quite a lot already," she added practically, with her usual hard-centred inconsequence, "and they're bound to appreciate in value. I should think a Hugo Lee original drawing might be worth a good deal of money one day." (She pronounced the word "munny" in the clenched-throat, Liverpool-Irish accent I remember from my earliest childhood.)

"Well you hang on to them," I said giving them back to her. "I wouldn't mind having a couple myself."

"I'll ask him for some," she said quickly.

"Oh no! Bridget, for goodness' sake don't pick me up on a casual remark like that—"

"Sure and it'll give me an excuse to go around to him tonight," she said seriously. I felt a slight flick of annoyance that it wasn't affection for me *or* a generous nature which was prompting her but quite unaware—she really is remarkably and selfishly obtuse at times—she went on: "That's fine. Thanks, Ruth, for the idea."

"Any time," I said rather ruffled and getting up crossly.

An inkling of my annoyance penetrating, she said: "I'm sure he'll give me some if I tell him they're for you."

"Surely!" I said struggling into my jacket. "He's a great admirer of mine!"

"As a matter of fact he is."

"Yes of course."

"No, really. I've told him heaps about you and he says you must be a *very intelligent creature*."

"That's very kind of him. Look, I've got to go, Bridget." She saw that I was really annoyed (quite disproportionately so for some reason) and said pacifyingly: "He's even asked me to bring you round. That's a *compliment* in case you don't recognize it. He's so damn reserved he can't bear to have people visit him most of the time. If I can get him to make a date though will you come? Maybe he'll ask Erik and you'll meet him too. Will you?" She ran after me as I walked to the cash desk and paid the bill, protested—but not too much—about at least paying her half, then said again: "Ah, come on now, Ruth. You might find it interesting. Seeing how artists live an' all that." We walked into the street.

"I've lived with one for years," I said pushing up your status a bit.

"I mean a real artist," she said, not meaning to hurt. (Nor do I, Francis.)

"Will you?" she said again looking into my face rather anxiously.

I do not quite know why but at that moment great tears came to my eyes. I could have broken down in misery and weeping standing there in the middle of the Finchley Road on that bright, summer evening. And I felt at last in its full force, not any longer to be denied, what I have been pushing away from me all these months; a bleak and bitter and weary desolation. Bernard—as he always is, to hell with him—was right. I have been filling my life and my thoughts this long, sad summer with the Zolds and their doings, with household matters, with walking alone through the pretty streets in the soft, milky, tender evenings, with reading, with writing letters . . . and suddenly I felt that I could stand no more. I had a sense of having slipped through the interstices of life into a floating dark where I had no name. I wanted to be a person, to be known. I wanted. . . . The wanting brought with it a sensation as if the dried, small, leathery membrane which had been my Self was reconstituting itself, becoming moist and full and palpitating, demanding a food . . . which was not there.

I looked down at Bridget. Her stocky little figure and slightly bowed legs appeared to me all at once as humble and requesting.

"All right," I said. "I'll come."

Even an evening with semi-phony, baby intellectuals will be better than nothing; so far have I sunk in my at last acknowledged, deepening despair.

It is, you will remember, my fortieth birthday today.

Ruth

❀❀❀❀❀❀❀❀❀❀❀❀❀❀❀❀❀

12th August

JESSICA is in Arcady! A young doctor at the hospital (I think he must be young enough to be her son!) has taken her to a concert. That is to say, he presented her with a free ticket (she is supposed—did I ever tell you this by the way?—to be musical) and took himself on another one. Anyway, he was there, sat near her, bought her an ice in the interval and—crown of crowns!—brought her home afterwards. This was yesterday evening.

For the last few days, and especially since last night, she has hardly stopped talking about the concert and the doctor . . . who is of course a combination of St. Augustine and Sir Alexander Fleming. The old woman is inclined to be a bit jealous and sniffy about this triumph, and Ginny as usual is indifferent to anything but television (though she has produced under Bridget's prodding some very curious pictures of flowers). The big surprise is Bernard who, though he adopts a chaffing attitude about Jessica's "boy friend," is secretly rather proud! A pleased, concealed smile twitches at his lips when they're talking about it. This has, I must admit, staggered me slightly. I would have expected him to be irritated by the incessant references to the doctor and Jessica's night out. But not at all! And on reflection I see that once again I have been stupid; both stupid and naïve. I am, as I have indicated to you before, in constant danger— I suppose out of some desperate need of my own—of building him up in my mind as some sort of saint-figure. This, as I keep reminding myself, is all nonsense. He is no more than human. He does not care for his wife at all. But it pleases his vanity a little to know that other men take notice of her. He is no more immune from, or uncaring about, the stamp of outside success than anyone else. After all, *she is his wife.* Any attention she may receive is a compliment, however oblique, to him. It is pleasant to him not to feel apologetic or irritable about her. So I see him, within an attempt at a sardonic attitude, trying to hide the gratified smile which he cannot help smiling now and then ever since the invitation was given.

There was another cause for pleasure and that was the actual presence of Dr. Phillips in his own living-room last night. Since the Independence Day party and Bessie Levitt a few days later for lunch there has been until a week ago not a soul to come into the house except Bridget. None of the people here on the 4th July have bothered to get in touch with him again let alone invite him back.

But within the last week this picture has suddenly changed. For instance having the doctor here for a chat over a drink (he seems a nice young man from the brief glimpse I caught of him, easy to talk to but what I think is described as a "wet") was pleasant for Bernard. He sat back, relaxed, for the whole time the visitor was here, talking pleasantly with an air of chatting to a daughter's boy friend.

It was normal. That was the thing. They were a family slotted into their place in society—like other families. Social contact with others, people coming in for a drink, the telephone ringing with a call that was not from a tradesman or —rarely—from the Vauxhall . . . these things were important to their life as a family. And now they were beginning! After the false start of Independence Day they are now really beginning to form the nucleus of an ordinary social life.

For the doctor has not been the only visitor. Mrs. Capes, Jessica's teashop friend, has been here too. She is a small, square, bony woman, alert, talkative, lower middle-class, landlady-shrewd. She and Jessica get on like a house on fire. Even Ginny has had a school friend here for tea now that her school holidays have begun. (The child is a dull little thing but her father is an architect!) The old woman must have combed that child's hair seventeen times for the event. She even called me to retie her hair ribbon though—since I am hideously clumsy in such matters (you would have done it beautifully!)—I was a broken reed and she was obliged to do it herself in the end—for the nth time.

And—most important of all—there has been Peregrine Soames. Yes, yes, yes . . . Peregrine, this year's Golden Boy in the British theatre. I suppose even you, sitting in Eversley Road, skipping the theatrical columns in the papers, have heard of Peregrine who, at precisely twenty-four has had three plays produced one after the other with considerable success in the West End.

Though with not *quite* such *réclame* as his manner might imply.

Yes, he has been here. Gordon, the agent who was here on Independence Day, knows him and apparently mentioned Bernard to him. Peregrine, who had been to Finland on holiday and was only just back, telephoned immediately. I answered the phone and told the elegantly lively young man's voice that Bernard and everybody else was out and could I take a message?

"If everybody's out then who are you?"

"I'm the housekeeper."

"With that charming voice? What typical American luck! I've spent years looking for—I say! I must come if only to see if I can entice you away. Would you care to keep house for me?"

I laughed non-committally and, I felt, inadequately and asked him again if he would leave a message.

"Yes. This is Peregrine Soames and would he please call me back as soon as he can as I want very much to meet him." He gave me the number and pleasantly hung up.

I heard Bernard speaking to him later that evening and half an hour later still speaking—or rather listening, with the receiver held six inches away from his ear—as I passed through the hall. He hung up a long quarter of an hour after that and came into the kitchen wearing a look of amused deprecation.

"That young man's some talker!" he said. "It's darn lucky I'm a natural born listener (though maybe you wouldn't know it, Ruth; with you I talk). I wonder what happens when he meets another talker!"

"Simultaneous combustion I imagine!"

He laughed and said a trifle self-consciously: "All the same I can take more of it! You know . . . that boy's just spent three quarters of an hour praising my work!"

"How *very* nice," I said warmly. "It's about time people started doing just that."

He gave me an embarrassed look then quickly shut it off and I realized—almost for the first time—that I had said practically nothing to him about his play. Going home from the theatre after the rehearsal that day the bus had been crowded and we had sat apart; and the scene afterwards had driven me from discussing the play or even—because it was now painfully related to it—referring to the rehearsal.

I felt remorseful and would have said something there and then if his mother had not come in with a curiosity which could not be restrained any longer and asked who had been calling him up. Her manner is not so hostile to me as it was before the scene, but curiously null. She had washed her own behaviour out of her mind and with it, apparently, mine too.

He took her arm, glad to be able to tell her something pleasant, and led her out, talking about Peregrine—as everybody in the house including Ginny now calls him.

He has been here three times. The first time I opened the door to him . . . and let in another world, full of sweep and dazzle. He came—invited for a drink that first evening—at six o'clock, in splendid evening dress, on his way to a party. He left at nine o'clock having talked non-stop through half a bottle of whisky and a pile of sandwiches I hurriedly prepared for the two of them in the big room while the women kept out of the way in the dining-room. Bernard had closed the communicating doors for once and I could see and hear very little of the visitor though his voice and laugh could be heard incessantly.

Taking in the sandwiches I did hear him say: "The *only* play in New York I found worth going to see. Quite tremendous impact."

Bernard murmured something like: "Not as good as all that," and Peregrine said: "Nonsense, my dear sir, it's not the slightest good being modest. You know perfectly well that it was by miles the best thing in the New York season."

"I wish I could say something about your own work," said Bernard trying to change the subject, "but I might as well admit it. I haven't seen it. In fact I've only been to the theatre twice since I've been here! Once to your Old Vic and once to see an Ibsen revival."

"My dear sir" (Peregrine has adopted a highly mannered lace-cravat style which is ridiculous but suits him) "I'll send you tickets for *Leamington Spa* immediately. It's been a tremendous hit with the coach trade! *Fleets* of coaches from Harrogate and Cheltenham and Buxton all madly jealous of old Leamington. (I've never been there in my life, incidentally!) And the carriage trade—what a delicious expression that is—has caught on too. So I'm in the money!"

"You see," Bernard was saying diffidently as I went through into the dining-room—he motioned me to shut the dividing door again—"I've been so busy with re-writing bits of *The Curtain* as well as drafting out a new piece that I simply haven't had time . . . and there's my family of course . . ."

Of course, I thought, as I shut the door. I knew very well why he hadn't gone to the theatre more often. He hadn't had the proper company to go with. Jessica's soft, brainless remarks on whatever they had seen had irritated him as it was. As for his mother, the theatre as a part of life hardly existed at all; on top of which she dislikes going into the West End. Did I say dislikes? She positively detests it. I don't think she has been into town three times since she has been here. Deeply and ingrainedly small town, she becomes, I know, profoundly uneasy away from the few, small streets she by now knows and clings to. It is quite a feat even to get her to the Finchley Road and she will not *ever* enter a big store. How they ever got her to his New York premieres I can't imagine.

Peregrine telephoned Bernard twice the following day, sent tickets for *Leamington Spa* the day after, came unexpectedly to tea the day after that and two days after that again. The second time he insisted on coming in to the dining-room for what he called "nursery tea" round the table, walked about with a cup in his hand looking at Ginny's pictures and making tactful, humorous comments, behaved very nicely to old Mrs. Zold who, unused to people being nice to her, could hardly open her mouth save to an ungracious mutter . . . and *talked.*

Have I told you what he looks like? He is slightly below medium height and rather solidly built—though he tries to disguise this with a lightly stylized grace of manner. He is, he says, as lazy as a cat, never gets up before noon, loathes physical energy for himself or in others, sunshine and daylight. All his energy is centered in his head. He has a round, baby face with an exceptionally clear, pink complexion and a good forehead. He must have had ringlets as a child but already, at twenty-four, is beginning to go bald. He came to tea wearing a gorgeous, brown and rust tweed suit, a waistcoat of what looked like thick, green felt with engraved, gilt buttons, and a large, topaz ring. Altogether there is a cultivated, Regency buck tang to him.

He keeps putting in a lot of what sound like bastard-German (but he assures us that they are Finnish) phrases into his conversation. Ginny laughs convulsively every time he does this. (It has just occurred to me that till now I have hardly ever heard that child laugh.) He tells stories, mostly about the theatre world, very well. They are nearly all scandalous or improper or both but so wrapped up that I doubt whether the others, apart from Bernard, realize what he's saying nine tenths of the time. When the old woman does catch on she laughs to herself while taking care to keep a bewildered air around her shoulders like an invisible scarf of innocence.

But above all he talks about Bernard and his work; talks with such plain and true admiration and understanding that my heart grows warm to him. Warmer I think than Bernard's. He is so totally unused to this kind of thing that he cannot quite take it in. He is suspicious of it. He does not believe Peregrine. And indeed I am (or I was at first) suspicious of him myself. Wrongly, however. For Peregrine, I am convinced, has no axe to grind here. The reason why this bright, successful, highly fashionable, young man has taken up the Zolds so wholeheartedly is, I have come to believe, a simple one. He has, theatrically speaking, the finest and most delicate of palates. He savours, he recognizes the quality of Bernard's work more I think than the author does himself. He has tremendous taste; a nose for the first class; and he admires Bernard as the source. He equates—for the moment anyway though God knows how long it will last—the man with his work.

And he is generous natured. They are, after all, rivals in a sense. Though Peregrine is much more successful. One of his plays is now in its second year. It is a very good play. I went to see it with Danny a year ago. (How strange! I have not thought of him for weeks and now I recall him only to wince at the jealous little remarks he kept making all through the performance, the slick, professional criticisms of the production. The meaning of the play, the thoughts behind the words, he didn't even notice. "But the theme . . ." I kept saying to him. "Oh yes of course," he kept answering perfunctorily and going back to the clumsy entrance O.P. of the star.)

They are, as I say, rivals in a sense. But in Peregrine there seems to be no consciousness of this, no trace of begrudging, of envy, of anything but a marvelling respect for the work itself of Bernard Zold. And, as I say, further to that he appears to like the man himself. He is anxious to take him around, to introduce him to people. He has invited him to luncheon at the Savage Club next week. Is not this nice? I am extravagantly pleased. Everything is looking up at last. Even my invitation to Hugo's studio has come, via Bridget, and we are going to go there tomorrow evening. It seems that we are all becoming a part of *life*. At last!

Ruth

❖❀❖❀❖❀❖❀❖❀❖❀❖❀❖❀❖❀❖❀❖❀❖

14th August

SOMETHING has happened, Francis. How am I to explain it to you, to myself? I cannot believe . . . It is against all rules, all probabilities. . . .

There are parts of Hampstead which are very ugly; streets of hideous, Victorian, yellow-brick houses. At the top of one of these Bridget's friend, Hugo, has his "studio." One large room with a skylight, one small one with a bed; and a tiny kitchen. He shares the bathroom which is two floors down.

Bridget and I arrived for "dinner." That is to say . . . Bridget brought some tins with her and set about opening them while Hugo, on her instructions, showed me round. The place was neither bleak nor "Bohemian" but (like Bridget's) drab, again furnished with bits of lower-class light oak. Such furniture as there was was crowded into the bedroom. The studio was almost completely bare save for the paraphernalia of his work, a couple of kitchen chairs and an old, scratched, stained table. He brought in a dirty easy chair from the bedroom and sat on the arm of it to eat when we finally settled down to dinner.

What did I expect Hugo to be like? I hardly know myself since the image has now been so blindingly superseded by the reality.

You know, it has sometimes occurred to me that all the critics who opinionate on anything, but particularly perhaps on matters of art, should be abolished. Perhaps this is too sweeping. Yet, when one experiences the absolute misconceptions which can arise from other people's descriptions it seems to me fatal to rely on anyone for any opinion whatever. Bridget's description bore no relation, no relation whatever to the reality of Hugo.

He opened the front door of the tall, narrow house to us and I saw him for the first time (symbolically?) in two lights: the dull yellow of the lighted hall behind him and the pinky-grey of the twilight in the quiet, mournful street behind us. He seemed anything but the brash rebel-artist, the scruffy version of the Peregrine bounce I had expected from Bridget's description, as he let us in and clumsily led us up the stairs after an abrupt, clutched, nervous hand-shake.

In the studio and all through the evening I was able to see him better and look at him freely—since he scarcely glanced at me—but to see his face before me now I have to go back (as I am doing again and again) to that moment of the door's opening and the appearance of his beautiful head glowing in the dusk.

Jessica's colour, as I have told you, is brown; a deep, dead-leaf brown. Bridget's is an enthusiastic red-brown. I am myself of the tribe but softened with ashy lights. Hugo is "brown" too but his is a glowing-pale, golden brown. His hair is chestnut gold. His face is long and curiously divided. The upper half is sexual. He has eyes like Pan, filmed, narrowed. The lower half is uncertain and young, the chin fragile. He has a full, carved mouth spoilt by timid writhings of the lips. He smiles too much. His nose is fine as a knife but the nostrils are diffident. He is slim and not very tall: a delicate, girlish, slender boy. But why go on with descriptions? They cannot alter desperate facts. I have fallen instantaneously in love with him. I think he has fallen in love with me. He is twenty-six years old.

Ruth

❂❈❂❈❂❈❂❈❂❈❂❈❂❈❂❈❂❈❂❈❂❈❂❈❂

16th *August*

THE WAY things work! Yes, I have seen him again. By that curious working of destiny which, as I have noticed before in my life, uses shamelessly the old, coincidental devices, I was having tea alone in a milk-bar near Belsize Park Underground when he came in for cigarettes. I pretended not to see him, keeping my head down while agitation boiled in me to my finger-tips. I prayed for him to see me and not to see me. Then he came up to my table and asked in a nervous mutter how I was. I answered him brightly, pertly. He sat down. I asked him how Bridget was. He asked me how Bridget was. We behaved as though we were both sixteen.

(He is not my *type*, Francis! That's the funny thing. He is not my type at all. I like them dark. I like self-assurance. I like cads. This is not my line of country at all. I must get out. I must get out of it—quickly.)

He said, looking helpless so that my heart twisted with agonized love, he was sorry he hadn't given me a nicer dinner the other night, he'd more or less left it to Bridget, but he'd do better the next time I came. . . . (*The next time* . . . I heard with a leap of the heart.) If I cared to come he added hastily when I said nothing. I must meet Erik who hadn't been able to come the other night. That would be very nice I said non-committally. He jumped up and said he had to go and almost ran out without suggesting any time at all for "next time." I sat on, flat, deflated, disturbed, wrenched, torn in half. I should have been more friendly . . . *I must scotch this thing at once.* . . .

What am I to do, what am I to do, what am I to do? I am still, but inside me there is an image of myself rocking backwards and forwards beating my folded hands against my breast. What am I to do? What am I to do? I repeat the words only as a steadier; a small release in repetition and rhythm of the stress within my heart. For of course I know very well what I am to do. I must guillotine. I must *chop*—as Bleu would say. I must kill.

If I don't, *I* will be killed.

My only luck in this business has been Bridget's cold which has kept her in bed and away from here since the visit to Hugo. I have told you hardly anything of the rest of that evening. It was, on the whole, sticky. Bridget tried hard to get her two "intellectuals" to sparkle or at least inform— as, to her way of thinking, we evidently do individually— but we did not do her credit. She kept explaining us to each other. "Ruth wouldn't agree with your ideas about—" "Hugo doesn't like—"

With a bit of prodding from her he nervously produced some of his canvases. We stood awkwardly about in that big, empty, drab attic he calls rather touchingly, his studio, on that rather chilly August evening examining them. He is talented perhaps but young, young. His larger work, unlike the animal sketches, is thin. He is unripe and needs experience. A love affair with a married woman? Yes, probably. It would redden and mellow and sweeten that hard, young green fruit of his talent. There was Barbara of course. But I have an idea that wasn't very important. Probably he exaggerated it in order to keep Bridget at arm's length; which he must certainly have found necessary. She can hardly keep her eyes off him. I think he puts up with it and is fond of her because she makes all the running and never takes offence. He finds her easy to be with. And adoration, an absolute devotion to oneself, holds such charm.

I think she senses that in the end he will not be for her. I see now why, in her shrewd way, she admits (even at her most besotted) to a willingness to settle for someone else and forget him if there were any reasonable substitute within view. But that is probably another of her virtues to him. She suffers, it is true. But her heart cannot be broken.

I am, as I say, thankful that Bridget has not been here to chatter, to ask me in detail what I thought of him. But I also long for his return. I could hurl blows on myself that I did not listen more attentively to all the talk she was constantly pouring out about him. Now I cannot remember it properly. He is Jewish. His family are rich. His father—or is it his mother?—has a roving eye. Many of the things Bridget told me about him are, as I have said, untrue. It is not that she has lied; it is that she projected him through the prism of her naïve conception of the artistic life; of what "artists" *ought* to be like; gay, amoral, careless.

There is one great irony in all this which I have not mentioned. Perhaps even you will smile in some twisted way if I tell you that the one thing I have been thankful for these last tormented days is the fact of my marriage! I hold to it like a rope. It protected me, saves me from some disastrous, ultimate folly. Thank God, thank God I am married! Could it have been some prevision, some sensed possibility that something like this may one day happen, which has prevented me from ever asking you for a divorce?

You know, I have sometimes reproached myself in a stupid, bad-novel way for not having been more honest with you over Danny. You did not even know I had left you till weeks afterwards. You let me go "on holiday" to London. I was tired, nervy, I made a scene. I had to "get away for a while," I said. And it is true I did not really know what I was going to do—or rather what Danny would suggest I do—when I joined him. Perhaps because I never said good-bye, because there were no dramatics, you have never really believed I have gone. Perhaps you think of me still as being "on holiday." And as for me . . . why have I never asked you for the finality of divorce? I do not know. I cannot explain.

For certainly I have no intention of ever returning to you. That is something which, in case I have not made it murderously clear already, I must emphasize again. I will never return to you, Francis.

But I thank God for the fact of marriage! Were it not for that, to what agonies might I not have committed my future. Even as it is my dreams fantasticate. Does not the machinery of divorce exist? And I would be good to him. . . . Only to have that chestnut-golden head against my heart. Only to have that strange, green, porcelain charm, which glints obliquely from his work, to my hand.

Such possession after two short meetings! It is witchcraft, nothing less. Have you been making revengeful images of me in some of your coloured clays? Stuck golden, poisoned pins in the heart? For if I go on there is nothing here but suffering. *I am too old.* I am not of the stuff which can carry such a situation. Were I divorced and free it would still be fated. I am obscure, penniless, ageing. He is talented and bright-haired. What could I offer? I have not even the gift of peace since my spirit, moaning and restless, is not quiet. To be loyal and talkative, a placid, helpful wife to young genius is not my role. I am no Mrs. Disraeli with a large fortune.

Thank God I am married! That fact alone keeps the more lunatic fancies at bay. But the others, God help me, persist, haunting my every thought, my every hour. My imagination has suddenly become a net against which, scooped suddenly from comparatively calm water, my Self writhes and leaps in the first shock of capture.

I feel again after all these years of quiescence the monstrous absurdities of adolescent imaginings; the melting, softness of sexual adoration, the raging curiosity, the fantasy life, the brilliant, impossible images of communication. Do we never grow old and wiser? No; only old and ashamed. Ah! the impatience, the unbelievingness with which we all at once realize the irrecoverability of life! We *must* be able to go back, we rage; to go back and start again. *What happened to our years?*

I have reached one of those moments when a cliché suddenly becomes brilliantly illuminated and meaningful for the first time. *We have only one life.* Only one life! How extraordinary that I should never have realized this before!

At all costs I must avoid seeing him again.

Ruth

❖❖❖❖❖❖❖❖❖❖❖❖❖❖❖❖❖❖❖❖❖

17th August

PEREGRINE'S invitation to Bernard to luncheon at the Savage Club did not materialize as he, Peregrine, had to dash away unexpectedly for a couple of days to visit his father. But he has asked him to a stag party at his flat this evening—which is perhaps better still. With any luck the atmosphere may be of that particular kind in which Bernard may be able to show himself at his best.

I am deliberately writing downstairs in the kitchen in order to be on hand when he returns. I am anxious over the party. I want Bernard to shine and feel at ease. I want this not only for his own sake but for mine since my obsession with Hugo—which grows stronger hourly—has produced in me a sense of guilt towards Bernard. It is as if he were my husband, not you. I find I cannot trace the source of this feeling. There is nothing between us. I do not think there has ever been the expectation of a sensual relationship—of a truly personal nature, I mean—towards one another in either of our minds. We owe each other nothing. We make no demands on one another. Harassed by his work and the constant drain of his family upon his nerves there have often been periods when there has been no communication between us at all. It is true that he has spoken as freely and confidentially of himself to me as I have spoken to him. But we have not pushed our friendship beyond its natural limits. We have been tactful, we have behaved with delicacy towards each other.

It is also true of course that to be involved in the rows and occasions and general strains of a family makes one after a time a part of them. But this still does not account for the acute sense of disloyalty—indeed dismay—with which I contemplate the possibility of his coming to know of my obsession with Hugo. I have a feeling it would distress him greatly. (He cannot be other than human. The deflection of my thoughts, my interest which has been so centred on this house, would hurt.) And he bears so much already. So much too much.

Mrs. Capes came to tea again this afternoon bringing with her a friend; a hospital Sister! Jessica, in her twinkling, demure, girlish way, became so excited about this marvellous prospect that she infected all of us with a feeling of its high importance. It was really quite absurd now I look back on it, but she has this gift of making one impressed by her small concerns. Even old Mrs. Zold took fire and announced that she was going to make some meringues. You know how even the worst cooks have one special thing that they usually manage to turn out with some success. Well the old woman's, it seems, is meringues. And sure enough, after a whole morning's work and an incredible number of eggs, two baking-tins of pale brown meringues stood very nicely risen and light on the larder shelf, waiting to be put together after lunch with coffee cream—another of her talents.

Again like all bad cooks, Mrs. Zold was inordinately proud of the one thing she can make reasonably well. And we were all, including Bernard, taken into the larder, one by one, to view the meringue cakes. "Have you ever seen anything so light?" she kept saying, picking up a shell and showing it. "And yet they're not so light but what they're just that little bit tacky in the centre. You know? You get a meringue just that much over-dry and they're nothing but sugar. The whole secret is you've got to do split-second timing so they're *done* . . . but that little bit tacky as well."

It is so seldom that she has anything to show off about that of course she overdid it and we were all exhausted with non-stop praise by the time lunch was over. All the same it was a distinct shock when Jessica came out of the larder after putting something away to say lightheartedly to her mother-in-law: "Say, Ma, something's happened to those meringues of yours."

The old woman jumped up and ran out into the kitchen while Jessica explained, still smiling and even laughing cheerfully, that she'd found Binkie, the kitten, in the larder trampling all over the cakes. "He's just smashed them to atoms," she said amused and laughing her soft, musical laugh. Bernard gave her one look and went out after his mother. I followed.

I found them both looking down at the two cake-tins full of broken, stoved-in meringues. Binkie, a fragile, pale-brown piece still caught on one whisker, was still darting in and out of the larder on some game of his own. I bent down and picked him up and smacked him as gently as I could make myself. I could have wrung his neck. "What a *shame*," I said strongly. "And they came up so beautifully. Oh, I *am* sorry. This wretched cat." In my pity and rage I gave Binkie another and much harder slap than I should have done and he gave a loud, frightened *miaou* and sprang out of my hands like a catapult.

The old woman, her head bent, was slowly picking up a few of the broken pieces in the tin and letting them fall again. "I wonder why it should have happened," she was saying in a strange, humble, patient voice which was entirely new to me. (It is the voice, I now realize, with which she encounters disaster.) Then she added, still with that touch of fatalism and meekness which suddenly—it was so extraordinary coming from her—cut me to the bone: "Well. It had to be, I suppose." She looked at the ruined cakes intently for a few moments longer, her eyelids blinked once, then picking up the baking-tins she went out saying: "I'll throw all this in the garbage can. Can't do anything else with it."

I looked at Bernard and saw that his eyes were suffused with pain.

"It's such a shame," I said, feeling not far from tears myself. "She'd taken so much trouble over them."

He stood there, his shoulders hunched, in the cold little room hardly bigger than a cupboard.

"If only *one thing* would go right for her," he said at last in a tone of soft, grinding bitterness. "Just one small achievement she could keep intact. God!" he said beating his hand rhythmically on the cold, marble shelf where the meringues had stood. Picking up a packaged half-pound of butter he pressed his thumb deep into the silver paper wrapper till his nail pierced it. He went on making precise indented patterns with the crescent of his nail all over the packet of butter. "God!" he said again. "What have they done, these foolish, unoffending creatures that they must have their tiny triumphs shattered? Why? What have they done that every small pride must be knocked from under them? These little, everyday prides are what we live by. *They are our life.* To take them from us, to punish such harmless vanities, to destroy such a pitiful, miniature buttress of an old woman's self-respect, her small prop. . . . She wanted to serve the cakes and have them praised; to vaunt a small talent. Was this so bad that she must be punished? Why? Why? I cannot understand this. Nothing we learn prepares us for these kinds of humble, foolish sufferings. There are no courts of law where such wrongs can be redressed. Are there now? We cannot say Give me back what has been stolen from me; that minute share of pride, of achievement, of ability to do *something* well which enables me to go on living. How to guard against the humbler vicissitudes . . . how to protect the helpless from their absurd anguishes, their painful, minuscule losses of the soul; how is this to be done?"

"Must you always feel that this is *your* job?" I said.

"If not me then whom? This *is* my job. It is what my talent —such as it is—is *for*. That much at least I have found out. To each his own function. And I am under no delusions as to what is mine. Other people, other writers . . . they serve other, greater purposes. They expose the follies of war. Or the temptations of power. Or the depths of crime and evil. Or the betrayals of passion. Or the social structures of society. I deal with none of those things. Important though they truly are, they are not my province. My country is the region of every-day hurt; the things everyone seems agreed are trivial and even ridiculous. To me they are not trivial at all. Though in attempting to show them as not I might render *myself* as ridiculous. Well . . . this is a risk I have to take. I have counted the cost—in terms of my own human dignity. And I am prepared to pay.

"What kills is to see the sufferings of others. How things eternally time themselves wrongly for some people! If only one could work Fate into dealing kindly with them. If one could only, even by sacrificing oneself, bring luck to others. But there is no fighting the grudges of heaven . . . And then —I have no help . . ." he said looking down as if ashamed. It was as near as he could bring himself to expressing his burning anger with Jessica for her amusement. I felt furious with her myself. "The heartlessness of pleasant, charming people!" he went on, half to himself. "The stunted imaginations, the rather pleased, gay, little malice. Though one can't really blame them too much either; since what they are set against is so unpleasing, irritating, ineffectual . . . and above all, absurd. But no allowances are made. No allowances are made. This is what angers me."

I began to move out of the larder and into the kitchen and, Jessica coming in at that moment to start preparing for her "distinguished" guest, we said no more.

Later

Well, my patient waiting up was rewarded—if rewarded is the right word. Bernard came in a little after midnight. He looked plain, his heavy eyelids dropping over his full, lustreless eyes. Fatigue and, I think, disappointment, made him paler and more porcine looking than ever, his forehead more bulging and shiny.

I asked him if he had enjoyed his evening. He lifted his eyebrows, looked uncertain, sceptical, half-amused; and very tired.

"Enjoyed?" he said sitting down creakily. "Fix me a strong cup of tea, Ruth, will you? Well . . . I guess so. In a way. It was . . . interesting. Yes. It was interesting anyway. There were compensations. For instance—who'd have thought I'd ever find myself guest of a famous, young dramatist in a bachelor apartment in Mayfair, London, England? Me! Bernard Zold! Three years ago an average guy in a small, American town in up-state New York. I kept sitting there and remembering this fact. It was something."

"Who else was there?"

He smiled to himself a little ironically. "A couple of writers —novelists. Bright young men. One actor; pretty bright. A young critic on a weekly. Nobody terribly, terribly famous— as Peregrine would say! I have an idea in fact that Peregrine was trying me out with his Number Four category of friends; seeing how I would shape up before letting me into any more distinguished circles!"

"How charming of him!" I said.

He made an irritable sound. "Don't be trite," he said. "And don't be silly about snobbishness—or Peregrine's kind of social caution. I don't hold it against him in the least. In fact he was quite right. Look . . . I'll tell you what I feel about snobbishness. Unless it's based on wealth or ancestry I've nothing against it at all. What's wrong with admiring brains and manners and accomplishments more than the people who lack these things. And if those with advantages prefer to consort with others of their kind—is that a sin? Walk down any Main Street on a Saturday night. Take a look at the toughs and louts and gum-chewing girl-morons. And tell yourself that, taken to their logical conclusions, all the arguments of the anti-snob brigade lead to ultimate absurdities; to the proposition, for instance, that those Saturday night roughs are as suitable company for an educated, fine, sophisticated mind as any other.

"But to get back to the evening. So Peregrine tried me out for size. O.K. This is something I don't condemn him for. What I—no, I don't condemn him for anything. But what I . . . regret . . . is that he made an error of judgement over me. He is more limited, less flexible than I thought. Well . . ." he made an open and closed gesture with his hands, "He's young. After all, he's still very young. In fact that was part of the trouble. Everyone there was young! And such *bright* guys. This actor now—he knew more about the drama than I could ever hope to. Everyone of them had had a university education—and not one of your redbrick institutions either! And every last one of them had that beautiful, English accent so when I hear it I could lie down and die from sheer envy. Everyone of them knew their company and their place and knew where they were in it. Oh, sure, they knew I was an older man and a stranger. But I guess they expected an American dramatist to be even more sophisticated than themselves. They sat around being witty, sprawling on their backs in their deep armchairs, fizzing with talk and epigram and mimicry and laughing with loud chortles. And they expected me to fizz too, and give off slow wisecracks and New Yorkerish comment and be knowledgeable in a smooth, glancing, Debenham Bleu way; or at least eccentric! Yes. Eccentricity would have helped a lot."

"And how were you?" I said gently.

"The way I always am," he said with a tired turn of his head. "Small town. Rather dull. Not very articulate. In fact a lot duller than usual if anything. You know, in the middle of everything else I found myself feeling really sorry for Peregrine! He worked like a maniac trying to draw me out. It wasn't really his fault that his tactics were just about the worst in the world he could have used. The more he pranced about trying to get me to rise the more I huddled into a fat, morose, nervous, middle-aged, lower-class ignorance sitting miserably in a corner. Ah Lord! what an evening!" He stroked his chin and smiled at me. But his eyes, those large, black, mournful eyes of his looked into mine, desperate and sad.

Changing the subject I asked him how the final rehearsals were going.

"That reminds me," he said. "You know I feel really sorry you've got to stay home on account of Ginny, the night of the premiere. I'd like you to have been there, Ruth. I think you'd bring me luck."

"Oh, that's all right," I said very warmly. "Of course I don't mind. That is . . . in a way I do of course because I'm longing to see it. But I can go in a week or so—"

"It should run that long!" he said.

"If that early rehearsal conveyed anything at all to me," I said slowly and earnestly (I was frightened of overdoing it since I know that he cannot accept praise save in minute quantities) "it is that that play will be recognized—box-office hit or no, one can't ever tell about that—as one of the most remarkable plays of our time. It is most great. It is a most great and beautiful play, Mr. Zold. I wished . . . I wished to tell . . ." My composure cracked and I could say no more.

He fumbled in his pocket and, glad to be doing something to break the moment, brought out an envelope and handed it to me. Inside were two front stalls for the second night. "Thought you'd like to take a friend," he said awkwardly and barely audibly. And getting to his feet, hardly listening to my thanks, went off to bed.

And, such are our natures, despite my inward nervous prayers and wishes for him, despite my care and anxiety that all should go well, despite my sinking heart that this evening should have proved of so little worth, should have opened no door for him . . . sitting here now, as I write, I can think of nothing but the tickets and Hugo. Shall I ask him to go with me or not? Such a perfect excuse to be given into my hands! What shall I do? What shall I do?

Ruth

◊}◊}◊}◊}◊}◊}◊}◊}◊}◊}◊}◊}◊}◊}◊}◊}◊

20th August

FIVE DAYS to go to the premiere. Even Jessica is beginning to feel the strain and is more out of the house than in it, spending hours of every day with Mrs. Capes. She is not affected imaginatively; she does not suffer with or for him. It is just that she dislikes tension of any kind and runs away from it. Her mother-in-law feels the situation much more acutely. She feels both for him and for their prestige as a family.

Her tensions, as usual, however, express themselves in the oddest ways. Bitten with a sudden and acute economy she goes about collecting bits of string and cardboard and putting them carefully away. It is as if she were saying:

If I'm careful and waste nothing God will reward me by making the play a success.

This attitude has led to one medium-sized argument already since Bernard made a special point about her buying —not making—a new dress for herself for the event. "I don't need it," she said, "and I can't afford it."

"For Pete's sake, Mama, I'm not asking you to afford it. *I'm* buying it for you. Here." He put down a roll of notes on the table and pushed them over to her. With an obstinate gesture she refused them. He spread his hands in despair. "Would anyone believe it?" he said. "What woman doesn't like buying? O.K. O.K.," he said as she still went on refusing, "I'll have to do what I did before . . . go out and get you something myself."

And that's what he did. I was present when he brought the dress in and handed it to her. The old woman never ceases to surprise me! For, instead of refusing or upbraiding him, she accepted it with every sign of genuine pleasure. It is true that when she tried it on she inquired suspiciously about the price (which he refused to tell her) and grumbled incessantly but the grumbles were her way of expressing gratitude. Conventional thanks are quite beyond her. But when she said ungraciously that the colour was too light, she was saying Thank You. And when she discovered the sleeves to be too long she was enchanted and took the gown off to her room to be altered, with a step like a girl's.

Bernard let out a long sigh of relief when she'd gone. "Happens every time," he said. "Give her a million dollars and she still wouldn't take any pleasure in buying."

"You don't have to ask *me* twice," said Jessica cheerfully, "or Ginny."

"Your life's been a whole lot different," he said shortly. "The fact is she can't buy because she feels guilty if she spends. The habit of poverty's been driven in too deep. But if she's *given* . . . that's different. No guilt. And, apart from that . . . there's another aspect. To be given . . . it's . . ."

He hesitated, with one eye on his wife, so that I again realized that he has long since given up trying to explain things to her, indeed feels embarrassed in the attempt, " 'to be given' is equated with 'to be loved.' "

"Why, Bernie!" said Jessica, "you're talking about your own mother as though she were no older than Ginny!" He flicked a glance at her, shrugged impatiently and went out of the room, leaving me with the job of admiring Jessica's new dress. This took half an hour without my realizing it. I still say she has the most remarkable gift I have ever encountered of absorbing one into her world of trivial detail without boring. I wish I could find out how it's done but this is the kind of thing which belongs with the alchemy of personality. There is no explaining it.

I am still no nearer a decision about the theatre tickets. A hundred times a day I tell myself that there is after all no harm in a friendly gesture. I shrink from the thought of a refusal—then I tell myself that that would be the best thing of all (that I should receive a snub) since that would cure me. Yet I hesitate. I hesitate. I cannot bring myself to destroy—not yet—such unexpected, iridescent happiness. You know for instance that I am not "musical" in your sense of the word. (Are *you*? Am I doing you one more injustice when I say that I have never quite believed it? There is a certain kind of middle-class pretension to artistic tastes which makes me shiver with irritation. It is common among schoolmasters, Civil Servants, professional men . . .) But those first weeks of a love affair . . . those are the only times of my life when I listen to music. Not for itself; but for the flowering charm, the open softness of my fancy which music—at the tender beginnings of love—sets free. How can I kill this delight so soon? Another week, another hour; before I break the carafe and spill the joy away.

Shall I ask him? Shall I?

Ruth

◑◐◑◐◑◐◑◐◑◐◑◐◑◐◑◐◑◐◑◐◑◐◑◐

21st *August*

HE HAS asked me! Not to the theatre but to dinner at his studio again. Only—it is for the 24th, the night before the premiere. And I . . . am hesitating. I tried to put it off but he said (wounding me) that it is his only free evening for a week. (Why? What else is he doing, where is he going?)

I hesitate because I fancy Bernard might need me that night. He is holding himself down—I *see* this—with an iron control which nevertheless I fear might snap. His tension takes, characteristically, a quiet form. Sometimes bad-tempered, even a little demanding from time to time about his domestic needs, he has become extraordinarily patient and uncomplaining about everything. He has given up asking for tea! He allows himself to be interrupted at his work without a murmur. He is more patient with Ginny, has bought her a whole lot of new books and paints and has even taken her walking on the Heath once. I thought at first that all this was his version of propitiating the gods but I have come to the conclusion that it is a kind of fearful prayer for modesty. He is, after all, in this enterprise, the king-pin. No matter what the others, the actors, the producer, anyone can do, he is the centre. By the words of his heart they will all be judged. I do not think he is made frightened by this thought (there are reserves in him) but he feels not only the responsibility of his position but also the egotism of it. I think this troubles him. And so in an attempt to redress the balance he makes no demands at all for himself.

This is all very well. But I am afraid for him nevertheless. I wish to be on hand to help on that last night before the play opens. Again a decision is being forced upon me. But at least the earlier one is resolved! Thank heaven I did not ask Hugo to come to the theatre. Bridget is taking him to the first night! She booked, it transpires, long ago. I feel obscurely shamed by this. I should have made some gesture of faith and interest too. But when I ask myself why I didn't I have absolutely no answer save that in some curious way I deeply wished to dissociate myself from the event. Perhaps I am too frightened of possible failure.

There has been one disappointment already. Craigie, the resident director of the Vauxhall, who always gives a reception after the first night of a new play, is ill and can't do it. Bernard hasn't said much but I know that he feels this as a deprivation: Craigie's on-stage parties after the show are famous.

His mother of course jumped in with the obvious remark which I and even Jessica had avoided. "Why doesn't someone else arrange a party?" she said. He shrugged. "What about that Wallace Grey? Can't he do it?" she persisted.

"I can't tell Wally or anyone else to throw a party for me," he said patiently.

"Well can't—"

"Look, Mama, if anyone ought to give a party it's *me*," he said.

"Well, why don't you?"

"Because," he said, still gently but with some strain in his manner, "the first thing you need for a party is people. I just don't know enough people in London. Just Wallace—and the cast. What does that make? Six. Throw in a coupla husbands and wives, one or two others perhaps . . ." (I guessed that the "perhaps" applied to Peregrine who has not been in evidence since his stag evening) "and what have we got? A dozen if we're lucky. That's not enough for that kind of a party. Besides . . . it wouldn't be the same anyway."

She looked argumentative but he turned away, and she said no more.

Well at least I know where Hugo will be that night! But

what shall I do about the night before? I must let him know by morning. Is he asking Bridget too? She has said nothing. Shall I go? Shall I not? I do nothing, it seems but ask questions of myself these days. I sway between decisions none of which will matter in the end; since the end is plain. The end will be an end. He cannot be a beginning for me nor I for him. (I suppose, knowing this, that you can bear whatever I say. Knowing its doom, you are not suffering over my love. I hope you are not anyway. You need not. Though I am perhaps doing you an injustice in this too. For what I would care about, were our positions reversed, is not the end but the beginning; the fact that I have been started into life by another; not *you*. This is what would bruise. This is where I would know that sickening drop of the heart. . . .)

There will be, as I say, an end. And if I had any sense at all I should make it now. Yet one taste of the terrible drug of emotional occupation has left me with a craving I cannot resist.

Yes; cannot resist. I have decided. I shall go to him on the 24th. I have a feeling that to do so is wrong; that to leave the house on that night is wrong. Bernard may need me in some way and I shall not be there.

But I shall go.

Ruth

❀❀❀❀❀❀❀❀❀❀❀❀❀❀❀❀❀❀❀❀

25th August

IT IS 10 P.M. The house is very quiet. Ginny is asleep in her bed and I am in mine, writing. They cannot be back for at least an hour and a half, yet I find my ear cocked to every sound in the street, the noise of every distant car. Bernard was at the theatre all day. He came home to bath and change and eat before going back with his two women. Their new dresses looked very nice.

I am putting off the telling. Only where shall I start? Too much has happened since yesterday; there has been so much for one short period of hours to bear.

I suppose it started with the argument between Ginny and her grandmother; something silly about Ginny's lunch which consisted of three tomatoes and a piece of cake. The old woman began sounding off about tomatoes causing acidity which—she said—was the cause of the child's paleness. (She has old-fashioned ideas about good looks; a Victorian ideal of red cheeks and tiny, pursed, rosebud lips. In fact, Ginny's thick, white skin is of that Scandinavian type which will never take colour.)

I thought that the whole thing had blown over by early afternoon (yesterday) but going upstairs after tea I heard a voice coming from the Zolds' bedroom, though both Jessica and Bernard were out. The door was not quite closed and something odd struck me as I hesitated on the landing. Going quietly nearer I looked in. The something odd was the light which at that time in that brilliantly sunny afternoon should have streamed through the door like gold. Instead there was a dull yellow glow which turned out to be, when I cautiously looked round the door, the result of Ginny having drawn the curtains tightly till the room was dark and then switched on the dull little tube of light fixed along the top of the dressing table mirror. Before the mirror the child was standing, her fists pressed down on the table before her. She was leaning forward and speaking softly to her reflection which swam before her in the dusky, yellow light and shadow. And she was saying in a soft, vindictive voice, horribly reminiscent of her grandmother's neuroticism: ". . . and don't think you can get away with it, Grandma. Because you can't. You wait. I'll tell about you. I'll tell daddy about you. And mommy. And everybody. You won't get away with it. *I'll see to that.* I'll *wish* on you! I'll do what *I* want, see?"

She curled her tongue right out over her lower lip and looked at herself consideringly. Then—as if rehearsing—she gave a scornful laugh and assumed a heavily scornful expression. Picking up one of Jessica's necklaces she put it round her neck and pulled the two ends tightly across each other as if strangling herself. "See? See?" she said, beginning to pant.

I pushed open the door and walked in pretending cheerful surprise at finding the curtains drawn. With a clumsy movement she whipped the chain off her neck. I went to draw back the curtains but, flinging herself forward, she tore them out of my hands. "No!" she shouted. "Leave them!"

"Don't be silly, Ginny. You're shutting out all the sun. It's a lovely day outside. Why don't you go out into the garden and play?"

"I don't want to," she said sullenly, her face still a dull, suffused red from the shock of my entry.

"Oh, come on now—"

"Go away! This isn't your room! Go away out. You leave me alone or I'll tell everybody."

"Tell everybody what?" I said. I caught her forearm. "Tell everybody what?"

"I'll tell!" she shouted. "I'll tell." And, without tears, began to scream.

I slackened my grip for a moment and she made a stumbling rush forward, fell on her mother's bed and began to roll and writhe and kick in full blown hysterics.

"Ginny, for God's sake—" I said and flinging myself on to the bed tried, without avail, to raise and quiet her. Still struggling, I managed with one arm, to pin her down on her back and had raised the other in order to bring my hand with a sharp slap against her face when, squinting from one half-open eye, she saw what I was about to do. I saw a look of satisfied malevolence cross her distorted face, her writhings became immediately less frenzied, reducing on the instant to a sort of stylized jerk, while she waited longingly for me to hit her. When I did, though with less force than I had intended, she gave a deep, satisfied sigh, a final, short, spasmodic, *manufactured* jerk—and lay quiet.

Manufactured! That was the horror of it. A child's screams and temper; that was nothing. But an artificial hysteria expressing some frightful, sullen grievance against life . . . that was something else again. Oh, poor child! I said to myself with sudden, painful sympathy as I sat there looking at her. All this because (like her father) she does not inspire love. And a nervous instinct, something born in her with her blood knows it. I see, I have always seen, in the movements of those plodding limbs an unconscious longing for grace; small, clumsy attempts at *being.* I remember an incident not very long ago when, trying to describe some dancer she had seen on television she had essayed a ballet movement, one solid, ungraceful leg stuck out behind her raised clumsily in the air till, attempting a floating movement of her arms, she had staggered and flopped, noisily and thumpingly, to the floor. She had not cried; only picked herself up and self-conscious and dumbly ashamed, walked ploddingly away.

Overcome with pity, I tried to talk to her as she lay, her glassy limbs sprawled on the bed, but she was entirely unresponsive and after a time I was obliged to leave her there, her eyes following me indifferently to the door.

It was time for me to start getting ready to go to Hugo. Still a little uneasy about Ginny, I debated whether to tell old Mrs. Zold to keep an eye on the child. In the end I decided not to. If anything was to set her off again it would be the old woman's fussing. Besides, Jessica was due back shortly. So I left it.

The situation had one selfish use for me, however. All

the time I was bathing and dressing I deliberately kept my mind on the problem of Ginny, working out in what terms I should present it to Bernard, trying to see what, if any, solution could be suggested to him. Though I found none—for after all what can any parent, however intelligent, however loving, do to make up to their children for the natural lacks they are born to?—at least the speculation kept me from thoughts of the evening ahead.

Not until I had left the house did I allow these full play.

What would we say to each other? On what plane of relationship must I endeavour to keep us both? What mask, what attitude must I put on—when my waist aches for its encirclement by that nervous, graceful, tweed-clad arm? When, like a wave of the sea, consciousness of him has roared into the dry, salt cave which was my life? When my mind is filled with rushing images of tender love, when I find myself unconsciously turning my face from side to side as though brushing my lips softly back and forth across his mouth.

Oh Francis, forgive me! For the first time I ask you your forgiveness if I am giving you pain. I do not mean to. I swear to you that I do not wish to pain you when I write my love. But I am driven, driven to use you for my own ease.

This time he had taken more pains to prepare for me. There was a vase of inexpensive flowers on the table; which now sported a new cloth, though a very cheap, cotton one. He had brought ready-cooked meat and a carton of potato salad and a lettuce; and some rather bruised peaches. I am not so enchanted that I do not see that he does not like to spend.

We hear so little in the accounts of love about the other kind of accounts; the money involved. The publicly upheld, social life takes it for granted that it is men who pay, who buy theatre tickets, meals, presents. . . . But the truth is very

different and involves much wretchedness for women. The
truth is that ordinary "decent" behaviour in such matters has
almost disappeared. Particularly is this so in semi-artistic
and intellectual circles. Danny now . . . there was a case in
point. He was not only mean; all his friends were too. But
that wasn't the worst of it. The worst thing was that all
these men took their attitude entirely for granted. There was
never the slightest sense of ashamedness about their un-
willingness ever to pay for anything if they could get out
of it. I can recall a hundred instances; like Danny giving
false information to a bus conductor (when the circumstances were such that we should have taken a taxi anyway) and expecting my approval of his disgusting, sixpenny
gain.

Men of course will deny their fault and accuse women
of rapacity. But at least nineteen times out of twenty they
are wrong. They do not understand that most women do
not require money to be spent on them. What they require
is the *wish* (which they equate with love) to do so. Men have
only to indicate, with sincerity, what they would like to do
if they could . . . and most women will gladly settle for what
they *can*. It is a matter of human dignity. It is a matter of
their need for human affection—and its exploitation.

(You are not like that, Francis. You were never mean
about money; yours is a different fault. You are generous
but not because you are *generous;* but because you wish to
be "correct.")

Hugo, son of a rich father, is a little mean. It makes no
difference to my absorption in him save to add one more
element of self-derision—but I see it. I see it in everything
Bridget has told me about him, in the cheap meat, the
bruised peaches . . . He gets no money from his father it is
true but can get what he likes from his mother who comes to
see him every week. In any case he is not short. He is not—
though he does live in a sort of garret—by any means the

starving artist; not an art-for-art's-sake man at all. He accepts any commercial work that comes along—and quite a lot of it does.

Though he is full of plans for what he calls "the big work," meaning producing enough oils for an exhibition, he is strangely naïve about their fulfilment. I am at a loss to know whether to encourage him or not. For I truly am not at all sure, now that I have examined his work more closely, that he has even a particle of the divine seed in him. What seems to me lacking is that holy *respect* for art, that oil of adoration given with a whole heart to its divine function which the creative faculty must bathe in before it will work at its fullest power. Hugo just enjoys playing the artist. It is all he can do not to wear a velvet jacket and floppy tie! He is also impatient and goes at everything with a sort of weak rush; whereas I have an idea that the true creator works in his medium with a kind of radiant patience. Bernard told me once during one of our conversations that the greatest joy of his life was the rich, slowly expanding ecstasy of detail with which his mind overflowed when engaged on the final draft of a play.

Hugo's canvases are pale; no apprehension of the real quick of experience enriches them. They have not even the rapid grace of his animal sketches. Yet they are touching. And he has certainly great faith in himself. Shy he may be but his is not the deeply analytical shyness of self-criticism. It is the simpler result of bad upbringing, the gauche social manners of the ignorant, *nouveau riche* society he comes from. He has never been taught to make himself polite and easy in order to save other people's feelings. And though he senses that somewhere he is lacking, he is, I suppose, too beautiful to have learnt this lesson the hard way. So he was at first tentative, a little suspicious of me in a blind, jerky way, unforthcoming, watchful; then suddenly boastful and as suddenly modest (since he wished to impress me) and finally childlike. When I stamped firmly on the first appearance of the dowdy, psychological jargon I had already heard at second hand from Bridget he accepted my strictures instantly, meek as a child. When he began giving me the usual orthodoxly unorthodox political opinions of bright young men I told him to keep the labour party for his other friends. "Talk about yourself!" I said. He laughed and said naïvely that if he did he would never stop.

"I'll tell you when to stop," I said in a bullying voice which pleased us both.

"Well what would you like to know?" he said making himself comfortable on the floor after dinner. He clasped his legs and looked over at me, his chin above his knees, to where I sat facing him in his dirty old armchair.

"How you spend your time. The pattern of your day. What time you get up in the morning. What time you go to bed. . . ."

"Very late. And I get up late too, I'm afraid," he said earnestly. "I can't bear mornings. I can't bear the day at all till it's well on. I mean I'm simply not human before eleven—"

"Right. It's eleven o'clock and you're up! What then?"

"Well . . . then I have breakfast. I don't like much breakfast," he said very seriously, "just tea and one slice of toast (sometimes I leave half even of that) and during the summer I sometimes have orange juice instead of tea—"

"No grapefruit?" I said indulging myself affectionately in his absurdity.

"Well, sometimes—when I can bother preparing it. It's better for me really than orange juice; less acid."

(Shades of old Mrs. Zold! I must bring them together!)

"My system has a tendency towards acidity," he said still dead serious; Jewish-anxious about his health. I longed to laugh and to touch his pale-gold, glowing face.

"And then?" I said.

"Well, I wash and shave and tidy up a bit and do some

shopping. And then I have late lunch—about two o'clock, or sometimes it's nearly three. And after that unless I've got to see someone about a commission or something I work. I work very hard. You might not think so but I do."

"What at? Precisely?"

"Well . . . you know; illustrations, posters, book jackets . . . the bread and butter jobs. The big work, the oils, I leave for the week-ends. My week's very organized," he said with pride, "though I am a late getter-up."

His late rising was so evidently a cardinal thing with him that the suspicion flashed across my mind that he had left home purely in order to do so; that the getting up late (and not the artist malarkey) represented the great ideal for which he was making his grand gesture against the bourgeoisie.

"And when you've finished your work for the day—what then?"

"I clean up the studio—and myself a bit, I'm always smothered in paint, I use barrels of turps and detergent. . . ." (I was so besottedly absorbed in every dull, enchanting, absurd detail it was all I could do not to ask him what brand!) "and either eat here or go out for a meal. It's usually rather late but there's lots of very good places open round here—d'you like spaghetti? I love spaghetti—and then by that time it's time to come home and go to bed and read. I read for hours every night. And then I fall asleep in my little couch," he said smilingly nicely at me, "and sleep the sleep of the just till the next morning. Oh! sometimes if I can't get to sleep quickly enough I get out of bed and make myself a cup of chocolate or Horlicks, I'm not very fond of plain milk, are you? Or I open a tin of soup. Only that doesn't always agree with me."

"No, well, it wouldn't," I said gravely. "Not late at night."

"Oh I've got a pretty good digestion on the whole," he said, "it's only occasionally it plays me up."

"Well, well," I said after a pause. "A blameless life!"

"Oh it is," he said eagerly.

Too eagerly by half, I thought, suddenly wrenched from my willing subjection to this picture of a shy, sunny, solitary life back to common sense. Surely it couldn't be all that blameless? Apart from Bridget and the as yet unmet Erik, there had been Barbara. . . . But perhaps they were isolated instances?

"I quite envy you," I said in a casual tone, "I wish I were self-sufficient enough to be content to be alone."

"Oh, I'm not *alone*," he said. "My goodness, that's my problem! Look over there!"

I looked towards the fire-place.

"*There!*" he said, pointing.

I found myself looking at the telephone. The receiver had been taken off and laid on its side.

"That's what I have to do if I want some peace," he said. "If I were to put that receiver back on again I can guarantee that in—"

He went on talking but in the gush of let-down fury which had engulfed me I hardly heard him. So much for the beautiful, shy, lonely boy and his solitary, contented, working life! So much for Bridget's "compliment" that I had been asked to go there as a rare privilege. I could have hit him! Even the fact that he hadn't wanted our evening together to be disturbed was no assuagement. And when, jumping up, he said: "Actually, I am half expecting a rather important call some time after ten," and put the receiver back on again I got up myself and in a raging bad temper said if it was that late, my goodness! I'd better go. He tried to dissuade me but with so little force that I almost threw myself out of the room, refusing his offer to accompany me at least as far as the bus if I wouldn't let him take me home.

"That's all I need," I said crossly, "to have Bridget or one of her friends see me with you."

"So what?" he said, standing at his front door, trying—but mildly—to detain me for even a few minutes more.

"Oh don't be silly, Hugo," I said, crosser than ever. "You know perfectly well it wouldn't do."

"I don't see why. I'm not married to her—or anyone else."

For some reason the phrase "or anyone else" cheered me a little and we parted amicably enough. "See you soon," he said as I walked off and that phrase too gave me pleasure—for about five minutes. And then the pleasure faded and I was left with the ruin of my evening.

Ruin it was; for many reasons. The unfulfilment of my sensual dream was one. But that deprivation I could have borne. Even in my most extravagant fancy I had hardly expected him to make any overt, physical advances at this stage of our acquaintance; though had I made them as I do believe he wished me to, he would have been delighted. But this was part of my dismay; that he was evidently (I saw it in a dozen tiny ways . . . his hesitancy, his smile, the occasional, tentative lift of his hand towards me and its slow withdrawal) going to leave it to me to make the running. And this I was determined on no account to do. The only possible terms on which I could enter on a relationship with him would be those of worship, of persuasive love so urgent from him as to overcome all my dreads of what would in any case be the inevitable pain. To deliberately court, of my own volition, such eventual grief would be madness. If he wished to spend *his* energy . . . then perhaps. But for me to spend mine? Oh no! That I would never do.

But there was another and equally strong disappointment; and that was my faint, persisting realization that the stuff of him was not what I had thought. He was no lonely, marvellous boy, no genius, no concerned, warm, young enthusiast, no poseur in the grand manner, even, like Peregrine. He was nothing but a suburban-Jewish, mother's boy with a slight talent, a rich home to fall back into when he got tired of playing Rodolphe . . . and a heart-catching shape to his golden-chestnut head. And his eyes, of course; those narrow, suffused eyes of Pan, tricking me—and Bridget—(and how many others?) into thinking we heard goat's feet clattering after us in the hot, golden silence of a pastoral afternoon.

I walked all the way home. As I turned into Honeysuckle Road I caught sight of the house with lights on, unaccustomedly at that hour of the night, in nearly every room. Letting myself in I found the old woman lurking about the hall, obviously lying in wait for me. From upstairs came sounds of movement; from the living-room, men's voices.

"There you are!" she said coming forward with a jerk. "I've been waiting for you."

"So I see," I said walking ahead of her into the kitchen. "It's not very late you know. Just gone eleven."

"I've been waiting for you," she said again, standing by the table her hands clutching the back of a chair, "to ask what happened with Ginny this afternoon."

I raised my hand and slowly drew my stole off from around my shoulders. "What d'you mean exactly?" I said.

"I'll tell you what I mean, Mrs. Holland," she said, so frightened and agitated by the strain of attempting a direct accusation that she couldn't use her voice properly. "We've had a time with Ginny I can tell you. It appears you scared that child into such fits this afternoon that she went out of the house all by herself to find her mother."

"I scared her?" I said. Then, slowly: "*What* did she do?"

"Went off to find Mrs. Capes' house—she's been there before of course, but not by herself—looking for Jessica. To tell her."

"Tell her *what*?"

"I guess you know as well as I," she said. "You hit that child this afternoon."

"Did she tell you why?"

"You're not denying it anyway," she muttered, at a loss. It was evident that she had expected me to do so and that all her furiously imagined dialogue with me before I came in had depended on that. I felt, in the midst of my general alarm, almost sorry to have deprived her of it—and simultaneously a flash of perfect comprehension of Bernard's sacrificial behaviour to her. All the same, I had to protect myself.

"Did she tell you why?" I said again.

"You had some argument . . . told her to get out of her mother's bedroom. And when she wouldn't you slapped her."

"*Mrs. Zold,*" I said with great firmness, "Do you seriously imagine—? well, let's get it straight first . . . what happened after that? She left the house?"

"How was I to know?" she burst out. "I was in the courtyard in back of the house. How would I know she'd gone?"

"And then?"

"She tried to find her mother at Mrs. Capes'. Of course she got lost. She didn't even have the proper address. I didn't even know she was out of the house till Jessica called to say not to wait supper for her she was staying out. And when I went to fetch Ginny for her supper she'd disappeared. God! I never want to live through another hour like that again. In and out every room in the house, up and down the street, round the neighbourhood calling 'Ginny' at the top of my voice like I was crazy. Finally I called the theatre and told Bernard I was half out of my mind with worry and he'd better come home right away."

"Was this during the dress rehearsal?" I said sharply.

"I guess so," she said without interest, concerned only with her own experience. I gave a sharp exclamation and— shrewd as ever in her own peculiar way—she said: "Play or no play—his child's more important." Under stress the truth of her real feelings about Bernard's work came out, raw, clear and unmistakable and, I saw, unalterable. (Perhaps even—who knows?—right. Who is to say that in her role of everybody's subconscious, she is not right to elevate life above art?)

"Anyway she's home now I gather?"

"Two of your policemen brought her back half an hour ago. She was found crying in the street. This three hours after Bernard called them. Three hours' nightmare that's all I can call it." "And all your fault," she was indicating with a look when Bernard came into the kitchen.

"Oh—Ruth," he said with evident relief when he saw me. "I'm glad you're back. Hold on a minute. The cops're just going."

"Now what's all this about you and Ginny?" he said coming back a few moments later and, brisk and straightforward as ever in a crisis, plunging in at the deep end.

"What did she tell you?"

He repeated in undramatic terms what his mother had already told me.

"I needn't say that I know perfectly well that it wasn't quite like that," he ended.

"How d'you know?" the old woman interjected rawly and irrepressibly. "You weren't there any more than I was."

"Mama! will you do something for me?"

"What is it?"

"Go to bed. You go on off to bed. You've had a hard day, all that worry and you on your own. Poor Mama!" He put his arm round her, smiled affectionately but led her firmly to the door. "Never mind. It's all over and nobody's hurt or anything. Everything's fine now. Say! you might take a look in at Ginny again and see if she wants anything. I think Jessica's gone to bed."

Given a job to do she trotted off docilely enough (though not without a darted glance at me) and then he turned to me.

"I suppose we'd better get it straight, just for the record," he said smiling but looking suddenly so pale and exhausted that I said: "What about a cup of prohibition liquor?"

"Fine!" he said.

I went to put the kettle on.

"I don't know why Ginny should have taken it into her head to do what she did," I said as I stood at the sink with my back to him, "but I'd like to explain just what really happened." I put the kettle on the stove and lit the gas. I took a quick look at him as I went to get the cups and saucers. He was lying back in the easy chair, his eyes closed, his face pouched and drawn and shiny-pale.

"What happened," I said carefully, "was that I found Ginny in your room sort of . . . muttering to herself. You know the way children do sometimes when they've got a grievance."

"What about?"

"What about?"

"What grievance was she muttering about?"

I hesitated. I was about to repeat Ginny's remarks to the mirror regarding her grandmother . . . but I hesitated, since to tell him just then when his nerves were already stretched to their limits could only cause him further worry and pain. Making a snap decision I said: "I really don't know exactly, Mr. Zold. Anyway, I went to—" I was about to say "draw back the curtains" but again I stopped since this would involve a description of the child's all-over curious behaviour, "went over to talk to her," I amended.

"And?"

"And she . . . sort of burst into tears and—or so I thought —just a touch of hysteria as well. It was nothing really, every child goes through these fits. So I smacked her on the cheek, not very hard, to bring her round."

"Did it?"

"Yes! I really thought it did. Otherwise, I assure you, Mr. Zold, I would never have left her."

I poured boiling water from the kettle into the teapot.

"I'm sure you wouldn't," he said sitting up and taking the cup I handed to him. "Of course you're not telling me the truth," he said looking up and nodding his head quizzically, "but I'm too darned tired to try and get it out of you— or deal with it if I could." He shook his head very wearily from side to side and sighed, once, very deeply. "I just wish it hadn't happened tonight, that's all."

"If only I hadn't been out," I said desperately. "It would never have happened in the first place—and even if it had I wouldn't have disturbed you at the dress rehearsal until I'd done everything I could myself first. At least I would have telephoned your wife to come home before bothering *you*."

"It wouldn't have made any difference. She'd gone to a movie with that appalling woman friend of hers and came home when all this was over. It takes a really rare genius to be always out at the right moment, doesn't it?" he said with mild unfairness. "It's not everybody's got a talent like that, you must admit!"

I said nothing and after a moment he gave an exhausted, sideways roll of his head on his neck, lay absolutely still for a few seconds, his hands on the wooden arms of his chair, then gripping them, he levered himself up and went to the door.

"All over!" he said before he went out. "A storm in a teacup—to coin a phrase. Forget it, Ruth. Or at least—forget it for the time being. In fact . . . what the hell am I saying? . . . *you* can forget it forever. But very soon now I'm going to have to start thinking hard about Ginny. Can't go on being a delinquent parent. She was crying in the street. My poor, clumsy child."

That was last night. This morning we were all back to normal again without another word being said (though

Ginny gave me one or two side looks, not sure how much I'd told of her behaviour) or at least as nearly normal as the premiere being only a few hours away would allow us to be.

And then, about three o'clock this afternoon, the telephone rang.

I answered it. A harsh, hoarse, male, American voice asked for Bernard.

"He's out," I said.

"Is any member of the family in, young lady?"

"I'm afraid his wife won't be back for about an hour. But Mr. Zold's mother is in."

"Put her on, will you?"

I called Mrs. Zold from her room and went to the kitchen. A few minutes later she came in in a great fluster.

"Wouldn't you just know! That was my older son, Jakie. They've just arrived this minute, he and his wife. Wouldn't you *know!* Today of all days! I'd better call Bernie right away. They're coming over."

She was almost out of the kitchen when I came to my senses and called after her: "Mrs. Zold! if you don't mind my saying. . . ."

"Yes?"

"Don't you think perhaps he might not want to be bothered about anything at all outside the theatre just for these few hours?"

"Why not?" she said, twitching and impatient. "It's his own brother isn't it? Family comes before other things." (Other things! The stupidity of it! As though he'd gone out to buy himself a pair of shoes.)

"Yes, but surely—" I began, struggling to hide my impatience.

She cut me short. "Say, have we got any cake in the house? Jakie's got a sweet tooth like you wouldn't believe. He can eat a chunk of angel cake head-size before you notice it."

She bustled off to examine the cake position. I followed her and said: "Look, Mrs. Zold, I know it's none of my business but Mr. Zold's nerves will be so much on edge till after the performance tonight . . . couldn't you . . . I mean . . . could you possibly not tell him that his brother's here. I mean, it might upset him. . . ." My voice trailed off as I saw the impossibility of saying to her that I'd overheard enough to know that Bernard had begged her to try and keep his brother away till after today.

She hesitated. Something of what I had not said belatedly entered her memory too. She said doubtfully: "Well . . . maybe you're right. I—but there's nothing I can do about it. They're on their way over right now."

"D'you have to tell them it's the premiere tonight? D'you have to tell Mr. Zold that they're even here till it's over?"

She looked uneasily away. "I don't see how I can't," she said. "And what'll Jakie say tomorrow when he finds out?"

All of a sudden I wanted to take her by her gaunt, narrow, bowed, obstinate shoulders and shake her violently into sense. "You foolish, foolish, old woman," I wanted to scream at her, "for once use your imagination. Must you spoil everything for him? Today of all days? Would you sacrifice him to that hard-sounding voice on the telephone?"

She moved away from me as if the silent demand I was making on her was being physically imposed. "My luck," she began to moan, pulling feverishly at her wedding ring. "He's not even in the house yet and already there's trouble. Already I'm being torn in pieces. What did he have to come today for? I never *told* him. I didn't write one word. My luck! My luck! And not a crumb of cake in the house," she went on in characteristic anti-climax. "Mrs. Holland," she said, "would you mind running over to the stores and getting some? One of those large—Madeiras d'you call 'em? They're very good. And a fruit cake. Oh, and maybe a dozen of those little cream cookies?"

"Yes, certainly," I said, "but—" I looked at her in mute appeal.

"Maybe it *would* be better not to say," she muttered looking frightened again. Afraid to say any more in case I tipped her the other way, I took the shopping bag and went off to the shops.

When I got back it was to find the visitors already there and Jessica, back from the hairdresser, prattling to them about the premiere. The old woman, now obviously deeply disturbed and regretful, came into the kitchen her eyes blinking and worried; too disturbed to keep me at a distance. "I'd have given every last cent I own in the world this shouldn't happen," she said. "I didn't have a chance to stop it, even. They all met on the doorstep coming in. Jessica let it drop right away. Bring the tea in will you?"

Jessica introduced me when I took in the tray. Not bothering to get up or even to break his sentence beyond a casual nod Jakie went on talking in his loud voice, sprawled in the biggest chair, one thick leg across the thigh of the other. He was like a bigger, coarser, looser version of his brother with small, sharp eyes as against Bernard's large, melancholy ones, in a heavy, jowled face, his thick lips loose over crooked teeth. His manner was at once both suspicious and hectoring. His wife was almost a duplicate of her mother-in-law! And—I could swear—almost as old! (He must have needed money badly at some stage and married her to get it.) Like so many thin, hunched, dowdy women she talked incessantly, droning away in accompaniment to her husband's raucous poundings. Their talk was simultaneous but independent so that it was difficult to disentangle what either of them was saying till every now and then he would force his voice still higher, drowning out everyone else, when with a nervous look she would fall silent.

"I'm sure sorry we can't spend your first evening in London with you," Jessica was saying with her usual, mild politeness, "but I guess you understand, Jakie." He gave her a cold-eyed look, jerked his chin and said: "Meantersay you can't get a coupla tickets? Bernie's the author isn't he?"

"Why, the house was sold out weeks ago," she said with some pride.

I saw his eyes widen and narrow as if the thought of so much notice being taken of the event angered him. "Premieres" (he pronounced it pree-meers), "are always sold out. Leastways after half the seats are given for free. Anyway, I'll speak to Bernie when he comes in."

"Maybe you'll miss . . . I mean . . . maybe he won't be back yet awhile . . ." said the old woman gabbling the words in a voice cracked with nervousness.

"So we can't wait? Say, you hear that, Thelma? We come a few t'ousand miles to see our own flesh and blood and we're being asked to go after five minutes."

"Now Jakie, who said about going? Did I say one word—"

"I guess we know when we're not wanted," said his wife in her dry mumble, looking sideways at the floor.

"You bet we do," he said making a sketched movement of getting up.

"Jakie! for God's sake what have I said already? I—"

"You said plenty already. You don't bother to invite us to this crummy, lousy premiere—"

"Did I know you were going to arr—?"

"It's not even in a big theatre like a Broadway production. You don't want we should stay and see Bernie, his Godamighty Highness, God forbid! We come off the plane and straight over to you. As God's my witness we never stopped even to check in at a hotel . . ." he paused for a second before going on, "we gotta sleep somewhere tonight—"

"I only wish we had roo—" began Jessica but the second's pause had told him what he wanted to know.

"Don't think we wanted to stay here, if that's what's biting ya. I can buy and sell a few hotels around this town without noticing. No! I come off the plane and rush straight off to my own flesh and blood, *my own flesh and blood*" (he managed to thrust a tremolo note into his harsh voice), "and what happens? Not even the offer of a bite of food."

"Jakie!" his mother cried out in outrage, "how can you *say* that? Why, I gave you your tea the minute . . . You've had lunch, you said so yourself. Thelma said. I asked her the minute she came in. Tell the truth, Thelma, didn't I ask you just the very minute you came into this house?"

Not giving his wife a chance to answer—though she would obviously have evaded doing so anyway—he stood up and began striding about the room. "So what can I expect from my ungrateful family anyway? Who paid for you to come over here anyway? Think the steamship company gives tickets away for peanuts? How many hundred dollars did it cost me so you could see Europe?"

I could hear his voice tearing on in this strain as I busied myself in the kitchen, his twisted version of the truth almost unanswerable. Jessica had told me long ago that *after* Bernard had bought all the tickets and made every conceivable arrangement, his brother had sent a cheque for five hundred dollars, not to him (since he would have sent it back) but to his mother. Since then he had sent to his mother occasional small sums, twenty or thirty dollars at a time. "She tells *me* when they come," Jessica had told me, "but she won't tell Bernie. He'd make her send them back."

"D'you think she ought to return them?" I'd asked her, curious as to her attitude.

"Me? Why no! Take what you can grab out of that creature, that's what I say to Bernie. Not that he listens to me."

The argument in the living-room had stopped. So had all conversation. Jakie had decreed silence since he was too upset to say another word. He was feeling sick and ill all over again with his mother's ingratitude. He had a good mind to take the next plane back. Old Mrs. Zold had twisted herself inside out with denials, protestations, weak, muttered assertions.

When I went in to clear away the tea things he gave me a curious look from his small eyes, a look of calculation so obvious that it almost seemed as if he were acting, not to say overacting the attitude. I deliberately refrained from taking any notice of him at all, only stood patiently while his mother asked him three times over if he was sure he didn't want some fresh tea made. (No objection to *him* drinking as much tea as he wanted!)

"And how long have you bin working here, may I ask?" he began on a high, elaborate, ponderously arch tone. He looked around to make sure everybody was noticing how friendly he was being to the hired help.

"Since Mr. Zold and his family arrived," I said turning my back on him to reach for a plate.

"Say! you don't talk like a Londoner!"

"I'm afraid I don't know what you mean," I said fitting two cups together.

"Stop me if I'm being *personal* but you wasn't born in this city, I'll bet."

"I come from Liverpool," I said shortly.

"Didn't I tell ya! What did I tell ya! Liverpool? Ain't that Lancasheer?"

"Yes."

"Hear that, Ma? Hear that, Thelma? I'm never wrong. I got an ear like Professor Higgins. Put me down in China an' I'll tell ya if the first coolie I meet comes from Pekin or Shanghai. See how I knew right off she came from Liverpool. I got the finest ear for an accent. How many Americans coulda told you that right off, Ma?"

"Sure, Jakie. You always had a talent for that even as a child," said the old woman brightening up as soon as he condescended to speak to her a shade more like a human being.

"So that's your home town, is it?" he was saying when the door opened and Ginny who'd been playing across the street with a very dull, little boy of six who occasionally asked her into his garden which had a swing, came in. "Come on in," he said forestalling his mother who would—I saw from the look on her face—have liked to run the child upstairs and tidy her up before letting him see her. She advanced slowly into the room.

"Why you surely remember your Uncle Jakie and Aunt Thelma?" said Jessica. "Go and say Hello to them now."

The child advanced in her wooden, expressionless way to within a yard of them. Thelma held out her hand and drawing her closer gave her a dry peck on the cheek.

"What about me?" said Jakie. "Don't your uncle rate a kiss too?"

He pulled her away from his wife and wedged her between his knees. She wriggled and tried to get away. He squeezed her tighter between his great fat thighs. Looking furious and sullen she struggled harder still. With a look of thunder on his face he opened his legs suddenly so that she nearly fell. "O.K." he said. "If that's the way you want to treat your uncle. . . . But you're making a mistake, young lady."

She ran over to her mother and stood beside her. Jessica said equably: "I guess she's got a bit of the artistic temperament like her father. She's quite a bit of an artist herself, you'd be surprised, Jakie. Run upstairs and bring down that little picture you did of the garden, Ginny. The one over your bed. You want to see this, Jakie. It's real good. Go on Ginny, you don't have to be shy. Bring it here."

She went off and, returning with the picture, handed it stolidly to her uncle. He took it in his hands, barely glanced at it then thrust it back at her. "Yeah. Kid's stuff," he said. "You ain't no great genius yet."

Ginny flushed.

"Hey, hey!" said Jessica though still pleasantly, "how do *you* know so quick?"

"Think I don't know about art and all that crap? I know a thing or two'd surprise you. Think your husband's the only one knows his way around? The *intellectual* in the family," he said with again such heavy, contempt that I felt a great, angry distaste boiling up in me.

I heard the front door open and close. And a moment later Bernard was in the room. He showed hardly any surprise, just stood there for a moment, his back to the door, one arm folded behind him. "Hello," he said. "So you've come."

"Yeah," said Jakie settling himself fatly into his chair. "We flew."

He made no attempt to get up in order to shake hands. Had Bernard wanted to do so he would have had to cross the room to him and bow his body physically before his brother. Rightly, he chose not to. But he did go over to Thelma and, putting one hand lightly on her shoulder, asked how she was. "I guess I'm fair enough, Bernie," she said nervously. "I was just telling Ma though I've been that low . . . I had the grippe three times—"

"Lotta talk about a coupla head colds," said Jakie on a growl. "Sneezes once and she's got pneumonia. I had the best doctor in town have a look at her. He cost me plenty that guy. Says there's nothing wrong with her. Nerves. That's all. Nerves! You wanna have my worries then you can talk about nerves."

"You want some tea, Bernie?" said Jessica.

He looked at his watch. "Don't think I'm going to have much time. In fact we'd all better eat dinner soon. You girls'll want time to put your glad rags on." He paused. "Say —I guess you know what's happening tonight, Jakie?"

"Sure. I've bin told."

"If I'd have known you—"

"You took good and plenty care we wasn't told before, didn't you? Sure. I know. I'm just your brother. You don't have to write and let me into anything that's going on, do ya? I'm just your businessman brother, not one of your intellectual buddies that don't have two cents to rub together."

"Since when am I in the habit of writing to you? Have you so much as written *me* a line—?"

"His egghead pals! *They* put money in his pocket—I don't think!"

I had left the room some moments before and was busying myself setting the dining-room table for supper but the communicating doors were open. Through them I saw Bernard's brother give a sudden leap out of his chair, stride with a fat, crude energy over to his wife and yank her to her feet.

"Come on. Get going," he said. "We're not staying here a minute longer than I can help." He made for the door—but not very quickly; his arms making large, deceptive gestures but his feet moving with remarkable slowness. I realized why when his mother jumped to her feet and ran after him with quite unnecessary speed, crying out: "Jakie! you can't go just like that! For goodness' sake, have you two got to quarrel the minute you meet up again? Is this what we came to Europe for?"

Jessica, for once showing sense as well as self-interest, had taken Ginny out of the room and there was only Thelma and myself to witness what was going on between the three of them.

"Jakie," said Bernard with a desperate patience looking at his watch again. "I've got to be at the theatre in two hours' time. *It's my first night.* It's *important* to me. If I had tickets for the show I'd give you them. I haven't. The whole house was sold out long ago. If you want to go down on the chance there's returns you can do so. I'll tell them out front to let you have first go at any that come in. But that's all I can do." He held out his hands incisively, palms upwards. "It's a *small theatre*. I can't manufacture a couple of seats out of thin air."

"You can have mine," said old Mrs. Zold suddenly. "Have my seat."

"Mama!" said Bernard.

"I don't care whether I go or not," she cried distraught.

"*You-may-not*," said Bernard grimly, "but I do. You're going to that theatre tonight if I have to carry you."

"You don't have to worry," said Jakie. "I wouldn't take the seat if you paid me. Think I've nothing better to do than have my pants bored off of me my first night in London? You can keep it . . . *brother!* Me and Thelma'll take in a real show. When we've settled on a hotel. Bye."

He moved again towards the door. Again his mother stopped him, crying with great agitation: "But where'll you be? I won't even know where you are!"

"I'll let you know," he said, then, as she looked relieved, added meanly: "Some time."

"When?" she said. "When, Jakie?"

"I'll call you," he said with deliberate vagueness and stalked out at last followed by his wife.

"At least stay for some dinner," his mother persisted, following them into the hall.

"Thanks!" he said sarcastically. "Some other time. Bye."

And they walked off down the front path, old Mrs. Zold trembling with misery and agitation, watching them from the front door.

There was only one thing for Bernard to do and he did it. He hurried her briskly upstairs, turned on the bath for her, took her frock out of the wardrobe and told her to get a move on or they'd all be late. "You have yours now. I'll bathe after we've eaten," he said firmly and, creating a continual bustle around her, managed to get her moving under her own steam, dear son Jakie pushed, at least for the time being, to the back of her mind. And finally they all went off leaving me with Ginny.

And now I am lying here waiting for them, totally unable to sleep or rest. I don't know what to think of first; of how difficult everything has been made for him? my own problems or his? of Hugo? or Ginny? or of certain kinds of natures which we like to believe don't exist . . . but do.

What is happening at the Vauxhall? How is it going? I lie and I pray—though whether for him or myself I hardly know.

I did not send yesterday's letter. They returned before I had finished and, putting on my dressing-gown, I went down to them.

The kitchen for once seemed alive; decorated and gay with the two women still dressed in their bright silks, Bernard in his evening clothes, programmes and chocolates strewn on the table.

"Go all right?" I said casually while quickly putting a saucepan of milk on the stove for their cocoa.

"Why, sure," said Jessica cheerfully kicking off her shoes. "They loved it. They really did, even you've got to admit, Bernie. Of course he won't!" she said turning to me. "Nine curtains! Would you get me my slippers, Ruth, there's a honey? Am I *tired!*"

She seemed in great spirits but her mood was nothing to go by. I glanced at Bernard but he looked just slightly more composed than usual. His mother was fussing about with a piece of soap and a ladder she had sprung in one stocking almost as soon as she'd entered the theatre, apparently, and which had thereafter occupied a good deal of her attention. I could not resist looking at Bernard again and raising my eyebrows questioningly. His lips twitched in a rather tender half-smile and he said soothingly, as if I were the one who'd been on trial that evening: "Not too bad, Ruth. I *think* it was all right." I nodded my head quickly and turned to the stove. "We won't really know for several days yet, you know. The dailies and the evenings will have their notices in tomorrow I suppose but that'll be Wednesday. Have to wait till Friday for the top weeklies—and two more days for the ones that really count—with a Vauxhall audience anyway . . . the Sunday heavies. Anyway there was one thing I felt really good about. You know, we were a bit hipped at the clash with that big musical that was also opening tonight?"

"Yes I know. Bother them!"

"Sure, but it was O.K. after all. Wallace tells me there wasn't a second string critic in the house from any of the important papers. They'd sent their top men, every one of them. That's . . . that's kind of an advance compliment. . . . You know!"

He was smiling and pleased in a way which I guessed he wouldn't have been if the reception of the audience in general hadn't been warm. And this he gradually—though I almost had to drag the actual words out of him—admitted. Though it was Jessica who told me of the number and enthusiasm of the curtain calls and his mother who kept telling me about a very handsome old gentleman who, walking out behind her at the end, had kept repeating: "Remarkable. Remarkable play."

Bernard had taken them backstage afterwards and introduced them to the cast and Wallace Grey had been very pleasant and the cast had been very hospitable in their dressing-rooms and they'd all had a drink. Peregrine had also been in the theatre and later, backstage. "You should have seen his girl friend!" said Jessica. "My! she was quite something something!"

Both the women were amiable and excited and inclined to optimistic prophecy which Bernard kept clamping down on till his mother, turning petulant, said sulkily, at last;

"For land's sakes, Bernie, stop pulling me down. Can't I even say for once when something gives me pleasure?"

I sympathized with the old woman! His determined pessimism, though largely unspoken, does seem to hang in the air, giving one sometimes a certain impatience with him. "Oh, come on!" one feels like saying. "Snap out of it!"

He laughed self-consciously and said: "Oh well, perhaps I'm wrong to keep telling you girls to hold your hosses. I guess I'm being over-cautious. Only—you can't *be* over-cautious in this racket. Sure, I know the audience seemed to like it. But so they did back home. That don't mean anything in terms of long runs as you know very well. Haven't we had experience?"

"I thought you didn't care about long runs, Bernie," said Jessica. "Haven't you always said that what you wanted above just everything else in the world was reputation?"

He looked at her with an expression of good-humoured tolerance (in itself an indication that he had been given reason for optimism that evening) and said: "Look! I'm like every other guy in the world. I want everything. Long runs, esteem, money . . . everything. But if I've got to choose just *one* of those things—then I'll take esteem. Not because I'm so darned high-minded. On the contrary—because I'm so calculating! I calculated long ago that reputation is the safest investment of all in the end. So if you only knew it I'm taking a pure, hard-eyed businessman's point of view!"

He smiled as he spoke, then yawned abruptly. "C'mon," he said. "Enough is enough is enough. Bed! Whichever way it is—I'm sure glad this evening's over. Thanks for the cocoa, Ruth. It was nice to come back home after all the excitement and find a friend."

"And find a friend." Those words haunted me as I lay awake long after we'd all gone to bed.

Do you recall in one of my earlier letters to you my speculations (jogged perhaps by Debenham Bleu's remarks) regarding Bernard's feelings for me? How I almost suspected a sexual colour to them? How absurd, how entirely wrong my readings were of the whole nature of this man. The truth is—I see it plainly at last—that he doesn't see me as a woman at all. As a suffering, lonely human being he is almost powerless to help—yes. But never as a feminine body. And I see why he does not see me as a woman. He does not *want* a woman. Oh yes! I sense this very strongly. The sexual instinct in him, discouraged perhaps by Jessica's deficiencies, never perhaps very powerful anyway, has turned into something else; pity. Or possibly responsibleness would be a better word. It is not that sex has forsaken him; he has forsaken *it*. In the rigours of his lonely duties he has no time for it. In the anxious complexities of his life, sex is too narrow a want. His crying need is for a friend. What an ultimate irony! Are you laughing Francis? That this should happen to me—who have never cared for friends, only lovers.

To Bernard—oh, this makes me smile!—I am a friend! Did I say smile? Yes I did but not, as you may think, in impatience or derision; only in wonder that I should have learnt friendship, the trick of it, so late, so unexpectedly. I thought that what I had for him was curiosity, a little human sympathy, a temporary filling of an empty space in my life. And now I discover that what I feel is a deep, personal, agonized concern for his welfare. It is—again I feel it necessary to repeat this—*not love*.

It has occurred to me that perhaps I have no capacity for love at all. For though I melt even to the thought of Hugo whose image swamps and decimates me, I also long to hurt him. I long to walk past him in the street with other men and laugh and leave him standing with an aching heart. My experience of him is like rain falling in sunlight on my hair; he is my April afternoon. Yet the very fragile stuff of him incites most vengeful feelings. I long to bring down a hammer and shiver that fine-blown glass to glinting fragments. He is not entitled to his being; he has not earned it. His face is too great a fortune.

I am led all over again into speculation on the influence of our physical selves. For what would I care for Hugo were some fractions of an inch of his bone and muscle arranged differently, if the traces of that pigment which make him so golden-pale and beautiful were absent? The thought of the world's subjection to such tiny differences of shape and colour infuriates me.

It is Hugo whose very failings fill me with delight.

But it is Bernard whom I wish to keep from harm.

Ruth

☼☾☼☾☼☾☼☾☼☾☼☾☼☾☼☾☼☾☼☾☼☾

26th August

ANXIOUS beyond words I was up at seven this morning only to find both Bernard and his mother down already. We spoke very little to each other. We were waiting for the papers to come through the letter-box. They should have arrived at a quarter to eight. At five to, the old woman, unable to bear it any longer, went to the front door to see if the delivery boy was coming. We heard the door bang— Bernard was stolidly eating piece after piece of toast and reading a magazine with concentrated inattention—then his mother came in almost flying apart with nerves and triumph clutching a great wad of newspapers under her arm. "Lying on the step!" she said. "If I hadn't thought of going to look . . . if I hadn't . . . they'd have still—Of course! How could he get them all in together?"

"He could have put them through one at a time," he said

calmly and even argumentatively though he at the same time stood up and reached out an imperious arm. "All of them, Mama," he said as she made to hold some papers back. And I saw that this was one thing he would always (his one touch of iron egotism) reserve for himself; the first reading of the notices.

"You could have gone down to Fleet Street and got them hours ago," she said. "Peregrine said he always did."

"I know. But I didn't choose. I didn't in New York and I don't here. I prefer to wait till they're delivered. It's my foible. You can't talk me out of it," he said in what were for him unusually quick, short, firm sentences. He made no move to open the sheets of newsprint, only held the thick wad of them between his hands in an iron-gentle grip. Then he walked out of the dining-room and into the living-room, ensconced himself (he was still in his dressing-gown) on the settee and, calmly and deliberately, with only one nervous ruffle of exasperation when two pages refused to separate, began to go through them systematically. His mother, still at the breakfast table, began helping me to clear some of the dishes away, subduing her movements—I had not thought her capable of such a restriction of herself—very carefully so as not to make a clatter. With one eye she watched him through the communicating doors cocking her head to every rustle he made. But she said nothing. She did not spoil it for him.

I was overcome with a sort of delighted admiration at her unexpected restraint. So much indeed that I could not prevent myself, as I moved round the table, from giving her warm, silent smiles. She smiled back and gave me the nearest approach to a wink that her face could manage. I noticed for the first time and with a start of surprise that she had blue eyes. I realize now that she must once have been quite fair and that that is where Ginny's blondeness comes from.

Morning sunlight, still at the back of the house, shafted through the dining-room window, dazzling us as we moved quietly about the table, but it did not reach the front room where Bernard was sitting, the light there seeming to come from a different and paler sun, its pale gleams reflected from the opposite side of the street.

Wanting to please him, wanting happiness for him, she remained silent. But when at last he called her she jumped as if electrically shocked and ran in and sat down beside him. He put his arm round her and gave her one of the notices to read. I looked at his head beside hers. He was indicating the column with his finger and reading it again, with her. And smiling.

"Not bad, is it?" he said when she had finished. He lifted his hand from her shoulder and poked her cheek with his index finger, playfully.

"*The others!*" she said.

He handed her another one. "Not quite as lyrical but not bad!" he said. She read it hungrily, her appetite suddenly voracious for praise.

"What does he mean 'with the exception of a dullish patch at the beginning of the second act'?" she said indignantly.

"He just didn't like that bit."

"I thought that scene just fine," she said. "He doesn't know what he's talking about."

He laughed indulgently. "He's entitled not to like just one little scene! He says some darned nice things about the rest. Damn it, Mama, you mustn't be greedy! Anyway, read this one. That'll do your heart good!"

Catching my eye as I was—I must admit—still hovering in the dining-room, he held up the ones she'd already read and I went over, grabbed them from him and read them rapidly, standing by the window. Then I looked up and said—*exactly* as his mother had done!—"The others!" He held them up and I went over, quoting "A subtle, powerful and extremely moving play" at him and beaming as I took more of the papers.

Jessica whom we had all forgotten came in with her usual placidly demure step. "Why, you've all beaten me to it this morning," she said. "Bernie, are they the notices? Quick, for heaven's sake. You'd better tell me. Are they good?"

"They're . . . not bad at all."

"Not bad!" his mother burst out. "Can you beat that? I'd like to see better ones, that's all. Just show me any play that's had better ones. . . ."

"O.K., O.K.," he said laughing. "They are pretty good. Here. Read 'em. I'm going up to get dressed." And he disappeared. But only to come back again to say, before he went upstairs: "Now remember! we're only a quarter out of the wood. There's the evenings, the Fridays and the Sundays. So don't crow too soon, girls! Hold it! You hear? That's an order!"

Washed and dressed Bernard came downstairs a little later and went to the telephone to ring Wallace Grey. He came away lively after a short conversation to say: "That guy must have nerves of steel. He was still asleep when I rang. Hadn't even seen the notices! Still, he's darn pleased. He's a *nice* guy. Talked about my success; as though all *he'd* done was shift the scenery." Doubling his fist he took a schoolboy punch at the air from sheer pleasure. "He's . . . he's got something, Wally," he went on. "Kind of a—I don't know what to call it . . . he's kind of a statesman instead of a politician. Know what I mean? He's got manners. It's a kind of a quality in him that's first class. He knows how to *be* with people; how to behave. He's like duck and orange— to the raw turnips most people are. Now I've gotta call the rest; all the cast. No, it's probably too early. No, maybe not. Well, I'll try Henry."

He spent the next hour reading the notices again and ringing up the entire cast one after another to congratulate them on their own mentions and thank them for their performances. Smiling and energetic he took Ginny up to Swiss Cottage, did some shopping, came home with duplicates of all the newspapers we'd already got and settled himself in the living-room for the hour before lunch, cutting out the reviews very carefully and sticking one lot into the exercise book he'd just bought. "I wouldn't even buy this," he said showing it to me, "till today. I was frightened of the tiniest move which might provoke Providence. I'm still frightened! But at least . . . well, I've got these." He held up the bundle of clippings. "They've *happened*. These words have been written and printed and circulated and read; and nothing on earth can change that now, can it?"

There was a ring at the front door and I went to answer it.

I showed in Peregrine! Dressed to kill too, in palest grey and lemon cashmere sweater.

"Congratulations! Felicitations! Salutations! and the whole Thesaurus to you, my dear chap. I'm delighted. You've made it! Of course, it's just the dailies. Never mind. Never mind. If the Sundays don't shout it up too I shan't speak to them! They so often contradict the dailies out of pure spite. Wally Grey's fantastically pleased. I had a long conversation with him (he's dying to do my new little thing though it's hardly born yet I told him he's got to wait till I've turned it upside-down and slapped its bottom) and he told me one of the things which pleased him enormously was the way most of the critics *got the point*. And when you think what it takes to get a point into their tiny—"

"Have you been over to see him this morning? My! you must have been up early—for you!"

"Oh no!" he said looking shocked, "I'm barely awake as it is. You know I'm never up before eleven at the very earliest. No. We all went down to the city and got the daily rags hot off, positively steaming, after the party."

"Party?"

"I suppose you went to another one," he said hastily, "it was just a few of the cast—"

"There's only five altogether," said Bernard smiling with exactly one half of his mouth.

"Yes, well, they weren't . . . anyway, Wally wasn't even prepared. It was all very sketchy and last minute and we ran out of Scotch almost immediately and all Wally had was half a bottle of vodka and some red ink from Yugo-Slavia. And brandy, thank goodness. He says he'll have to get married again if only to have someone check the liquor supply. Don't quote me but I have a pricking in my thumbs which tells me Lorraine might like the job. She's been going around with Cosmo Match but that's all over, I happen to know. I know old Cosmo terribly well; he came over one evening and told me the whole story. She's treated him terribly badly. I must say I hope she doesn't get her hooks on Wally, he's too nice a boy. It's a pity Frinton Chalmers wasn't representing the Daily Bubble and Squeak last night, wasn't it. They sent old Weston and although he's done you proud it's not quite the same as a quote from Chalmers. Maddening! But it happens to the best of us. Anyway! what I really came round for—apart from congratters (I have to use Public School usages sometimes just to thank God I never went to one)—is to say Morty Davy the playwright is terribly anxious to meet you and can I bring him over one evening? And someone else is too—old Rodericsthal. You've heard of them both I'm sure."

"Sure, I'd be delighted to have them come over."

"Fine. Well that's settled then. Only you don't want them both together do you? Or do you? Well anyway, we'll see."

"Stay and have some lunch won't you?"

"Thanks all the same but really, really not. I have a date with a stuffy, Yankee bore—oh I adore nearly every American I've ever met but—truth even if it kills!—when an American bores, brother! he does an outsize job. Look, I

simply must go. Where is everybody by the way? I haven't
seen anyone but Ruth swishing in and out of the dining-
room reminding me, I can't think why, of an O'Neill play.
What d'you think of those *superb* notices, Ruth?" he called
out.

"Yes, they are superb," I said coming forward into the
front room. "They're . . . like treasure. It must be," I said
strongly to Bernard (I could not bring myself to look at
Peregrine without anger), "like taking possession of some
marvellous pieces of gold. They're not just valuable in themselves. They're *rare*. They're something no money in the
world could buy. A few people earn them. Just a few in the
whole world. And you're one of them. Everybody else has
to make do with inferior satisfactions; large quantities of
dross to make up for their poverty in gold—"

"I *must* go," said Peregrine. "Give my love to everybody.
I'll ring you as soon as I've had a word with old Morty. And
Rodericsthal. Many, many congratulations all over again."

I heard the front door shut with a feeling of profound relief that the others, particularly his mother, hadn't been in
and heard Peregrine's brick drop, the clangour of which was
still ringing in both Bernard's ears and mine. As it was it
was bad enough.

He came back into the living-room and sank down on to
the settee, puffing out his breath exaggeratedly. "Even at
twenty-four that boy's staggering. What'll he be like at forty-
four?" he said in a conversational voice.

I glanced at him. He had picked up a magazine and, his
head bent, was flipping over the pages. But I saw that he
was wearing the self-conscious, stricken smile of those
deeply, socially wounded.

"Burnt out—or just possibly a flaming genius," I said.

"Oh not the first," he said with genuine distress.

"Could happen," I said firmly.

He sighed. Picking up the scissors he had been using on

the newspapers he tapped the handle against his teeth. "Well . . . at least he'll have had his fun," he said.

"Is that so important?" I said—the more stoutly since I knew that what he meant by "fun" (the being part of whatever is still lively, intelligent and charming in our society) *was* important. Or at least . . . it was important to him since his alternatives were so deadly; deadly and deadening.

"Yes," he said quite simply, showing his hurt.

"You may have to . . . you may have to live without it," I said slowly with a feeling of being cruel to be kind.

"Yes, I know. But it isn't only that. It's the being deceived." (He meant Wallace Grey.) "I know," he went on awkwardly, "it's very probable that it was a sort of casual, last minute arrangement. I don't think, no, I'm *sure* Wally wouldn't have deliberately left me out of any formal invitations that were being handed out. Though one never knows of course. I guess I wouldn't bank even on that. But the not telling me this morning, the pretending he hadn't seen the notices yet. . . . Oh, I see *why*. I even see that in a cock-eyed sort of way he was being careful to save my face. Those good manners I was talking about before. Though that is, it has always seemed to me, precisely the point where such situations give themselves away. Funny isn't it how people will deny till they're black in the face that a social snub is anything more than a trivial thing compared with matters of real importance; yet they'll always go to immense pains to conceal such 'trivial' things from you. I wonder why, if they're really so unimportant? Perhaps they are. I don't know. . . ."

His voice thinned and faded on the last words, then sank into silence. We heard the others beginning to converge on the dining-room for lunch.

"But I can't deny," he said at last getting up slowly and moving towards the dividing doors, "I can't deny that my pleasure has been spoilt. Stupid! Such a stupid, small thing when weighed against these." He tapped the bundle of cuttings lying on the bureau. "But it burns, Ruth. It chars my heart."

And the question which burns in my heart is: Did Peregrine do it on purpose? It must have occurred to Bernard too. Another betrayal? Is that the eternal equation of life? Must a triumph always be balanced by a betrayal? Is that the rule of life?

The afternoon was curiously empty. During the strain of these last weeks none of us seemed to give any thought to the day *after* the premiere. Jessica took her mother-in-law and Ginny out for some shopping, Bernard disappeared upstairs to his study and I was left to prepare their supper which I was leaving ready for them before I left for the theatre. I had asked a woman I knew in my "Danny" days to go with me; an actress, about my own age, not a bad sort. Though I had work to do, the sunny silence of the house oppressed my spirits and I was terribly glad when a little after four Bridget appeared. I had forgotten, in the stress of everything else, that it was her day for Ginny's lesson.

I asked her while she was waiting for Ginny to come in what she had thought of the play: though what I was really longing to hear was Hugo's opinion. Her enthusiasm surprised me. No less than the critics she had, with gamine shrewdness, "got the point" of what Bernard was saying immediately. Her response was such that for the first time I began to feel a flutter of excitement as I envisaged the possibility that the play, apart from being so rare in quality, might perhaps have the luck to strike some deep, contemporary chord of feeling at exactly the right time for tremendous, popular success.

"And what did Hugo think of it?" I asked as soon as I decently could.

"Sure and I can't understand that boy at times," she said. "There was meself going overboard from the minute the curtain went up and he sitting there stone cold. Of course I know everyone's opinion is purely subjective," she added hastily, "and either a thing hits you—bingo!—just like that —or it doesn't. I guess it's because he's pretty satisfied with his life really," she added shrewdly, "though I didn't realize that till recently. I mean, if you haven't been through the mill yourself you can't get what the play's about at all, can you? D'you know, I still can't believe it was our Bernard that wrote it. Can you? I must say my respect for him has gone up miles. Hugo and I were in the circle but we saw the family in the stalls—"

"So Hugo didn't like it?"

"Not really. In fact, to tell you the truth, I think he got a bit bored. I hope you're not, Ruth. You're going tonight aren't you?"

"I won't be bored," I said pushing my vexation and even anger with Hugo to one side for the moment.

Nor was I. My admiration only deepened as I sat there (the house practically full) to something like awe. Rounded out from the bones of the skeleton rehearsal I had witnessed I now saw the play in all its strong, delicate, lyric fullness and bloom. Though perhaps, it occurred to me afterwards, the most remarkable thing about it was its realism, the constant recognition it brought one to of those usually glossed over movements of the mind which result in our minute-by-minute consciousness. Every word we utter has, so to speak, its history. And in this sense *The Curtain* is a historical play; original, profound, numinous.

Felicity, Danny's actress friend, insisted on taking me for supper afterwards in return for the ticket. It was so long since I had been anywhere in town that I found I was enjoying myself greatly. She's a nice woman; very intelligent, divorced, perhaps a little embittered, but pleasant to be with.

When she told me she had had a small part in Peregrine's first West End production I asked her what she thought of him. She began to laugh. "At the beginning, the middle, or the end of the run?" she asked.

"Was there all that variation?"

She nodded briskly. "He's quite a boy, Peregrine. Quite a boy. But my goodness he's going to have to watch his step pretty soon."

"Why?" I said, extremely interested.

"He's going to run out of people. Well perhaps not yet awhile, there's always some new face or other coming up. But sooner or later."

"How d'you mean?"

"Well," she said. "For instance. At the beginning of the run we all adored him. At the end of the run we still adored him in a way (he's the sweetest boy) but we all avoided him. Now how can I explain . . . ? Well you see, it's like this. He's a truly kindhearted, warm, amusing boy. He's quite uninhibited about expressing admiration if he feels it. He's generous —and you don't always find that in the profession whatever the legend may be—and as I say, he's *sweet*. He truly is. He'd do anyone a favour. *But* (and it's a terrible 'but') cutting across all his virtues like a great, big, ugly, jagged crack across a china plate is this . . . how the hell can I describe it? . . . sort of irrepressible, incessant, conversational malice. It's not deliberate, it isn't that he's really malicious at heart— like some! It's more like a nervous tic that he can't control. I've been told he had a terrible stammer as a child. I suppose conversation came hard to him. So to make himself listened to he discovered that the easiest way was to bitch. And now he's lost the stammer but kept the habit. And he knows just how to use it. He's tremendously intelligent. The trouble is, he's so *young*. He's hardly out of the schoolroom even now. That first play of his was put on while he was still at Cambridge. He's a baby. And he hasn't learnt yet that even in the theatrical world—where my God! there's malice enough and to spare—you can go just that little inch too deep. So far, as fast as his wounding-remark-dropping has set one group against him, his entertainment value, his generousness, and that amusing Regency-Buck line has got him into another. But frankly I don't see how the supply is going to last forever."

"He seemed to like Bernard so much," I said cautiously, not wanting to give away what the young man's admiration had meant to Bernard.

"My dear, of course he did! That's one of the nice things about him. He adores modest people. He worships real talent. But he's got into the habit of wearing malice—like a dinner jacket (and for much the same social reasons)—and now he can't take it off."

When I got home it was to find the kitchen in minor uproar. Jakie had telephoned to say—to issue a curt declaration —that they were all going to Windsor with him tomorrow, that he was hiring a car, that he couldn't be bothered with English food and they were to bring supplies with them. All this at eight o'clock in the evening! When I came in I found the larder, the refrigerator and the store cupboard had all been ransacked by the old woman and the spoils heaped in confusion on the kitchen table.

"Are you going too?" I said to Bernard in an undertone after I had thanked him again for the tickets and congratulated him on the way the play had gone over. I was, still in my theatre dress, standing at the sink washing lettuces so that they didn't have to be done in a hurry in the morning. He gave me a warning frown to keep my voice low and said: "I have to this once or he'll take it out of everybody else."

Feeling (unfairly) rather impatient with him at my having to start all this work at that hour of the night—to say nothing of the shambles there'd be to clear up in morning—I said rather crossly: "Oh now, what on earth can he do?"

He shrugged. "I can't tell you what he'll do; that's something I've always found impossible to forecast since I can't force my imagination along the sort of paths his takes. I've tried often enough—" He broke off as his mother came in. Fortunately she was too distracted to give us the sharp, suspicious glance she usually gave on the rare occasions she actually caught us talking to each other. But when she had gone out again he said: "There's no knowing what he's capable of doing. But at least if I'm there it'll be one grievance less."

"What beats me why doesn't he stay away from you when he dislikes you all so much."

"Hah! why indeed? that's a question! Why, Jakie wouldn't give this pleasure up for anything. He's only regretting all the years he let go by when he hardly came near us. All that energy stacked up doing nothing except knocking over a couple of business competitors now and then and letting go at Thelma every once in a while just to keep his hand in. He only married her for her ten thousand dollars when he had to have the money good and quick" (I was pleased to note how right I'd been in my guess) "and now he's stuck with her. Anyway, that's how it was till a couple of years ago when suddenly, wham! it strikes him little brother's making something boil back there in Allegra and it's time for him to go home. Big scene. Big, big fatted calf. All those years wasn't a week went by Mama didn't weep for want of her Jakie, her beloved first-born. So you can imagine what happened when he showed up again. And what he didn't promise that first week! There was going to be a coronation for Mama! Queen of his heart she was going to be crowned—" We both looked round quickly as his mother appeared suddenly in the kitchen again.

"Just don't you bother with any more tonight," she said to me, "I'm sure you're tired. I guess I am. I'm going to bed right this minute. You coming Bernie?"

"Sure," he said. Then, as she hovered round waiting for

him actually to go out of the door with her, he shrugged his shoulders and went.

Well, at least this excursion to Windsor will leave me with most of the day free tomorrow. I wish I knew what to do with it. It is strange but, much as I thirst for Hugo, I do not particularly want him tomorrow. Or at least, I feel that now. The fact that he did not like the play, was actually bored by it (I have no reason to doubt Bridget's word on this—indeed it seems to me only too likely to be accurate) has shown me more than anything else could have done how far he is from the creature I had desired him to be. Oh dear! Oh dear! I keep saying to myself, rueful and disappointed; not so much in him as in the loss of a dream. It saddens me, Francis, I am perhaps absurdly saddened because—it seems—there are no marvellous boys left in our society. Oh, I suppose they *might* exist; in Camberwell or Nottingham. But somehow I have a feeling that they are all now extinct. No fiery imaginations transcending attic walls burn in our cities. Yes, there are still a few attitudes of this kind being struck no doubt. But there is no marrow in them; they are hollow, weightless, based on fashionable rebellion rather than genius. They're as quickly on television as any of their despised, cream-painted public figures: a lot of little, pernickety twig fires, no blaze. And Hugo isn't even that—just an oil stove with a neat little ring of blue flame.

My beautiful, third-rate boy. I do not want him tomorrow.

What do I want? I don't quite know. But there is a picture at the back of my mind struggling to come forward. It is a picture . . . I recognize it now. It is—of all things!—the stretch of promenade from Seacombe to New Brighton on the Wirral side of the Mersey. I don't think it means much to you; for some reason you and I hardly ever went "across the water." The fashion for doing so is as dead in Liverpool (amongst the middle classes anyway) as the Edwardian carriage processions in Hyde Park. The post-war, motor car age killed it. But in my childhood and adolescence (something you never wanted to hear about . . . why? why? I tried once to show you a house I had for a time lived in as a child, to explain to you my memories of it, and you turned sullen and walked away) in those years, as I say, it was the thing in our small, lower middle class range of amusements, to go there. How well I remember at this moment, though I had forgotten them for years, those short, sunlit journeys across the bright river. I remember the crowded decks of the ferry boats and the extremely deep, boxed in, slatted wooden benches on the decks and the little, barrel-shaped, wooden spools slung all round them. I recall the wide, gently moving, glittering patches of different colours on the water where the sandbanks came nearer to the surface; and the handsome shape of the Liver Buildings receding as we drew towards the other side. The boats would turn right round as they came up to the floating jetties at Seacombe or Egremont or New Brighton. The sailors would throw their ropes and make them fast, then they would slide back a part of the bulwark, lower a gangway and we would all troop on to the pier and up its slatted way with glimpses of river and sand between the rough planks. Then we'd be through the turnstiles and out into the busy, seaside world.

When I was at school it was still the thing to do to go to New Brighton on Sunday evenings in the summer and walk up and down the crowded esplanade. It was our Ascot where we dressed to kill in our best frocks and tried to get off with the boys. "Clicking" we called it: "fellers" we called them. "Clicking" like life itself was I think more innocent then than it is today—but drab, drab, drab. Palely diluted sex— there was no discrimination, just the difference in sex was enough—an occasional backwards glance and giggle, that was the peak excitement of our early teens. It was all mean and meaningless like the whole of lower-middle-class life in

the thirties. Extravagance was a poached egg on toast on
the veranda of the corner café. Glamour was the shopgirl
with the extra, lurid frill or curl. Backwards and forwards
we strolled along the wide, crowded promenade, past the
small booths, past the waxworks, the minute fairground,
the fortune teller, the "best" hotel, the bucket and spade
shops . . .

Going home, streams of people would flock down the
wooden piers and wait, densely packed in a sort of com-
pound behind a movable barrier for their turn to get on a
boat. Ah! those summer, Sunday evenings with the crimson-
streaked sunsets fading across the river and the huge,
penned, melancholy—raucous crowds waiting for the ferry
boats in the long, grey dusks . . . the lowering, tearing
sadness. . . .

No one who has not lived it can know the grey meanness
of provincial, lower middle class life at that time. However
good one's home—and mine was good of its kind—the
senses were starved of all taste, all grace. It was not so
much the lack of material things; it was the social climate
which was unbearable. No one who has not lived in it can
know or feel what this climate was like. No wonder it has
hardly been touched on by our writers; since to re-create it
would make wretched both writer and reader. And to make
it palatable with magical caricature would be to falsify.
Writers about this life—as Wells and Bennett knew—are
under enormous handicaps. For there was no *salt* there.
There was no humour—only unbelievably inept catchwords.
There were liars certainly—but no invention. There was no
quickness of understanding; only clumsy, sometimes hurtful, more often stupid remarks. The weak were utterly defenceless in that society since there was no *intelligent*
goodness; only, sometimes, good nature. Excellence amongst
the lower middle class of that time was suspected and de-
rided beyond all reason: the tone, the way to be, was muted,

grumbling, mingy. Our lives were like our kitchen-living-rooms in winter; gritty with the smoke from the blackleaded grates, luke-warm, draught-ridden. We struggled through our every day like so many badly cooked potatoes; half-raw. Everything was coarse, petty, tepid and, worst of all, ignorant. There was absolutely no knowing of what anything was really about.

Perhaps the true working class was different; I don't know. But even there I have an idea that novelist's convention has created a picture which did not really exist. For what is always forgotten is that the writers always, *always* portray the exceptions. For every touching, poor young couple making love outside a tenement front door there are thousands of poor, young couples who are grossly uncouth, insensible to love and only concerned, calculating or stupid, with sex, indifferent to politics, shrill over money, utterly devoid of appeal. The falsifications about them are of course no greater in degree than the falsifications about the upper classes. But the realities are harder to live among than anyone outside can ever believe.

Yet it was not a picture of those New Brighton Sundays which first struggled into my consciousness just now. It was—how could I have forgotten it for so long when I once knew every yard?—a sudden image of the stretch of promenade between Seacombe Ferry and New Brighton. It was to Seacombe that I used to go, playing truant from school on occasional mornings of early summer to walk the two miles along the front to New Brighton. Those curiously joyful, stolen mornings walking escaped and alone in windy, sparkling sunlight along the deserted, fresh esplanade . . . those are the hours which I suddenly—from who knows what subconscious necessity?—recall. And all at once I long with a kind of bleak passion to be walking there again with on my left the little, red brick houses primly gazing across the water at Liverpool, the shelters, the gates of the small, charming park, the 16th century cottage tea-room (where sometimes, with a sense of doing something classy and above my station, I would stop for coffee); and on my right the glittering river and green, slabbed rocks and the ribbed, hard sand. I ache to be there alone, young, in salt air, the handle of my heavy school case rubbing hard segs on my palm. That is where I should like to be tomorrow. And whom.

Ruth

✿✦✿✦✿✦✿✦✿✦✿✦✿✦✿✦✿✦✿✦✿

28th August

THE FRIDAYS have come and are—with one slightly carping exception—as enthusiastic about the play as the dailies. Thank heaven for that! Advance bookings are hotting up too. Though the real test will come at the end of the six weeks' season which is all the Vauxhall usually allows for preliminary runs. After that it's for the West End impresarios to decide whether to take it for a canter in theatreland proper.

What did I do yesterday? When they had all gone off I telephoned Hugo and asked him to have lunch with me here. The invitation was hardly out of my mouth when he accepted with most flattering alacrity. No! he is not so careful with his money that a free lunch attracted him! He was genuinely longing to see me again. When I opened the door to him he almost took me in his arms. With an effort he recalled to himself the brevity and casualness of our friendship so far. Even then he would I think have risked it but he is utterly uncertain of what my reactions would be. He does not want to risk losing me. I took heart from his timidity (how charming a quality when allied to beauty; how dimin-

248

ishing when not) and became playful, egging him on to dis-
close further distractingly adorable absurdities about
himself. I am prepared to believe Bridget when she describes
him as sullen and abrupt (and even intellectual or what
passes for such with her) at times. But he is not like that
with me. Indeed our conversations amuse me enormously
when I think about them afterwards. So much of them is
exactly like those between very small children. "My father's
got a gold watch." "Mummy's buying me a red coat with
little buttons all the way down." We exchange information
about ourselves in exactly that way. It is mostly information
about him since he no longer asks me anything about myself. To do him justice he did at first today. But when I told
him very briefly that I was separated from my husband he
asked me no more questions, only said, rather nicely I
thought: "Poor Ruth. That's not very happy for you."

"You must have known already, though? I'm sure Bridget
must have told you. She's such a chatterer."

"She's a very good sort," he said making me feel vaguely
reproved. "She's got a wonderful nature. She's a wonderful
friend."

I looked at him in exasperation. Didn't he know that girls
like Bridget are always wonderful friends to beautiful young
men? If she'd been a wonderful friend to someone like Bernard now . . . that would have been rather better evidence
of a wonderful nature.

"Why don't you marry her?" I said abruptly taking the bull
by the horns. To my great pleasure he blushed scarlet.
"That's rather a personal question," he said with an attempt
at dignity.

"Of course it is. That's why I'm asking," I said jovially.

"I mean I don't mean that *Bridget* is personal. I mean
there's absolutely no question . . . she's a wonderful *friend*,"
he said falling back on the same words.

"But not to marry?"

"No, not to marry," he repeated, relieved I had given him the phrase.

I looked at him consideringly wondering whether to try further shock tactics. "Have you a girl friend you do want to marry?" I said at last.

He looked embarrassed and murmured something about his having lots of friends, male *and* female.

"I *bet!*" I said mock-grimly. "I bet the girls queue up ten deep!"

He blushed even deeper, began to answer in an incoherent mumble then faded into silence.

"Well, if you haven't chosen one yet, then I shall choose one for you! Now! What kind of ideal girl do you have in mind?"

Trying, rather touchingly (he has very little sense of humour) to play up, he said, not looking at me: "I'm not very fond of 'girls' at all. I prefer women."

A marvelling, chuckling, ridiculous, rich happiness seemed to well up from my centre at these words. Sailing, in my delight, rather too close to the wind (since I am determined not to encourage my own heartbreak), I said: "Well that shouldn't be too great an obstacle to your getting married. Now all we have to do is to find the right *woman*, free, white and thirty-one, get you together and leave you to go down on one knee and say 'Darling, will you m—' "

"That's one thing I *don't* do," he said.

"What's that?"

"Use words like 'darling,' " he said lifting his chin and looking stubborn.

"Oh!"

"I just don't believe in using words like darling and . . . and all the rest of them," he said looking very stern and ridiculous.

"But why ever not?"

"They falsify relationships" (I saw where Bridget had

picked up her jargon), "by smearing sentimentality over what ought to be true feeling. If the emotion's genuine enough between two people it doesn't have to be expressed in sloppy words of endearment that don't mean anything."

I lifted my eyebrows, suppressed a rather hysterical chuckle, and said: "I think they're rather nice words. Don't you think if you want to please your ideal woman—when you find her!—that you ought to learn to use them? She'll almost certainly want you to. Now come on! Have a go! Just try saying the word."

He looked at me uncertainly.

"Oh come on," I said playing with fire. "Say after me: 'darling.' "

He made a tiny, impatient movement with his head which immediately took away some of my pleasure in the game. Nevertheless I went on. "Say: 'darling,' " I said teasingly.

He looked cross. Turning his head completely away from me he said, muttering: "I told you. I've never used the word in my life."

"Then it's time you started," I said firmly. "It's not so difficult! Two simple syllables . . . are they so hard? I know! We'll do it as we used to do at Drama School. *Now!* say after me . . . Dartington Hall."

My poor lamb! As I told you, he has hardly any sense of humour at all. (Neither have you! All your sympathies, in this account, will be with him.) My playfulness appeared to that narrow suburbanism of his which is never very far beneath the surface as something quite alien and suspicious. He couldn't get the hang of it at all; had no idea, as a more truly sophisticated young man would have had of how to respond. I think his spiritual home must be with you in Liverpool!

He gave an impatient exclamation and said: "Dartington Hall," in a quick mumble, humouring me.

"Right! No difficulty with 'Dar' was there? Come out quite easily. Now try the word 'lingering.' "

He clicked his tongue impatiently and said "lingering" very quickly then sat back and gave me a broad, tolerating smile. "Really!" he said. "Aren't we behaving just like two silly kids!"

And there it was again! The old, frustrated, screaming irritation I felt with suburban-provincial ideas about sophistication. This, *this* is the blind, rigid barrier one comes up against in raw societies. It is not the "highbrow" interchange of ideas that is missing so much, it is the knowing when and how to be silly with style. Dons can delight in nonsense, celebrated barristers can indulge their wives with baby talk, dukes and editors play incredible games at parties . . . but in the suburbs we mustn't "behave like silly kids."

I felt suddenly bored to death with Hugo and my own passion for him. Jumping to my feet I said: "Come on, I'll show you the rest of the house before you go." He followed obediently, commenting on the furniture and decorations with—I must be fair—some shrewdness (I could almost wish that the occasional flashes of perception which he sometimes shows did not occur since they unsettle without satisfying) but asking nothing about the family . . . increasing my suspicion that he has no real interest—despite his many "friends"—in people at all. When I opened the door of the spare bedroom Bernard uses as his study he gave but a cursory glance inside. Feeling irritated I said: "This is where something like genius works. Aren't you interested?"

"Genius?" he said with a faint air of surprise.

"Oh I forgot," I said standing rather tensely on the landing. "Bridget told me you didn't like the play."

"I didn't *dis*-like it," he said.

"But how could you not—but how can you be so mild about something so marvellous?"

"I didn't think it marvellous. I mean, it held my attention
—more or less—though I thought it a bit slack technically."

"Perhaps the theme didn't appeal to you?"

"Well I don't quite know what the theme was," he said
screwing up his eyes and looking rather helpless. "I mean . . .
there were these five people sort of bringing in the present
and the past simultaneously (I suppose that was the idea
wasn't it?) and having to make decisions about their future
and so on. Well that isn't very original is it?"

"Put like that it isn't," I said, angry and feeling helpless
in my turn for being unable to put into words just how
Bernard's originality did come in. "Look. Take a Chekhov
play. It's usually in three acts, the people act and talk in a
normal, undistinguished way, there's no fantastic or violent
happenings on the stage, there's no wild experiment with
technique . . . and yet what Chekhov gives us is a profoundly
moving and original view of what life is, what people are
like . . . and that's what Mr. Zold does too."

"Well maybe I'm just too stupid to see it!" he said with
such a tender, charming smile at me that my heart began
to pound with love again. We were standing in a shaft of
mellow, glowing sunlight on the landing outside the door
of my room which I had not yet shown him. We stood
there facing each other, his light, hazel eyes looking into
mine. He had seen the rest of the house. He must have
known that behind that last door was my bedroom. If I
wished he would follow me into it. But he was going—I saw
it in his eyes—he was going to leave it to me to make the
last decision . . . and the first gesture.

And this I was not going to have. In the silent, gentle,
remorseless tug of war that was going on between us we
were each trying to persuade the other to persuade us. Both
of us—he perhaps from sloth, perhaps from out of the
mild, untried vanity of his nature, I from deeper motives—
were leaving it to the strength of the other's passion.

I had left Bernard's door slightly open and I stretched out my hand to close it. Hugo's head jerked; his eyes followed my hand in acute sensitivity to my every movement, then back to my face. Yet still he left it to me. And I, in full knowledge that this might be the end, that I may be refusing something which might never be offered again, by Hugo or by life itself, nevertheless refused. I cannot say I know why, even now; for though I feared future grief it was not that which stayed me, but rather that I found myself in the grip of a curious, struggling obstinacy of feeling I could not combat. Out of the *ewigkeit* there had come upon me an astonishing, new sense that where, up till now I had rushed upon experience, only anxious to *have* it without regard to right or wrong, now I was not prepared deliberately to choose wrong. When I say wrong I do not mean Ten Commandments morality. I mean . . . I do not know what I mean.

Had Hugo made my choice for me, pushed me upon it, I would not have resisted. I do not think I have yet reached the strength of thrusting away delight should it be forced upon me. But I seem to have arrived, without my realizing it till now, at a strange, passive, half-way place along the moral road where I will not put out my energy to *seize* what I now know—though I cannot say how I have arrived at this knowledge—to be punishable experience.

"This is my room," I said and added gaily, "but I'm not going to let you see it! It's so untidy I'd be ashamed to!"

He held my eyes with his for one moment longer then said with an effort: "Just as you like, Ruth."

All of a sudden, though my determination did not alter, I felt that I could not endure that his eyes should not have looked on my room, my personal possessions, the bed on which I lay, the mirror into which I looked each day. Opening the door but keeping hold of the handle I said: "Two seconds! Just a quick look!"

He walked in, stood in the centre of the room, looked quickly round then joined me on the landing again. Gauchely (he should not have done it just then) he looked at his watch, then said: "My goodness, it's nearly four o'clock! I didn't realize it was so late. I'd better be getting along."

"Yes," I said leading the way downstairs.

"Thank you very much for a very good lunch," he said to me at the front door. His face was most beautiful in the sunlight.

"You're very welcome," I said, my heart breaking.

"See you soon," he said in his usual formula and went off down the path.

I went back into the empty, bright, afternoon house, my limbs so heavy with anguish that I could hardly walk. All I could tell myself in comfort was that sooner or later, whatever had happened that afternoon, he would be walking away from me down some path or other for ever. And . . . "Better sooner" was all I could say, holding the phrase to me like a shield. "Better sooner."

Ruth

✿✦✿✦✿✦✿✦✿✦✿✦✿✦✿✦✿✦✿✦✿✦✿✦✿

29th August

WELL AT LEAST the Almighty was good to me in one way since the family came back from Windsor the other day in such a state of war and disintegration as to absorb all my attention for the rest of the evening.

"Did you enjoy yourselves?" I asked innocently, going into the hall as they all trudged in. Only Jessica answered me. "It certainly is an interesting place that old castle," she said, but even her voice sounded abstracted as, with unaccustomed briskness, she hustled Ginny upstairs. The child had been crying. "Put her to bed right away," said Bernard.

Jakie who had been parleying with the driver of the big, hired car came heavily through the front door and called brusquely: "Bernie!"

Bernard, who had his hand on the kitchen door, turned his head.

"Here!" Jakie barked beckoning him over though he could easily have gone to him.

"Yes?"

"You got any dough? I didn't draw enough yesterday—"

"How much do you want?"

"Er . . . you got five pounds?"

"Five pounds?"

"Sure. I'll let you have it back tomorrow."

Irony in every line of his body Bernard counted five pounds out of his wallet into Jakie's exceptionally large, brutal-looking fingers; the nails like his mother's, square and milky. Without bothering about niceties, like saying "Thank You," Jakie went back to finish with the driver. Then he came back into the house again, and said to Thelma who had sunk down on to a chair in the hall and was sitting there passively: "C'mon!" She looked up startled and old Mrs. Zold who had been upstairs during the interchange about the money and was just descending called out: "Aren't you going to stay and have supper with us, Jakie?"

"Nah! Me and Thelma'll be getting along. We need a proper meal after those lousy restaurants. The hell with them; who'd they think they was pickin' on? Some sucker that don't know a dime from a dollar? Nah, we're goin'. Anyway, tell ya the truth whether you like it or not I've *had* my family for today. I reckon I've had just about as much as I can take. Spend money all day long, rent an automobile so you don't have to walk any place, take you to restaurants —and what do I get? *Moanin'!* That's what I get. I've had enough. Let's go. I'm starvin'."

"Why didn't you keep the automobile if you're in such a hurry?" said Bernard mildly.

"*Because, brother,* I wasn' goin' to let that chiseller take another nickel outa my pocket. Think I didn't know what he was up to? Fiddling the charge so he could make for himself on the side. No wonder he turns nasty coming home. Knew he couldn't get his cut, not with anyone like me around. We'll pick up a taxi at the toppa the road."

"The subway's not five minutes away—" began his mother ever ready to save money.

"Say, listen, Ma, I've had a bellyful today an' I'm tired. Get that? I'm tired. I'm not fighting my way onto no subway."

"We-ell," she said nervously with one eye on Bernard, "I, I guess we ought to say thanks for the trip out, Jakie. I sure hope you enjoyed it. It surely was interesting to see that castle and the river and all. Didn't you think so too, Jakie?"

"I told you! I seen it before," he said with a scornful, impatient movement of his great, gross body. "Think I never bin to Europe before! Lemme tell you something you don't appear to have took in. I bin to Europe *three times,*" he said, wagging his face within an inch of her. "*This is my third trip.* I'm no greenhorn that don't know his way around. I bin all over. France, Spain, Italy. . . . First time I came was in '48. I spent four months just travellin' around. Boy! was *that* a vacation. Yeah, '48 that was."

" '48?" said Bernard in a cool voice. "That was the year I had the accident and Mama was having trouble with her eyes. That was the year we didn't eat so good."

He stared calmly at his brother who had swung round to stare at him, his eyes going a dull, inflamed red.

"What're you trying to imply?" said Jakie, his face actually seeming to enlarge as his rage caught fire. The old woman pulling immediately at Bernard's arm was twittering about going into the dining-room, she was sure supper was ready and Thelma, still sitting on the hall chair her eyes half closed, was muttering something rapidly to herself.

"D'you want I should repeat it?" said Bernard trying to calm his mother's frenzied hand on his sleeve. "That was the year we didn't know which way to turn."

"Listen—"

"Jakie!" shrieked his mother suddenly as he started to approach Bernard, his eyes almost black-red with suffused blood. He stopped short, but not too close to where Bernard was standing, thrust his head forward and said: "That settles it! That wraps it up! You don't get me in this house again. If it weren't for Ma standing right there next to you I'd wade into you so you wouldn't be writing no more plays with that wise guy head of yours because I'd've knocked it off your shoulders. This time I'm really goin'. As far as I can get from as Goddammed ungrateful a set of chisellers . . . see if I ever spend another dime on a family that's nothing but a—" He let go a string of abusive remarks. Then he flung out of the house, almost kicking Thelma before him, and was gone.

He was hardly out of the door before his mother began weeping and bewailing and reproaching Bernard for having provoked him.

"*I* provoked him! Mama! What're you saying? In heaven's name get your proportions right. All I did was state a couple of facts he didn't want to hear. *That's all.* Do I have to not only take everything he cares to dish out but also protect him from any possible prick of his own conscience? Compare what I do with what he does. Take today's behaviour alone. Good Jesus Christ . . . *how much am I supposed to take?* Look! we've been out for a day before without him, haven't we? Didn't it all go off reasonably quiet and pleasant? We took food with us, we went comfortably on one of those green coaches, we had a day out. It was peaceful, wasn't it? It was *normal*. What happened today? *You* insist we take every high-priced can of food we got in the house, stay up late preparing the night before, pack everything . . . and what happens? Comes lunch-time and Jakie looks over everything we brought, then says *he's* off for a proper meal and leaves the rest of us sitting in that automobile in that shutaway, dusty parking lot for *one and three quarter hours* waiting for him to come back. Even the chauffeur was pitying us. We don't dare leave, *you* say, case he comes any minute and finds us gone. When he finally turns up he's fit to burst with temper because, so he said, he'd been over-charged in the restaurant. So who does he take it out on, finally? The kid! Ginny! eight year old Ginny. And why? Because when we did get on up to the castle she wanted to see the Doll's House—and that part costs sixpence to go in. I'd have taken her in myself the minute we saw it if he hadn't started creating so we all had to walk away before his screaming brought the cops around. Right! So we walk about, Ginny crying, till *he* decides he's had enough. So then we start looking for some place we can have tea. *How long* did we walk around with you dropping off your feet, half dead with exhaustion, till we found a cheap enough joint that he decided wasn't going to swindle him. *And what kind of a place was it?* Where you had to wash the cups with hot water from the water jug and wipe them on your handkerchief. But that still wasn't enough for your first born, was it—?"

He stopped. His mother who had been sobbing out huge sighs while he was talking had suddenly torn her hand from where he had been holding it urgently between both of his and crying, "I don't want to hear no more! I can't stand it! I can't stand it, I tell you!" had fled upstairs.

Jessica, who was always extremely sensible when it was a matter of keeping out of unpleasantness, had been busying herself with Ginny's supper which she'd taken up on a tray. She came down now and, coming into the kitchen where I had been standing, listening and watching through the open door, said to me: "I guess we'll eat now, Ruth, if it's all ready. I'll tell Bernie to go fetch his mother down."

What inducements, what exhausting arguments he had to use I do not know, but she came down, watery and resentful, to sit at the supper table. None of them spoke very much at first until, when they had nearly finished, Jessica said: "Ooh! what a blessing to have that voice out of my ears! If I were Thelma I'd have gone stark crazy by now. The way she puts up with him . . . it's something to see! What beats me is the way she sticks with him. You'd think she'd hate his guts by now. Sorry, Ma, I know he's your son and all, but I guess I'm entitled to say something once in a while. But the way he *treats* her . . . beats me why she hasn't left him long ago. She must *hate* him."

"She doesn't hate him any more than Mama does," said Bernard, "and for some of the same reasons. She admires him—just like his mother does. Don't you, Mama?"

His voice carried a bitter, grinding note I had never heard from him before. I saw his mother flush and raise her napkin to her lips.

"You've no right to say that, Bernie—" she began.

"No right!" he said with a look of suffering irony on his face. He struggled for one more moment to control his sense of bitter grievance but all at once it was too much for him. Picking up a knife he flung it with all his force back on the table. "*No right!*" he repeated. "And what Divine Right does he have that he should smear and ruin my life every time he touches it? When Papa died did he even come home for the funeral let alone the week's mourning? Three weeks later he comes over for one day to snoop around and see if he'd left any money anywhere he could get his hands on. He was *entitled* he said, to *claim his share*, he said. Like we hadn't been skinning ourselves to keep him in the Home. Remember Mama? You started preparing lunch for him but as soon as he knew his father hadn't had a dime to leave he upped and went. Wouldn't even give you the pleasure of staying for a meal, of feeling that your own son had come to see if you needed help—the way sons do when they're human beings. And that time it came up about me going to college and getting a degree . . . *no!* He comes over again hot foot, specially primed to get at me through you, nagged at you, blew himself into one of his great, synthetic, tempers at the idea of me, his two-bits brother, getting himself an education—and frightened you into talking me out of it. We could have managed it then, between us. It could have been done. But no, you had to let yourself be influenced—when you weren't even beholden to him for one red cent! That was the cool, almighty irony of it! He didn't even have the *right* to say a word. He gave us *nothing.* But you listened to him. Oh yes, you listened to him. Like you listened to him today in that café—"

"Bernie—!" said Jessica interposing for once between them.

"Oh you don't want to hear either!" he said, his voice high and violent. "You want to forget it too, don't you? You want to forget the picture of you and me and Ginny wedged in back of that table so we couldn't get out. And Jakie and Thelma and Mama sitting on the other, free side. And Jakie pulling out a handful of money to leave his lousy three cent tip. And spilling coins all over the floor. And sprawling back on his chair saying: 'You pick 'em up, Ma.' And she did it, by God! She did it! Went down on the floor picking up his Goddammed pennies for him before I could get out to stop her. *I told you not to!*" he suddenly shouted out at his mother.

Jessica said something to the old woman who was sitting at the table perfectly still, her face blank. She did not answer. She had, by an effort of will, made herself stone deaf.

Jessica got up and spoke to her again. Then, taking her arm she pulled her to her feet. "Come on, Ma," she said, "you'd best go to bed." She gave her husband a look and said: "Don't you know by now it's no use, Bernie? You're the one that's smart—haven't you learnt *that* yet? She'll never change. So you might as well get used to it. *She'll never change.*"

She took her mother-in-law, moving with a curious, stiff, dazed, goose step, upstairs and Bernard—as I had known he would—came into the kitchen. He sat down in the easy chair, his breathing harsh, his face agonized.

"Can I give you anything?" I said.

"No. No. Not yet. You go on in and clear. You can make me some tea when you've finished in there."

I went into the dining-room. When I came back into the kitchen his breathing was a little easier but his colour was still ghastly. I put the kettle on and began stacking the dirty dishes in the sink.

"And yet she listens to him," he said suddenly.

"Why?"

He attempted to shrug but was too weary to do more than sketch the movement. He sighed, a deep, tearing sigh.

"Or don't you know why?"

"Sure, sure I know. Two reasons. One; he's rich—"

"And you're famous!"

"Oh that!" He laughed shortly. "Believe it or not all that had gone out of my head. It's as though it has never happened. Strange, isn't it?" he said, his face lined and puzzled. "It was only two nights ago . . . the applause, the occasion, the achievement, the sense of success . . . and today, in my usual, everyday state of wretchedness, I'd forgotten all about it! It might never have happened. In fact I find it difficult to believe it did. You see how nothing counts against the day to day of living."

"All the same, to value his money so much above your achievement," I began rather angrily.

"No," he said, sitting up wearily to drink his tea. "How many times do I have to knock this into your head!" he said with the acerbity of fatigue. "You're making a mistake. She's not like that. In her heart Mama doesn't value the wrong things. It's just that she's been at other people's mercy so much she can't help giving first place to what would raise her in their eyes. If you live in a society where only the dollar counts—and when you've always stood socially as nothing— then you value money, *need* money, because without it you won't be accepted. I've told you this before," he said still irritable. "Don't be so damned dense. It's *not the money,* it's the respectability, the acceptance, the position in society which it represents. Life with my father made her long for respectability, *long* for it. She wants respectability like Becky Sharp wanted it. It is her passion. My 'fame' as you call it; that isn't the same thing at all. Indeed, it is an embarrass- ment. It's . . ." he shook his head as if to clear it, "it's alto- gether too much for her, for what she wants. I've overshot the mark. Her modest wish is to be ordinarily happy, safe within reasonable, social limits, normal, *respectable.* Play- wrights aren't *normal.* They're a useless luxury, a mink coat to a housemaid, in our world. (D'you think her neighbours back home admire me? They're frightened of me!) But money . . . that's normal."

"You said there was another reason why she listens to your brother."

"Yes," he said. "Yes." He paused then said with a kind of hesitant shyness; "I suppose, because he was . . . born in love. There is no getting over the accidental timings which affect our lives. She came as near, I suppose, as she ever came to happiness with my father at the time of Jakie's conception and birth. So that whatever he does he is as- sociated for ever with the colour of the rose. She refuses to believe that the rose tint faded long ago, that then was the fragile illusion and everything since has been reality. She needs to believe in good; that the long greyness is temporary, a mistake, that the time of the rose is bound to return. *He* is associated with it; and *I* am associated with humiliation and pain. There is no educating of such instincts. They are more powerful than any systems of justice we can devise. Because of them whatever my brother does she will never let herself know. He can hit her; he nearly did once . . . he made to hit her in front of me. But when I went to hit *him* she ran between us, clutched *my* arm, held *me* back, restrained and implored *me* . . . she dared not let herself admit his behaviour to her consciousness; she could not stand the knowledge. She has a delicacy of heart that you would not believe; only it has been bruised, bruised, almost to insensibility. You do not know her, Ruth. You know only her silliness, her sometime injustice, her ignorances. But I know her mutilated goodness, her crippled innocence which cannot and will not bear the knowledge of hopelessness and wrong. She must close her eyes in order to live."

"So you must bear her knowledge for her?"

"I try. But sometimes—being no more than human—I fail. I try reason—though I know very well that reason quite simply does not apply. It is like using marmalade to polish shoes. It does not fit the task. If only life *were* amenable to reason . . . but reason fails; and sooner or later we shall all have to accept this fact. Some other method will have to be worked out to deal with the nature of man. Though what it will be I do not know."

I had finished the dishes and was wiping my hands on the roller towel. Looking over at him I saw that he was leaning forward, his hands loosely on his knees, his face jowly, puffy and exhausted, his gaze inward. And all at once I felt a vast, scathing impatience with him. "Don't!" I wanted to shout at him . . . and, "Do!" Don't just accept and analyze and try to understand. *Do.* Do something to life and yourself. *Make* your fate.

He looked up and caught my eye and—as ever—my thought.

"Yes. I know," he said with an ironic twist of his lips. "This is the point where I too feel impatient with myself. 'Doing' is always more attractive than 'not doing.' Even when it's not a very pretty sight. It's more natural, more in harmony with our deeper instincts. The very absurdities of 'doing,' the pushings and indignities and contrivances always seem more valid than any amount of dignified—but fatal—acceptance. (I'm still analyzing! Oh well . . . !) D'you think I too haven't a sort of respect for grubby persistence, that I don't recognize that a fierce, stupid, clinging, howling grip on life is a kind of proof of our indestructibility? But," he lifted one shoulder, "*ce n'est pas mon métier*. As it is, for instance, Jakie's. Whatever else he is he's consistent in his behaviour with what he *is*. For that matter in my own way so am I. But he's much luckier than I am since what he is *appeals*—believe it or not! Sophisticated people will pretend that it doesn't, they will invent other reasons for tolerating Jakies—as they did for tolerating Hitler, some of them. But the truth is that the coarser and more brutal the egotism the greater its magnetism for everybody's subconscious. Naïve people hardly even pretend about this.

"As for 'doers' one of their charms is that they seem to find solutions to their problems. (I say 'seem' but perhaps that's patronizing. Maybe they even do.) But the weapon of 'doing' is one which I am unable to use. Not unwilling . . . *unable*. I am not built for combat; it is against my nature. So that I cannot alter my ills any more than I can change the weather. I cannot alter or bypass the outrageous fact that so often it rains in what should be my summer. I may be affronted—or saddened—by such weather, but I can do nothing only live on and through it. There is—for such as I—no escaping the rains of July. And I suppose—in a way —I do not really want to escape them; since they keep me living and green. They are necessary to my crops. My slow insufficiencies for life are not, after all, so killing for my work. My griefs are my food. I am learning to hold them to my heart since without them I would be nothing. Without them I would be dry."

He left me a few moments later looking less strained but terribly tired. And I am left here thinking of what he said —and acknowledging unwillingly its truth. The sword which fits our hand is the only one we can successfully employ. Other people's swords are useless.

Though I do not ordinarily think of it, I am reminded just now of his Jewishness. I have an odd feeling that he personifies in himself the whole role of the Jew in the historic life of the world's soul; that he is obliged (not by choice but rather by a mystical necessity) to exemplify the suffering, the humane, the pacific, the enduring, the compassionate strands in the composite human nature of society. That these are mistaken for cowardice, lack of will, failure of energy . . . the misunderstanding is an intrinsic part of the very role itself.

At least Bernard knows his own climate. I do not yet know mine. I can only wait through my present weather with its treacherous, April-Hugo gleam for the inevitable change of sky.

Ruth

❀❀❀❀❀❀❀❀❀❀❀❀❀❀❀❀❀❀❀❀❀

30th August

WHAT, I wonder, did you do with yourself today? Some gardening perhaps if it was as warm and sunny in Eversley Road as it was here. How *do* you fill your time, Francis? Now that I am not there to frame it for you. Perhaps you were out with the photographic club or sketching somewhere in Cheshire? Or you went on a day excursion to see your parents? How they must hate me. Poor Francis. Poor

Francis. Poor me. Poor everyone. How the gross unhappiness of all our lives overwhelms me. I try sometimes quite desperately to think of someone I know who can reasonably be described as happy. I would never begrudge such a state; I only wish I could find it—somewhere. One happy creature —and I would believe the condition attainable. But I do not see it.

If only the weather were grey! But the sun shines on and on. I am melancholy in this perpetual sunlight. If I could afford the eccentricity I would be like—was it Aubrey Beardsley?—who always kept his curtains drawn against it and lived for the night. Sunshine is only bearable to crisp natures, to the vastly occupied or to children. I have never really liked it. Perhaps subconsciously I too prefer rain in July.

Strangely, I have a feeling today for Eversley Road. It is that curious affection we sometimes feel towards even a miserable past. The act of re-creation in the memory seems to make holy our every experience. Though there are some which are brutal or shameful at the time.

Brutal is the word for one of Bernard's reviews in the Sundays. It fills me with rage every time I think of it. Most of today's notices were good. One of the heavies was beautiful in its understanding, perfect in its comprehension of the "time of day" element in the play. But another one was murderous—within its two short paragraphs at the tail of a long, insipid notice about the insipid musical which also opened during the week. Infuriated, it seems, by the lack of political content in this "play about ordinary people" the critic, Peter Spaid, took it into his head to complain peevishly, in nasty, stabbing little sentences about Bernard's entire conception which he called—the least of his phrases—"ethically juvenile." To hell with him. He also referred quite gratuitously to the fact that the author was a Jew and an American with a sort of implied query of "Who let *you* in?"

Bernard took it quietly enough. His mother seized of course on the Jewish reference and made a four-course meal out of anti-Semitism. The really vocally indignant one was Jessica who, with her occasional, rather touching loyalty, musically defended her husband at great length if without much insight to me all the time I was preparing the Sunday dinner. I only gave half an ear to what she was saying since I was waiting for the telephone to ring. I was expecting Wallace Grey, Peregrine perhaps, or some members of the cast, to ring him up, to congratulate him on his rave reviews, to commiserate or reassure or sympathize in some way over the Spaid knifing. And though he said nothing I knew that Bernard was waiting too.

He waited, all through the sunny, Sunday morning, sitting about with newspapers in the living-room and, after lunch, in the courtyard, resisting all suggestions that they go out somewhere, till after five o'clock. Then he came into the house and said he would take Ginny for a walk. When they came back he deliberately refrained from looking at the telephone message pad. I came into the hall and said quickly to cut short his suspense: "I wonder if the phone's out of order, Mr. Zold? I've been expecting a call all day but it hasn't rung once."

"Better call the exchange and ask them to test," he said and went upstairs.

I was so angry that I found myself uttering idiotic, schoolgirl invective under my breath. "The beasts! The beasts!" I kept muttering to myself, seething as I remembered that even the day after the premiere it had been he who in his excitement had rung up every one of *them*. Not one of them had troubled to call him. He had not noticed this at the time and neither had I. But now it came back to me—as it must have done to him; as it must even have occurred to his mother and his wife. For once neither of them said anything. But for the rest of the evening the cold omission, the absence of anyone at all from the world outside to join with them in either their pleasure or their hurt weighed like a sad and heavy stone on each of us. Even my anger failed, turning, as theirs had done, to something worse. We were, all of us, ashamed. They were ashamed (and I felt it with them) of their isolation, their lack of friends, the uncaring, almost uncanny, silence with which his fate, good or bad, had been met. Whatever the ultimate impact of the play, he himself had failed. It was this fact which lay over us all like a layer of smouldering, gritty cinders. He had failed with this society, too. New world, old world, lively America, civilized Britain . . . neither cared anything for him as a human being in society. He had failed the integration test. There was no place for one like him; and no friends, no friends.

This was the reality behind achievement, behind public praise, behind the discussions of his work which must certainly be going on somewhere, behind the "name in the papers." He had held out his play like a man holding up a poster, saying: "This is me. This is what I am really like." And they had stopped to admire the poster all right—but had gone on ignoring the man.

There is something wrong, wrong, wrong with the cultural class of this country. What is the matter with them all that all they want is surface personality? A man like Zold comes amongst them and they treat him as if he were a hog among gazelles. Is there no curiosity left in them, no good-mannered warmth, no sympathetic comprehension of his difficulties, no generous overlooking of his inadequacies, no acceptance of diffident difference, no wanting to know more of the delicate springs of high talent behind the awkward mask? It seems not. And that being so I am ashamed for *them*, for our society, for our trivial, lazy, dried-out world.

Ruth

❂❂❂❂❂❂❂❂❂❂❂❂❂❂❂❂❂❂❂❂❂

31st August

WELL at least we were spared Jakie yesterday. But he walked in this afternoon, Thelma trailing at his heels as usual, as though no threats, no abuse had passed his lips only a few days before. He was apparently in a good mood; which showed itself in him in a kind of coarse energy, his loud voice braying all over the house. The mood of course had been engendered by the Spaid review which he had cut out and brought with him. He read it aloud, rolling some of the phrases triumphantly round his tongue and repeating them several times until even his mother said, trembling: "If you don't stop that this instant, Jakie, I swear I'll run out of the house and not come back. It's . . . it's cruel mean," she said almost inaudibly, glancing towards the courtyard where Bernard, who had not said one word to his brother, had gone to try and escape from the sound of that voice.

"Say, Ma, can't you take a joke?"

"It's not a joke," she said and went on with considerable bravery: "You're not being fair. You're just not being fair. Bernie had the most wonderful notices in the other papers. Why'nt you read those out loud?"

"The others!" he said. "Pooh! Second raters. *This* is the leading Sunday newspaper in this country."

"That's just not tr—"

"Everybody knows, what this paper says *goes*. Think I don't know what's influential and what ain't in this country? This guy Spaid: he's the leading dramatic critic in *Europe*. He knows what's what in the theatre. You can't kid me. My, he sure gave your smart boy a going over, all right, all right. Yeah. Me. I wouldn't be surprised if the play folded in a week. You mark my words, Thelma! You heard me. You're a witness. It'll come off in a week. You mark my words. Say don't we get any tea?"

His mother, jumping nervously, came into the kitchen to ask me to hurry up with the tea and to put out every cake they had in the house for Jakie's inspection. When I took the tray in he was sitting sprawled in an armchair, the cat, Binkie, was on his knee and he was playing with it, giving him his big knuckle to bite. When his mother told him to put the animal down and go wash his hands before touching any food he didn't answer, only went on playing, making Binkie leap and clutch at his fingers. "See that!" he said admiringly, watching the cat's determined, ferocious leaps, "see that energy! See the life in that animal! Got more spunk than a dozen men I know of. That's what gets me. Spirit! Life! That's what counts in this world. That's how to get what you want—and keep it!" He gave the cat a piece of cake then tried to get it away from him again, Binkie, all claws and vibration, resisting with absolute will till Jakie, giving up, let him keep it. "What's mine is mine!" he said. "That's his motto. And that's mine." He made to touch the cat approvingly under the chin but suddenly, for no apparent reason, Binkie hunched himself together, put out a vicious paw and scratched a long tear down his sleeve. Then, with a quick duck of his head, the cat made for his hand but Jakie caught him in time and threw him to the floor.

"Jakie! Did he scratch you, Jakie?" His mother came fussing over but he pushed her away saying, "Nah. He didn't touch me, the bad-tempered little beast . . . Say, what'd he go do that for? I didn't do nothin'."

He looked over at the cat as the animal sat a few feet away from him, looking in his direction with a curious expression of malevolence in its green eyes; an expression of sudden, shocking hurt on his own gross face as he realized that even the cat disliked him.

"Will you please go and wash your hands, Jakie," his

mother repeated firmly and—somewhat to my surprise—he rose and did so. I saw that there were certain areas in which she still retained a rudimentary authority over him; in health for instance. And that that authority, exercised against such odds, was yet another cause of his ascendancy over her. The occasional bossing he allowed her tasted wonderfully sweet. Not all Bernard's tact and care and attention compared in pleasing with Jakie's rare submission to her commands.

Conversation over tea—with Bernard sitting completely silent and absorbed in a newspaper, his brother casting furtive, resentful glances at him—was sticky. Even Jessica's melodious flow was dammed and made jerky by her brother-in-law's habit of abruptly bursting in on every remark no matter who was talking or what was being said, with violent interjections which after a time dried everybody up. Having thus deliberately created his own desert he then became bored with its emptiness and complained loudly about the dullness of his company.

For some reason this stung his mother far more than anything else he had either done or said. Flushing angrily, she began, in an attempt to prove him wrong, to talk. No great conversationalist at the best of times, wretched with nervous tension, in the attempt to impose some consequence on her ramblings she hit as usual on the grumble. Not for grumbling's sake but to fill the silence, to make a noise like life. She grumbled at their clothes, at the weather, at the furniture in the house, at London Transport . . . most of all she grumbled at English food.

"You just never tasted such stuff in your whole life," she said, talking about some ready-made cole slaw we had once bought from the delicatessen. "You should have tasted it, Jakie."

He yawned, a great, cracking yawn; (he can do nothing, make no gesture without a touch of insult).

"I just can't imagine what they thought they were making. We certainly don't fix it that way back home. It was all *wrong*," she said persistently and (I must admit) boringly.

Bernard looked up and, breaking his long silence, said irritably: "It's not wrong, Mama. It's just the British way of doing it."

"No one's going to tell me that's the right way to make cole slaw."

"It's right for *here*. They like it that way here. It's not *wrong*: only different," he said patiently.

"Don't tell me about cooking, Bernie. I was making cole slaw before you were born. In the first place you just don't slice cabbage that way. It's got to be very fine cut—"

Jakie gave a loud, artificial snore to indicate bored contempt with their conversation.

"*You* cut it fine. They don't. Why can't you get it into your head that what you do isn't the only right way. You shouldn't be critical at differences. You should be *interested*."

Yes, I know the argument was a trivial and boring absurdity. But the essence of it was not absurd at all. What Bernard was trying to do was save her from the megalomania and narrowing insularity of old age. Even at this late hour he was still trying to open and liberalize her mind, to extend it beyond herself, to give her more resources not less.

Jakie, opening one eye, said with heavy irony: "Fact is, Ma, you're not clever enough for Bernie these days. You wanna educate yourself a bit before you talk to him."

Flushing and taking him dead seriously (in his shrewd, peasant way he had poked at a secret resentment of her own) she said: "My younger son can think that if he likes. Nobody's going to stop him. If his mother's conversation isn't good enough for him time he went elsewhere."

"And what about your older son, Ma? Don't he rate a word of appreciation? I'm no egghead pickin' on you every other word. I'm just an ordinary, commonsensical guy."

"You're ten years older, Jakie," she said still ridiculously taking him seriously. "It's natural you should have more experience in life. I'm not blaming Bernie for thinking he knows it all. He'll learn by and by. Give him time," she said with absurd patronage, "he'll find out a thing or two 'bout life."

The week's papers which had contained so many columns of praise for Bernard's knowledge of life, his profound and original insights into the nature of human experience, were still strewn all over the room. Yet, with the exception of Bernard himself (and me, listening and watching as usual) they had all completely forgotten them! His family—it was incredible but it was true!—no more related his achievement to *him* than the world in general had done.

"I suppose you never contradict Mama, shout her down, humiliate her," Bernard said, opening his mouth at last out of sheer exasperation.

"I got a right to speak my mind," said Jakie lumbering himself up in his chair, spoiling for a row, his boredom gone.

"Yes? You got a special dispensation from the Pope to give out kicks?"

"I'll tell you what right," Jakie gritted out, scrambling up with his gross, rapid, fat movements to glare at his brother. "I got three hundred thousand dollars worth of rights!"

"Oh! sure! The dough!"

"That's right, *brother*. The dough. You show me better rights, that's all."

"No one has *any* 'rights' to humiliate any other human being."

"Spare me the philosophy, bud. When I want your two bit sermons I'll ask for them."

"Now, Jakie," said Jessica intervening mildly, "you ought to know that money isn't just everything in this world. There's other things—"

"You name 'em."

"Why . . ." she said hesitating. Her eye fell, belatedly, on the newspapers. "There's Bernie's career for instance. . . ." Jakie's thick mouth twisted into an expression of utter contempt and she added hastily, "and there's health—"

"I'll tell you somethin' you don' appear to know," he said sitting down again and crossing his legs vindictively. "You know what health depends on? Money! Pure and simple. Money! Wanna know why I get sick to my stomach so often to this day? I'll tell ya—"

"Say, Thelma," said Jessica with her usual blandness in escape tactics, "you want to come up and see the bracelet I was telling you about? It's just the cheapest thing. And it's so *pretty*."

"Sure," said Thelma jerking out of the semi-conscious state which was her last line of retreat from her husband.

The two women were hardly out of the door before Jakie was repeating after an elaborate, bad-tempered pause at the interruption: "You wanna know why I got ulcers? I'll tell ya. It's because we ate cheap when I was a kid. Remember the square inch of rotten meat we—"

"Jakie!" his mother said clenching her fists to her chest in anguished outrage, "how can you? How can you say . . . there was times I starved myself—but never my children. *Never my children.* When did I buy bad meat? How you can sit there and—"

"Ah, cut it out, Ma," he said uneasily knowing he had gone too far.

"Dog!" said Bernard drawn at last into open war. He jumped to his feet. "Dog! to sit there and accuse Mama when you know as well as I do what she went through to keep us all alive—Get out of the house!" he shouted suddenly. "I can't stand any more of this. Go on! Get out!"

Jakie rose slowly and deliberately and putting an expression of profound injury on his face said: "O . . . K. O . . . K." He nodded his head conveying slow, deep threat. Then he looked at his mother. "You want I should go, Ma?"

With her right hand, in a gesture of absolute panic, she

pulled desperately at the ring finger on her left, her elbows held out stiffly at right angles to her body. She opened her mouth to speak but Bernard forestalling her said: "Let him go, Mama. D'you hear? Let him go."

Looking at Jakie she said: "Let me alone, Bernie. Let *me* speak."

"Mama—"

She turned and gave him a cold look, her panic all of a sudden gone. "I'll speak to Jakie," she said.

"You can't," he said, "you never have and you never will. Let me. Once and for all, let me."

"*Will* you leave me alone," she said moving her shoulders pettishly.

"I want to protect you!" he cried out suddenly in a tone of agony.

It should have moved her. But instead, incredibly, she grew angry with *him* and, Jakie forgotten (he was listening to the argument between the two of them with a grin of glee on his face) flounced, grew sulky, would not listen; and finally attacked him. "You're one to talk about my giving in to your brother. What about yourself? Did you take Ginny in to see the Doll's House or not?"

He lifted both his hands and shook them slightly, saying half to himself: "How can I . . . ? Look, Mama . . . the situation was such . . . I had to make a choice . . ."

"What choice?" she said scornfully. "You couldn't have slipped off with her and taken her in?"

"And left her with the idea that her father's so subservient that he has to hide and scuttle from his own brother? I've suffered from that kind of conditioning all my life. I've been crippled, *irreparably damaged* by such indignities. I'm trying to save *her* from them. Which was worse for her at Windsor? To take away her treat? Or to expose her to the spectacle of her father being furtive and undignified? Those are the kind of damned decisions—and not only about Ginny—that

I have to make every hour of my life. Not between good
and bad—dear God in heaven if only it were that simple!—
but between indignity and saving my self-respect. How
many times do I support *you*—at what cost to myself!"

"Who asks you to?" she muttered angrily. "Keep your support. I don't want it. I lived my life without it for long enough.
I guess I can go on that way."

"*What* way—" he started then shut up. Screwing up his
eyes in pain and hopelessness he turned away.

And yet—for all Bernard's love and pity and sense of
outrage on her behalf, for all his attempts to help her—I
see that in some ways she was right. In wanting to fight her
battles for her he was undermining her fiercely held on to
belief in herself. However incompetent, however fumbling,
she had fought through life in her own way, she had endured, she had survived.

"Quite right, Ma," said Jakie. "Time you told that son of
yours—"

"What have I done in my life to deserve all this?" she
cried out suddenly with a wild movement. "What happiness
have I had at any part of my life that I should have no peace
even now? Better I should have had no children at all than
they should tear me in half between them."

"There should be no tearing in half, Mama," said Bernard
in a tone of low, controlled tensity. "Only take sides with
what is right. That's all you have to do. Open your eyes and
see what's right and what's wrong. See who suffers and who
causes suffering."

"*You* talk of suffering!" said Jakie abruptly. "You! What
d'you know about it? You wanna be told a thing or two, baby
boy. I've kept my mouth shut long enough all these years.
Now *you're* gonna hear a few things you don't know about
this family. You're gonna know about my last years at home
before I lit out on my own. And not before time—or I'd've
gone nuts too!"

His mother made a sudden, arrested gesture then stood stock still, the colour draining from her face. Then, cocking her head in a desperate attempt at diversion she said: "I think that's Ginny at the door, come back from over the road." No one took any notice.

"*Now. I'll tell you*," said Jakie. "*I'll tell you* about suffering. I'll tell you about being a kid of fifteen with a crazy father to go after whenever he broke loose. I'll tell you about, havin' to go lookin' in gutters all over the neighbourhood, nights, till I found one he was lyin' in—and bringin' him home, babblin' and screamin'. Yeah. Remember Ma? Remember?" he said, boring the word into her with no regard for what the recollection might do to her. "Screamin' all the night through. But that was only the start, wasn't it, Ma? There was other things besides that. Things that wasn't so good, what with the neighbours an' all. Sat'days, when the other kids was at the ball game," he said to Bernard, "I was takin' him to hospital to have his 'injections.' We was tryin' to save him from being committed, see.

"How old were you when all this was goin' on? Five? Six? Seven? What did *you* know? *You got off light, bud.* You never had to hold your raving father down in the middle of the night while Ma ran for the doctor, didya? You don't like me, do ya? Well, you're not the only one. There's a lot of people around don't like me." He turned his head suddenly, from side to side a wildly vacant, bewildered look on his face. "But if I'm not popular I know the reason why. An' I'll tell you for why for free. You don't want no fancy psychology to explain *me; ever.* Them nights was my psychology. They was my college trainin'. I got my education all right, all right. That's why!"

He paused, then sank his bullish, brooding head into his shoulders. And I saw that at the heart of that graceless egotism lay a seething molten core of injury and ignorance and shame at the ugliness of life. I saw that he regretted and

278

was blindly appalled by his own behaviour, bewildered by the whole, dreadful shortage of love and respect. Almost I saw the tremble away, the terrified, averted head from the knowledge of the uselessness of money.

Bernard had taken a pencil out of his pocket and was pressing the blunt end into the centre of the cleft between his lower lip and his chin. His head bent forward he was looking at Jakie from under his eyelids. He glanced at his mother who was sitting down now absolutely immobile on an upright chair, her face turned to the wall, then back at his brother again.

"D'you think I was born blind and deaf?" he said at last in a quiet voice. "D'you think, young as I was, I don't recall . . . All right! So you bore the brunt of it. For a time. But I bore the *fear. I listened to those screams too.* I saw Mama's face—" he looked over at her again but she sat on, still as stone, her face still turned to the wall, "when she'd been with him. I remember the night—after you left home but before he was put away—when she had to wake me in the middle of the night and we both had to get out of the house he was that violent. Mama went for the doctor and I stood shivering in the porch, in the dark, in the rain, the sounds of smashing and destroying coming from the house . . . and then we went to those Winebergs for the rest of the night and all the weeks following till we got him committed at last."

"The pity," broke in his mother suddenly, talking in a soft voice to the wall. "The pity! The pity!" she repeated. "The degradation was bad enough. Keeping out on the streets all day without a cent in my pocket till Bernie was out of school. Daytime you're in the way in other people's homes. That's something I learned that summer. Couldn't go near my house while *he* was there, couldn't work, couldn't get my machine. No clothes. He'd ripped up what few I'd had. Six weeks that hot summer I had to go out on the blazing streets in my heavy old winter coat; I'd no dress fit to be seen. We ate charity. Oh they were good, them Winebergs, I guess. Bernie never went hungry in that house. But the pity, the explaining while we lived with them . . . 'Phil Zold's wife,' to any of their friends that called. And then I'd get the looks. Will I ever forget those looks! Pity! That's what I got from those people. They were good," she said, her voice roughening, "but ignorant, common people. They were low-class folk, those Winebergs. They took us in and they were kind enough. But they were low class. They'd always been lower class than my family. Coarse. That fat Dorothy with her yelling laugh and her dirty nails and her sleazy underwear. And then all of a sudden there I was, down near the bread-line, right down at the bottom with my child. Lower than them. Taking their charity. I guess they kind of liked that in a way. Folks like despising; it makes them feel good. I tried to pay back; I did their washing for them. And sometimes for the neighbours. I'd take Bernie and hope they'd give us both a meal."

She turned her head at last and looked over her shoulder, at Bernard, at Jakie—who, all the time she had been talking had been attempting to break in, fidgeting, tapping, looking at his watch, anything to stop himself hearing.

"So if it's suffering you want to talk about, I guess I got high marks in that examination. I've passed with honours. You're not in the same class with me, neither of you. So I don't want to hear no more."

Her quiet, flat voice ceased and there was a moment of silence in the room filled with pain. Then Jakie, the twist of vanity in his nature unable to bear it, deliberately destroyed her moment of dignity. Letting out a loud, coarse snort he said: "My oh my! The tragedy queen! You wanna get Bernie to cast you in his next pro-duction, Ma!"

But she had spent her life being slapped, and only said: "Bernie, you better go fetch Ginny from across the road. It's time she had her supper and went to bed."

When Bernard had gone Jakie said with guilty truculence: "We better be going too, Ma. I'll just call Thelma down."

"Hey!" he bawled going into the hall and standing at the bottom of the stairs. "Thelma! we're goin'. Make it snappy, I wanna eat."

The two women came down and Bernard came back with Ginny just in time to hear Jakie say to his mother, one hand clutching his chest: "You know something, Ma, I don't feel so good. You any idea who's a good doctor in this town? I don't wanna alarm you, Ma, but I don't feel so good these days. I bin told I gotta take it easy. So, *with your permission*," he said with a suffering, heavy-invalid air, "I won't be comin' around for a day or two. I can't take these scenes any more. Too much for me. They make me ill, Ma, and that's a fact."

"Just as you like," she said indifferently.

His eyes widened with anger but managing to control it he stepped with a stiff, invalid's step to the front door. "So long then," he said indifferently in his turn without a backward glance and, leaning showily on Thelma's arm, trudged down the path. His mother and his brother watched them go, the old woman's face expressionless, Bernard's ironic, almost smiling. Then, putting his arm about her shoulders, he drew his mother inside and, shutting the front door, led her into the living-room.

"You ready to eat?" he said sitting her down and making her comfortable with cushions.

"Soon," she said mechanically. "When it's fixed."

"Ruth," he called in through the dividing doors, "we're ready if you are."

"I'm just setting the table," I called back. "Won't be a minute. Everything's cold so you can start right away soon as I've got everything on."

"Fine," he said. Through the dividing doors I saw him standing behind his mother's chair and rhythmically stroking the straight, grey wisps of hair back from her forehead and face with firm hands. "That better?" he said.

"Yes, Bernie," she said. "Your hands feel good. So cool."

She rubbed her closed eyes and he immediately put his palms coolly and firmly across them. "All right?" he said.

"Yes, Bernie. Yes, son," she said. And, taking his hands from her eyes for a moment she smiled backwards at him, keeping her hands on his as they came down again across her vision, interposing a peaceful dark between her and a world which, it seemed, could not forgive her for being. It was all at that moment that he could do.

Yet I cannot help wondering if he—or any of us—can be sure that we are wise to make any attempt to shield another. For who is to say what experience is for? If, with Jakie for instance, the spectacle of misery and madness brought some kind of pitiable ruin to his nature, with Bernard that same experience brought him to strength; and beyond that, to art; to the creation of a great and teaching beauty. How can we prophesy the fruit of experience? How can we know the end of all that we endure?

Ruth

❂❂❂❂❂❂❂❂❂❂❂❂❂❂❂❂❂❂❂❂❂

10th September

THERE HAS BEEN no word from Hugo: nor, I know, will ever be again. I swim in and out of common sense. *This is a good thing* I tell myself those moments when I am busy and at peace and the strong thoughts of him are diminished to no more than faint, pleasant wisps of memory; when I am deeply grateful to be free of the problem of him. But then come moments of a strange, empty, golden loneliness which I can hardly bear without a feeling of terrible inner deprivation. When I long for him at "Bernard's hour," five-thirty to six p.m. No! long for him is not exactly right. I long to be going to meet him, I long to stand outside a Tube station at the evening rush hour waiting for him. I long for the *occupation* of him. Especially now; now that I need distraction from what has occurred.

We had visitors again last night. True to his word at last Peregrine brought along the two men who were "anxious to meet" Bernard; Morty Davy, present champion of the Impulse School of playwrights, and Rodericsthal, a historian of sorts—or so he describes himself.

Davy seemed quite enthusiastic when *The Curtain* was first mentioned, standing up and sitting down several times, as he talked about it and The Drama generally, with a rather gauche and self-conscious litheness. When he *was* sitting he couldn't keep still, constantly folding his arms behind his head, slithering down in his chair till he was almost lying on his back, sitting up abruptly to sort of act out the pose of "enthusiastic argument." His skimpy, shrunken sweater and craggy face, the streaked hair over the stern forehead, the bitter-diffident lips are all part of the uniform appearance of the Impulse School.

He and Peregrine were well away with each other when they arrived, Peregrine the Regency Buck temporarily in abeyance to Peregrine the "Impulse" man; the newest American style of acting to which nearly all the younger playwrights have taken with great enthusiasm. Morty Davy's second disappointment of the evening (his first was that we had no gin and all Bernard could offer him was sherry or whisky) was his host's indifference to—and indeed ignorance of—this latest fashionable School of Drama. In fact he could hardly believe it.

"Oh but . . . but you haven't heard those *marvellous* records of Dubby Dubow?" he said in his gulped, soft, redbrick-nasal voice. (In fact he isn't redbrick either but technical college evening class.)

"No," said Bernard politely but rather shortly. "They've managed to pass me by."

"But you *must* get to hear them," said Morty, "they're so, *you* know, so marvellous, you know."

"Maybe when I get back home," said Bernard.

"That reminds me," said Peregrine, "are you staying on over here whether or no *Curtain* gets on the Avenue?"

Bernard shrugged. "You're asking me something I don't know the answer to myself."

"Such a hellish will-they won't-they period," said Morty. "I've been through it *all*. I *know*."

"Well, at least they've extended the run at the Vauxhall for another couple of weeks," said Bernard. "By the way, I saw your play last week."

"Did you actually traipse all that way out to that benighted suburb?"

"I certainly did."

"I—er—hope the journey wasn't a dead waste of time."

Jessica (did I mention?) had gone off to see her friend that evening. The old woman, though Bernard had asked her to stay and meet the company, had insisted that she had some sewing to do in her room. I had therefore gone into the unlit dining-room and was watching and listening through the not-quite-closed dividing doors. Standing there in the dark I saw from the expression on Bernard's face that Morty's question was proving an embarrassing one. He hadn't liked his play. I found myself speculating with a good deal of interest on what he would say. Would he be truthful—or kind?

"Not at all," he said. "The second act alone would have been worth it." (He had chosen to be kind.)

There was a pause. Then Morty said with strained casualness; "What would you say were its chances of reaching American audiences?"

"You mean . . . would it get across to them? The meaning?"

"Yes."

"Well . . ." said Bernard rather doubtfully, "it's kind of hard to say. What I mean is that in a way we've sort of got our *avant garde* behind us."

"I don't *think* I would describe myself as *avant garde* exactly," said Morty with a rather affronted laugh in his voice.

"Well no," said Bernard reasonably, "perhaps that's a wrong description of your work."

"I mean, I'm as much against that as I'm anti-traditionalist. You know," said Morty.

"Anti-me he means," put in Peregrine, elegantly jovial.

"Oh, well," said Bernard polite but anxious to be exact, "I wouldn't say you're anti-either really."

"You wouldn't?" said Morty sounding more affronted than ever.

"No, well . . . No! what I'm trying to say, I think, is that the actual texture of your writing is traditional. But the form lends itself to *avant garde*—or more precisely, *fashionable*—interpretation. Especially by the actors."

"You think *The Ten Shilling Note* was badly acted?"

"Oh, Lordy!" said Bernard with a rather embarrassed smile aware that in some mysterious way he was managing to offend Morty with every innocent word he spoke. "Look! I'll be frank. I'm not crazy about the kind of acting where you have to have the characters springing onto step-ladders all the time and declaiming their credo with outstretched arms. I think what your character of Les for instance was saying was true and important and touching. But I didn't like the—if you'll pardon me for saying this—way he was saying it. And I don't think, for that reason, that the play made the impact it should have done. And put over like that in America that may well be a strike against it."

"Fair enough. Fair enough," said Peregrine. "Ferdy!

you're most terribly quiet. You haven't said a word. Not like you! Utter!"

Rodericsthal began to say something but was over-talked by Morty who was saying in a high, hurt gabble: "Of course one's original conception, one's ideal performance gets muddied over by the time . . . But you see I don't think one ought to be too smug about—"

"Talking of ideal performances," said Rodericsthal cutting in very smoothly, "you know, Shaw used to say to me—of course I only knew him in his latter years—that any serious theatregoer in England would be much better off at home *reading* his plays than in the theatre watching them. One of his typical remarks, not meant to be taken seriously of course . . . quite unlike Galsworthy who was sincere in every syllable he uttered. Too worthy, not enough gall for nowadays though. You know, I don't think I ever heard Galsworthy. . . ."

Morty was standing before the fire-place holding his glass of sherry between his thin, graceful, dirty fingers, the pose of his meagre body . . . I hardly know how to describe it; like a self-conscious, nervy, jerked-elbows attempt at man-about-town perhaps? Peregrine, who was being rather unusually quiet for him, was spread with ease in one armchair, Bernard was facing him and Rodericsthal was sitting neatly, small feet together, in the low, fireside chair. He's a small man, about seventy I would say, with a neat, round head of pure silver hair and a powdery but still handsome face spoilt only by his slack lips which looked—as old men's do sometimes—chapped and purple as if he'd been sucking a blue pencil. Now talking non-stop in a peculiarly mellifluous and hypnotizing way, the talk of a well-polished and long-experienced conversationalist, he had got on to the Basque country where he'd once worked—with the benevolent interest of Maynard Keynes he said—on an investigation into its almost medieval social structure.

"Virginia too was fascinated by every detail she could

pick up about the place," he said. "She was even planning a holiday there at one point but it didn't come off for some reason. Exotic, queer country . . . though the Bloomsbury set was far more fascinating than any Basques!"

"Personally speaking, as they say (as though anyone ever speaks any other way!) I'd certainly have stayed put in Tavistock Square," said Peregrine. "Those medieval lavatories. . . ."

"You have to crouch of course," said Rodericsthal merrily, "but like everything else there's a knack to it. Couldn't do it now you know, not with my arthritis. But it was fun then. Everything was fun then."

"Did the Bloomsbury set have *fun?*" said Morty with nervy, thin contempt.

"Oh they did, they did," said Rodericsthal. "Those evenings . . . what talk, what talk!"

"Were you actually a part of that circle?" said Bernard sitting forward with interest.

Rodericsthal smiled, a little patronizing in his amusement, as if Bernard was being childishly naïve. "They *were* glamorous I suppose, up to a point. Part of the glamour of course was the exclusiveness. Invitations to Bloomsbury weren't so easily come by. . . ."

"Walpole was kind of thrilled—" put in Bernard but Rodericsthal, not too pleased to see that his host knew something about the period, went on: "There was a kind of 'royalty' feeling about them. And even when you did receive an invitation you still had to prove yourself. You had to— as they say nowadays—give value. Of course there were other circles. Wells was a great party giver too. I used to wonder how his wife coped. She was a frail little thing to look at. And then there were the great houses—and the great hostesses."

"Too infernally boring from all accounts; chinless Dodos and horsefaced Margots—" said Peregrine.

"Oh no," said the old man with a slightly irritated flash

of his eye. "I don't think so. But of course," he said modestly, "I wasn't really a part of *that* world. Though it might have been at Londonderry House that I met Max—"

"*That's* who you remind me of!" said Bernard snapping his finger in the air. "I've been trying to think all evening. All those pictures and descriptions of him. . . . Did you know him well? D'you think yourself you look like him?"

"I like to think so," said Rodericsthal demurely, avoiding the question of whether he had in fact known the incomparable Max well. "Of course," he went on, "I dabbled a little in writing too. Apart from my subject I mean. I remember G.K. thought one of my tiny pieces worth a word or two. They said he was anti-Semitic you know but it wasn't true. It wasn't true at all. After all, he knew *I* was a Jew; yet he couldn't have been more friendly. A big man in every sense of the word. I lived a few doors away from him at one time. We saw a lot of each other."

"In the street?" said Peregrine, innocent-impudent. He was beginning to look bored. Morty was wandering about the room examining books and pictures.

"In the street—as you say," said Rodericsthal equably. Smoothly changing the conversation he started to talk to Bernard about various famous names in America. To my absolute surprise—though I realize now that it was entirely within character for him not to have mentioned it before— I heard Bernard admit to having met several of them (which was more, I gathered, than the old man for all his familiar tone had done). He explained with typical self-deprecation that it just so happened that he'd appeared on the same television interview programme with one, had been asked to a luncheon where he'd been introduced to several more, had found himself at one big theatrical party ("the only one I ever was asked to!" he said), where he'd talked with others.

This revelation had a curious effect on his visitors.

Slightly ill at ease with him, for no appreciable reason, before, they now began to dislike him! Rodericsthal (I suspect —and I am almost sure I am right—that he is nothing more than a ragbag collection of remembered gossip and small encounters with the Names he had been dropping so liberally; I suppose he manoeuvred this visit itself on the same principle of getting a foot in the door of anyone who's made an impression) resented him because he was so honest and deprecating that the bland, shrewd, polished little man felt the contrast with himself as a violent criticism. Morty because Bernard bewildered him by not fitting the categories he understood, being neither bright and angry nor despised traditional nor mannered, smart as paint fashionable. . . . And Peregrine because he had liked the idea of being the one to dole out "contacts" to Bernard; and now found that his benevolence had been, if only by a little, anticipated. Bernard's very modesty, his very reluctance to use, till it came out by accident, the prestige counters he'd had hidden away, flummoxed and angered them. They would not believe it was modesty and interpreted it as sly arrogance. But when, as he talked on it became obvious to them that he was *not* trying to impress, that furthermore his work had made a great impression before he'd ever met even one person of influence, that he had known no one at all who could have helped him, that he had sprung from utter obscurity into high reputation by the sheer quality of his work and nothing else . . . they were shocked! They were, all three of them in their different ways, so geared to the notions of publicity, contacts, smart talk, the selling of one's direct personality, that they were totally dislocated by the fact of Bernard's getting on without them. And so, waspish, uneasy, his very modesty became their harsh accuser, they began to get their own back.

"Of course, the publicity racket over there is quite unbelievable. I've made the trip three times and I still don't believe what I saw with my own eyes. I don't believe my own experience," said Peregrine.

"Anything you like to say about America or the Americans is not only believable; it's only too likely . . . *you* know . . . to be true," said Morty without bothering to insert a "present company excepted" even into his voice.

"That's on their home ground," said Rodericsthal (a more experienced rapier man) with a slight but cold smile at Bernard. "What they do when they're abroad is even more fantastic. As for the Yank at table. . . . Have you," he said to Peregrine, "ever been in a restaurant when American tourists are demanding dinner? I remember one in Rome. The bangings on the table. . . . 'Pasta! Pasta!' this great waddling Yankee kept shouting across the room. 'Don't we get any service around this joint?' " He shook his gnomish, silver head ruefully. "Impossible!" he said. "With all due apologies!" he said with a half-look at his host.

"I actually saw an American—you may believe this or you may not, as you please," said Peregrine. "But I swear it to be true—carving his name on the *Parthenon* only last summer. When I caught him at it he said he'd only wanted 'a lil of all that posterity stuff' himself! 'Say,' he said, 'I didn' mean no harm. I wuz just *identifying* with all this art jazz.' "

Morty and Rodericsthal both burst out laughing, the latter hugely enjoyed his own amusement, keeping up his high-pitched shrill bleat for some moments. When they had quietened down Bernard, who had smiled but not laughed, said thoughtfully: "And yet you know, he had a point! I'm not defending what he did. Of course not. Who could? But, say . . ." with a quick movement he opened and shut his fingers, groping for a way of presenting his ideas, "you know what that guy was *feeling* was a sort of reverence. Not for what are called artistic values so much as for the idea of 'greatness.' He probably saw the Parthenon as something less than the Waldorf-Astoria. But the fact that it has survived from antiquity to be revered as it is is something, a fact, which impresses him. I'd say at a guess that it affected his rudimentary sense of marvel just as much in a way as it would have an educated man. So that even to touch the stone of one great pillar linked him so to speak, with greatness, gave him a sense of being near it. This is important; and it shouldn't be despised. Don't you see?" he said rather imploringly stopping short before the invisible, hostile, noncomprehending wall of the others' half-attention. When none of them answered he plunged in again with a kind of desperate candour.

"You see," he said, "I know what that guy was feeling because I've felt it myself. Not now! One of the more appalling things that happens when you enter the world of the arts—even in a small way—is the loss of the sense of awe. You rub up against the third rate and the second rate and soon even the first rate becomes a little diminished as well. The nearer you come, the less marvellous, the less transforming. But before that happens . . . I remember," he said with again a somewhat disorientated conversational plunge, "when I first went on a trip to New York—I was just out of high school . . . I went to a bar I'd read somewheres was a Eugene O'Neill haunt. I remember sitting there over a beer waiting to catch a glimpse of him. It wasn't just fan worship or rubber-necking or art snobbery. It was an *experience;* both the waiting and the eventually seeing him."

"Tanked—as they say—to the eyes no doubt," said Peregrine.

"Sure, sure . . . he was tight I guess," said Bernard impatiently, "but that's not what I'm . . . the point . . . you see . . . I sat there taking quick peeks (from a distance) at his hands. I imagined their movements in writing. I looked at the shape of his head. I thought about the bone of that skull enclosing the forms and activities, the very factory of genius. And you know what!" He gave a deprecatory laugh at his own youthful absurdity, "I would have given anything at that moment for a lock of his hair!"

The amused, sceptical smile on Rodericsthal's lips broadened. Peregrine was looking down at his own knees and frowning. Morty Davy's expression was at once bewildered and contemptuous. But none of them said a word.

"Oh you can laugh at this if you like!" said Bernard again giving a small, rather forced laugh himself. "But since that day I've never been able to despise the people who tear buttons off a movie star's coat—*or* condemn the initial-carvers. You see—" he clicked his tongue in the exasperated attempt to convey what he meant, "the impulse is not a bad one. Deep in ordinary people's hearts is a sense of magic, reverence, awe . . . a longing for something great. To touch, to hold in one's hand an object which has been touched or made by someone great (or even—which is just as important in a way—someone they think is great . . . the object in a way doesn't matter, it's the 'feeling of reverence,' the intimation that there's something beyond their own lives) or to be within actual, physical sight of someone whose experience they believe to be more magical than theirs . . . this is a natural, a good feeling. They feel in touch with *something else* . . . their own heart-rending obscurity lessened. I can't condemn this. Yes, common sense tells me that when the idols are false the worship is useless. And yet . . . to be without the impulse to worship at all is even more terrible. To revere *nothing;* surely that's the ultimate disaster? To carve one's name on a sacred piece of wood or stone is no more than a wish to be part of eternity. That quivering obtrusiveness of the mob . . . sure I know it can be horrible. But it's infinitely moving too."

"Upon my word, Bernard," said Peregrine with uneasy lightness, "you'll be defending the litter louts next!"

Absorbed in their conversation I had noticed nothing else. But at that moment I felt in the dark a small flicker of

movement at my side—and turned to find that old Mrs.
Zold had silently joined me. I gave a small gasp of guilt but
she said nothing, only reached out an arm and very carefully
pulled the folding door a crack wider so that we were both
able to see into the room a little more. (I realize that—like
me!—she has done this before.) We continued standing
there in, on my part anyway, uneasy alliance, listening to
the conversation which had turned on the more familiar,
easy beat of class distinction. This was Morty's country
where he felt most at home but his jerky argumentativeness
was being gradually flattened out by Rodericsthal's socially
expert flow of easy, informed-sounding talk. This Morty
found difficult to cope with since his educational equipment
was not strong enough for the expression of his ideas. Indignant but uncoordinated, he hadn't the agile flexibility of
Rodericsthal or his sheer smoothness in the conversational
technique of presenting fact. On top of this he was, I believe, handicapped, consciously or not, by the knowledge
that, son of a small clerk, he wasn't even real working class
but as lower-middle as Bernard.

For a few moments, while he and the old man argued,
their shared hostility towards their host shifted to a slight
antagonism between themselves. "But there *is* a sheer physical difference," Rodericsthal was saying, "that one can't get
away from. The working class chap—say what you will, but
you can tell the difference."

"If you don't eat enough when you're young—" began
Morty.

"I once went down to a Kentish hop farm," said Rodericsthal, "and saw university students working side by side with
some East End boys. You should have seen those working
class lads. As big and brawny . . . but my dear Davy, one
can't get away from it. One could *tell*. Identically dressed,
doing identical jobs you could still distinguish between the
classes. I recall—"

Morty subsided rather sulkily but cheered up when the old man, switching his attitude to the working class in order to win him back (he obviously cannot bear not to be popular), got on to the poverty of the Italian peasants. "You young men," he said genially including Peregrine who had been looking more and more bored, "want to raise your sights when you're talking about poverty. You think the British working family hard done by. Go to Naples as I did only six months ago and you'll come back thinking we don't know what the word means. Poverty! they live in conditions of such gross squalor—"

"But that's just not . . ." said Bernard leaning forward and interrupting. "I must argue this one, Rodericsthal. Look! I know only too well what poverty means—"

"*How* do you know?"

"How?"

"Yes, how?" said the old man resenting the interruption to what was evidently one of his standard speeches. "You know what it means in theoretical terms," he said petulantly.

"Oh no," said Bernard surprised. "Oh no. I'm probably the only one of you in this room who has actually known what it's like to be hungry!"

"When?" said Rodericsthal rudely.

Bernard looked at him uncertainly for a moment before saying with a laugh: "Well now, you don't want the story of my life, do you?"

"We've only got your word for it."

There was a second's pause then Bernard, attempting to overlook the rude, disbelieving tone, said: "Well anyway, the point I'm trying to make is that even when economic conditions are at their worst, there *are* compensations that somehow or other we've lost on our own better-housed, better-fed level. It's at least arguable that social loneliness is almost if not quite as bad as physical hunger. I've no statistics but I believe the number of suicides, the incidence of mental disease is higher—"

"These Italians were picking crusts out of dust bins," said Rodericsthal. "You think that kind of existence—"

"American ash-cans are so full of half-eaten steaks and whole chickens—" began Peregrine not really caring about the argument but unable to resist his usual scathing impulse.

"Yes! That's just what I feel. You know!" said Morty jerking into the discussion. "With so much conscienceless waste going on—as a matter of national *policy*—I don't know how any American can hold his head up—"

"I'm not defending the economy of my own country," said Bernard. "Far from it! What I'm trying to say is that there are different kinds of hunger. You're talking about the brute, physical kind. (And don't let anyone think this doesn't exist in the States either.) But what I'm saying is that life in a slum, however hard, very often has *something* which life in say a prosperous new factory location hasn't got. Now surely," he said good humouredly, "this can't be questioned! Half the social commentators in both our countries are investigating the loss of human affections, human relationships. . . ."

"All hungry together. That certainly makes for a fine fellow feeling," said Rodericsthal impatiently.

"But surely you've read—" began Bernard, his high voice squeaking a little in astonishment.

"I remember Laski countering your sort of argument. . . ."

The old man went on talking (with a childish determination to dominate the conversation) not about Laski's argument but its effect on more than one occasion on the various literary intelligences who had been listening to and finally defeated by him. "They used your approach," he said to Bernard with a most curious note of grievance in his voice, "but I assure you by the time he'd finished with them their lines of defence had been shattered. Completely shattered."

"Well—what *was* his argument?" said Bernard in a pacific, willing to be convinced manner.

"*Read it!*" said Rodericsthal with sudden boorish petulance, his handsome little face pink with temper.

"O.K." said Bernard, "I will! But at least you'll grant me this. Conditions have moved on from thirty years ago. It's not, after all, the same world. Things, ideas we thought would work we've now discovered won't. Needs have been discovered that money won't cover."

"Well," said Rodericsthal with heavyish sarcasm, "I wouldn't be as well up as you in modern economic theory. I'm just a poor, benighted historian."

"But . . . ah, come now, Rodericsthal, you must admit to change. After all nothing stands still."

There was a pause. And I realized that in fact that was exactly what was at the bottom of the vain old man's ill humour. He *had* stood still. He had either not read or not digested anything new since the Thirties; perhaps even the Twenties.

But there was something else behind his hostility. Something which was connected with his early days. I think, I am *sure,* that something in Bernard's way of thinking, his entirely human angle on experience, had touched off a recollection in the old man of his encounters with the artistic intelligences of his youth. He had (I guessed) always, with his lack of perception, his unoriginality, his stereotyped academic approaches been made to feel an outsider, tolerated occasionally but never really accepted by the first class creative imaginations he had known. Bernard had unconsciously recalled the snubs he had received from those touched with genius. Bernard had anything but a first-class mind. His education was negligible. But the artistic quality of him was of that very first imaginative rank, utterly without vulgarity or pretentiousness which the historian had so resented in those others. And—even worse—his host hadn't even the backing of class or education or breeding. His superiority was entirely his own, was unconscious—and so was unforgivable.

Bernard was still attempting to argue the case for social isolation being almost as bad as physical privation. "But look," he was saying desperately against the thickening hostility in the air—Morty was saying with an insultingly contemptuous twist of his thin mouth: "Typically middle-class get-out,"—"Look. I know what it is to be hungry."

"So you keep saying," said Rodericsthal peevishly, "but what does that prove?"

"It doesn't *prove* anything at all. It's just that I'm therefore able to measure degrees of misery from first-hand—"

"What do you mean by 'degrees of misery'?"

"What do I mean—?"

"I'll tell you what I think," said Rodericsthal with a sudden, spiteful drawing together of his small body, "I think you've deliberately closed your mind against everything I've been saying. You haven't taken in a word I've been saying. You've—you don't mind my speaking my mind . . . ?" (Bernard gave an astonished, helpless, polite shrug) "you've been showing the typical Yankee ignorance and Yankee arrogance that we've all come to expect from people like you."

(I felt the old woman's body beside mine quiver with the silent shock I was myself experiencing at this uninhibited, sudden explosion into childish invective.)

" 'Degrees of misery'! What do you mean by vague, high-sounding phrases like that? Define your terms."

"Why, surely," said Bernard with desperate lightness. "I mean for one thing that there is no confining suffering to one kind of human experience. Surely that should be self-evident?" he said, turning as it were humorously for confirmation towards first Davy and then Peregrine. The latter,

avoiding his eyes, said nothing at all. But Davy, after giving
him a jerked, sideways stare, said: "I agree with Rodericsthal. You've got to define your terms."

"For crying out loud!" said Bernard, "we're all reasonably
intelligent men aren't we? We all have a reasonably similar
idea of what we mean by 'suffering'—"

"Oh no we haven't," said Morty and the old man with
simultaneous and malicious triumph.

"Well I don't know that we—" began Peregrine but
stopped. He was reluctant to side with any minority and was
moreover bored and annoyed with Bernard for not handling
the evening more adroitly. And I must say that in a way I
almost sympathized with him. I could have shaken Bernard
for having no idea how to protect himself, for not being
shrewder, for his patient courtesy with what was turning
into sheer, embattled rudeness, for his handicapping sense
of what was due to a guest . . . though there was no answering sentiment in them about the kind of behaviour which
was due to a host.

For, when Bernard, trying to normalize the atmosphere,
stood up and offered them another drink, Rodericsthal
nodded but, when Bernard brought a couple of bottles over
to him holding them poised ready to pour and saying:
"Which?" he went on talking to Peregrine, keeping Bernard
standing there like a lackey holding the bottles foolishly
before him till the old man paused long enough to say
indifferently: "Sherry I think," before turning back to Peregrine.

If only he had thrown the liquor in the old man's face!
Or else had agreed hypocritically with them and their
fashionably stereotyped outlooks. But there was—I saw it—
a maddening quality about him, a kind of humble intran-
sigence which both angered and frightened them. If he had
matched their bad manners, if he had turned on them they
would have sighed with relief.

For what, finally, was inflaming them beyond all else was, I saw, the touch of "holy fool" about him, a kind of deliberate, almost lazy innocence. He was refusing to admit the fact of their really shocking behaviour. But the more he tried to remain explanatory and polite, the more he refused to acknowledge that they were being vicious and nasty beyond all social limits, the more they hated and baited him. Peregrine, who should have defended him, retreated out of the conversation altogether and sat restlessly flicking through a magazine.

"But don't you see?" Bernard said impatiently at one point, "there's a kind of *flux* in human nature which the academic mind is sometimes too stiff—and to be truthful, too wooden-headed at times—to take account of." He meant no harm, no insult, the remark was nothing compared with what they had been throwing at him, but Rodericsthal, in his spiteful, small-minded way, decided to take umbrage on behalf of the academic mind in general.

"One or two historians I know—some of the most brilliant minds in the country—wouldn't take kindly to being called wooden-headed," he said through his loose, purple lips.

"Now *did I say. . . .*"

"Oh yes you did!" said Morty. In other company he would never have supported Rodericsthal's position but the chemical dislike he felt for Bernard as a man overbore his own principles.

The argument went on with Bernard entirely at their mercy. He took pains, answering seriously and pleasantly all the perverse, hair-splitting debating points Rodericsthal and Davy continued to throw at him. Strained to breaking point he remained good humoured, even to making small jokes against himself. He behaved towards them as though they were civilized and this a pleasant discussion between friends. (This was what he had come to London *for;* intelligent talk with intelligent men: and—with deliberate blind-

ness it seemed—he could not let the dream go.) At one
point, goaded almost beyond endurance, he took one of their
stupidest methods of argument, an idiotic bolting down
some non-sequitur hole from the bottom of which they
lurked and sneered at him, and used it mildly against themselves, laughing apologetically even as he did so—as if he
were insulting *them* by even the smallest use of so paltry a
weapon—and said with a strained smile: "I can use that
kind of answer too you know. But it simply doesn't get us
anywhere. Now does it?"

"That's true," said Peregrine from behind his magazine
but so lack-lustrely that they only paused for a moment,
nonplussed, then, with a kind of hysteria of spite, started
on Bernard again with a heightened degree of virulence I
could hardly believe I was hearing.

I suppose in all comings together of men there are times
when suddenly, for no really cogent reason, façades break
down and deep under-currents of hatred break to the surface; the catalyst, I suspect, being very often innocence. I
realize now that I saw in that room last night every reasonless lynching mob in the world. I saw the hatred of small,
rigid natures for what is open and vulnerable. I saw the
secret wish in the souls of limited and narrow men to destroy whatever is generous, benevolent of will, innocent in
intention. I saw the hatred of the academic mind for the
artist; I saw—and the knowledge terrifies me—that in our
contemporary dementia our guilts are so great that we cannot bear the unconscious reproach of virtue.

I saw more. I saw in this house last night what the world
does to those who will not answer back; who hold, not hate
but patience with their enemies; that patience which eternally provokes the slap of outraged littleness. I saw, and
understood for the first time, the concentration camps; and
those who stood by and watched the old Jews scrubbing the
Berlin pavements. I saw vain, dry, begrudging, vicious man.

I saw a kind of crucifixion.

But worst of all was that his mother saw it too. Rodericsthal finally wound up by saying—he had been hiding some of his hatred of what Bernard was all along by talking behind the smokescreen of "you Americans": "You're blinded you know. So blinded, like all your countrymen, by your own fat living that you've lost the capacity to feel. American imagination is dead; choked with its own gold. You're so self-righteous that you can't produce art, only squeals. Your play," he said to Bernard, "is, if I may say so," he said with travestied politeness, "one long squeal."

"I wouldn't say squeal," said Morty flinging his thin legs about, "Whimper! A capitalist whimper at the idea of losing privilege."

"I thought you said earlier on that you rather liked parts of it," said Bernard. He had got up and was standing against the fire-place looking round at the ring of his tormentors attempting, even now, a polite pleasant expression on his face. He still could not believe what was happening.

"Oh I still say *technically* you've managed to pull off—"

"There's no solid core to the play, Zold," said Rodericsthal, "it's just a bag of sentimental fat. There's no *bones*, no social framework."

"Them's mighty hard words," said Bernard smiling a terrible, ashamed smile as he fought (still!) not to know what they were doing to him. Peregrine let out a loud, undergraduate chortle. He too was trying not to know. Bernard turned to look at him and Peregrine's laugh stopped in his throat. He said quickly, holding up the *New Yorker* he had been flipping over: "How much further out can they *get!* Seen this drawing?" Bernard half held out his hand still maintaining a normal manner though his eyes were stricken. But Peregrine—as if he had finally decided to come down against him—turned the magazine sharply away and passed it across to Morty. It is possible that he did so from sheer embarrassment, a kind of unnerved gaucherie at the whole wretched situation. But the effect was of final betrayal. Rodericsthal, smiling, said: "I'm afraid you haven't made out a very good case for yourself, Zold."

"I guess it's good enough for me in my own mind," said Bernard in an abstracted voice.

"You're just one against three. Three against one, Zold! If you're the good citizen of a democratic country you're claiming to be then you've got to admit that it's the majority vote that counts! No! you'll have to admit defeat. You're a defeated man, Zold," he said with a laugh. He stretched his short little legs out in front of him and put his two small feet demurely together. "You might as well go home. I'm afraid the British won't support you!"

For the first time I saw Bernard wince as he (like me) superstitiously, applied the words to his uncertain position over the transfer of *The Curtain*. "Oh come off it, Ferdy," I heard Peregrine say but I'd turned to old Mrs. Zold who had given a gasp of pain and moved forward as if to go in to them. I grasped at her arm to prevent her and after a moment's silent straining away from me in the dark she slackened and gave in. I knew that she could do him no good in there. There was nothing she could say. What *could* she say? That she had bequeathed the habit of willed unknowingness upon him? That however much he struggled with those elements in his nature which brought him to defenceless indignity he would never entirely overcome them? If she went in there. . . .

There was a faint sound from her as we stood there together in the dark. I bent my head thinking she was saying something to me but she was saying in a humiliated, whispering moan under her breath: "My son. My poor boy. . . ."

The impact of her pitiful suffering, the outrage which was being wrought upon them both becoming all at once too abominable to bear, I put my arms about her shoulders and led her, unresisting, away.

I think I once wrote to you before about a particular feeling I have about Bernard. He is one of those creatures whom, I am convinced, no amount of celebrity treatment would ever spoil. Given honour and courtesy he would never become demanding, boastful, egotistical. He would know how to retain proportion. He would not enlarge himself beyond his natural limits. But the converse of this does not obtain. Treated wrongly as he nearly always is by everyone, treated as less, far less than he is by everybody he knows, he not only fails to maintain his proper size but suffers constant diminishment. He has no idea how to defend himself. Though he thinks he knows the face of evil he has such a bad memory for grievance that attack comes to him always with an astonishment which paralyses. Before he is able to remember and believe that human nature is able to do this he is already half beaten to the ground. If only he were able to manufacture bitterness or rebellion. I say "manufacture" because that is the precise definition of what we do. I manufacture my grievances against you for instance. Bitterness is not a purely spontaneous feeling; it is *made*. And the reason why it is made is because it gives—or seems to give—more dignity to pain. We don't any of us mind being caught in attitudes of bitter rebellion since such attitudes have become socially attractive. The great contemporary shames are humility and fortitude. By some mysterious process the *yelp*, the complaining protest has become the virile thing. A whole era of civilization has become mass-hypnotized into making nothing of endurance. And so Bernard's virtues have become nothing but weights to drag him down.

Powerless to protect him in any other direction, I stayed talking to his mother as she lay stretched and motionless on her bed till she began to revive from the state of grey pain to which she had been reduced. If only, if only she had been too stupid to understand what had been going on. But, as I have said before, as Bernard has said before, she is not stupid; she is not stupid at all.

One thing more I did for him—as I heard the front door close, the men's voices as they went down the path, Peregrine's loud, guilty laugh. I got her promise that she would not tell him that she had witnessed his humiliation. "I beg of you, Mrs. Zold," I said almost weeping myself, "I beg of you. It would only make him feel a hundred times worse. Keep it to yourself. It's the only thing you can do for him." She promised at last. And I can only hope that when —as inevitably she will—she tells him it will be when he can bear it.

Not now. Not now.

Ruth

❖❖❖❖❖❖❖❖❖❖❖❖❖❖❖❖❖

20th September

NEW TERM starts for you this week, doesn't it? A fresh school year, new faces to be memorized—in accordance with your "system"; scenery to be painted for the school play. I used to help in the productions the first few years of our marriage. You cannot deny this. Perhaps I should have gone further; "tried" a child too. The limited people would certainly say so. "Your marriage would have worked if you'd had a child," they would say. But what a huge, silly myth this is. Having a child is no more a remedy for my kind of unease than having a car or a hobby. They are all "something to *do*." Oh yes, there are overtones. The "look! it's alive!" sense of wonder, the constant interest of change in a child as it grows, the mystic sense of creation . . . *I* did it. With my body I *created*.

But heavens! what a lot of pother over "the child" as an essential ingredient of happiness. Ask a dedicated soldier, a cabinet minister, a fine actress, a great doctor—let alone a true artist; to none of them is a *child* of absolute first importance. Only to the third-rate, to the otherwise unoccupied, personality, to those who cannot live off their own quality is it so. I want to live *in myself*—not through another. One of the stupidest conventions I know is that of parental sacrifice. Since at what point in the endless chain of generations does this cease? At what moment in time does loving parent cry "Hold! Enough! The benefit stops here. With *me*."

I have almost entirely stopped thinking about Hugo. It was not so difficult really. I have been saved much unhappiness for—older or younger—he is not really my kind. The fibre of his mind, his reactions, his tastes, they are all a little vulgar and third-rate. And I—whatever my other faults— am not vulgar. At least, I don't think so. Worse even than his vulgarity was his lack of sympathy. And worse than that again his lack of all knowledge of his lacks. He has, I found out, a great opinion of himself (though he has not the remotest idea in the world what the nature of experience is, what human beings are made of) simply because he is accepted and entirely at home with the shoddy-sophisticated fringe world of the arts. Without a grain of wit himself he has instinctively known how to buy his way into their smartly knowing society with his face. An insipid, shrewd boy with a light talent. And so I am lucky. There was nothing in him for me to regret the losing. (Does this information gratify you? How do you feel when I tell you this? I find that my knowledge of you is fading and I can make no guess. You are receding from me, Francis; taking on mystery. *This should please you.*)

Jakie has erupted again. He has offered to take his mother to Paris next week! Bernard, though increasingly worried

about his own situation (there has been a half offer, with-
drawn then made again, to put *The Curtain* on in the West-
End) has spent some time talking it over with her. Jakie is
taking a flat there for a month and is making a great point
of giving her "one hell of a time." With her hatred of change
though, I doubt if she will go for all his persuasion.

"It's plumb crazy, Ma, comin' to Europe and not even
seein' Paris."

"Bernie says we might go for a few days before we go
home."

"Bernie! What Bernie says! What'll he do it on? Coffee
beans? Now look! I'm offerin' you the chance of a lifetime
an' you're not only not sayin' thank you. You're not even
takin' it. D'you get that!" he said to his wife. "An apartment
in Paris! Every comfort. An' she's not decided if she wants
to come or not. Can ya beat it?"

"I wouldn't want you to think me ungrateful, Jakie. It
isn't that."

"Then what is it?"

"I guess I don't want to leave Bernie just now he's that
worried and all."

"I told ya! I told ya it wouldn't run. Didn' I, Thelma? Remember? Those were my very words."

"We don't none of us know whether it's going to go on
or not. So you can quit talking out of turn, Jakie," she said
with some show of spirit; not much but a distinct advance
on her previous attitude towards him. The advance is paral-
leled by a disgruntled gentleness towards her younger son
since the night of the long knives—which I can hardly think
of myself without an inward grimace of pain. For at least
forty-eight hours after that evening Bernard was hardly
visible. What he went through, what hopes he finally buried,
what residual heaviness of heart will stay with him perhaps
for the rest of his life, I do not and will not ever know. The
wound went too deep for him to fall into his usual habit of

confiding in me. And of course he has no idea that anyone else in the house knows. The hurt has gone deep into his mother too but with her it has taken a simpler and more belligerent form. She is in some ways more difficult than ever simply because he has given her so much pain. For instance, someone who has something to do with his London agents telephoned him yesterday. In the course of the conversation the man at the other end must have mentioned Gordon, the agent who was here with Debenham Bleu that night.

"Sure I know him," said Bernard. "How is Gordon? I haven't seen him in months."

When he put the telephone down at last his mother pounced on him.

"Why d'you have to ask after that Gordon?" she said so violently and suddenly that he gasped.

"*What* in— what d'you mean?"

"I thought you didn't like Gordon."

"Well I'm not crazy for him—"

"So what d'you want to ask how he is for? You should worry how he is."

"Look, Mama, let's be reasonable. I don't particularly like Gordon but there just isn't any reason in the world why I shouldn't ask after him if he comes up in conversation."

"Well, you shouldn't have," she said. "All I know for sure about that man is that he don't give a row of beans how *you* are."

"It was just . . . talk. The sort of thing you say when you can't think of anything else to say."

"Well you just keep your dignity," she said obstinately.

He gave her a questioning look then shrugged his shoulders and said no more.

Though as I say he has not discussed that night with me (nor do I wish him to since I could not bear it) he has dropped remarks in general which I find disquieting; where they are not saddening. He has been damaged—perhaps permanently. I see the black bruise on his nature—and fear that it may never heal.

"People's social lives terrify me," he said when we were talking about something or other the other day. "So much balance is involved, so much struggle for footing, such a bracing of strength is needed for the facing through of difficulty. I tell you there are times, Ruth, when I long only to sink out of all necessity to communicate with another human being. I find myself thinking of gutters, of a peaceful descent into oblivion. How I long to give up, to *sink*. . . ."

"What about your work?" I said.

"That too. To abandon all claims and longings; to touch bottom and want nothing. . . ."

Even the thought of such release held out an invitation of such strength and enticement that it was, I saw, with a sense of actual tearing out of the roots of happiness that, with a rubbing of his hand down one side of his face, a moment's look into space, a resigned clutch at the nape of his neck he went upstairs to work once more.

And again: yesterday he got on to his old topic of loyalty echoing what I once wrote to you: "When I read about your 18th and 19th century literary figures," he said, "there's a kind of warmth comes off the page that's been captivating me for years. I've only just managed to put a name to it. Know what it is? Friendship! All those people . . . take Coleridge for instance. Now *there* was an appalling personal life. And yet his friends were generous, forgiving, warm. Sure, I know he had a remarkable personality. That helped. But go back a bit further, to Oliver Goldsmith say, who had no personality, couldn't talk. Oh sure, Dr. Johnson laughed at him a little—but he loved him too. Whatever time you turn to in the past it seems to me you could find this warmth between human beings. They all had friends: people who didn't mind their failings, friends who weren't stupid and loyal but intelligent, of high intellect and talent—and loyal. It's only now that no one has any real friends any more; no one they can turn to with trust."

Slightly hurt I wished—but did not know how—to put in some claim on my own behalf but he forestalled me saying with a half smile: "Present company *always* excepted, Ruth!"

And finally, only this evening before he went out. . . . He was going down to the Vauxhall to meet a potential backer but came into the kitchen an hour before he was due to go and sat down in the fireside chair to talk to me as I sat cleaning the silver.

"Did I tell you about this guy, Chevening?" he said.

"The backer? Not much. A captain of industry?"

"Yes. Something like that. All the dough in the world. But I doubt he'll open up for *The Curtain*."

"He'll be mad if he doesn't. What's holding him back?"

"Nothing!" said Bernard.

"Well then?"

"It's not that he's holding back. It's just that nothing's prodding him forward. Like a lot of rich men he's depressed about himself. He doesn't really care about the money. What he wants is to feel the whole enterprise is alive and important and—in the current catch-phrase—*meaningful*. Like with Peregrine's last play. He backed that, you know. Gave him the biggest kick he's had in years. What with Peregrine's chatter and charm. . . . *He* called me up yesterday, by the way."

"Did he?" I said rather astonished. "What did he want?"

"Mr. Peregrine Soames," said Bernard with an ironic smile, "requested from Mr. Bernard Zold an introduction to one, Philip Woodger, well-known liter-airy figure just arrived from New York. He happened to know I'd met him casually once or twice back home."

"You didn't do it, did you?"

"Yes. I called Woodger, told him Peregrine wanted to meet him and made arrangements for Peregrine to go over to his hotel for drinks."

"Didn't—?" I began and stopped.

"Oh sure, Woodger asked me along too. But I bowed out."

"Why, for goodness' sake?" I said impatiently.

He shrugged. "I didn't particularly want to meet up with Peregrine again," he said.

"Then why bother to do him any favours? Unless of course he's going to do you one in return."

He shook his head with a wry half-chuckle. "This isn't costing him so much as a cup of coffee," he said.

"Then *why*—?" I stopped again as I remembered that I wasn't supposed to know what had happened that evening with Rodericsthal.

He looked down, folding his full lips inward. Then he said: "It has become interesting to me recently to see just how far in outrage people will go; how much uncaring, casual insult, how much sheer want of delicacy is going to be exposed. To have Peregrine calmly call me up and ask me for favours—when he should be running in penance to do *me* one: to have him make cool demands on me when he should be down on his hands and knees—why, I wouldn't lift a finger to stop this display. *I'm enjoying it,*" he said with light emphasis. Then, his voice changing, becoming suddenly rough and charged as with a buried rasp so that I narrowed my eyes and shivered slightly with unease, he said with a single bang of his fist on the arm of his chair: "*I am beginning to welcome it*, Ruth. I am developing a taste for insult and injury. Only—" leaning forward he made a vicious snatch at the air, "I haven't had near enough yet. The appetite grows by what it feeds on. I find myself picturing in vengeful fantasy great, satisfying injuries done to me . . . I bleed with pleasure. . . ." He stopped suddenly, sat back, as it were, from his near hysteria and smiled at me with his large and melancholy eyes.

"Don't look so shocked, Ruth! Don't be so shocked now. *Don't you know I'm human too?* That I can be corrupted too?" His voice rose again. "When you live with insult, eat it for your daily bread, then the greater in scale the better. There comes a point in humiliation when it becomes a kind of ecstasy. There is, I tell you, a kind of conceit in anguish which can throb in the soul like sexual pleasure. I would not dispense with it. But to reach that condition the scale must be large; one must feed grossly. Ah! I could almost thank Peregrine for the dirt he has thrown upon my human dignity."

"You . . ." I said with pain, "you . . . must not speak like that. It is not right. It is not . . . suitable."

He surveyed me, my hands, dirty with polish, trembling on a silver candlestick. "You mean," he said with a complete return to his normal manner, "that it doesn't fit the saint image you're always trying to make out of me."

"You're not foolish enough," I said wildly. "Only fools are saints."

He gave a half laugh then quickly caught it back and said, teasing me: "The sainted fool is a very respectable figure after all."

I stared with a kind of seething vacancy at the candlestick. Then I looked up and saw that he was laughing openly.

"My *dear* Ruth," he said in the most affectionate voice. "*No.* I am not one! So don't keep thinking the category would suit me. Besides—you are paying me no compliment, only removing me from life; from the necessity to consider me as a human being. Saints are irrelevant. They are no great value to us in the world since they are too simple. They do not apply. To be simple is to be selfish. It solves nothing. *I* am not simple. I'm not a fool and not a saint. I'm the sorry mid-twentieth century substitute; the worrier, the conscience man, the anxiety bearer. No more than that, I assure you. In fact, during these last months . . . less. I have shrunk in England; lost moral weight. Some of my beliefs have been sweated off me. I expect less, give less; just an occasional twitch against the cords that bind me to show I'm alive.

"There is a picture," he went on, "which has haunted me all my life; that famous illustration—you probably know it —of Gulliver in Lilliput. The immense man tied to the ground with innumerable strings while the tiny Lilliputians swarm all over him. How it haunts me! The strength, the bigness tied to the ground by the small, pinching strings. I imagine it constantly, the trying to pull oneself away and the wincing, plucking pinches as the strings pull on the flesh. All my life, but *all my life* I have felt in my body those innumerable, tiny stings of pain, the tearing and bleeding and futile, exhausted falling back in despair; captive to the end."

He left for his appointment just as his mother came in fussing about a missing book—one which had come with the house—and which she obviously suspected me of having either lost or stolen; so that between turning the house upside down looking for it and suppressing my irritation I had no time to think of what he had been saying. And all I have been feeling since is a deep uneasiness, a sense of helplessness. I see him drifting from me on a small raft, drifting towards some black and tainted waters. And I have no rope, nothing which will help. I am on a raft too. But mine is becalmed and still. I wish to help him—

I am no use to him at all.

Ruth

❍❥❍❥❍❥❍❥❍❥❍❥❍❥❍❥❍❥❍❥❍❥❍❥❍

29th September

IN MY last letter . . . did I say that I wished to help Bernard? Did I speak of him as a soul in danger? This is what I *did*.

Four days ago Jakie issued an ultimatum. His mother was to come to Paris—or she wouldn't lay eyes on him again for as long as *he* could help . . . and on, and on; whereupon she consented. Indeed, not only consented but, with a complete reversal of her usual extreme fear of change, became caught up in a determined frenzy to go. I think it is possible to understand why. To begin with, she is flattered to be wanted. This is—and understandably—a great thing to her. Then, she wishes to boast afterwards of having had "an apartment in Paris." This seems to her (though she would not know the word) immensely *chic*. These are good enough reasons—but there are others. One of them is, believe it or not, a kind of vestigial "sportiness." When teased about going to Paris she responded like a young girl; chuckled a little, blushed almost! I would not now be surprised if told she had been coyly flirtatious in her youth. When I think of that innocent coquettishness crushed beneath the loaded misery of her marriage I feel desperately pitying. But I must admit that my pity is diminished by the other reason I have detected for her sudden voraciousness for the trip.

She wanted to get away from Bernard. She wanted a holiday from his everlasting demands on her for good behaviour. She is tired, too, of suffering for him, of having to watch herself, of curbing her irrationality, of smothering the constant, anarchic impulses which rise continually within her temperament and are the complement to her equally strong desire for respectability. However badly Jakie behaves she does not have to put on moral "manners" for him. And so she equates Paris with release.

Bernard did not want her to go. "I don't know, I don't know," he said to me a couple of days ago. "I can't stop her. If she wants to go I've no way of stopping her. But what's *he* getting at? If there's one thing for sure with Jakie it's that he does nothing for nothing."

"I think myself he just wants an audience to boast to,"

I said. "He wants to show his mother how powerful he is, to parade his money."

He put the flat of his hand across his mouth and looked speculative. "Maybe you're right at that," he said thoughtfully. "But there's some game he's playing too. I know him. Nothing that Jakie touches can be relied upon to go forward normally. If you asked him the time he'd twist the answer around and send you away not only without the information but most likely snubbed to the hilt as well."

That was two days ago.

At five o'clock this afternoon Jakie and his wife were supposed to collect the old woman on their way to London Airport. By *two* o'clock she was ready, packed and waiting and raging with restlessness. At five past two the telephone rang. It was Jakie to say with his usual brusqueness that he'd decided not to call for his mother. He and Thelma would meet her at the airport.

"For the love of Pete," said Bernard angrily, "didn't you know this before? You'll *have* to come for her. Everything's been fixed. What in hell d'you think you're playing at, lousing everything up before you've even started?" He held the receiver away from his ear, his face darkening while Jakie's voice rasped through it, his mother fidgeting round him saying, "What? What's happened?"

"No, I can't," he said finally. "I've an appointment at five-thirty right down in the West End. I *can't* take her, I've got to see this man I tell you. It's important for me. It's not something I can duck. You'll have to stick to the arrangement. No, Jessica can't take her either. She's taken Ginny out for the afternoon. They've already gone and they won't be back before six. *Are you crazy?* How can she go by herself? You know she can't. She'll panic—or lose something."

"No I won't," said the old woman at his elbow, divided between petulance, independence and terror. He put out one hand and touched her arm. "I'm not letting you go off by yourself. *Don't you know your son?* Wait a minute," he said into the telephone and put the receiver down on the hall table. "Ruth," he said coming to the door of the kitchen, "you heard?"

"Yes."

"Jakie! I might have known! Mama," he said turning back to face her. "Are you *sure* now you want to go? *Are you sure?* You're not there yet and already he's starting—"

"Sure I want to go," she said nervously. She lifted a hand and touched, as if to remind him, the new hat she'd bought specially for the trip and I saw a spasm of pitying tenderness cross his face.

"Yes, well . . ." He turned back to me. "Ruth . . . ?"

"Of course I'll take her," I said promptly.

He heaved a sigh of relief. "O.K. Thanks a lot, Ruth. What this household would do without you—" He took up the phone again, told Jakie that I would be bringing his mother, warned him to look after her and hung up. He stood quite still for a moment looking down, his face worried. Then he braced himself and said to his mother: "O.K., crisis over. Now all you have to do is sit down and relax till it's time for you to go. If you leave here about a quarter of five that should give you plenty of time. And me too. I can still be here to see you off before I get down to see Chevening."

"It's still on then?" I said to him in an undertone when his mother had gone off to sit in the front garden.

"Chevening? He's teetering. The producer's had a go; Craigie, the resident director at the Vauxhall's had a go. . . ." He laughed. "We'd have put in Lorraine but she's not his type! He likes 'em dark and dimply!"

"This is very important to you, isn't it? Chevening's your last chance?"

"Yes," he said briefly.

"Then tell me something," I said. "If . . . I mean, if she

were his type and it lay in your power to . . . throw him
Lorraine and get his backing . . . if it were in your hands . . .
would you do it?"

"Would I pimp for the sake of my 'art' d'you mean?"

There were some crumbs on the kitchen table. He pressed
his fore-finger down on one hard enough to make it adhere
to his skin then brought it up before his eyes and looked at
it. "I can't answer your question," he said at last squinting
at the crumb.

"But surely—" I began.

"But surely!" he said laughing on a curious note. "What
did you expect? A shocked 'Oh no!'? I can't answer your
question," he said and walked out of the kitchen.

Suddenly I felt I couldn't stay another moment in the
house. Going into the living-room I said hurriedly, "I'm just
running up to the shops, there's one or two things I ought
to get in."

"Surely," he said without looking up from his newspaper.
"You've plenty of time. Just so long as you're back before
five."

"I'll only be an hour," I said. Then I added, hovering in a
way untypical of me (as you know), "Is there anything
you want while I'm out?"

"No thanks," he said turning the pages of his paper.

I hesitated a moment longer, the sudden, slight antagonism between us, sprung absolutely from nowhere save my
hesitant question—a question of a kind I had put to him
many times before with no fear of touchiness in reply—
giving me a feeling of hot upset in my chest. Then I left the
house.

The walk to Swiss Cottage calmed me a little. Shopping,
which I always find soothing (how you hate it, Francis!)
made me more tranquil still. And it was such a beautiful
day; all September gold and deep blue sky. Why do people
say autumn is sad? To me it is the most cheerful season in

the year, when everything stirs and wakes. I love autumn as I love Mondays. It is a time of *life*.

And then I met Bridget. Did I tell you—I sometimes forget what I have written—that she has been away on a sort of working holiday for some weeks; helping out at a holiday art school somewhere down in the West country.

"Sure and it was not exactly what you'd call a rest cure!" she said greeting me with her usual pop-eyed enthusiasm and a more strongly Irish accent than usual. "All those tired Whitehall men relaxing on to canvas and doctors' secretaries painting their *dreams!* Enough to put you off Harley Street for life! Not that *we* didn't plug the medical angle. 'Art therapy is *good for you*'; that's how we advertise."

"It's been good for *you*," I said inspecting her. She looked very pink and red and untidy—not to say shaggy—but extremely cheerful. She plunged into a babble of her experiences without so much as a word of inquiry about the Zolds. But that is typical of her. She is like a child with a child's narrow concentration on only one interest at a time.

"What are you doing round here anyway?" I interposed after a few minutes. "You're not due to start Ginny's lessons again till next week."

"Sure well . . . about that . . . I don't think I'll be carrying on."

"Oh, *Bridget!*" I said with a sense of loss. "Why ever not? We'll miss you."

She squinted sideways at me. "Well the truth of it is," she said at last with a kind of merry triumph, "I'll probably be getting married quite soon."

"Good heavens!" I said with an inward flicker of disquiet. "Who to?"

"A perfectly *sweet* man I met at the School. That's why I'm around here today. He asked me to have a look at some shops that are up for sale."

"Shops?"

317

"Sure. He's an estate agent. He's got his own office and all. I'm to work with him and help him expand. He says I've got a real good head for it. D'you know what a conversion lease is?"

"I can't say I do," I said absently, still absorbed by a most curious and ludicrous relief that it wasn't Hugo she was marrying. She began to pour out a stream of property dealer's jargon much as she had once poured out art jargon . . . and I saw that Bridget the Business Woman (already she had that busily important swing to her shoulders) had now taken over from Bridget the Bohemian—perhaps permanently.

This idea was strengthened when she began talking about marriage to her Walter. "He's a sweet lamb," she said, "but he's got to be watched. He's too easy going by half; spends too much money on other people. But I'm going to stop all that," she said firmly. "I'm not going to have all that extravagance when we're married."

There was a ring to her words which fell oddly on my ear. Then I realized that what I was noticing was a kind of gleeful adoring of her position in being able to *say* those words. The possessive sentence was lovely to use. It defined her status. I smiled half sadly to myself as she went on talking of her plans. How strongly the managing-helpmeet, suburban-housewife note was sounding already! How swiftly Bridget, the gay, attitudinizing little Bohemian had gone. She couldn't get into her semi-detached quickly enough!

"How's Hugo by the way?" I said casually as we began to move away from each other.

"My *dear!*" she said with a slight recrudescence of her old manner. "He's off to Nassau!"

"*Is* he?" I said. "Lucky devil! Wish I could afford it."

"Sure and it wouldn't be him that's paying!" she said. "It's this woman!"

I had already taken a couple of steps away from her but at this I stopped and turned. "Woman?"

"Oh well, you know Hugo! He's always a bit cagey. But I gather some woman a lot older than himself offered to take him with her—and he accepted. He was laughing about it when he told me; sort of teasing. Well—I laughed back this time. He's terribly immature really. I mean set a boy like that up against a real man of the world, someone who has to compete with hardheaded businessmen—"

I left her at last still babbling about the mature realities of commerce and walked away in a state of irrational and trembling shock, the words "some woman older than himself" *beating* at me. I was assailed violently by a feeling I have had before; that what I had, from scruple or fear, refrained from taking, others with no better right were now enjoying. I had made my gesture for nothing.

I had gone perhaps a third of the way home when I, as it were, came to. I looked about me, at the road, the traffic flashing past. I looked down at the shopping bag I was carrying. Then I glanced at my watch. It was a quarter past three. I could just manage to get to Hugo's flat and back by five. *I had to see him.* There was something—though I did not know what—that I must say to him. I began to walk quickly in the hot, ripe sunshine through the streets, the rhythm of my pace increasing with the mounting urgency of my thoughts; images rising and breaking in repeated frenzy within my mind. My hands ached and clenched with the frightening, sensual wish to twist between them his slight, pale-gold fragility. He is not very tall; lightly built; I had a raging longing to hold and crush those small and delicate bones between my palms. I bit my lips as viciously as if I were biting his, my legs stiffening as I forced my stride along the hilly, Hampstead pavements.

I slowed down when I came in sight of his house half-way up the ugly steep street. I wiped the perspiration from my face and neck and between my breasts, combed my hair and powdered my nose. Then, my legs suddenly weak almost to collapsing, I walked up the steps and rang his bell. I waited for over a minute leaning against the lintel and trying to breathe more slowly. Then I rang again. I rang four times before I would admit to myself the fact that he was not in. Then I sank down on the top step and holding myself rigidly upright covered my eyes with my hands. When I took them away again I saw a woman approaching. She turned in at the gateway of the house and climbed the steps looking questioningly at me as I sat there. She took out a key and I said to her: "Excuse me but do you happen to know what time Mr. Lee will be back?" "I really couldn't say," she said. "He doesn't keep regular hours at all."

"I know," I said. And then I added, "It's a nuisance though. I've come such a long way and he *said* he'd be back by now."

"Is he expecting you?"

"Oh yes," I said in an "Of course," voice.

"Well, if you'd rather wait inside . . ." she said and putting the key in the door she opened it and let me into the narrow hall.

"I know the way," I said quickly as if to prove that I really was a familiar visitor and ran quickly up the stairs to his attic rooms.

I was hot and fatigued but I could not rest. Going into the studio I prowled about, turning sketches between my fingers, slanting canvases away from the walls. His work was so little a part of him, contained so little human essence of any kind that after a few minutes I could not be bothered with it. Besides, the room, facing north and very quiet, all at once looked so hollow in the afternoon light, so empty and lonely, that I ran out of it and into the bedroom. This, though tiny, looked human, the deep, gold sun pouring in on the clutter, the dirty, comfortable armchair, the neat but poor-looking bed. I poked around, opening drawers full of nothing but clothes, looked in cupboards . . . I could see nothing of interest. What I was really looking for was something acutely personal from which I could prise out the mystery of his life. But there was only an odd postcard or two from friends on holiday (one from the elusive Erik whom after all I never met), some bills and receipts from art dealers, letters from publishers and editors about commissions, past and present—and a snapshot of a family group, obviously his own; father, mother, son and daughter on a suburban lawn. I took this over to the bed and, lying down full length, held it in the air before me.

Hugo himself was hardly recognizable. For one thing, he was holding a tennis racquet! His sister looked plain; a tall, dark girl with a bony face. The parents looked quintessentially parents; the father very Jewish, dark and broad, the mother small and fairish. Hugo evidently takes after her. The whole group looked profoundly, profoundly uninteresting; dull to the nth degree. I gazed and gazed at the insipid little piece of stiff paper and the tepid lives caught upon it. There *must* be something more to him than that. I sprang up and put the snap back where I'd found it. Then I opened the wardrobe door again and began systematically going through the pockets of every garment I found there; again with no result. A sudden chiming from somewhere in the house reminded me about the time. I looked at my watch. It was a quarter past four. Another ten minutes and I would have to go.

I sank down on the narrow bed again and turning back the shabby counterpane laid my face against the greyish pillow. It smelt vividly of his brilliantine bringing him suddenly, almost palpably before me. I slipped my hand into the bed . . . and then I found myself, with feverish deliberation, taking off my clothes one by one till I was completely naked. I got into his bed and lay there, one hand over my eyes. My head felt hot, my hair rough, my feet chill. The sheets smelt of his body. My heart pounding I sank into a red blackness of confused, tactile images.

I saw, or rather felt, the huge, tight curled chrysanthe-
mums of autumn now in bloom, crushed their large, crisp,
petalled coolness in my hands, ached to *eat* them . . . I made
an O with my thumb and forefinger and encircled Debenham
Bleu's corrupt and slender ankle. I remembered you, your
bones and weight . . . (I turned my face deeper into the
pillow). I imagined tears to my dry, burning eyes—and then
love with an unidentified body. My own body softened, I
stroked my beautiful arm, touched my breast, laid my face
against my naked shoulder, stretched myself down the
narrow bed . . .

I held the wheel of a great, fast, open car and drove,
streamed in the air; conjured the breast of a swan moving
against lapping water. I remembered a hill in Wales and
slipping in the damp earth as I climbed. With a spiteful and
rancorous joy I hallucinated the confrontation of love between Hugo and some unknown woman; then saw two
bright, blue umbrellas carried by a man and a woman along
a rainy, country road; . . . then felt the rain itself in warm,
heavy, blinding drops.

The excited drumming of my heart sickened me at last.
Opening my eyes I turned to the room again. The sun lay
on it, thick and sticky, horribly yellow. I looked at my watch.
It was ten to five. If I could get a taxi, I thought, I could
still be in time. Yet, clenched in inertia, I did not move.
"Bernard!" I thought—then remembered the small coldness
of his manner before I left; and again did not move. Long
moments passed. I grew thirsty but did not stir. I heard the
front door bang below and waited for Hugo's step. But
whoever it was stayed downstairs.

Moving at last I got out of bed, dressed, tidied everything
back to the way it had been before, picked up my shopping
bag from a chair—and saw beneath it a letter. I read it,
standing near the door. It was from his mother telling him
that all arrangements had been made for the trip, that

when his father joined them in Nassau he was to remember
not to argue with him and spoil everybody's holiday. . . .

It was five-thirty. I let myself out of the house and walking
slowly reached Honeysuckle Road at six. I met Jessica and
Ginny on the corner returning from their afternoon out and
we strolled to the house together, Ginny talking so much
about the Zoo that nothing much was said about the old
woman's departure.

When Bernard came back from seeing his mother off they
had had their supper. I went into the dining-room where he
was eating alone and said: "I must explain. And apologize."

"You don't have to," he said without raising his eyes from
his plate.

"But I *must*—"

"You don't have to," he repeated.

"I want to tell you what happened . . ." I began and waited
for him to say "What?" He said nothing. I felt the explanation I had been concocting begin to slip from my mind.
Clutching at the outline again I said: "I didn't mean to
let you down. What happened wasn't my fault. Really not,"
I said earnestly. (I wanted my excuse to carry conviction
not for my sake but for his.) He reached for more butter.
"What happened was . . ." Again I paused waiting for him
to say "What?" or "Yes?" or *something* from which I could
launch my story. When I saw that he wasn't going to help
I still tried to get it out—but it wouldn't come. Just one small
word from him, an inquiring look even, would have released
it. But this, his generosity tried too far at last, he would not
give.

Stumbling, I said: "Can you see Chevening tomorrow
instead?"

"Nope. He's off to West Germany in the morning."

"West Germany?" I repeated, shaken.

"Yes. Business deal. Me, I wouldn't set a foot in that

country. But . . . business is business!" he said, lilting and parodying the phrase. He stood up from the table.

"Then what's going to happen about the play?" I said in panic.

He turned his hand palm upwards in a "Who knows?" gesture and left the room.

With his perceptions, no fabricated explanation in the world would have done. I see that now. He knew with his nerves that I had no genuine excuse to offer, that what I did was at least partly in revenge; an extortionate price for his tiny coolness. That I, no different from anyone else, was prepared to give nothing, sacrifice nothing, concede nothing to *his* needs . . . while demanding from him nothing less than perfection. The world forgives him nothing and begrudges him everything. If he was not sure of this before he is now. And it was through *me* he had to learn this. Through me!

And so what am I to do now that the hot, shameful insanity of this afternoon has gone? I feel cold to the bone; my guilt infinitely worse because of its timing. To crack so heavy a blow across his already bruised heart. To destroy the last loyalty on which he leaned. And for what? *For what?* For a momentary, sexual hysteria over a cushioned, negligible boy. And for that to have sacrificed him. No! not just him. He is, and has always been, more than himself. He was like an affirmation; a spirit of good in my life. And to have killed it! To have killed it!

Ruth

P.S. He has never demanded. I tell you, Francis . . . I tell you . . . He should have *demanded* from me. It is not right. He should not have left me free to choose my own behaviour. Was it my fault? It was his. *His.*

❀❀❀❀❀❀❀❀❀❀❀❀❀❀❀❀❀❀❀

4th October

HE HAS GONE to Paris. Though he has spoken little to me these last few days I have been aware that he was uneasy about his mother. He begged her, before she went, to write to him without fail every day, but apart from a postcard on arrival there has been no word from her till this morning. I read the letter when they were out of the room and think myself that it is disquieting. She writes that she has hardly been out, feels exhausted and unable to eat, that Jakie is grumbling and Thelma not well. There is a postscript: "I don't think much of this apartment."

Before he went he said to me: "I may just possibly have to stay over another day. Maybe you'd just keep an eye on things till I'm back." He does not reproach, you see; nor sulk; nor elaborately forgive. Though I would willingly go down on my knees in apology I know that he does not want it. It would be no use because what I did was the result of what he *was*. The thing he cannot forgive or forget is the element in his own personality which time after time invites betrayal. So now, forced to it at last, though his manner is normal I sense that ice is beginning to form in his nature. He is trying to freeze to the point where he cannot feel. I find this inexpressibly painful.

Ruth

❖❖❖❖❖❖❖❖❖❖❖❖❖❖❖❖❖❖❖❖❖❖

5th October

THEY ARE BACK! He brought her home with him this morning. She looked frightened, haggard, weary to death and glad, pathetically glad, to be home again. I am glad too, both for her own sake, poor woman—she has had a terrible five days—and for the warming, melting effect she has had on him. Her need has unfrozen him. He hovers round her, asks her a dozen times a minute if she is comfortable, does she want anything, takes her hand, pats her shoulder.

I heard most of the story from Jessica. Bernard had been only too right about his brother. The truth was that— physical illness being about the only thing which frightens Jakie into being human—Thelma has for long made the most of her ailments. Genuinely asthmatic she persuaded her husband to fork out for a series of treatments by some new drug discovered in a Paris clinic. She should of course have gone in as an in-patient. But Jakie, baulking at the extra fees, compounded the typical economy of taking a small apartment and getting his mother to look after Thelma.

"That apartment, Bernie told me," said Jessica shaking even her indifferent head with anger, "was on the fifth floor! With *no elevator*. Can you beat *that*? And such a poky, tiny place that Ma had to sleep out of it anyway in a room the size of a box that they keep, Bernie told me, for the *maids*— big, healthy, country girls. And it was on the floor above! *He* was out all day of course (and most evenings too, if I know him!) doing the town. So except for the doctor once a day they didn't see a soul. They were like two prisoners up there. And Thelma sick and ill from the shots. . . . How that man has the *nerve* . . . I don't know. I just don't know at all. All I can say is that I'm sure sorry for that Thelma."

"She's probably used to him by now," I said dryly. I had long ago made up my mind that Thelma, though not to be compared with her husband, was not particularly likeable either. It was not that he had crushed her so much as that she was peevish by nature.

I am sorry that it should have been old Mrs. Zold who had to pay the price, but overjoyed to see the change in Bernard back to his old, warm, affectionate concern for his mother and equally his old manner to me. I had feared him scarred beyond healing. But I had underestimated the generosity woven into his nature.

There has been one other good result which I witnessed with my own eyes. Bernard was hovering over his mother as usual when she turned and—putting *her* hand on his for a change—said: "Oh, I missed you in Paris, Bernie. My good son. I missed you. You're very good to me." It was as near as she could go, even now, in condemning Jakie. But I have no doubt at all that Bernard considers it worth having come all the way to Europe to hear those words. It is not that he wants to be thanked for his own behaviour; but that he needs to believe that good eventually prevails. That, to use his own words, in the end quality is all.

Ruth

✪❯✪❯✪❯✪❯✪❯✪❯✪❯✪❯✪❯✪❯✪❯✪

10th October

THE CURTAIN came off last night. It is not going to the West End. And the Zolds are leaving. The second quarter of their lease on the house is up and they have decided not to renew it, but to go back home. I knew of course that this might happen. I have half expected it for some time. Yet, having refused to allow myself to think about it, the news came as a shock.

Bernard told me this evening. He had been out to dinner —invited belatedly but just in time by that very famous old man, perhaps our greatest living writer, Sir Trevelyn Reece, O.M., who had sent him a charming letter full of praise for his play.

"It was *something*," said Bernard pacing about the kitchen, teacup in hand, too excited to sit down. He had come in after twelve and everyone else was in bed. He nodded his head. "It was something, Ruth. One doesn't live on such things of course. As an occasion it will recede. The remarkableness will fade. But the lesson. That I hope never to forget."

"What lesson?"

"The lesson is . . ." he paused and breathed deeply through his nose. "The lesson—what I mean is that the small people are small, but the big people are big. *Big*. Only how to get near them? That's the problem. There are so few, they're so surrounded, so shut away from those who need them. Trevelyn Reece . . . I was scared blue of meeting him after what my experiences have been. But you don't know, you can't imagine; the courtesy, the true kindness, the instant comprehension, the lack of all pretentiousness. He is not 'sweet.' He is very shrewd. I would not like to cross him. And he does not suffer fools—but he did not think *me* a fool!" he said laughing at his own pleasure in the statement. He put down his cup and, raising loose fists in the air with a gesture of delight, said: "I *breathed* there, Ruth. For the first time in my life I breathed in congenial air. Not that I can compare myself with him. *I* am not great as he is. But to know that *greatness can be*. That was the marvellous lesson. Bogged down in all the littleness I thought that that was all there was. That size and generousness had vanished from the world. But now . . . *I have seen it.*" He sat down in his favourite chair and leaned back with a smile at the ceiling.

"Perhaps he'll ask you again," I said.

He brought his gaze down, turned to look at me and said: "No. No, I don't think he would. He's an old man and a frail one. It was a great compliment that he asked me at all. His wife told me that in the hall before I left. And he is in some ways rather shy himself. It was very strange! I saw my own shyness mirrored exactly in him! It is a great effort for him to meet strangers.

"And then, another thing. I'm not so naïve that I would expect a friendship between that man and myself to develop. It wouldn't be possible. Our sympathies may chime but our . . . our ambiences couldn't be further apart. There is no *social* level common to us. He is old now. And although he's shy he's also worldly in a way I could never be. His past is so tremendous, encompasses experiences and people, marvels and wreckage of a kind I could never. . . . He is a *very great man.* And I? What am I? I say to you again— what am I? A middle-aged, small-town, raw American of infinitely limited experience; struggling in a puny way with the small, desperate plights of average men; a difficult child, an inadequate wife, an injured mother. I have no friends, no talents, no possessions to boast of, only the one gift which I have neither the authority nor the quickness to make full use of. How can I think in terms of friendship with the truly great? The wonder is that I came as near as I did to that great man. To expect more would be greedy. It would be . . . ill-bred."

He paused again, put up a forefinger to scratch his cheek, then said very gently: "Besides, I shan't be here."

"You are going home," I said. I was sitting at the table, my elbows on it, my hands supporting my chin.

"Yes. I've decided that we must go back to America.

329

There's no point in staying here any longer. The play—"
He stopped.

"It was my fault," I said.

"Ah, now, cut it out, Ruth—"

"It was my fault," I said again. "And now you are going
because of that. I have brought my own retribution—"

"Cut it out!" he said again. I began to speak wildly and
getting up he came over to the table and putting a hand on
my shoulder said: "Will you shut up now and let me speak.
I want to tell you something—about the play. I'm glad you
did whatever it was you did that afternoon and made me
miss my date with Chevening. Remember you asking me
before you went out if I'd do something—to use an old-style
expression—dishonourable for the sake of it? Remember
me turning snappy?" I nodded. "That was because I'd decided to do just that very thing—no! not throw him Lorraine! But Chevening had said as how he'd be prepared to
back me if I'd do one little thing; change the last act of the
play! He didn't like it. Wanted something a bit more upbeat.
'Optimistic'! That was his word. Optimism. If he used it
once he used it a hundred times. I met guys like him before.
They get their teeth into one word like they'd just invented
it and thrash it to death. Well, anyway . . . I was going to
agree! So you see!" He tapped my shoulder with one finger.
"You did me a good turn after all. Sure, the play's not going
on. But in its new form it wouldn't have run a week anyway.
All I'd have gotten out of it would have been self-hatred. *So*
. . . you can quit reproaching yourself Ruth. Unless of course
you're enjoying a little guilt!"

"I *am* guilty," I said, "all the same. However it turned
out, I betrayed you, used you—"

"And what the hell d'you think I've done with you?" he
interjected. "D'you think I haven't known and realized all
these months that I've been using *you*? The only creature
in the world to whom I have ever been able to talk. My

luxury!" he said affectionately. "You have been my great, self-indulgent luxury that I haven't been able to resist! D'you think I haven't had qualms? Lord knows I don't want to flatter myself. But you *might,* you just conceivably might have come to regard me as a man—instead of a voice yacketing away at you at every possible moment."

"Yes," I said. "I sometimes wondered myself if . . . though . . . I mean I don't flatter *my*self either."

There was a moment's silence between us. Then I turned my head and saw his hand resting, loosely curved, on my shoulder. He saw my movement and, lifting his arm, stroked the back of his hand against my cheek. I felt the smooth surface of his hand against the smooth, warm surface of my cheek. And, by some mystery of sympathy, I felt my face against his hand as *he* felt it. The effect was most strange; most delicate and sensuous and loving. But it was a gesture between us of farewell.

Taking his hand away he touched, very briefly, my forehead and my hair. "You have a very beautiful brow," he said. "Gentle."

"Gentle-browed!" I said in mock-vexation. "I've heard that before! I expect something more original from a literary gent."

"Don't look to literature for *anything* Ruth. That's my advice to you. It's a very bad guide in some ways."

"Why?"

"Because literature is dramatic and life isn't."

"What *is* life?" I said idiotically.

"You expect an *answer!*" he said laughing at me. "All right! A confused endurance; that's what life is. When the winds blow we lift and turn and when they are still we settle. But we don't control them."

"But *you* do in a way. Art is a kind of tiller."

"A tiller?" he said thoughtfully. He took a few steps about the kitchen and stopped by the sink. "I think perhaps . . .

not a tiller. Not a steering mechanism . . . more like a prism refracting a special colour.

"I recall once," he said putting his hands behind his back and leaning against the sink, "how once, after my first play was put on and I was wondering if I'd ever be able to write another, someone I knew quite well said something sneering about it, some snide remark (I can't even remember now what it was) which left me acutely depressed for hours; not so much by the remark itself I guess but that it should have come from a 'friend.' When I got to thinking of the envious malice behind it I was overwhelmed with a sort of deep, melancholy misery.

"And then . . . a little later on that same evening I turned the radio on for the news . . . and there was a dance band playing an old tune I used to dance to—oh, sure, I went to dances as a young man!—years ago. Something called *Long ago and far away*. Came from a Rita Hayworth movie. Such silly words! 'Chills run up and down my spine, Aladdin's lamp is mine . . .' that sort of . . . But the *tune* you know. And suddenly my whole imagination began to work, to recreate those years of my blind and anguished youth, its few moments of joy, the *feel* of things, the sense of time then and time now. And this lifted me into that miraculous *other country*. And I found *The Curtain*.

"Ah!" he exclaimed stretching his arms wide, "you do not know what it is like, that marvellous sense of thaw after a period of frozen imagination; how the mind gradually begins to hoist and fill like a sail; how the light changes and the wretched becomes bearable; how all one's faculties begin to melt and sing. That soft, strong, loosening joy—like the beginnings of love, like the opening of a rose . . . *I feel it now*," he said bringing his arms down again but clumsily so that he knocked a cup off the draining board on to the floor. But it didn't break. He bent down and picked it up. "No dignity, you see," he said shaking his head and smiling at the cup. "But what does it matter? How lucky I am after all! I can *use* my indignity. Ruth! At this moment, I tell you, I could get down on my knees and worship my own imagination, my only gift from God; oblique, unpredictable, a slanting light . . . but my particular blessing."

"Yes," I said expressionlessly. I had twisted round in my chair to look at him. Something of the sad envy I was feeling must have shown in my face for he said instantly: "Don't! Don't, Ruth. Don't envy me."

"Not in a bad way—?" I said incoherently.

"No. I know. But don't. The moments are so rare. They do not make a life. Look, I'll tell you! There are strangenesses about the place of art in an artist's life. What—I sometimes ask myself—has my work to do with my getting mad at Ginny for eating three ice-creams in a row and getting sick to her stomach? Or me sitting around Sundays reading the papers like fifty million other guys? That power of the imagination I was talking about; it's separate. Even at the best of times, it's separate. It doesn't relate to the rest of me, to my life, my circumstances. It doesn't *connect;* it's just an annexe I've been lucky enough to build. Most of the time I live in a house worse than yours."

I remained twisted round in my chair still facing him; but I could not speak.

"What will you do," he said at last, "when we go?"

"I don't know," I said. "When will it be?"

"A week, ten days maybe. There's nothing to keep us."

"I don't know," I said again.

"Go back to your husband?"

"No."

"Then what?"

I shrugged my shoulders and said: "I seem to have arrived at a brick wall."

"Yes," he said. "I know that wall. But I have always seen it at the end of the long corridor which is one's search for joy. You walk on and on through the corridor thinking that sooner or later you *must* emerge into happiness. And then you're at the end of it—and you see that there is still no happiness, that joy is unlikely and always was—and there is nothing but the blank wall. It is a terrible moment—or it would be if on the same instant something else didn't happen. You find that though you can't get through the wall you can turn sideways and, so to speak, by-pass it. This by-passing . . . it comes about if you loosen your grip on the *idea* of happiness, when you realize that unhappiness is nothing to be ashamed of. Admit it, hold it to you, forgive your pain. It is not an enemy. It is there to tell you something. Be patient. Don't blame. Don't force. It is necessary to flow with one's fate.

"You have been very good to us," he said before he left me.

Ruth

24th October

THEY have gone. I have tidied the house, put piles of rubbish out for the dustmen to remove, hoovered, dusted . . . Save for an odd stain or two here or there everything is as it was the day I sat in this room and wrote to you six months ago.

They all bought me presents before they left, as I did them. We exchanged them at a rather embarrassed little ceremony last night. They bought me perfume (Jessica), handkerchiefs (Ginny), a brooch (old Mrs. Zold), and a superb handbag (Bernard). I bought them a necklace (Jessica), a bracelet (Ginny), a scarf (the old woman), and a five-year, leather-bound diary (Bernard).

I am waiting now for the house agent's representative to

come and check over the inventory. As soon as he arrives I shall be free to go. You will want to know where of course. Well let me tell you what happened an hour ago. The Zolds had only just gone when the telephone rang. It was Peregrine.

"They've gone," I said. "You've just missed them."

"Thank goodness I've caught you!" he said. "No, it's all right. I heard they were off the other day and called them up then to say good-bye. No, it was you I wanted to catch."

"Why?"

"Why? 'Why?' she says! Ruth, angel, you haven't forgotten you promised *faithfully* you'd come and housekeep for *me* one day? Well . . . *le jour de gloire est arrivée!*"

"I did nothing of the sort."

"Oh yes you did! You've forgotten!"

"How could I have—?"

"Let's not argue about it anyway," he cut in swiftly. "The point is—when can you come? If you want a little holiday first then I won't—"

"Hold it, hold it!" I said laughing in spite of myself at the sheer warmth of feeling wanted.

"If it's a question of salary there are still a few hundreds in the bank my creditors don't know about. I can raise whatever—"

"Oh no, no," I said. "It isn't that."

"Then what's holding you back for the Lord's sake? You must know that as these jobs go and though I say it myself and all that, it's a jolly good one. You'll love my flat. I entertain a good deal one way and another. There's a lot of interesting people in and out. You'd find it fun I promise you."

"Yes, I'm sure I would. It's just that you jumped it on me so suddenly."

"Well, you've had at least four minutes to consider it now. You can't want any more. So will you come? Come *now*.

335

Dump your bags, take a few days off if you feel you must . . . then come back and settle in. Drat it! I *need* you, Ruth," he said his voice going up in mock alarm. "I need your protection! Lorraine's on my tail! Wally Grey won't play so now she's shaking her shining, golden mane at me. And you never know. She might just strike at a melancholy moment and get me!"

I began to laugh again. "Oh dear!" I said. "So I'm to save you from a fate worse . . . Oh, we-e-ll! I suppose I'd better! All right. As soon as I've finished here."

I rang off feeling a great lift to my spirits. Peregrine was not exaggerating. To live with him would be at last to live with "style." Not ten minutes before all I had to look forward to was a room in the flatlet house run by Jessica's friend, Mrs. Capes. And now a door had opened. Swept with excitement I almost waltzed back into the living-room.

And now, an hour later, I am sitting here waiting to hand over the keys—and leave not only the house but Bernard for ever. But I am not going to Peregrine. I rang and told him so five minutes ago.

Why? Let me tell you about a woman I happened to meet when I was living with Danny; a Leftish, public-spirited woman who has worked very hard for certain kinds of human betterment. We were left together for half an hour in a pub one evening and she started telling me how a man whom she knew slightly through a friend had taken her out to dinner. During their conversation over the meal he'd told her quite casually, without remorse or shame, of the way he had deliberately deceived and betrayed their mutual friend. Yet she went to bed with him that night. Not for love or irresistible passion; just for . . . "why not?"

It is this contemporary "why not?" that I find at last so terrible, so *terrible*. If no one is to suffer the consequences of his acts, if we condone everything, admit no necessity of punishment, apply no moral sanctions, feel bound by no loyalties; if we march for morality in public and condone or commit great treacheries in private. . . . No! This will not do. We forgive too much. I will *not* forgive.

No! I will not go to Peregrine; though it is with reluctance with a dragging, unwilling effort that I range myself against that gay and for the most part, lovable boy. Do not think I make the choice with ease. I am irritable, querulous; my heart sinks. But the issue is clear. That I see it is my only wisdom. How can I forgive, through Peregrine, that great, failing sickness of our society; the lack of moral delicacy in the life of everyday? It is because of this lack that he has hurt and insulted a good and admirable man. It is with this lack that I struggle in my own nature. And so I must not support his acts. I must not support or live by expediency. I must not support Bernard's enemies. No, I have not caught saintliness from him! I am not giving up my whole self. If I were of that stature I should attempt to bring you happiness. I should return to you. But that I cannot do. At least . . . but no. No! But this much I can do. I can refuse Peregrine's offer. I can refuse the universal, shrugging acceptance of the indolent, the worldly, the indifferent, the disloyal. I can make a gesture, a private choice; not yet enough I know, but a tiny count for good.

It is not much; but it is something I am impelled to do. I have a sense as of a great hand pressed against my back; not hard, not propelling, but gently firm and directing. I feel that I am being moved forward as if by soft winds along some path I am reluctant to pursue. It may be that that path leads back to you—or to some ordained place where my soul will be forced into employment of a kind I do not want. I do not want to go towards this place. I clutch at my Self. I do not want . . . but the great hand presses. I have an intimation that one day the small gesture will not suffice, that I may surrender to the entire pull of good. I fear that I shall find goodness not too difficult but too easy. One has only to say to oneself: "It can be done! I can stretch out my hand and not withhold it," . . . and one *can*. It is *done*.

But I do not want to, Francis. At least . . . not yet. In a while. When I have more strength—or more weakness. In a while. But not yet. Not yet. Not yet.

Ruth

A NOTE ON THE TYPE

THE TEXT of this book was set on the Linotype in a face called PRIMER, designed by RUDOLPH RUZICKA, earlier responsible for the design of Fairfield and Fairfield Medium, Linotype faces whose virtues have for some time now been accorded wide recognition. The complete range of sizes of Primer was first made available in 1954, although the pilot size of 12 point was ready as early as 1951. The design of the face makes general reference to Linotype Century (long a serviceable type, totally lacking in manner or frills of any kind) but brilliantly corrects the characterless quality of that face.

Composed, printed, and bound by
The Haddon Craftsmen, Inc., Scranton, Pa.
Typography and binding design
based on originals by
GEORGE SALTER

A NOTE ABOUT THE AUTHOR

GERDA CHARLES was born in Liverpool, England. She attended many different schools as a result of much moving about and managed to get in only three years of high school. Her first novel, *The True Voice*, was published in England in 1959. Her short stories have appeared in *Vanity Fair* and *Jewish Chronicle* (one of which was reprinted in *Pick of the Year's Short Stories*) and she has done critical articles and reviews for the *New Statesman* and *Midstream*. She has edited an anthology of Modern Jewish Stories and broadcast as fiction critic for the BBC. *The Crossing Point*, her second novel, was the first to be published in this country; *A Slanting Light* is her third. Miss Charles has for some time now lived and worked in London.

July 1963